CASTLES IN THEIR BONES

LAURA SEBASTIAN

HODDER

First published in Great Britain in 2022 by Hodder & Stoughton
An Hachette UK company

This paperback edition published in 2023

1

A CIP catalogue record for this title is available from the British Library

Hardback ISBN 978 1 529 37295 3
Trade Paperback ISBN 978 1 529 37296 0
Paperback ISBN 978 1 529 37387 5
eBook ISBN 978 1 529 37302 8

Printed and bound in Great Britain by Clays Ltd, Elcograf S.p.A.

Hodder & Stoughton policy is to use papers that are natural, renewable and recyclable products and made from wood grown in sustainable forests. The logging and manufacturing processes are expected to conform to the environmental regulations of the country of origin.

Hodder & Stoughton Ltd
Carmelite House
50 Victoria Embankment
London EC4Y 0DZ

www.hodder.co.uk

For my brother, Jerry.
Because even when we fought with each other,
it was always us against the world.

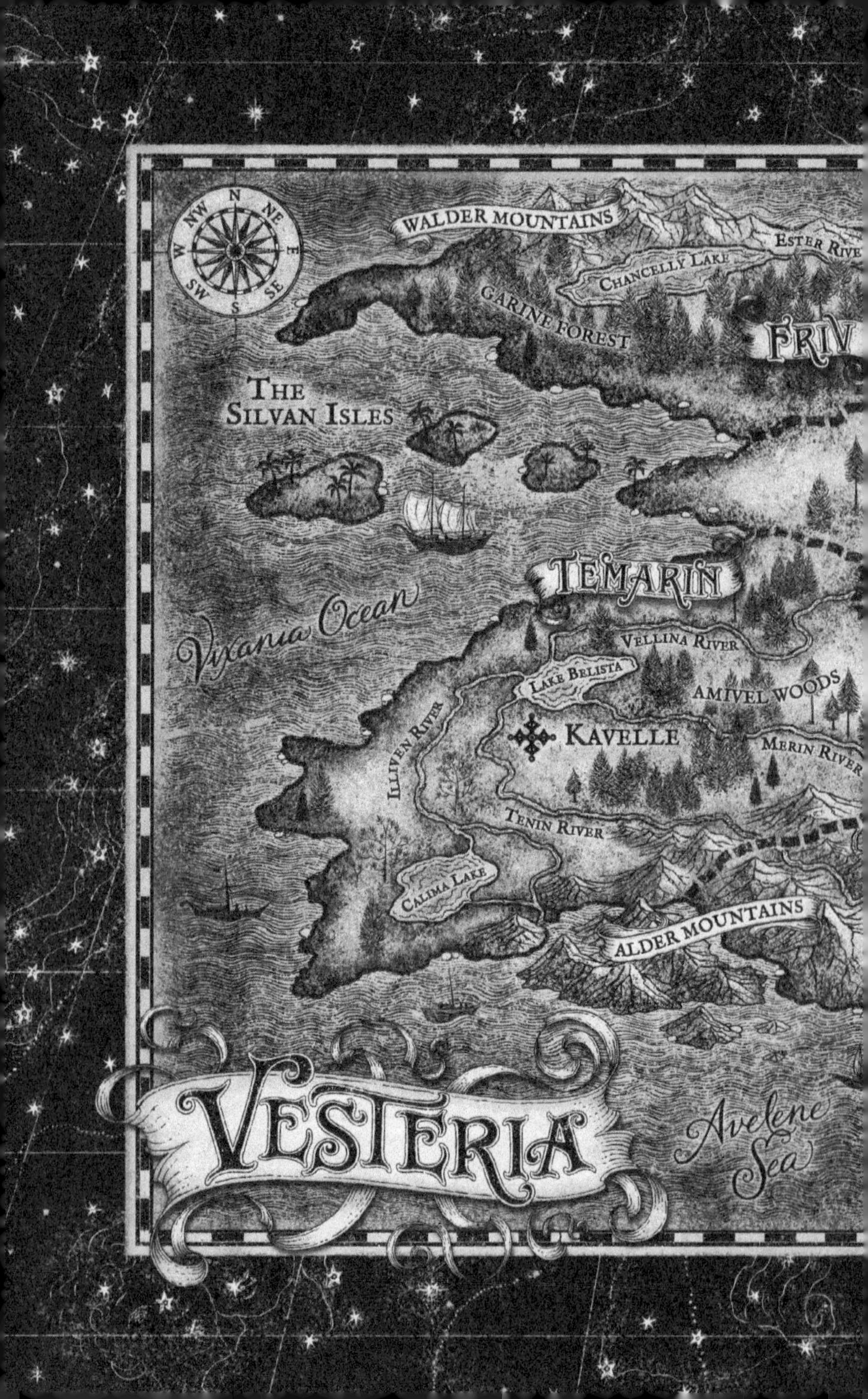
Vesteria
Walder Mountains
Chancelly Lake
Garine Forest
The Silvan Isles
Temarin
Vixania Ocean
Vellina River
Lake Belista
Amivel Woods
Kavelle
Merin River
Illiven River
Tenin River
Calima Lake
Alder Mountains
Avelene Sea

CRISK MOUNTAINS
TACK MOUNTAINS
NOTCH LAKE
TACK RIVER
LAKE OLVEEN
NOTCH RIVER
TREVAIL FOREST
TENAL RIVER
ELDEVALE
BESSEMIA
DALCINE LAKE
HAPANTOILE
Whistall Sea
NEMARIA WOODS
CARINO RIVER
KELLIAN FOREST
LAKE SULIMO
PUREEN WOODS
AZINA RIVER
CELLARIA
VALLON
VULIA WOODS

The Royal Families of Vesteria

Bessemia

House of Soluné

Emperor Aristede (deceased) — Empress Margaraux

Princess Beatriz

Princess Daphne

Princess Sophronia

Friv

House of Deasún

? --- King Bartholomew — Queen Darina

Bairre

Prince Cillian

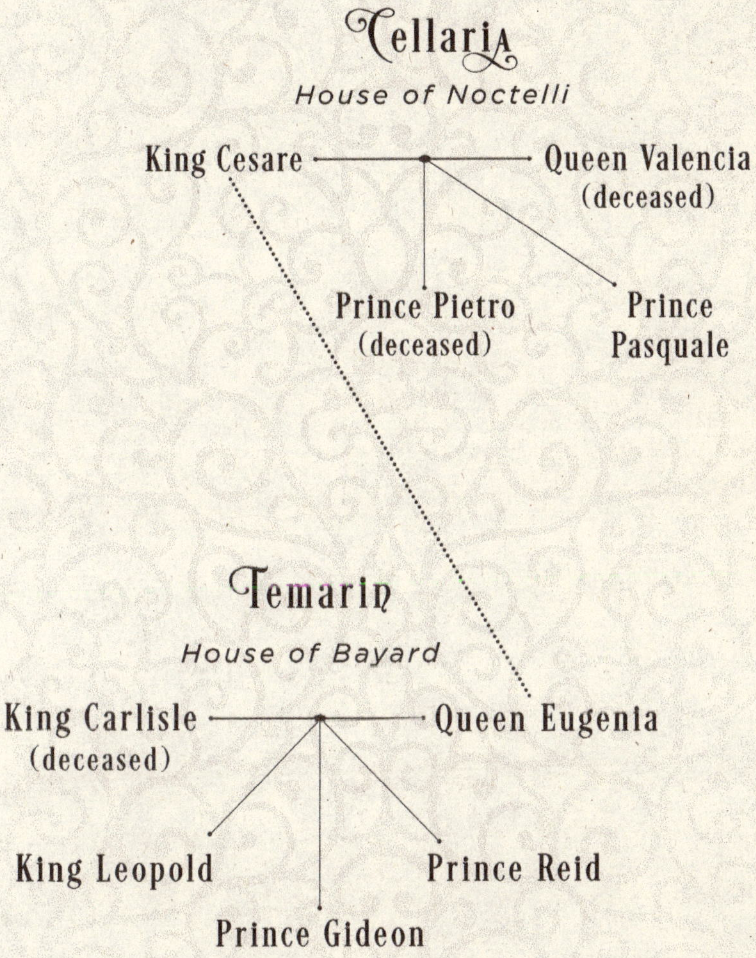
Cellaria
House of Noctelli
King Cesare
Queen Valencia (deceased)
Prince Pietro (deceased)
Prince Pasquale
Temarin
House of Bayard
King Carlisle (deceased)
Queen Eugenia
King Leopold
Prince Gideon
Prince Reid

It is said that the stars shine brighter on the princesses' birthday, but the princesses themselves think that is balderdash. The stars look the same as they always do, and this year, on the night before the three of them leave their home and one another for the first time in their lives, everything—the stars included—seems far darker.

The sounds from the party drift through the palace as the clock nears midnight, but the princesses have abandoned the celebration, Daphne plucking a bottle of champagne from an ice bucket while Beatriz bats her eyes at the server and Sophronia keeps a lookout to ensure that their mother doesn't see them. They have done their duty, danced and toasted, shaken hands and kissed cheeks, smiled until their faces ached, but they want to spend their last few minutes of girlhood the same way they came into the world sixteen years ago: together.

Their childhood rooms haven't changed much since they were moved there from the nursery—still three identical white rooms connected to a shared parlor, each with the same white canopied bed piled high with silk pillows, the same birch desk and armoire, inlaid with gold in a pattern of vines and flowers, and the same plush rose-colored rug stretching across the floor. The shared parlor is full of overstuffed velvet seating and a grand marble fireplace carved to represent the constellations that moved across the sky at the time of their birth—a full moon of inlaid opal at the center, surrounded by the constellations: the Thorned Rose, the Hungry Hawk, the Lonely Heart, the Crown of Flames, and, of course, the Sisters Three.

Rumor has it that Empress Margaraux had tasked the royal empyrea, Nigellus, to use magic to ensure they were born when the Sisters Three crossed overhead, but others say that's ridiculous—after all, why would she have wished for three girls when a single boy would have been far more helpful?

Others whisper that the Sisters Three was the constellation that Nigellus had pulled a star down from to grant the empress's wish for children, though none appear to be missing. But she must have wished, on that everyone agrees. How else could the emperor have suddenly fathered three daughters, at the age of seventy, when his last wife and his countless mistresses had never fallen pregnant?

And then there is the matter of the princesses' eyes—not their mother's brown or their father's blue but the star-touched silver that only graced those conceived with magic. Those with stardust running through their veins.

Daphne

Sitting on the rug before the mantel, Daphne can't help but glance at the constellations as she adjusts the skirt of her green organza dress around her like flower petals.

Babies born beneath the Thorned Rose are known to be beautiful.

Those born beneath the Hungry Hawk are ambitious.

Lonely Heart children are known to sacrifice more than others.

The Crown of Flames offers its offspring power.

And the Sisters Three bestow balance and harmony.

There are exceptions, of course—Daphne knows of plenty of people born beneath the Thorned Rose who did not grow up beautiful and many born beneath the Crown of Flames who became chimney sweeps and cabbage farmers. But still, more people believe in the omens of the stars than don't—even Daphne, logical as she is about most things, takes the daily horoscopes laid out with her breakfast to heart.

Her eyes keep drifting to the mantel as she struggles to open the stolen bottle of champagne with her glass nail file. After some digging, the stopper comes loose with a loud pop that makes her shriek in surprise, the cork careening into the air and hitting the chandelier above, making the crystals chime together. The champagne bubbles over onto her dress and the rug, cold and wet.

"Careful!" Sophronia cries out, hurrying to the adjoining powder room for towels.

Beatriz snorts, holding three delicate crystal glasses to the mouth of the bottle, letting Daphne fill them up almost to the brim. "Or what?" she calls after Sophronia. "It isn't as if we're going to be here long enough to get in trouble for ruining a rug."

Sophronia returns, towel in hand, and begins mopping up the spilled champagne anyway, her brow furrowed.

Seeing her expression, Beatriz softens. "Sorry, Sophie," she says before taking a sip from one of the glasses and passing the others to her sisters. "I didn't mean . . ." She trails off, unsure of what, exactly, she did mean.

Sophronia doesn't seem to know either, but she drops the sopping towel on the floor and sinks down on the sofa beside Beatriz, who drapes an arm over her shoulders, rustling the taffeta of her rose-pink off-the-shoulder gown in the process.

Daphne looks at them over the rim of her champagne glass, downing half of it in a single gulp before her eyes fall to the wet towel.

By the time that's dry, she thinks, *we'll have left this place. We won't see one another for a year.*

The first part is tolerable enough—Bessemia is home, but they have always known they would leave when they came of age. Beatriz south to Cellaria, Sophronia west to

Temarin, and Daphne north to Friv. They have been preparing for their duties for as long as Daphne can remember, to marry the princes they've been betrothed to and drive their countries to war against one another, allowing their mother to sweep in and pick up the shattered pieces and add them to her domain like new jewels for her crown.

But that's all for the future. Daphne pushes her mother's plots aside and focuses on her sisters. The sisters she won't see again for a year, if everything goes to plan. They haven't spent more than a few hours apart in their entire lives. How will they manage an entire year?

Beatriz must see Daphne's smile wobble, because she gives a dramatic roll of her eyes—her own tell for when she's trying not to show her emotions.

"Come on," Beatriz says, her voice cracking slightly as she pats the sofa on her other side.

Daphne stands up from the rug for an instant before falling onto the sofa beside Beatriz gracelessly, letting her head drop onto Beatriz's bare shoulder. Beatriz's strapless sky-blue gown looks terribly uncomfortable, its corseted bodice digging into her skin and leaving behind red indents that peek over the top, but Beatriz doesn't appear to feel it.

Daphne wonders if hiding her feelings is a trick Triz picked up during her training with the palace courtesans—a necessity, their mother said, to fulfill her own objective in Cellaria—or if that is simply how her sister is: only two minutes older but always managing to seem like a woman, when Daphne still feels like a child.

"Are you worried?" Sophronia asks, taking the daintiest of sips from her glass.

Despite the fact that they are triplets, Sophronia has a lower tolerance for alcohol than her sisters. Half a glass of champagne for her is the equivalent of two full glasses for Daphne and Beatriz. Hopefully one of her attendants in Temarin knows that, Daphne thinks. Hopefully someone will keep an eye on her there, when Daphne and Beatriz can't.

Beatriz snorts. "What on earth would I be nervous about? At this point, I feel as if I could seduce Lord Savelle in my sleep."

Lord Savelle is the first part of the empress's grand plan—the Temarinian ambassador in Cellaria, he has been responsible for keeping the peace between the countries for the last two decades, the longest they have gone without war in centuries. In compromising him, Beatriz will reignite that conflict and add a few extra logs to the fire.

"Cellaria alone would make me nervous," Sophronia admits, shuddering. "No empyreas, no stardust, no magic at all. I heard King Cesare had a man burned alive because he thought him responsible for a drought."

Beatriz only shrugs. "Yes, well, I've been preparing for it, haven't I?" she says. "And the king's increasing paranoia should make it even easier to incite war. I might beat both of you back here."

"Sophie would be my bet," Daphne muses, sipping her champagne. "She's the only one of us marrying a king instead of a mere prince, and I'm sure Leopold would declare war on Cellaria if she simply fluttered her eyelashes and asked it of him."

Though she means the words as a joke, they're followed by an uncomfortable silence. Sophronia looks away, her cheeks turning bright red, and Beatriz shoots Daphne a dirty look. Daphne feels as if she's missed something, though it isn't the first time. The three of them are close, but Beatriz and Sophronia have always been just a bit closer. Which is fine by Daphne—after all, she has always been the closest with their mother.

"Beatriz is the prettiest of you—she will have no trouble swinging the hearts of the Cellarians. Sophronia is the sweetest and she will win over the Temarinians with ease," the empress said to Daphne just the day before, her voice like that of a general dispatching troops. The words deflated Daphne, until her mother leaned toward her, pressing her cool palm to Daphne's cheek and blessing her with a rare full smile. "But you, my darling, are my sharpest weapon, so I need you in Friv. Bessemia needs you in Friv. If you're going to take my place one day, you must prove you can fill it."

Shame and pride go to war inside Daphne and she takes another sip of her champagne, hoping her sisters don't notice. She supposes she can't fault them for keeping things from her—she has her own share of secrets.

Logically, she knows her mother was right to ask her to keep that from them—she has never mentioned making one of them her heir, and knowing it will be Daphne will only stoke jealousies. Daphne doesn't want that. Not tonight, especially.

She lets out a sigh, slumping farther into the sofa's cushioned back. "At least your princes are handsome and healthy. One of the Frivian spies says Prince Cillian has been leeched so many times, his skin is covered in scabs. Another said he's unlikely to live another month."

"A month is plenty of time to marry him," Beatriz points out. "If anything, it should make your job much easier. I can't imagine he'll get in your way, and Friv is such a young country as it is, it will be easy to take advantage of the chaos surrounding the death of the only heir to the throne. Maybe *you'll* be the first one of us home."

"Hopefully," Daphne says. "But I can't believe I'm going to be stuck in cold, miserable Friv while you're off relaxing on sunny Cellarian beaches and Sophie gets to attend those legendary Temarinian parties."

"It's not like we're going to relax on beaches or enjoy parties, is it?" Sophronia reminds her, but Daphne waves the words away.

"Well, it will make for a better backdrop than snow, gray skies, and more snow," she grumbles.

"No need for dramatics," Beatriz says, rolling her eyes. "Besides, you have the easiest assignment of all of us. What do you have to do? Steal the king's seal? Forge a few documents? Admit it, Daph."

Daphne shakes her head. "You know Mama—I'm sure there will be more to it than that."

"Stop," Sophronia interrupts, her voice cracking. "I don't want to talk about this anymore. It's our birthday. Shouldn't we at least make it about us and not her?"

Daphne and Beatriz exchange a loaded look, but Beatriz is the first to speak.

"Of course, Sophie," she says. "Shall we toast?"

Sophronia considers it for a moment before raising her glass. "To seventeen," she says.

Daphne laughs. "Oh, Soph, are you sloshed already? We're *sixteen*."

Sophronia shrugs. "I know that," she says. "But sixteen is when we have to say goodbye. By seventeen, we'll be back here again. Together."

"To seventeen, then," Beatriz echoes, raising her own glass.

"To seventeen," Daphne adds, clinking her glass with theirs before the three of them gulp down the last of their champagne.

Sophronia leans back against the sofa cushions and closes her eyes, apparently satisfied. Beatriz takes Sophronia's empty glass and sets it with hers on the floor, out of the way, before leaning back beside her, staring at the vaulted ceiling, where whirling arrangements of stars have been painted in glittering gold against a deep blue background.

"Like Mama always says," Beatriz murmurs. "We're three stars of the same constellation. Distance won't change that."

It's a surprisingly emotional sentiment coming from Beatriz, but Daphne feels a bit sentimental herself right now, so she curls up beside her sisters, throwing her arm around both of their waists.

The tall, marble-faced clock in the room strikes midnight with a loud chime that echoes in Daphne's ears, and she pushes her mother's words from her mind and holds her sisters tight.

"Happy birthday," she says, kissing each of their cheeks in turn and leaving behind smears of pale pink lip paint.

"Happy birthday," they each reply, their voices weighed down with exhaustion. In seconds, they're both asleep, their quiet, even breaths filling the air, but try as she might, Daphne can't join them. Sleep doesn't claim her until a sliver of dawn sun is peeking through the window.

Sophronia

Sophronia can't cry, not in the presence of the empress, not even in the carriage on the way to the center of Bessemia, the place where she and her sisters will say their final goodbyes. Tears sting at her eyes, make her throat burn, but she forces herself to hold them back, aware of her mother's critical gaze, always hungry to find fault—in Sophronia, it seems, more so than in Daphne or Beatriz.

"Tears are a weapon," Empress Margaraux likes to say, her full, painted mouth pursing. "But one that is wasted on me."

Sophronia doesn't intend to use her tears as a weapon, but she can't help the torrent of emotions ripping through her. She forces herself to hold on to her composure, aware of her mother sitting on the bench across from her, silent and steadfast and strong in a way that Sophronia has failed to master, no matter how many lessons she's had.

The carriage hits a bump, and Sophronia uses it as an excuse to wipe away a tear that has managed to leak out.

"You have your orders," their mother says, breaking the

silence. She sounds dispassionate, almost bored. As if she is on her way to a weekend in the country instead of saying goodbye to all three of her children at once. "I expect updates as you progress."

"Yes, Mama," Daphne says.

As they sit side by side, it's impossible to deny the resemblance between them. It's more than the ink-black curls that frame their heart-shaped faces, more than their heavily fringed eyes—Daphne's a star-touched silver, like Sophronia's and Beatriz's, their mother's a warm and liquid amber—more than the freckles that dance over the bridges of their sharp cheekbones and upturned noses. It's the way they sit, backs ramrod straight, legs primly crossed at the ankles, hands gathered in their laps. It's the set of their mouths, pursed and turned down at the corners.

But there is warmth in Daphne when she smiles that Sophronia has never seen their mother match.

The thought makes her heart hurt, and she looks away from Daphne, focusing instead on the velvet seat cushion behind her sister's shoulder.

"Yes, Mother," she echoes, hoping her voice comes out like Daphne's, level and sure. But of course it doesn't. Of course it wavers.

Her mother's eyes narrow and she opens her mouth, a reprimand at the ready, but Beatriz gets there first, a cold, wry smile on her full lips as she throws herself once again between Sophronia and the empress.

"And if we're otherwise occupied?" she asks, lifting her eyebrows. "From what I've heard, life as a newlywed can be quite . . . busy."

Their mother drags her gaze away from Sophronia, focusing it on Beatriz instead.

"Save it for Cellaria, Beatriz," she says. "You'll send an update, coded—just as you've learned."

Beatriz and Daphne both grimace at that, but Sophronia doesn't. She took to cryptology far more naturally than her sisters, and though she loves them, she can't deny that excelling at something they struggle with sends a thrill of pleasure through her. Especially because Sophronia excels at so very little. She lacks Beatriz's mastery of flirtation and disguises, can't match Daphne's skills with poisons or a lockpick, but she can break a code in half the time it takes them, and craft one almost as quickly as that, and while they all studied economics, Sophronia was the only one who actually enjoyed poring over tax laws and budget reports.

"And I don't suppose I need to remind you that your newlywed lives are merely for show," the empress says, and now her eyes rest so heavily on Sophronia that her skin begins to itch.

Sophronia's cheeks heat up and she feels her sisters looking at her too, with some mix of pity, sympathy, and, in Daphne's case, a dose of confusion. Sophronia hasn't told her about the conversation her mother took her aside to have a week ago, the cold look in her eyes as she asked Sophronia, without any sort of preamble, if she was developing feelings for King Leopold.

Sophronia didn't think she hesitated or gave any reason to doubt her when she said no, but her mother heard the lie all the same.

“I didn’t raise you to be foolish enough to think yourself in love,” she said, pushing a folio of documents into Sophronia’s hands—reports from their spies in Temarin. “You don’t love him. You don’t even know him. He is our enemy, and you will not forget that again.”

Sophronia swallows now and pushes the memory aside, and the information in those documents along with it. “No, we don’t need any reminders,” she says.

“Good,” the empress says before her gaze falls on Beatriz and her frown deepens. “We’re nearly there, fix your eyes.”

Beatriz scowls, even as she reaches for the emerald ring on her right hand. “It itches, you know,” she says as she twists the emerald and holds the ring over one eye, then the other, letting a green drop fall from the ring and into each. She blinks a couple of times, and when she looks across the carriage again, her eyes have gone from silver, like Sophronia’s and Daphne’s, to a brilliant green.

“I assure you, you aren’t nearly as uncomfortable as you’ll be if the Cellarians see your star-touched eyes,” the empress points out. Beatriz scowls again, but she doesn’t protest. She knows, just as Sophronia does, that their mother is right. In Bessemia, star-touched eyes are only somewhat rare, found on children whose parents used stardust to conceive them. They aren’t the only royals to have silver-hued eyes—many an ancestral line has only been continued due to copious amounts of stardust and, in rare cases, assistance from an empyrea. But in Cellaria, magic is outlawed, and there are plenty of stories of Cellarian children killed for having silver eyes, even though Sophronia wonders how many of those children had eyes that were merely gray.

The carriage pulls to a stop, and a quick glance out the window confirms that they've arrived at their destination, the clearing at the center of the Nemaria Woods. Their mother stays seated, though, her gaze moving slowly from one sister to the next.

If Sophronia looks closely, she thinks she sees a touch of sadness in her mother's expression. A touch of regret. But as soon as it appears, it's gone, sealed away behind a mask of ice and steel.

"You'll be on your own now," the empress says, her voice low. "I won't be around to guide you. But you've trained for this, my doves. You know what to do, you know who to strike, you know where they are vulnerable. In a year's time, we will rule every inch of this continent and no one will be able to take it from us."

As always, Sophronia feels her heart swell at the mention of that future. As much as she is dreading the next year, she knows it will be worth it in the end—when the entire continent of Vesteria belongs to them.

"There is only one tool I have left to give you," their mother continues. She reaches into the pocket of her gown, pulling out three small red velvet drawstring pouches and passing one to each daughter.

Sophronia opens hers and empties its contents into her palm. The cool silver chain slithers over her fingers, a single diamond dangling from it, smaller than her pinky nail. A quick glance confirms that her sisters' gifts are identical.

"It's a bit plain for your tastes, Mama," Beatriz notes, her mouth pursed.

It's true—their mother's taste tends to run gaudier: heavy

gold, gems the size of croquet balls, jewelry that shouts its price at top volume.

As soon as she thinks it, Sophronia understands.

"You want these to go unnoticed," she says, glancing at the empress. "But why? It's only a diamond."

At that, her mother's stoic mouth bends into a tight-lipped smile.

"Because they aren't diamonds, my doves," she says, reaching out to take hold of Daphne's chain and her wrist. As she speaks, she fastens it in place. "I commissioned them from Nigellus. Use them wisely—if at all."

At the mention of Nigellus, Sophronia exchanges a furtive glance with her sisters. Their mother's closest advisor and the royal empyrea has always been something of an enigma, even as he's been a regular feature in their lives since birth. He's kind enough to them, if a bit cold, and he has never given them reason to mistrust him. They aren't the only ones who are wary of him—the whole court dislikes him—but they fear him and the empress far too much to ever do more than whisper about it.

Sophronia can count all of the empyreas on the continent on two hands—each royal family employs one, except in Cellaria, and there are a scant handful who are nomadic either by nature or by training. While the power to bring down stars is natural for them, it is a gift that requires extensive study to control. An untrained empyrea is said to be a dangerous thing, allegedly able to bring stars down by accident and make their wishes come true simply by giving voice to them, though there hasn't been an empyrea born in Bessemia in her lifetime.

"Stardust?" Beatriz asks with a touch of derision. "A bit of a disappointment, really. I could have found a vial from any merchant in town for a few hundred asters."

Beatriz is the only one of them who speaks to their mother that way, and every time she does, a bolt of fear goes through Sophronia, though in this case she has to agree. Stardust is not exactly a rarity—every time a starshower happens in Vesteria, reapers comb the countrysides, gathering the puddles of stardust that remain, bringing in pounds of it to merchants, who bottle it up and sell it alongside their fine jewels and silks, each pinch good for a single wish—not strong enough to do much more than heal a broken bone or disappear a pimple, but valuable all the same. Stardust can be found in the inventory of any merchant worth his salt, except in Cellaria, that is, where starshowers don't occur. According to Cellarian lore, stardust isn't a gift from the stars but a curse, and even possessing it is a crime. To Cellarians, the absence of starshowers is viewed as a reward for their piety and a sign that the stars smile on the kingdom, though Sophronia wonders if the truth of it is the opposite, that the lore was written as a balm to convince Cellarians that life is better without the magic they don't have natural access to.

The empress only smiles.

"Not stardust," she says. "A wish. From Nigellus."

At that, even Beatriz goes quiet, looking at her bracelet with a mix of awe and fear. Sophronia does the same. Whereas stardust is a fairly average luxury, a wish from an empyrea is something else entirely. Usually, such wishes are made in person, with the empyrea wishing upon a star and using their magic to pull the star down from the sky. The wishes made that way are stronger, without the usual limits of stardust, but there are only so many stars, so they must be used only in the direst of circumstances. As far as Sophronia knows, the last time Nigellus wished on a star was to end a drought in the Bessemian countryside that had lasted months. His action doubtlessly saved thousands of lives and kept the rest of Bessemia's economy from plummeting, but there were many who thought the cost too high. Sophronia could still see the place in the sky where that star had once hung, part of the Clouded Sun constellation, which signified a change in weather. Sophronia wondered what constellations were missing stars now thanks to the creation of these baubles.

"And it's in the stone?" Beatriz asks, looking somewhat skeptical.

"Indeed," their mother says, still smiling. "A bit of alchemy Nigellus has come up with—the only three in existence. All you have to do is break the stone and make your wish. It's strong magic, strong enough to save a life. But again, they should only be used when you have no other options."

Beatriz helps Sophronia clasp the bracelet around her wrist, and Sophronia returns the favor for her. With that done, the empress looks at each of them, giving one final nod.

"Come, my doves," she says, pushing open the carriage door and letting in a burst of bright morning sunlight. "It is time to fly."

Beatriz

Beatriz has to squint when she steps out of the carriage, the sunlight blinding her and making her eyes itch even more. The chemist who made her eye drops told her that she would become accustomed to the sensation, but she's practiced using them a few times now and she's not sure that will ever be the case. Loath as she is to admit it, though, her mother's right—it's a necessary discomfort.

When her eyes adjust she sees three matching open-topped carriages that must have preceded them from the palace—all painted powder blue and gold, Bessemian colors, and each pulled by a pair of pure-white horses with ribbons wound through their manes and tails. Beside each carriage is a small silk tent. One Frivian green, one Temarinian gold, and one Cellarian scarlet, each flanked by a pair of guards dressed to match.

The Bessemian delegation that accompanies them surrounds their carriage, and Beatriz spies a few familiar faces, including Nigellus with his cold silver eyes and long black robe. Even under the heat of the noon sun, there isn't so much as a bead of sweat on his alabaster forehead. He must be her mother's age, at least, but he looks closer in age to Beatriz and her sisters.

Surrounding each tent is a cluster of well-dressed men and women, their faces all blurring together—the delegations of nobles sent from each country to escort them. The Cellarian party is by far the brightest, dressed in colorful shades—some of which she can't put a name to. They look friendly enough, all wide, beaming smiles, but Beatriz knows better than most that looks can be deceiving.

It doesn't matter how many times Beatriz has heard her mother go over the official handoff, she still doesn't feel prepared, but she tries not to show her nerves, instead keeping her back straight and her head high.

Their mother kisses each of their cheeks one last time, and when she gets to Beatriz, her lips are thin and cold against her skin and then it is done. No show of sentimentality, no parting words, no declarations of love. Beatriz knows better than to expect anything different. She tells herself that she doesn't even want any of that from her mother, but she finds that it still stings when the empress moves away from them, leaving the three sisters in the center of the clearing, caught both literally and figuratively between worlds.

Daphne takes the first step, as she always has as long as Beatriz can remember, walking toward the Frivian tent with her shoulders squared and her eyes fixed straight ahead. She tries so hard to mirror their mother's coldness, but she can't stop herself from looking back at them, and in that instant, Beatriz sees the uncertainty plain in her eyes. In that instant, Beatriz wonders what would happen if Daphne said no, if she refused to go into the tent, if she disobeyed her mother. But of course she doesn't. Daphne could sooner catch a falling star in the palm of her hand than go against the empress's wishes. With a final half smile at Beatriz and Sophronia, Daphne steps into the tent, disappearing from view.

Beatriz glances at Sophronia, who has never been able to hide her fear like Daphne.

"Come on," Beatriz tells her. "We'll go together."

Together until we can't be, she thinks, but she doesn't say that part out loud. They follow Daphne's lead, and before they disappear into their own tents, Beatriz gives Sophronia one last smile that her sister's wobbling mouth can't quite return.

She hopes Sophronia won't cry in front of the Temarinians—that shouldn't be their first impression of her, and their mother has always stressed the importance of a good first impression.

As soon as Beatriz enters the candlelit tent, she's besieged by an army of women speaking in rapid Cellarian. Though Beatriz is fluent in the language, they all speak so quickly, with a range of different accents, that she has to listen carefully to make sense of what they're saying.

"Bessemian fashions," one woman says with a scoff, pulling at the full, lacy pale yellow skirt of Beatriz's gown. "Pah, she looks like a common daisy."

Before Beatriz can protest, another woman chimes in, pinching Beatriz's cheeks. "There is no color here, either. Like a porcelain doll without any paint—flat and homely."

Homely. That stings. After all, what is she if not beautiful? It is the one value that has been assigned her: Daphne is the charming one, Sophronia the brainy one, and Beatriz is the pretty one. Without that, what value does she have? But Cellarians have different standards—they want beauty that is loud and dramatic and overstated. So she bites her tongue and lets herself be poked and prodded and talked about without speaking a word. She lets them pull her dress over her head and toss it to the floor like an old rag, lets them unlace her stays and pull off her chemise, leaving her naked and shivering in the chilly autumnal air.

But at least now, the snide remarks cease. She feels their eyes on her, appraising.

"Well," the first woman says, her mouth pursed. "At least we know she eats. Some of these Bessemian women have no softness to them—no breasts, no hips, no flesh at all. At least I don't have to tailor clothes for a skeleton."

The woman pulls a new shift over Beatriz's head, then laces her into a new corset. Where her Bessemian corset was so tightly laced she could scarcely breathe in it, this one is looser. It seems designed to emphasize her breasts and hips rather than to make any part of her smaller.

A petticoat follows, more voluminous than any Beatriz has worn before, even to a formal ball. It is so wide it will be difficult to fit through doors, let alone into a carriage, but at least the material is light. Even through the layers, her skin is cool. She feels the rustle of a breeze that blows in through the tent.

Finally, the dress itself. Ruby-red and gold silk damask with a low neckline and wide shoulders, baring more skin than anyone in Bessemia would dare before sundown. Without a mirror, it's difficult to tell how it looks, but the woman in charge of her dressing gives her an approving nod before conceding her place to the woman who seems to be in charge of cosmetics.

After that, it's a flurry of brushes and paint, of hair pulled and curled and piled, of metal combs scraping over her scalp and leaving it raw. Of cold paint brushing over her eyes and cheeks and lips, of powder dusting on top of that. It's tiresome, but Beatriz knows better than to complain or even flinch. She's learned how to stay perfectly still—a living, breathing doll.

Lastly, the seamstress and the hairdresser help her step into heeled slippers crafted from the same material as her gown.

"She is quite lovely, isn't she?" the woman in charge of cosmetics says, eyeing her with her head tilted slightly to the side.

The seamstress nods. "Prince Pasquale ought to be very happy with his bride."

"Not that he's happy about much," the hairdresser replies with a snort.

Beatriz smiles and dips into a slight curtsy. "Many thanks for all of your hard work," she says in perfect, unaccented Cellarian, to the surprise of her attendants. "I am truly looking forward to seeing Cellaria."

The hairdresser speaks first, flustered and red-cheeked.

"A-Apologies, Y-Your Highness," she stutters. "I meant no disrespect, to you or the prince—"

Beatriz waves her words away. Her mother has stressed the importance of endearing herself to her staff. They're the ones who know the most, after all. And the comment about Pasquale is nothing she hasn't already heard from her mother's spies, who have described him as a sullen, moody boy. "Now, shall we?"

The seamstress hurries to hold open the tent flap for Beatriz to step through, into the bright sunlight once more. She sees that she's the last to emerge, her sisters already piled into their respective carriages, each surrounded by the delegation of fawning courtiers.

Both of them look like strangers.

Sophronia resembles an elaborately crafted pastry, swamped in a sea of bejeweled chiffon ruffles in shades of lemon yellow, her blond hair curled and piled in a towering hairstyle ornamented with all manner of bows and jewels. Daphne, on the other hand, wears a green velvet dress that could be called plain only in comparison to theirs, with long, narrow sleeves and bare shoulders, and delicate flowers embroidered on the bodice in shimmering black thread; her jet hair, in a single braid down her back, highlights the severe sharpness of her bone structure.

They both look beautiful, but they also already look so different. In a year, they might be strangers altogether. The thought makes Beatriz feel sick, but she tries not to show it. Instead, she walks delicately toward her own carriage, careful that the heels of her slippers don't dig into the soil and make her stumble. A guard hands her up into the carriage, and she settles into the empty space between two Cellarian women with matching red lacquered mouths.

The women immediately fall all over themselves paying her compliments in stilted Bessemian.

"Thank you," Beatriz replies in Cellarian, much to their relief, but she barely hears the rest of their chatter.

Instead, she watches her sisters. Her driver urges the horses into motion and the carriage jerks forward, heading south, but she keeps her eyes on them until they both disappear from view.

Daphne

Daphne thought she would be able to see the moment she left the country of her birth. She's imagined a place where the fertile green grass and blooming flowers stop short and give way to the hard brown earth and patches of snow that make up Friv's terrain. She's imagined she would feel it in the air, that she would exhale the fragrant, fresh air of Bessemia and inhale the frigid, dead air of Friv.

Instead, the change happens gradually over the three-day journey north. The flat earth turns to rolling hills, those hills slowly go bald, the trees around her begin to grow wild and skeletal, their branches twisting toward a sky that seems to appear slightly grayer every time she blinks. At each inn they stop at, the accents of the innkeeper and the other patrons grow rougher and sharper, though they still speak Bessemian.

They will reach the border today, and then there will truly be no going back.

This is a mistake, Daphne thinks as she watches the world around her shift and change into something unrecognizable and dark. She wants to go home, to the palace where she learned to walk. She wants to run back to her mother and feel safe and comfortable in her shadow. She wants to wrap her arms around her sisters and feel their hearts beat as one, just as they were always meant to.

The longing is so strong that her throat goes tight under the lace of her new high-necked gown and it feels like she's choking. For a second, she lets herself imagine what it would feel like to tear it off, the stiff velvet plush beneath her fingers as the material gives a satisfying rip and she's free to breathe deeply, the skin of her throat no longer itchy and hot. Already, she misses the unstructured pastel dresses of her girlhood, how she could always find herself reflected in Sophronia and Beatriz, the same features, refracted like facets in a diamond.

She tries not to think of her sisters as she last saw them, strangers with strange faces, varnished and corseted and pinched and prodded until she had to squint to find them.

"Are you all right?" her companion in the carriage asks. Lady Cliona, the daughter of Lord Panlington.

Daphne supposes the king sent her to be a source of comfort during this trip, that Daphne is meant to be grateful to have someone her own age to travel with instead of a stiff matron with narrow eyes and pursed lips.

She recalls everything she knows of Lord Panlington—former head of the Panlington Clan before the Clan Wars ended and Bartholomew became king of a united Friv. Panlington was a formidable warlord and one of the last of the clan heads to swear fealty, though since the war's end, he's been one of Bartholomew's most loyal courtiers—a few spies have even used the term *friend*.

She knows significantly less about Lady Cliona—only that she's his sole daughter, though he has five sons. Cliona is said to be his favorite. The spies said that she was notoriously headstrong, bold, and hopelessly spoiled. They didn't explicitly say she was beautiful, but there was mention of six marriage proposals rejected over the last year since she turned sixteen, so Daphne had assumed.

Now, sitting across from her, Daphne's surprised to find that she isn't a traditional beauty—at least not by Bessemian standards. Her face is more freckles than unblemished skin and her copper curls are riotous, barely restrained in a chignon. Her features are too sharp, lending her an air of severity that makes her look older than her now seventeen years. But over the last three days, Daphne's realized she has a quick, dry wit, and she's seen her wrap everyone from the carriage driver to the innkeepers to the guards around her finger in mere seconds.

Daphne decides she likes Cliona—or, at least, the girl she's pretending to be likes Cliona.

"I'm fine," Daphne tells her, forcing a smile. "I'm nervous, I suppose," she continues carefully. "Prince Cillian and I have only exchanged a few letters over the years, but I don't know anything about him. Have you met him?"

Something flickers over Cliona's expression, gone too quickly to say what it was, but Daphne files it away. "Yes, of course," Cliona says, shaking her head. "We grew up together at court. He's very kind, and very handsome. I'm sure he will adore you."

Daphne tries to look relieved, but she knows that isn't the truth—not the whole truth. Prince Cillian is dying, and everyone seems to know it. The last report from the spies said he hadn't left his bed in three months and was getting worse each day. He just has to live long enough to marry her, she reminds herself, though a little voice in her head chides her for her callousness—it sounds an awful lot like Sophronia.

"And the rest of Friv?" Daphne asks. "I've heard it's still a . . . tumultuous country. How do they feel about a foreign princess set to be their next queen?"

There's that look again, the fleeting glimpse of wide eyes and pursed lips. The look, Daphne realizes, Cliona gets right before she lies.

"Why, I'm sure they will adore you as well, Your Highness," Lady Cliona says with a bright smile. "Why wouldn't they?"

Daphne leans back against the carriage seat and looks her new companion over. "You aren't a very good liar, are you, Lady Cliona?" she asks.

Cliona freezes before managing a bashful smile.

"When I was a child my mother used to say the stars blessed me with an honest tongue, but these days it seems more like a curse," she admits.

Daphne laughs. "Is Friv so full of liars that you feel hindered by truth?" she asks, raising her eyebrows.

Cliona laughs too, shaking her head. "Aren't all courts?"

They ride for a few hours more in bursts of small talk and stretches of silence, until the sun is high overhead and the carriage comes to a stop beside a wide, rushing river, the sound of it so loud Daphne hears it even before the door opens. More carriages are gathered on the other side of the river, all of them painted dark gray except one that is a bright lacquered green with gold and black accents, drawn by two pure-black horses bigger than any Daphne has ever seen.

This is where Bessemia meets Friv, she realizes—the Tenal River marking the border. There are plenty of footbridges across, as well as wider bridges that are part of the trade routes, but here there is not a bridge in sight.

"Tradition dictates you make the crossing into Friv on foot," Cliona says, seeing Daphne's bewildered expression.

"On foot," she repeats, frowning. "Through the water, you mean?" When Cliona nods, Daphne can't help balking. "But it will be freezing cold and I can't possibly keep my balance."

"Someone will make sure you don't fall," Cliona says, waving a dismissive hand before her eyes catch on someone waiting at the riverbank. "See? There's Bairre."

"Bear?" Daphne asks, confused and a little alarmed. She peers out of the carriage, but she doesn't see any bears—only a crowd of strangers. Cliona doesn't have a chance to answer before a footman offers a hand and Daphne steps down onto the ground.

Still Bessemian ground, she thinks, but the distinction doesn't give her much comfort.

Cliona doesn't stray far from her side, and when she offers Daphne her arm, Daphne accepts it. The terrain is unfamiliar and her new boots are too tight and the last thing she wants is for her first impression in Friv to be of her falling flat on her face.

A first impression lasts forever, you must ensure you make a good one, as her mother liked to say. Daphne repeats the words to herself now, hoping she will not find a way to be a disappointment before even setting foot in Friv.

A boy waits at the bank, and when they approach, he bows his head, but his expression is difficult to read. His chestnut hair is curly and overgrown, blowing wildly in the wind and hiding his eyes. He's handsome, Daphne thinks, but in that moody, wild way that yearns for a haircut, a bath, and a glass of champagne to alleviate his pinched frown and tense jaw. There are dark circles under his eyes, standing out starkly against his pale skin, and she wonders when he last saw either his bed or the sun.

"Bairre," Cliona says—not *a* bear, Daphne realizes, but *the* Bairre. As in King Bartholomew's bastard son. He gives Cliona a curt nod before his eyes fall on Daphne and he bows. "Normally, your betrothed would be the one to escort you across, but given Prince Cillian's health . . ." She trails off.

At the mention of Cillian, the boy flinches—*Bairre* flinches. There hasn't been much information from the spies about Bairre, even though he's been a regular presence at court his entire life. The story is, he was found in a basket on the palace steps when he was a few weeks old, mere days after the Clan Wars ended. There was nothing on him but a note with his name, but the king didn't hesitate to claim him as his own, raising him alongside Prince Cillian despite Queen Darina's protests.

"Your Highness," Bairre says, his voice as chilled as the wind blowing off the river. He looks back at the river and the group of courtiers waiting on the other side.

Daphne follows his gaze, taking in the sparse harshness of the land with its gray skies and bald trees, the patches of overgrown weeds. She tries not to flinch at the sight of the courtiers in their drab velvet gowns and ermine cloaks. Already, she yearns for the soft beauty of Bessemia, the frills and silks and sparkle. Looking at the women now, she can't find one piece of jewelry among them, not a hint of rouge even. The people are all bland and colorless and Daphne can't imagine she will ever feel like one of them.

Friv is a harsh, joyless land, her mother told her. *Filled with harsh, joyless people. It is a land shaped by war and hungry for blood.*

Daphne shudders.

"You could try to smile," Bairre says, his voice jerking her out of her thoughts. "They did come all this way to greet you."

Daphne forces herself to smile, knowing he's right. She can hate it here—nothing can prevent that—but the people can't know it.

"Let's get this over with," Bairre says, his voice tight.

Daphne shoots him an annoyed look and opens her mouth to retort but then forces herself to bite her tongue. After traveling for three days, leaving behind her sisters and her home, and now getting ready to plunge into frigid water, she is ready to bite anyone's head off. But insulting the king's bastard will get her nowhere, so she simply lets Cliona take her boots off, knotting the laces and hoisting them over her shoulder. Bairre lowers himself into the river with a splash, holding an arm out to Daphne.

The river rushes so wildly that it looks ready to knock

Bairre over, but he holds firm. That, at least, gives her some comfort, and she takes hold of his arm. With her heart beating so loudly she thinks they can hear it across the river, she lets him help her into the water.

The cold knocks the breath from her lungs, and she has to keep herself from crying out. The water goes up to her hips, soaking her velvet dress and making it so heavy she has to struggle to keep upright, holding on to Bairre's arm so tightly she fears she's bruising his skin.

Cliona is in the water next, taking Daphne's other arm, and together the three of them make their way across the river in slow, measured steps.

"You're going to crack a tooth if you keep chattering your teeth like that," Bairre tells Daphne, his voice even and unbothered by the cold, though he seems to be quite bothered by her.

She glances sideways at him, eyebrows knitted. "I can't help it," she says, her voice quivering. "It's *cold.*"

Bairre snorts, shaking his head. "It's practically still *summer,*" he tells her.

"It's freezing and I'm wet," she says. Though she doesn't mean it to, her voice comes out like a whine. If her mother were here, she would reprimand her with a sharp tug of the ear, but at least Daphne doesn't cry. If she does, she knows there will be no stopping it, so instead she clenches her jaw and keeps her gaze straight ahead. She puts one foot in front of the other and thinks of a warm fire in the hearth and a cup of hot tea in her hands.

When they arrive at the other side of the river, a man reaches down to help Daphne out of the water, but it's only when she's safely on Frivian soil with an emerald-green flannel blanket draped over her shoulders that she sees the gleaming gold crown resting on his brow and remembers that she needs to curtsy.

"Your Majesty," she says to King Bartholomew, the words she's meant to say dim and far away in her mind. She's meant to recite some sort of formality, some promise of loyalty, but all she can think of is how cold she is.

King Bartholomew's smile is kind, though, a beam of warmth that Daphne clings to. "Welcome to Friv, Princess Daphne," he says in Bessemian before turning to where Bairre is helping Cliona out of the river.

"How was the crossing?" he asks Bairre in Frivian.

Bairre looks at the king, not bothering to bow even when Cliona manages a shaky curtsy. Instead, he shrugs, scowling.

"I don't see why it was necessary now," he mutters, eyes flickering to Daphne.

King Bartholomew flinches before shaking his head. "There are bigger things at stake, Bairre."

Bairre laughs, the sound cold and harsh. "Bigger things?" he asks. "What, trade routes and a *cannadragh* princess are more important than—"

The king silences him with a look before his eyes shift to Daphne, huddled in the warmth of the blanket and trying to make sense of what she just heard.

"Your mother assured me you took well to your studies, including Frivian," he says, smiling, though the smile appears strained. "I apologize for Bairre's manners. We have a tent set up for you to change into some dry clothes. Lady Cliona, will you escort her, please, and change into something dry yourself? King or not, your father will have my head if you catch your death."

Cliona dips into a curtsy. "Of course, Your Majesty," she says, taking hold of Daphne's arm and steering her away, toward a burlap tent set up between two towering pine trees.

"What were they talking about?" Daphne asks.

"I'm not sure," Cliona admits, biting her bottom lip.

"And that word?" Daphne presses. "*Cannadragh*?"

"There isn't really a Bessemian equivalent," Cliona says. "The closest would be *soft*, but that isn't quite right. It's used to describe someone who is accustomed to a luxurious life."

Daphne can read between the lines—he called her a snob.

Sophronia

It's taken two days to cross into Temarin, and another day to make it to the outskirts of Kavelle, the capital city, but the trip has been relatively smooth up until now. Sophronia isn't sure if it's the bumpy road or her nervousness about finally meeting Leopold face to face that makes her stomach churn, but perhaps it's some combination of the two, along with the new Temarinian corset, which has been laced so tightly she can scarcely breathe without feeling the whalebone stays biting into her rib cage.

It's all she can do to focus on taking slow, shallow breaths while listening to her carriage companions ramble on in rapid Temarinian that she can only understand about three-quarters of. She thought she was fluent in the language, but then she's never practiced with anyone who's been drinking so freely.

One of the women, Duchess Henrietta, is Leopold's second cousin once removed, and the other, Duchess Bruna, is his aunt on his father's side. When they introduced themselves to her earlier, Sophronia smiled and nodded, like she hadn't been forced to memorize the Temarinian royal family tree before her sixth birthday. Like she doesn't know that Duchess Bruna's husband has a fondness for gambling and women that has left the once-illustrious family deep in debt, or that Duchess Henrietta's eldest son bears a striking resemblance to her husband's valet. It's strange, after so many years of knowing their names and the names and ages of their husbands, children, and other relations, to finally meet them in person. It's almost like characters from a book coming to life before her eyes, if those characters turned out to be loud and inebriated.

She turns her gaze out the window, to the quiet forest on the edge of Kavelle, trying not to think about what lies ahead. In another hour or so, she will finally meet Leopold. It's a strange thought—they must have exchanged hundreds of letters over the last decade. Letters that started out stiff and forced, a few stilted words, but in time grew to pages upon pages detailing private thoughts and particulars of their day-to-day lives. In some ways, she feels like she already knows Leopold better than anyone else in the world, except maybe her sisters.

But she doesn't, she reminds herself. The dossier her mother gave her has proven that. The Leopold she thought she knew wouldn't have tripled taxes on his subjects in order to increase his own wealth. He wouldn't have evicted two dozen families and razed their village in order to build a new hunting lodge. He wouldn't have had a man executed for publishing satirical illustrations of him. But the real Leopold has done all of that and more since taking the throne last year.

She doesn't really know him, not any more than he knows her, and she cannot forget that again.

Everyone in Temarin is our enemy, Sophronia, her mother said when she gave her the dossier. *Fail to remember that and you've doomed us all.*

Duchess Bruna clears her throat, drawing Sophronia's attention back to them. She tries to remember what they were discussing, what she's been asked. Something about Bessemia, something about her mother.

"She asked if the rumors about your mother were true," a soft voice says in Bessemian. The lady's maid who helped her get dressed this morning at the inn, though she didn't say a word to her then. Sophronia is surprised to hear how well she speaks Bessemian, without a touch of an accent.

"Which ones?" Sophronia asks the duchesses in Temarinian. Though she's in earnest, the women think she's made a joke and dissolve into laughter. Sophronia looks at the lady's maid again. She's around Sophronia's age, with blond hair almost the same color as her own that's been pulled back into a tight chignon, pretty but without the ornamentation and ostentation that seem to define Temarinian beauty.

"You speak Bessemian very well," Sophronia tells her.

The girl's cheeks turn pink and she drops her gaze. "Thank you, Your Highness. It's my native tongue, which is why the duchess wished that I accompany her on the journey. I grew up not far outside the palace."

Sophronia glances at the women to find them watching her, measuring her up. She doesn't know which one is the girl's employer, but it hardly matters.

"What's your name?" Sophronia asks her.

She opens her mouth to answer, but Duchess Bruna gets there first.

"Violie," she snaps at the girl. "Fetch my fan. This heat is infernal."

The girl—Violie—hastens to open up the reticule she carries, pulling out an ornate golden fan and passing it to Duchess Bruna, who immediately begins fanning herself with it.

"Poor dear," she adds, looking at Sophronia. "You must be sweltering as well. This carriage is a hothouse."

"I'm fine, thank you," Sophronia says. If anything, she thinks, there's a chill in the air, though the two duchesses have finished off a bottle of champagne between them, so perhaps that is the reason behind their warmth.

"Such a dear girl," Duchess Henrietta says, clicking her tongue and taking another long sip from her cut-crystal champagne flute.

The carriage veers sharply to the left, jerking Duchess Henrietta's flute out of her hand. It shatters on the floor of the carriage, spilling champagne all over Sophronia's silk slippers.

"What in blazes was that?" Duchess Bruna demands, snapping her fan shut and pushing open the carriage window. As soon as she does, the sound of frenzied shouts fills the carriage—Sophronia counts five voices, two of which she recognizes as the coachman's and the footman's.

"Not another robbery," Duchess Henrietta says, sounding more annoyed than alarmed. She rolls her eyes and closes the window again. "These woods are becoming a nuisance."

Sophronia peers out her own window to see a group of three masked men, each holding a dagger. One holds his blade to the throat of the footman while the coachman searches the bench, looking for something.

"They're going to hurt the footman," Sophronia says, alarmed. She doesn't understand why the other women are being so calm about it—the men have daggers and the only defense the women have is the empty wine bottle. Sophronia supposes she could make a weapon of that, if necessary, though that would lead to an awful lot of questions from her companions. But the duchesses are acting as though the shattered champagne glass is the worst of their problems, and even Violie doesn't seem particularly troubled.

"Not to worry, Your Highness," Duchess Henrietta says with a wan smile. "Unfortunately, it's becoming quite common in these parts—ruffians looking for easy coin—but the coachman is prepared with enough money to secure safe passage. It's only a temporary delay."

She sounds certain, but Sophronia's unease doesn't subside. She turns her attention back to the window.

The coachman holds out a white velvet pouch tied with a gold tassel and one of the thieves takes it, peering inside and weighing its contents in his palm. He pockets it, giving the man holding his dagger to the footman's throat a nod. The footman is released, and Sophronia notices that he doesn't look particularly troubled by the experience either.

"I didn't realize the crime rate was so high in these parts," Sophronia says, closing the curtain.

"Desperate people will do desperate things, Your Highness," Violie says softly.

"Ungrateful people, you mean," Duchess Bruna snaps.

Though she can't say as much, Sophronia is more inclined

to agree with Violie. The drastic increase in taxes in Temarin will have been enough to make many people desperate.

The sound of horses' hooves approaching interrupts. The three thieves hear them too and start to run, but in seconds, a dozen horses appear down the road, ridden by soldiers with pistols raised.

"Halt!" one of the men at the front shouts. Sophronia recognizes his uniform by the gold epaulets and the three yellow stripes on his sleeve—the head of the king's personal guard, though what he's doing here she isn't sure. The three thieves must know it too, because they all freeze, their hands going up. The guard dismounts, still holding his pistol, and walks toward the thieves. "You are under arrest in the name of His Majesty, King Leopold."

He grabs one of the thieves by the back of the neck, yanking his mask off. The boy can't be more than fourteen and looks on the verge of tears. The guard removes the masks of the other two and they look even younger, though the guard seems unfazed by this. "Cuff them!" he shouts, and his men dismount and do as he bids, binding the boys' hands behind their backs, more roughly than seems strictly necessary. One of the boys cries out when his arm is bent at what looks to be an unnatural angle.

"King Leopold wanted to surprise you by meeting the carriage," Duchess Bruna says. "And what fortuitous timing he has."

"Princess Sophronia, are you in there?" the head guard shouts toward the carriage. "You're safe now."

Sophronia's hand tightens on the door's handle and she thinks that perhaps the guards are more frightening than the thieves were. But she knows her role in this play, so she opens the carriage door and allows the footman to help her out into the afternoon sun, lifting her gloved hand to shield her eyes. She beams at the guard, offering him a bright smile that shows all of her teeth.

"Oh, thank you, sir," she says to him in Temarinian. "We were so frightened."

The guard bows low. "I'm sorry your first impression of Temarin was so coarse, Princess," he says.

"Sophronia!" a voice calls. She turns her attention back to the retinue of guards, and then she sees him and despite everything, her heart stutters. She knows him right away even though he looks a bit different from the last portrait, which was sent two years ago—his bronze hair is longer, curling around his ears, and his features appear sharper, most of the boyish roundness whittled away, but more than that, he's *real*. Not oil and canvas, confined to two dimensions and to stillness, but flesh and blood and life. She didn't know he could smile like that.

She gives herself a mental shake. *Did he smile like that when he sentenced the artist to death? When he forced those villagers from their homes?*

In seconds he's off his horse and coming toward her, and then she is caught up in his arms, her arms around his neck. Somehow, he even *smells* like she imagined he would, like cedar and some kind of spice.

When they pull apart he has an embarrassed smile on his face and Sophronia belatedly remembers their audience. She glances around to see the two duchesses, Violie, and Leopold's guards all watching them, their expressions a collection of amused and bemused. Even the thieves are staring, though they only look afraid.

"Apologies," Leopold says, dipping into a bow and kissing the back of her hand. "I just can't believe you're actually finally here."

Sophronia forces a smile, trying to control her rapidly beating heart and the flush she feels working its way over her cheeks. "I can't believe it either," she tells him.

And that, at least, is true.

Leopold helps her onto his horse in front of him, holding the reins on either side of her waist as they make their way through the woods and toward Kavelle and the palace. Word of their arrival must have spread, because people are pouring out from the villages on the outskirts of the city, waving and cheering for Leopold and Sophronia, who wave back. Not everyone cheers, though. She notices that a good quarter of the crowd stands in silence, watching them go past with stony expressions and hard eyes. But they don't dare to jeer—not that Sophronia can blame them. The execution of the illustrator served as a dire warning.

Leopold's guards surround them on every side, and the carriage holding the duchesses and Violie brings up the rear of their entourage. The three thieves are still cuffed, walking beside the guards' horses.

"What will happen to them?" Sophronia asks Leopold through her smile. Her cheeks are beginning to ache, but she holds on to it, smiling at the peasants who line the pathway, her hand raised in a constant wave.

"Who?" Leopold asks, confused.

"The boys," she clarifies, nodding toward one of them, trailing beside a guard on their right.

"Oh, the thieves," Leopold says, and she feels him shrug. "Not to worry—crime is taken very seriously in Temarin. They'll be properly punished."

He says the words like a reassurance, but Sophronia is far from reassured. Did he think the illustrator was *properly punished* as well?

"They're so young," she says, forcing her voice to stay light and airy. "Perhaps some mercy would be appropriate—no one was hurt, after all."

"But you could have been," Leopold says. "And my mother says it's important to set an example or the crime rate will only climb higher."

Leopold's mother, Dowager Queen Eugenia, was only fourteen when she was sent to Temarin from Cellaria to marry King Carlisle and secure the truce that ended the Celestian War. Sophronia knows this because her mother often used it as an example of her own kindness in waiting until her daughters were sixteen to marry them off. Their spies have reported that, since King Carlisle's death a year ago, Queen Eugenia has become more involved in Temarinian politics, helping to advise Leopold, who was only fifteen when he took the throne.

"They're about the same age as your brothers," Sophronia points out, thinking of the younger princes, Gideon, fourteen, and Reid, twelve. "Surely your mother would be sympathetic."

"My brothers would never rob a coach and threaten to kill a footman," Leopold replies.

"I can't imagine these boys did it for fun. Look at that one," she says, nodding toward the youngest-looking of the three. "He's skin and bones. When do you think the last proper meal he ate was?"

Leopold doesn't speak for a moment. "You have a soft heart, I admire that, but they made their choices. There must be consequences."

Sophronia tries to mask the unease working its way through her as her mother's words come back to her, echoing in her mind with each clip of the horse's hooves. *He is our enemy, and you will not forget that again.*

Beatriz

For Beatriz, the carriage ride to the Cellarian palace in the city of Vallon passes in a blur. The ladies in her carriage—tired from the first several legs of their journey—fall asleep soon after they depart the last inn, leaving Beatriz to stare out the window, looking for hints of Vallon in the distance.

She knows she's going to miss her sisters. She already feels the space left by them in her heart the way she used to feel the space in her mouth after losing a baby tooth. She can't help but prod it and marvel at the loss, but she's also hungry for Cellaria, hungry for change, hungry for a taste of the power her mother has always guarded so carefully, like a dragon in a children's story.

While she has a moment's peace, she turns her mind to the mission her mother set for her.

Charm the Temarinian ambassador, the empress told her. *I want him so wrapped around your finger that he will leap from the cliffs of Alder if you ask it of him.*

It will be easy enough—this is what she was raised for, after all. Raised to charm and seduce and curl people, men in particular, around her finger. She has an arsenal of courtesans' tricks at her disposal: how to laugh and touch a man's arm, letting her touch linger an extra second; how to smile in a way that shows the dimple in her cheek; and most importantly, how to deduce quickly and accurately what is desired of her and how to fulfill that desire. How to become the blushing innocent. The bold seductress. The shy romantic. The brazen wit.

Everyone has a fantasy, and Beatriz has learned how to embody every last one. It is simply a matter of reading people.

Everything she knows about the Temarinian ambassador, Lord Savelle, indicates that he will be easily charmed. A widower in his forties, he's spent half of his life in the Cellarian court, barred from using stardust for any purpose. Her mother's spies say that he is disliked and distrusted by everyone at court, but by none more so than the king himself, who wastes no opportunity to insult him. For his part, Lord Savelle appears unruffled by the attitudes of the king and his court—he is in Cellaria to do a job, and by all appearances he has done it well. In the nearly two decades since the end of the Celestian War, peace between Cellaria and Temarin has been kept—a difficult task, given the rumors of King Cesare's quick temper and rash impulsiveness. The Cellarian spies credit Lord Savelle with singlehandedly preventing the king from declaring war on what he viewed as the heathen Temarinians no fewer than a dozen times.

Beatriz is sure Lord Savelle must be lonely.

You want me to flirt with an old man? Beatriz asked her mother. *He's old enough to be my father.*

The empress didn't like that—didn't like any sort of questioning of her instructions. But Beatriz was never as good as her sisters at holding her tongue. If she were to be honest, she never really tried. *I expect you to do whatever it takes to win him over,* the empress said coldly. At Beatriz's horrified look, she laughed. *Oh, please, Beatriz. Playing the part of the prude doesn't suit you. You'll do what needs to be done.*

The other ladies in the carriage stir when they begin to cross over a bridge leading into a walled city with colorful spires peeking over the walls, and Beatriz forgets her mother, forgets those instructions and how nauseated they make her.

"Ah, Vallon," one of the ladies says, wistfulness in her voice. She's the closest to Beatriz's age, but still at least a decade older.

Bianca is her name, Beatriz remembers, the Countess of Lavellia, who is insecure about the size of her ears and has a reputation for bullying the younger ladies at court. They haven't even gotten to court yet and Beatriz has already seen those rumors to be true—not in an overt way, the countess knows better than to be openly rude to her future queen, but there have been barbed compliments and withering looks and cutting laughs in her direction.

Each time, Beatriz grits her teeth and pretends not to notice, even when the other ladies smirk and titter behind their hands. Her mother has taught her many things, most of them unpleasant, but chief among them is patience.

She leans closer to the window, trying to see as much of the city as she can, but even at this distance, it's too big.

Bessemia's capital, Hapantoile, could fit inside it at least thrice over.

Suddenly, Beatriz—always too loud, too bright, too boisterous—feels as small as a mouse in a cathedral.

They draw closer, over the bridge and through the city gate, a great, gilded thing set with a rainbow of jewels that glitter in the afternoon light, making it look like it's alive. Then it's through a labyrinth of winding streets, past brightly colored town houses and manors, gardens blooming with flowers Beatriz can't begin to name, people in fashions that in Bessemia would be considered gaudy and ostentatious. The whole city bustles and glows with a light Beatriz never imagined possible. The cacophony of city sounds hits her ears like the sweetest music.

"It's beautiful," she tells the ladies in Cellarian, her face pressed so close to the window that her breath fogs it every time she exhales.

But even the city is lackluster in the shadow of the palace. It looms over everything, a large white structure with too many windows and balconies to count and an arrangement of pillars along the entrance. In the sunlight, the white stone seems to glow with a light of its own.

Beatriz has always thought the Bessemian palace is the grandest in the world, but when she steps out of the carriage and stands before the Cellarian palace, she realizes just how small her home is.

She tries not to gape openly and instead focuses her attention on the group of people gathered in a line, facing her. Each one is dressed more outrageously than the last. One woman wears a sweeping orange gown with sleeves the size of watermelons. Another wears a hat that resembles a monarch butterfly, dripping in more jewels than any chandelier Beatriz has ever seen. Another man wears a suit of red-and-black-striped satin and boots with ruby-studded heels.

At the center of the line is King Cesare, recognizable by the gold crown atop his head and the bejeweled velvet cape around his shoulders. Beatriz has heard stories from some of the Cellarian women in the Bessemian brothels about King Cesare, most of whom used a past dalliance with the king to advertise themselves—who wouldn't want to bed a woman good enough for a king? In his youth he was said to be the handsomest man on the continent, and even now, in his fifties, she can see the shadow of that. They say he has so many bastards that a day has been set aside in the calendar to commemorate all of their birthdays at once.

Beatriz can feel her heart speed up as she shifts her gaze to his right, where his only living legitimate child stands at his side, marked by his own golden crown, less ornate than his father's but every bit as regal.

Prince Pasquale.

He looks like Beatriz imagined, more or less, though the portrait she received of him some years back took some liberties. His shoulders aren't quite so broad, his stature slighter. But the artist captured his eyes perfectly—the same wide hazel gaze that looks better suited to a child, curious and also somewhat terrified. When those eyes meet hers, he tries to smile, but it's a close-lipped thing, tight and insincere.

A crowd lines the stairs that stretch up to the palace,

shouting townspeople who cheer as Beatriz begins her ascent. One of the ladies from the carriage hastens to lift the long train of her gown, which spills out behind her like a trail of fresh blood.

Her legs ache when she finally reaches the top, but she manages to dip into a deep curtsy before King Cesare.

"Welcome to Cellaria, Princess Beatriz," the king says, his voice booming enough that even the crowd gathered at the base of the steps can hear. He reaches down, placing one smooth finger beneath her chin and tilting her face up toward him. Beatriz meets his gaze as he looks her over, his expression critical. For an instant, her heart stops beating—what if he can see through the eye drops? She used them last night, careful to put them in just before she fell asleep so that the servants who woke her in the morning didn't notice. The apothecary said the effect would last a full twenty-four hours, but what if something went wrong? Will the king have her killed on the spot? After what feels like an eternity, he smiles widely and lifts her back to her feet.

"A beauty!" he proclaims to the crowd, taking hold of Beatriz's hand and holding it up. The crowd erupts again into cheers.

Cheers for her, cheers in her honor—but they feel hollow to Beatriz.

"My son is a lucky man," King Cesare continues, taking Prince Pasquale's hand in his other one and joining it with Beatriz's. The prince's hand is clammy in hers, but he gives hers what she imagines is meant to be a reassuring squeeze. Halfhearted as it might be, she appreciates the gesture, but when she tries to meet his eyes, he continues staring out at the crowd, sweat beading on his forehead though the weather is mild and breezy.

"I know we all had our worries that a Bessemian princess would be too corrupted by magic to make an appropriate future queen," King Cesare continues, and Beatriz feels a bolt of unease shoot through her, though she is careful not to lose her smile. She holds her breath and waits for him to continue.

"But Empress Margaraux has assured me that Princess Beatriz has been raised Cellarian in both customs and faith and she follows the true path of the stars. Isn't that right, my dear?"

Beatriz opens her mouth to recite the line she's been practicing for years, the denunciation of magic and Bessemia's heathen ways. She is even ready to throw in some fist-shaking or dramatic swooning, depending on how the audience responds. But she never gets the chance.

"And why should we trust the word of that whore?" a man shouts from the crowd. "A woman who sleeps with a demon empyrea in exchange for her petty heart's desires?"

Beatriz has to stifle a laugh at the idea of her mother and Nigellus together. She knows her mother has had many lovers over the years, but the thought of Nigellus among them is absurd.

"I would not," the king says. "My ambassador has confirmed it, as have the spies we have in the Bessemian court. All have described Princess Beatriz as a pious and devout girl. While her heathen sisters used stardust to wish for ponies and jewels, Princess Beatriz refused every bit of stardust ever offered to her."

It's a lie—almost as laughable as the thought of her mother and Nigellus—but Beatriz knows that those ambassadors and spies are all hypocrites, all willing to tell the king whatever Beatriz's mother ordered in exchange for a few vials of stardust of their own. Those who did refuse were met with horribly unfortunate accidents.

"It is true," Beatriz says, looking out at the crowd from lowered eyelashes. "I have counted the days, waiting to be rid of that horrid place. I feel truly blessed to be here, before you, in a far more civilized country, and I am infinitely grateful to King Cesare and Prince Pasquale for rescuing me from such a nightmare. If I never see a mite of stardust again, I will thank the stars every moment of the rest of my life."

It might be a tad overdramatic, but it does the trick. Even the man who shouted looks placated.

"A true treasure! If you aren't careful, Pasquale," King Cesare says, leaning close to his son's ear, though everyone within fifty feet can hear him, "I might have to steal her away from you."

Before Beatriz can process his words, the king places a hand on her backside in plain view of the thousands gathered and squeezes. She can barely feel his touch through the layers of petticoats and the bustle, but heat still rises to her face.

She shouldn't be surprised—she's heard more stories of his lasciviousness than she can count, stories about noblemen's wives and scullery maids and seemingly every type of woman in between. Yet shock freezes her in place and for an instant, she feels like a doe before a hunter. But her mother didn't raise does, she reminds herself, swallowing down the bile in her throat. She raised vipers.

"Your Majesty," Beatriz says, forcing her mouth into a coquettish smile when all she wants to do is slap his hand away. "You ought to know that if you have to resort to stealing a girl, you're doing something wrong."

For a second, there is silence, and Beatriz worries that her mouth has gotten her into trouble, that she has shown her fangs and claws too early. *Patience,* her mother has always cautioned. Before she can apologize, though, King Cesare throws back his head and laughs loudly, dropping his hand.

"And a spitfire, too," he says with an approving smile before his eyes shift to his petrified son. He lowers his voice, speaking this time only for Beatriz and the prince. "Perhaps you'll learn a thing or two from her, my boy."

The term of endearment doesn't soften the words, and Prince Pasquale flinches like he's been physically struck. King Cesare doesn't see it—his attention is already focused once again on the crowd.

"These two lovebirds won't have to wait too long—as planned, their wedding will take place tomorrow evening. . . ." He trails off, glancing back at them with mischief in his eyes. "But for now, I don't suppose a kiss would hurt anyone."

This time when Prince Pasquale looks at her, fear is plain in his eyes. His hand trembles in hers.

Stars above, Beatriz thinks. *He's never kissed a girl before.*

In all of her training for this, she has been led to believe that Cellaria is a land of pleasure and loose morals—completely at odds with its strict attitude about magic—and she expected to find a prince who was his father's son, a confident debaucher with a string of broken hearts in his wake. Instead, Prince Pasquale is a nervous boy, looking at her like she's some sort of dragon come to swallow him whole.

The crowd is waiting and watching them, excited for a show, and Beatriz is nothing if not a performer.

"Pull me close to you," she whispers to Prince Pasquale, who stares at her, alarmed.

"Wh . . . What?" he asks.

"Just do it," she replies.

Prince Pasquale swallows, eyes shifting to his father, to the crowd, then back to her. His hand still in hers, he pulls her toward him, and Beatriz presses her lips to his.

In the eruption of cheers and whistles, no one notices how uncomfortable a kiss it is, but Beatriz does. It isn't just that it's clumsy the way most first kisses are with a new person, it's the fact that it's cold—only lips touching, his hand dutifully placed on her back just so. There is no spark to it, no warmth, no romance at all.

But the crowd wants to see a great love story unfolding before their eyes, and Beatriz isn't about to disappoint them. When they break apart, she smiles, biting her lip and summoning a blush to her cheeks just as she learned to do from the best courtesans in Bessemia.

You're a toy to them, one of them, Sabine, told her. *If you can become what they want you to be, they'll burn the world down in your name.*

She knows what Cellaria wants her to be, the passionate beauty, the blushing bride, the princess madly in love with her prince. Looking sideways at Prince Pasquale, she realizes she doesn't have the slightest idea what he wants her to be. But she's determined to find out.

Daphne

A scant half hour after emerging from the river drenched and freezing, Daphne finds herself in a dry, new gown almost identical to the green velvet one she wore before, a thick ermine cape draped over her shoulders to ward off the chill that works its way even into the carriage she shares with King Bartholomew and Bairre. Neither of them seems to feel the cold, but when Daphne remarks on it, Bartholomew gives her a small smile that doesn't reach his eyes.

"You'll grow used to it, in time," he tells her.

Daphne thinks she would rather burn alive than stay in this miserable place long enough to *grow used to it,* but she pretends to find the words a comfort.

King Bartholomew glances at Bairre, whose attention is focused out the window, before looking back at her. He seems to steel himself for something—hardly a good sign, Daphne thinks. The king takes a deep, steadying breath before he speaks.

"There is no easy way to say this and I'm still struggling

to say it at all, but Cillian died six days ago, the night after Cliona and the others departed to meet you."

Daphne laughs. She doesn't mean to, but after all the stress and sleepless nights and change over the course of the last few days, she can't help it.

"You aren't serious," she says, but when Bartholomew and Bairre only look at her with anguished eyes, her laughter dies. "I—I'm s-so sorry," she stammers, "I didn't mean . . . I'd heard he was ill, but I didn't think . . ."

"None of us did," King Bartholomew says, shaking his head. "Until a few months ago, he was the picture of health. We always assumed his illness would pass. It didn't."

His words are clipped and matter-of-fact and Daphne can see the general he was before he was king, a man more familiar with death than life. But even that hasn't prepared him for the loss of his son—beneath the placid exterior, there is pain in his eyes.

"I'm sorry," she says, and she means it. She didn't know Cillian, not really. They've shared letters over the last few years and she's thought him kind and clever, but she isn't Sophronia, imagining herself in love with a boy made of words. Any sympathy she feels, though, is quickly drowned out by panic that she tries her best to hide. What does this mean for her mother's plan, for her own future?

"Thank you," King Bartholomew says. "It's difficult for a parent to lose a child, just as I'm sure it was difficult for you to lose your father."

Daphne doesn't correct him, though the truth is that she rarely thinks about her father. He died when she was only a few days old. She couldn't mourn someone she'd never known, and besides, her mother has been more than enough.

"I always looked forward to Cillian's letters," she says instead, another lie that falls easily from her lips. "I was very much excited to finally meet him."

"I know he felt the same, isn't that right, Bairre?" King Bartholomew says, looking at his son.

Bairre gives a jerky nod but doesn't speak.

"However," Bartholomew continues, "I am a king first and everything else second, even a father. And as much as I would like to take the time to properly grieve Cillian, I must ensure my country's well-being. We need the trade routes our alliance with Bessemia promised."

Daphne frowns. "I'm sorry, I'm confused," she says. "I came here to seal an alliance through marriage. If Cillian is dead—"

"Cillian was my wife's and my only surviving child, but there were others. Ten total. Six born alive; three of those survived a week. None survived two."

"I'm sorry," she says again.

King Bartholomew shakes his head. "The reason I am telling you this is so that you understand: we can have no more children together. The stars will not give us any, for whatever their reasons might be. And a united Friv is too young—too fragile—to endure should I die without an heir." He pauses, looking at Bairre, who sits up straighter, his face suddenly ashen. "However, I do have an heir."

"You must be joking," Bairre practically growls. "Cillian has been dead six days and you want me to replace him? To just step into his life, his title, his betrothal like a pair of hand-me-down boots?"

King Bartholomew flinches, but his gaze on his son remains steady. "Friv needs a clear future. Legitimizing you is the only way to give her one." He doesn't wait for Bairre's response, instead turning to Daphne. "And this way, our treaty with Bessemia will still stand. I have written to your mother already. Her agreement arrived just before you did. An updated contract is being drawn up as we speak."

Of course she has, Daphne thinks. One Frivian prince is much the same as another. She doubts her mother even spared the matter a second thought.

"Is it a request?" Bairre asks his father, his voice shaking. "Or a royal order?"

The king doesn't answer at first, though he suddenly looks much older than his thirty-seven years. "You are my son," he tells Bairre. "And I believe I have raised you in such a way that you will know the difference."

If Bairre does know the difference, he doesn't say as much. Instead, he looks at Daphne for the first time since she entered the carriage. "And you?" he asks, the words scathing. "Are you all right with agreeing to marry a stranger?"

Daphne holds his gaze. "I was always going to marry a stranger," she says before looking at King Bartholomew. "Whatever it takes for the treaty to hold."

If the Bessemian palace is the crown jewel of the country, the sun around which all life revolves, the castle Daphne steps into that evening is the long shadow of Friv, a distillation of its wildness and savagery. There isn't a hint of gold glowing beneath the light of the candles, no shining enamel paint, no glistening marble. It is all stone and wood, narrow hallways lined with thick wool rugs in shades of gray, and sparse décor. Where the entryway of the Bessemian palace is bright and decorated with gilded paintings and porcelain vases stocked with fresh flowers, the entryway here is dimly lit, with only a handful of oil portraits framed in naked wood.

Daphne pulls her ermine cloak tighter around her shoulders.

"I must check on the queen," King Bartholomew tells them as soon as they're inside. "Bairre—will you see Daphne settled in?"

The king doesn't wait for an answer before hurrying off down the dark hallway. Daphne and Bairre remain, cloaked in an awkward silence.

"I'm sorry," she says when the silence becomes too much. "I can see you cared for him."

He doesn't answer right away. "He was my brother," he tells her, finally, as if it's that simple.

And it is. Because even though Daphne doesn't like Bairre, she cannot imagine what it is like in his mind right now. If it were Sophronia or Beatriz dead, she doesn't know how she would even continue to breathe.

"I'm sorry," she says again, because there is nothing else to say.

He nods once before looking at her, his silver eyes intent and red-rimmed. Star-touched, Daphne thinks, though this, too, was part of the spies' information. She has never quite understood it—what woman would wish for a child only to give him up? Bartholomew wasn't even king at the time of conception, just another soldier. So much about Bairre is a mystery.

He offers a brief, halfhearted bow. "There's a guard at the end of the hall who will show you to your room," he tells Daphne before turning on his heel and walking away, leaving her alone in a strange castle, in a strange country, with her world off-kilter.

Daphne paces the length of her bedchamber. It's smaller than the one she had in Bessemia, but she's grateful for that—the tiny room traps the heat from the fireplace better than a larger space would. The thick pine-green velvet curtains insulate the room from the bitter outside air, and the bed and chaise are piled high with furs in shades of white, gray, and brown. A woven gray wool rug, patterned with curls of green ivy, covers the stone floor nearly wall to wall.

It has been hours since she arrived, and the clock in the corner shows it is nearing two in the morning. Her attendants have come and gone after changing her into a flannel nightgown. Despite the late hour and the busy day, she can't find sleep. She can't do anything but pace while her thoughts unspool.

Prince Cillian is dead.

It doesn't change anything, not really. She was sent here to marry a prince, and so she will. Nothing will change but the name on the marriage contract. It's what her mother would tell her if she were here.

But that isn't the whole truth. She's spent her entire life

preparing to marry Cillian, learning everything about him, figuring out how to make him fall in love with her so that he would be clay in her hands. She knew about his obsession with falconry and archery, that he once found a baby rabbit with a broken leg and nursed it back to health himself, how he forfeited a horse race when he realized his competitors were letting him win. She understood how Cillian worked, and how to use it to her advantage.

Bairre, though, is a mystery she doesn't understand and doesn't like—a feeling that seems mutual. The tactics she had planned for Cillian won't work on him. She will have to start from scratch.

There is a part of her, too, that can't stop thinking about Cillian's letters, the boy she knew inside and out even without meeting him. She wasn't Sophronia, losing her head and heart over a few kind words, but when she thinks of Cillian, cold and lifeless, she feels a pang of something deep in her chest that might be grief.

It won't do. She shakes herself and tries to focus.

The seal.

She originally planned to give herself a few days to settle in and figure out how to steal the king's seal while avoiding notice, but now, with everything feeling more tentative, Daphne latches on to the one solid thing she can do. And, she reasons with herself, given the late hour and the prince's recent death, the castle will be quieter than usual, allowing her the perfect chance to snoop.

She slides her cloak on over her nightgown and picks up the candle from her bedside table. She slips from the warmth of her room into the cold and empty hallway.

The Bessemian palace never felt dark. Even in the early hours of the morning, it was always bright and bustling. Servants would start bringing coffee and breakfast to courtiers' rooms even as other courtiers were just coming home from whatever ball or banquet had begun the night before. It was never quiet, not like this.

It's unsettling to Daphne as she tiptoes down the pitch-black hall, the candle casting a small aura of light, just enough to see a few feet in front of her.

Part of her wants to return to her room, but she knows she might never get another chance like this—even if she is caught, she's new enough that she can widen her eyes and claim she got lost trying to find a glass of water.

She knows her mother keeps her seal in her office, hidden away in the locked drawer in her desk. It seems as good a place to start as any. The layout of the castle is strange to her, but she remembers the way she came from the entrance, the same way Bartholomew went when he left, which means she must be in the royal wing. The king's office should be here as well, but it will be more accessible, closer to the castle entrance, so that he can hold meetings without visitors having to pass through his family's private halls.

Of course, it would be easier if it weren't so *dark*. It takes nearly half an hour of wandering to find the entryway she came through, never passing another soul along the way. It sets her teeth on edge. For the last sixteen years, she's seen guards posted outside each door—her own included. It's all she's ever known, so the sudden absence of them feels like a nagging fly, darting around forever just out of reach.

There are guards standing outside the front hall—she

sees their outlines clearly through the windows—more than twenty of them in her line of sight alone, and each with a rifle in hand. Given the absence of guards inside the castle, that many outside strikes Daphne as strange. What sort of threat are they worried about?

She goes to the first door down the hall of the royal wing and presses her ear against the wood, listening for voices. It can't be a bedroom—who would want to sleep so close to the entrance?—so when she hears nothing, she carefully pushes the door open.

A sitting room, with plush velvet furniture and floral curtains. A small harpsichord sits in the corner, though it looks neglected, the keys covered by the lid and the sheet music kept on a high shelf with a thick layer of dust over it.

A gallery is next, another sitting room, a library, but no sign of an office.

Daphne has all but given up when she finds a locked door—a promising sign. She pulls the pins from her hair and crouches so the lock is eye level. Lockpicking is a delicate process, and one that requires patience in spades, which is why Daphne has always enjoyed it more than her sisters. It takes time and effort to displace all the pins in the lock's barrel, but nothing is more satisfying than when she's finally able to lever the hairpins to turn the door's handle.

She withdraws her hairpins from the lock as she steps into the room, hastily shoving them back into her hair. Her earlier instinct proves right: it is the king's office—a moderate-sized room dominated by an oak desk, the walls lined with wood-framed paintings of various battles Daphne can't name. The only paintings she recognizes are a cluster of smaller ones just behind the desk showing the queen, young and rosy-cheeked, a young Prince Cillian, and Bairre at six or seven. Even then he looked surly, seeming to stare at her straight through the painting.

There is no time to waste. The top of the desk is covered only with sheaves of papers, a feather quill and inkpot, and a heavy marble paperweight. Most of the drawers reveal nothing of note. More papers—orders for merchants, correspondence from a cousin in the north, several original versions of royal decrees that have been issued over the last decade.

None of the drawers are locked, but none of them contain the king's royal seal, either.

She could keep looking, try another room, but it is nearly morning now, and the castle will be waking at any moment.

She leaves the office just as she found it and slips from the room, making her way back to her bedroom to get a measly hour or so of sleep before dawn.

Sophronia

The wedding happens more quickly than Sophronia expected. No sooner does she arrive at the palace than she is accosted by a group of servants and shoved into a gold silk gown that fits her perfectly. She has a thousand questions on her lips, but as she is herded down the Temarinian palace's gilded hallways there is little opportunity to ask them, and she is suddenly so nervous she worries that if she opens her mouth, she won't be able to control what comes out.

Two guards stand at the end of the hallway, and when they see her and her retinue of maids approaching, they offer low bows before pulling open the tall filigreed doors behind them.

The royal chapel is full with more people than Sophronia can count, all dressed in elaborate finery—embroidered gowns of bright silk, tailored suits edged with precious metals, and so many jewels that Sophronia's eyes hurt just looking around the room. It's almost enough to outshine the night sky above, showing through the glass roof. When she looks up, she understands the haste. The sky is littered with stars in their various constellations, but Sophronia can make out the vague shape of the Lovers' Hands—a constellation that is said to look like two hands clasped together, though Sophronia can never quite see it. Regardless, it is the sign of romance and unity and an ideal sign to marry under. Already, she can see the Stinging Bee rolling into view from the east and the edge of the Wanderer's Wheel encroaching from the south. In just a few more moments, the Lovers' Hands will be gone.

Sophronia quickens her pace as she walks past hundreds of Temarinian courtiers, feeling their eyes on her all the while, toward where Leopold is waiting at the front, dressed in a suit of white and gold with a yellow satin sash over one shoulder and a gold crown around his brow. With his suntanned skin and burnished bronze hair, he looks every inch the gilded king.

She has imagined this moment more often than she would ever admit aloud, even to her sisters, back when Leopold was a hazy idea made up of pretty words on paper. She thought she would be giddy to find herself walking toward him, that she would catch his eye and they would smile at each other, and the rest of the chapel would fall away.

But the truth of it is not so romantic. She's far more aware of the crowd around her, their heavy gazes and murmured words, than she is of Leopold, and even when he does catch her eye and smile, it doesn't feel like a comfort. It feels like a lie.

Which is a good thing, she reminds herself. It *is* a lie, and so is she.

Sophronia reaches the front, coming to stand beside

Leopold, who takes her hand in his. She barely hears the royal empyrea—Valent, she remembers from her lessons, Temarin's version of Nigellus—give his speech about partnership and unity and the bright future of Temarin. He places a hand on Leopold's shoulder and a hand on hers.

"It is time for blessings," Valent says, looking from one to the other. "Your Majesty, what do you wish of the stars?" he asks, his gaze settling on Leopold.

Leopold tears his gaze away from Sophronia and looks at the empyrea, clearing his throat.

"I wish the stars to grant us trust and patience," he says, the words unwavering.

Sophronia's heart stutters. *Trust and patience.* It is what a peasant might wish for on their wedding. Every wedding she has attended among the nobility in Bessemia brought less sentimental wishes—many were blunt enough to simply wish for children, but others wished for wealth or fortitude. She has heard men wish for their wives to stay beautiful and women wish for their husbands to stay faithful. But never has she heard someone wish for trust or patience, let alone both.

Her own prepared wish suddenly seems crass—*I wish the stars to grant us prosperity.* Her mother worded it for her, crafted it to seem about their marriage as well as Temarin as a whole. Now, though, it doesn't seem right at all. Saying that will make her sound cold. Her mother has always said that the best-laid plans are the most adaptable ones.

"I wish the stars to grant us love," she says, holding Leopold's gaze. As soon as the words leave her mouth, she worries it was the wrong thing to say, that it makes her sound too naïve or unworldly, not at all like the queen she will be in just a few short moments. But then Leopold smiles at her and the gathered crowd lets out a cacophony of sighs and pleased murmurs and Sophronia realizes that the lovestruck princess is *exactly* what they all want her to be.

Valent lifts both of their hands up toward the stars, tilting his head back the way she always saw Nigellus do when he communed with the stars on her mother's behalf.

"Stars, bless this couple—King Leopold Alexandre Bayard and Princess Sophronia Fredericka Soluné—with trust, patience, and love as they are joined together under your holy light as man and wife."

There is thunderous applause as Valent releases their hands and Leopold kisses her in front of the entire court. It is a chaste thing, just a brush of lips that barely lasts a second, but it's enough to seal their vows and make her now, officially, Queen of Temarin.

Afterward, at the wedding ball, Sophronia sits on a throne beside a husband who is far more of a stranger than not, and she can't stop stealing glances at him while the dance floor below fills with whirling courtiers dancing in a jewel box's array of silks and sipping from delicate crystal flutes of champagne. In his wedding regalia, grinning like a fool, Leopold is so handsome and boyish that Sophronia can't quite reconcile him with the king who had children thrown in prison just a few hours ago.

Unaware of the torrent of thoughts tearing through her mind, he takes her hand in his and kisses the back of it, letting his lips linger just a second too long on the silk of her glove.

"Are you enjoying yourself?" he asks.

Yes, she should say, but after all the letters they exchanged, she suspects Leopold knows her better than almost anyone, so she offers him a shade of truth.

"It's a bit overwhelming," she says, lowering her voice to a murmur. "I only entered Temarin this morning, and now I'm its queen. And we're *married*. A few hours ago, we'd never even met in person. It all happened so quickly."

Leopold frowns slightly. "Do you wish we'd waited? I thought—"

"No," she says quickly, offering him a smile she hopes is bright enough to mask the lie. "No, I'm glad to be your wife, and your queen. I've been looking forward to it for so long. It's just so much change in such a short period of time. It almost doesn't feel real."

He smiles back and shakes his head. "I know what you mean," he says before pausing. "Do you remember what I told you about when my parents took me on a trip to the Cellarian border to meet my uncle Cesare and my cousin Pasquale for the first time?"

Sophronia nods. Pasquale will be Beatriz's husband, if they haven't already married. She remembers comparing her letters with Beatriz's, noting how the two princes expressed similar feelings of excitement and nervousness about meeting each other, though Leopold had sent Sophronia five full pages, while Pasquale barely managed to fill one.

"I looked forward to it for months," Leopold says. "And the entire week of the summit passed in a blur. I know I had fun, I remember playing on the beach with Pasquale and hiding under the banquet tables at night so that we could avoid our bedtime, but it all went so quickly. That's a bit what this feels like."

Sophronia bites her lip. He sounds like the boy who wrote her letters. But that boy doesn't exist, and neither does she, really. Not the Sophronia he thinks he knows, at least. If he knew her—*really* knew her—he would run away screaming. But strangers or not, it is their wedding, and she is meant to be the lovestruck young bride. "Then we should ensure that we enjoy every moment of it," she tells him.

Leopold grins and rises to his feet, pulling Sophronia with him. "A dance, then?"

"I thought you'd never ask," Sophronia says, following him out onto the dance floor, where the other couples give them a wide berth. The orchestra begins to play a *glissant*—Sophronia's favorite. She notices Leopold watching for her reaction. "You told them to play this for our first dance," she says, her smile feeling slightly more genuine.

"It's your favorite," he says, lifting their joined hands and settling his other on the curve of her waist. She rests her free hand on his shoulder and they begin to twirl across the dance floor.

It feels like she's danced with him a hundred times before. They move together perfectly, and though Sophronia has danced more dances than she can count over the years, this is the first time she's truly felt comfortable with a partner.

Love is an illusion and a weakness, her mother is fond of saying. *And I will not tolerate weakness.*

Sophronia shudders.

"Are you all right?" Leopold asks, concerned.

"Fine," she says, a little too brightly. "Just tired—it's been such a busy day."

Leopold looks like he doesn't quite believe her, but before he can press her further, the song comes to an end and there's a tap on her shoulder, and she turns to see a boy of around fourteen with the same bronze hair and sharp features as Leopold.

"I was wondering if I might have the next dance with my new sister?" he asks.

Sophronia smiles. "You must be Gideon," she says, letting go of Leopold's hand to take his. "And I would be honored."

"Try not to break her toes, Gid," Leopold says, pressing a quick kiss to Sophronia's cheek before leaving her to dance with his brother.

The orchestra begins to play a much faster *devassé*, and Sophronia lets Gideon sweep her through the quick steps and turns. He's a couple of inches shorter than she is in her heeled slippers, but they make a good go of it and by the time the song ends, Sophronia is breathless and giddy, and then Leopold's other brother, Reid, is there to take the next dance. He is barely twelve and blushes madly the entire time, tripping over his own feet twice and hers three times.

"Sorry," he mumbles to her, staring down at the floor studiously. "This is the first ball I've been allowed to attend—I should have paid better attention in dancing lessons."

"You're doing fine," she assures him. "At my first ball, I knocked over a bowl of punch and then slipped in the puddle. The court spoke of nothing else for an entire week."

Reid glances up at her and smiles shyly. "I've always wanted a sister," he admits.

"We're a good match, then," Sophronia tells him. "You with two brothers, wanting a sister, and me with two sisters, wanting a brother."

He smiles at her, looking somewhat more relaxed. When the song ends, she's intercepted by a tall, stately woman with dark brown hair pulled back in a sweeping chignon, topped with a demure tiara. Even without it, Sophronia would have recognized her from the sketches made by her mother's spies: Queen Eugenia—the dowager queen, now that Sophronia is here.

She thinks of her mother's instructions, the specific ideas on how to push Temarin into war with Cellaria. *Leopold rules Temarin, but Eugenia's hand is in every action he takes. In sowing tensions, start with her—many have not forgotten their hatred of the onetime Cellarian princess.*

As Sophronia stands before Eugenia now, she finds herself unimpressed. She expected Queen Eugenia to have the same energy as the empress—the kind that radiates power and influence. But if she weren't wearing a crown, Sophronia suspects the dowager queen would all but disappear.

"Your Majesty," Sophronia says, dropping into a curtsy.

"*Your* Majesty," Dowager Queen Eugenia replies, one corner of her mouth quirking up in an amused smile as she dips into her own curtsy. She glances at her youngest son.

"It's time to say good night, Reid. It's past your bedtime," she says.

"Yes, Mother," Reid says, giving Sophronia one last bow before skittering away.

"You must be positively exhausted after the day you've had, my dear," Queen Eugenia says, guiding Sophronia off the dance floor. "I've sent Leo to fetch some water for you, but would you like to sit with me while we wait for him?"

"That sounds lovely," Sophronia says, following Queen Eugenia back toward the thrones. A servant is quick to bring another chair for Queen Eugenia and set it beside Sophronia's, and though it looks plush and comfortable, Sophronia is all too aware that a year ago, the throne she is sitting in belonged to Eugenia.

"You and Leo seem quite taken with each other," Queen Eugenia says.

"I feel so relieved," Sophronia tells her, remembering that the dowager queen was once in her position. She knows she can endear herself to her through that connection. She lowers her voice to a whisper, like they are two friends sharing secrets. "You wouldn't believe the thoughts that went through my head—that he would be hideous or cruel, that all this time it was his valet writing me those letters."

"I'm sure he had some similar thoughts," Queen Eugenia says. "Stars know I did when I came here close to two decades ago, though I admit I was . . . less relieved."

She says the words carefully and Sophronia glances at her with a furrowed brow, as if she doesn't already know how unhappy their marriage was. "In his letters, Leopold mentioned that his father could be a difficult man," she says cautiously.

"We came to understand each other, eventually," Queen Eugenia says. "Admiration and respect grew, even if romance never did." She shakes her head. "I don't know why

I'm telling you this—just to say you aren't alone, I suppose. I've been where you are now, only younger and with a husband who terrified me, in a court full of people who hated Cellaria after a decade of war, and hated me for my association with it."

Sophronia tries to imagine what that was like—fourteen years old, in a strange and hostile land. Eugenia hadn't been raised for it the way Sophronia has been, trained from birth in Temarin's language and customs, taught to navigate court politics and control every situation she found herself in, taught not just how to survive in a foreign country, but how to conquer it. Eugenia had only been a girl—young and frightened and cut off from everything and everyone she knew.

"When I was young," Queen Eugenia continues, "my mother told me that a queen always hopes for sons—not just to ensure the line of succession, but because it's easier. Sons you can keep, daughters you only borrow. I don't think I understood her at the time, but I never saw her again after we said our goodbyes on the Cellarian border."

Sophronia thinks of saying goodbye to her own mother just a few days ago. Had the empress been sad to see Sophronia, Daphne, and Beatriz go? It would only be a year, but that was a year longer than they'd ever been separated before.

"Perhaps I was lucky, after everything," Queen Eugenia says, giving Sophronia a smile that reminds her of Leopold. "I had three sons. None of them will be sent off to foreign lands, never to be seen again. And now, I have a daughter I get to keep."

Queen Eugenia takes Sophronia's hand in hers and squeezes it, sending a bolt of guilt through Sophronia, though she manages to hide it with a smile.

"I would not wish my first years here in Temarin on anyone, Sophronia, and I will do everything in my power to ensure you have an easier time than I did."

A lump rises in Sophronia's throat and she looks down at their entwined hands, suddenly struck by the urge to cry. She has known Queen Eugenia for only a few minutes, but already the queen has shown her more affection than her mother ever has. It will make it that much harder to betray her.

It's nearly dawn before Sophronia and Leopold are able to escape the party and make their way to their bedchamber. It's the first time Sophronia has seen it. The room is large, with a ceiling so high it is cast in shadow. The walls are painted a soft cream color, complemented by gold molding and polished oak furnishings. The oversized four-poster bed is dressed in gold silk.

The bed.

In all the chaos of the day, Sophronia nearly forgot to worry over this. She is a married woman now, and that marriage isn't official until it's consummated. Her mother has emphasized the importance of consummation so often, Sophronia knows it by heart. If their marriages aren't consummated, nothing else they do will matter. The sooner it is accomplished the better.

"Alone, finally," Leopold says. He takes her hand and

pulls her toward him, into a kiss. It's nothing like the kiss they shared during the wedding ceremony—that was only a quick press of lips; this is something so much more. Leopold kisses her like he wants to devour her, his arms twining around her waist to hold her close. And she finds herself kissing him back, even enjoying the feel of his mouth against hers. There was a time when she looked forward to this.

She knows what comes next. Her mother sent Sophronia and her sisters to lessons with courtesans so that they wouldn't freeze in this exact situation. She learned all about the mechanics of the act, but nothing can prepare her for when his hands move over her hips, up the curves of her waist, when her hands move of their own volition, sinking into his bronze curls, anchoring his mouth to hers as if she will die if he stops kissing her . . .

Then she thinks of those thieves—those *boys*—in the woods. She imagines them huddled together in a cold, dank prison somewhere, frightened. She thinks about the blood and tears of Leopold's people, the people he doesn't care about at all. He cares about her, that seems obvious, but it isn't enough to erase the rest. It isn't enough to dull the repulsion she feels when he touches her.

And that is why she forces herself to break the kiss, bringing a hand to Leopold's chest to put some space between them.

"I'm sorry," she says. "It's been such an overwhelming day and I'm so tired and we don't really know each other yet, do we? Can we . . . wait?"

She almost expects him to say no—the courtesans told

her and her sisters that some men could be forceful—but instead Leopold smiles and kisses her forehead.

"Don't apologize. We have the rest of our lives, Sophronia. We'll only sleep," he tells her, nodding over her shoulder to one of two gilded doors. "Your dressing room is through there—there's a bell you can ring to summon a maid to help you change into your nightgown."

Sophronia watches him leave through the doorway to his own dressing room, relief flooding through her. Soon, the marriage will have to be consummated. But not tonight.

Beatriz

A lady never drinks so much that she loses her wits, Beatriz's mother was fond of saying, her gaze always lingering a bit longer on Beatriz than her sisters, as if she somehow knew that Beatriz always ended up drinking the most, though Beatriz doesn't think she'd ever really lost her wits.

Now, though, she feels the edges of her mind blurring, turning malleable and hazy as she sits beside her skittish new husband in the banquet hall, Cellarian courtiers approaching every few minutes to offer their congratulations and, she suspects, to try to pick up more gossip.

Prince Pasquale fidgeted throughout the wedding ceremony, his hands twisting in front of him, and though his suit is made from light linen and the air in the chapel was cool, he was dripping in sweat. The worst, though, was how clear Prince Pasquale's hesitation was when he said, "I do."

Beatriz is an unwanted wife, and everyone at court knows it.

She needs her wits about her, and she knows her mother was right. She shouldn't drink any more—should certainly eat something—but when a servant brings her a fresh glass of red wine muddled with berries and citrus fruit, she takes another sip. Then another.

If Daphne were here, she would take the glass from her hand. She would call her self-destructive. She would tell her to focus, that somewhere in this thick crowd of courtiers is Lord Savelle—and the sooner she makes his acquaintance, the better.

But Daphne is not here and Beatriz does not want to focus. If she does, she will feel the eyes of the Cellarian courtiers measuring every inch of her, looking for the flaws that have the prince so disinterested in her. She will be aware of the whispers, the speculating that has already started, that will only grow wilder and louder. This is not how this night was meant to go.

Beatriz understands rumors, how they work, how to start them. She knows that the right rumor, wielded with precision and the right timing, can be enough to bring a person to ruin. She can do it herself, with such grace that it is practically an art form. But she's not sure how to weather that weapon being turned against her.

Beside her, Prince Pasquale is nursing the same glass of muddled wine he was initially served, and when the servant offers to refill it, he shakes his head and waves them off.

"You don't enjoy wine?" she asks him, the first words either of them has spoken to the other since they were pronounced man and wife.

He turns his gaze to her, large hazel eyes blinking like he'd forgotten she was there. Maybe it's the wine, turning her mind soft and sentimental, but he suddenly reminds her of a puppy she had as a child that followed her everywhere, always staring at her with eyes like that, soft and perplexed, a pathetic whimper constantly in the back of his throat.

She was relieved when Sophronia took responsibility for the creature, though it wasn't something they ever discussed. It was simply understood between them: Sophronia knows how to take care of helpless things, Beatriz doesn't.

"Not particularly," Prince Pasquale says, dropping his eyes from hers to focus on his lap, his hands fidgeting. Now that he's removed his gloves, she can see he bites his nails—they are so short and ragged that the skin around them has been torn up as well.

She waits for him to continue but realizes that he has no intention of elaborating. She should say something witty now, she knows this, but with the wine buzzing through her, her wits are just out of reach.

"You could smile, you know," she says, before she can stop herself. "Pretend to be happy about this so people stop wondering if I'm hiding a thicket of thorns between my legs."

The prince actually *blushes* at that—his face turning as red as the wine in her glass.

"No one thinks that," he mutters. "Trust me, they aren't whispering about you. They're whispering about me, and I'm quite used to it by now."

Beatriz rolls her eyes. "You don't get it, do you, Your Highness? We are married now. They aren't only whispering about you, they're whispering about me, too. Me more, maybe, because I'm new and foreign and a woman so it is inherently more fun for them. So please, paste a smile on your face, laugh at my jokes, and pretend that marrying me isn't absolute torture for you."

That gives him pause. He frowns, looking at her again with those pitiful puppy eyes.

"It isn't torture for me," he says softly. "It's just—"

Before he can say more, two new courtiers approach, a boy and girl near Beatriz's age, both with pale blond hair and fine bones that make them look like a matching set of porcelain dolls, the kind that are kept high on a shelf, looked at and never touched. Though he must outrank them, Prince Pasquale gets to his feet when they approach, and their bow and curtsy are afterthoughts.

"Congratulations, cousin," the girl says, stepping toward Prince Pasquale, the train of her lapis-blue silk gown spilling over the stairs behind her like a splash of clear sky on a summer's day. She takes hold of his arms, rolling onto the toes of her jeweled slippers to kiss him on each cheek.

"Gigi, Nico," the prince says to them, nodding toward the girl and boy in turn. "I'm glad you're here."

"As if we would miss the wedding of the century," the girl, Gigi, says with a bright grin.

"And don't be rude, Pas—introduce us to your beautiful bride," the boy, Nico, adds.

Prince Pasquale's cheeks turn bright red and he mutters something, gesturing from Beatriz to the two newcomers, who Beatriz feels certain must be siblings. Though he's mumbling too much to be sure, she thinks their names are Gisella and Nicolo.

"A pleasure," Gisella says, taking hold of Beatriz's hand and dipping into a deep curtsy. "But call me Gigi—we are family now, after all."

Beatriz smiles. "Then you must call me Beatriz," she tells her.

Nicolo goes one step further; when he bows and kisses her hand, his eyes linger on hers, his lips pressed to the back of her hand just a touch too long before he straightens up.

"Enchanted," he says. "You're a lucky man, Pas."

Prince Pasquale mutters more at that, too quietly to be intelligible, but at least with his cousins he seems a bit livelier. Nicolo calls for more fruit wine, so Beatriz has another glass. And another. And another.

It is after midnight when Beatriz is ushered into the bedroom she will share with Prince Pasquale. Her mind buzzes pleasantly as she's moved about by her attendants, arms and legs raised and lowered so that she can be stripped to her skin and dressed again in a soft pink satin nightgown. She wants nothing more than to crawl into the inviting, plush bed and sleep.

But her attendants keep glancing at her with knowing eyes and smug smiles, and she remembers that tonight is her wedding night and she is not meant to get much sleep.

Beatriz knows what will happen. Her mother explained it to her and her sisters when they were quite young, and then in the last couple of years, she's heard more details from the courtesans who gave them lessons in seduction. The princesses are supposed to be virginal and pure, of course, but that didn't mean they couldn't learn the art of undoing a man with a touch on his arm, or making him fall in love with a single look across a room.

Now, though, she isn't sure. It is one thing in theory, but when Prince Pasquale enters in his nightshirt and the attendants all scatter from the room, tittering like a flock of parrots, she suddenly doesn't know what to do.

Start with a kiss, a Bessemian courtesan told her once. *Go from there.*

After their earlier mishap of a kiss, Beatriz should be wary, but her mind is too blurry with wine to linger long on that. All she knows is that she's supposed to kiss him, so she stumbles toward him, the marble floor cold beneath her bare feet. She has to steady herself with her hands on his shoulders before pressing her mouth to his.

She is too drunk to care that it is a bad kiss, not just because he is thoroughly unresponsive, but because she doesn't really want to be kissing him, either. He pulls away, placing a hand on her waist to keep her from falling and lets out a long sigh, a thousand words on his lips that he kills with a shake of his head.

"You're drunk," he tells her. "I'll help you to bed."

Relief and embarrassment course through her in turn as he pulls back the duvet and tosses the many decorative pillows to the floor, helping her into the bed before pulling the duvet back up, tucking her in the way her nanny used to. Her eyes are so heavy that she begins to fall asleep immediately, though she's still aware of his footsteps, padding around to the other side. She waits for him to join her.

She's heard warning stories about men who like women

like this, helpless and unable to protest. Maybe all of that shyness, all of that awkwardness, is hiding something darker. Distantly, she's aware that she's holding her breath until she hears him lie down, though the bed doesn't give beside her. She forces herself to roll over, but the wine has made her limbs heavy and it takes more effort than it should.

When she opens her eyes, she sees him lying on the velvet sofa beside the bed.

"At least take a pillow," she tells him, though the words don't feel like hers. She's already half asleep, falling deeper with each second. "And a blanket."

She's asleep before she knows whether he heard her.

Daphne

Daphne expects it to only be the king and queen at tea the morning after her arrival, but when she steps into the parlor she finds Prince Bairre there as well, sitting across from his father at a small round table, Queen Darina between them, all of them dressed in black. The sight of Bairre glowering into a delicate porcelain teacup is almost enough to make her laugh, but he looks so adrift that all she feels is pity.

When Daphne steps into the sitting room, the king rises to his feet, followed belatedly by Bairre.

"Daphne," King Bartholomew says. He tries to smile but fails as he gestures for her to join them.

"Thank you for thinking of me in this difficult time," Daphne says.

"Of course," the king says, taking his own teacup into his hands. "I wanted to let you know that the new marriage contract has arrived from Bessemia, ready for your signature, and Bairre's. It's happening quickly, I know. But it's in Friv's best interests to see this settled."

And in Bessemia's, Daphne thinks.

At the mention of the prince's name, Queen Darina lets out a whimper, setting her teacup down with a clatter that echoes in the silent space. King Bartholomew sets his free hand over hers, holding it tightly. Queen Darina has covered her face with a black veil that falls to her collarbone, allowing her expression to be visible but casting it in shadow. Daphne can just make out sharp features, bone-white skin, and dark eyes that focus on nothing.

"I'm not sure we will ever stop reeling," King Bartholomew continues. "But Friv depends on us, so we must carry on. Bairre, you're my child by blood and the only one I have left."

"According to a note, on the word of a whore," Queen Darina bites out, her voice sharp-edged and brittle.

The king flinches, but he holds his ground. "It's what Cillian would have wanted."

Daphne might not know much about Bairre, but she knows this is a cruel card to play. Bairre goes a shade paler, though after a moment, he inclines his head in assent.

King Bartholomew gets to his feet and crosses the room to a writing desk in the corner, where he picks up a piece of parchment and a quill in an inkpot, bringing them back to the table and laying the document between Daphne and Bairre.

"After Cillian's death, the country is holding its breath, waiting to see what will become of it," King Bartholomew says. "I would like to reassure our people that we are still here, that we still have a plan to ensure that Friv remains secure not just for my lifetime but beyond."

Daphne scans the document. Though it's written in elaborate Frivian script, she understands it well enough. It appears identical to the contract her mother signed as her guardian when she was mere weeks old, betrothing her to Cillian. She's seen it a few times in the years since, her mother bringing out her copy of it for Daphne to read once she was old enough to understand what it meant.

Don't sign anything unless you know it forward and back, her mother's voice whispers through her mind.

Daphne picks up the piece of parchment, reading it more closely, but it's all there—the outline of the alliance, the trade route provisions, promises of support in the face of war.

When Daphne finishes reading, she takes the quill from the inkpot and touches it to the line awaiting her signature. It's only then that she looks at Bairre, who is watching her every movement with wary eyes.

For just a second she hesitates. She doesn't want to bind her life to his, doesn't want to call him her husband.

But a prince is a prince, and she will do her duty.

She signs her name in jet-black ink before holding the quill out to Bairre.

He doesn't take it right away, and for a moment she thinks he might refuse—and what would happen then? He looks at her and she tries to smile, to reassure him, to entice him, maybe, but his expression remains stony and closed off, a fog-draped thunderstorm.

Finally, he exhales and presses the tip of the quill to the parchment, signing his own name beside hers.

She looks at them together, the delicate looping letters of her full name, *Daphne Therese Soluné, Princess of Bessemia*, and there, beside it, a simply scrawled *Bairre,* with a *Prince of Friv* hastily added after it.

King Bartholomew takes the contract and draws something out of the pocket of his jacket. When he holds it up, a jolt goes through Daphne—his seal. It is a heavy gold thing the size of a lemon with a long handle and a flat end. She can't see the design of the seal itself, so she watches as the king places a ball of wax below the signatures and holds the seal up to the flame of the candle for a moment, letting it grow hot. When he's satisfied, he presses the seal into the wax. Daphne watches, rapt. She's heard about the seal, but it is a different thing entirely to see it in action. King Bartholomew must feel her eyes on him, because he looks up at her.

"An invention of Fergal, our court empyrea," he tells her, releasing the seal and holding up the contract so she can see. "I understand your mother has one as well."

"Yes, but she's never let me see it up close," Daphne lies.

"No? Here, take a look, it's quite impressive."

The seal is still warm, the yellow wax glistening, pressed into the crest he designed for himself when he took control of Friv—the Northern Star. The star looks easy enough to replicate, but that isn't what gives Daphne pause. At the center of the seal, a few drops of crimson have mixed in with the wax, blossoming over the yellow.

"For authenticity's sake. See the barrel here?" He motions to the handle of the seal. "It holds a store of my blood mixed with a pinch of stardust."

He passes the contract to Daphne so that she can see the seal up close. What looked like a drop of crimson from afar is, in fact, an incandescent violet shimmer that reminds Daphne of a bruise.

"How will anyone know it is your blood?" Daphne asks. "It could be anyone's, no?"

"As of now, the only three people who own seals like this are me, King Leopold, and, of course, your mother. If one of us needs verification, an empyrea can provide it with a bit of stardust. Now it is official," he continues, looking from Daphne to Bairre. "We will declare Bairre a prince of the realm tomorrow evening, and the two of you will be wed in a month's time."

A month. Not ideal, but Daphne can't exactly protest. Not that she gets the chance. The queen stands up so suddenly her teacup topples over, spilling the weak tea all over the white tablecloth.

"You brought this curse on all of us," she tells King Bartholomew, each word laced with poison. "This was your doing. You might as well have killed our boy with your own two hands."

She doesn't give Bartholomew a chance to reply—though he doesn't look like he has a response anyhow. Instead, she turns and stalks out of the room, mourning veil streaming behind her like smoke.

When King Bartholomew chases after the queen, Daphne is left alone with Prince Bairre, an uncomfortable silence settling so heavily over them it's smothering.

"I'm sure Queen Darina is hurting worse than anyone," she says finally. "She didn't mean it."

"She did," Bairre says, not looking at her. "She's been saying the same thing for months, ever since Cillian got sick. My father says she's distraught."

Daphne frowns, filing that away in her mind. Friv is a more superstitious country than Bessemia, but she isn't sure what kind of curse Queen Darina referred to. But as Bairre said, she's distraught. Daphne pushes the thought away and focuses on him instead.

"It isn't every day a bastard becomes a prince," she says, taking a sip of her tea, which has gone cold.

Bairre doesn't say anything for a moment, instead staring at her like she's suddenly grown horns.

"My brother is dead," he says slowly. "And suddenly I've had his life forced upon me, his title, his betrothed, his position."

"I didn't mean it like that," she says quickly. "I have two sisters, and I cannot imagine what hell I would go through if anything happened to them. But you'll be king one day—something that was impossible before today—"

"Something I never wanted," he interrupts, shaking his head. "Not all of our lives revolve around a crown. Difficult as it might be for you to believe, I have no desire to be king. I was quite happy to be the bastard brother of a real prince."

It *is* difficult for Daphne to believe, but she knows better than to say as much. He already thinks her a snob; she isn't about to prove him right.

"And what would you rather do, then?" she asks, unable to keep a touch of derision out of her voice.

He blinks at her, silver eyes unreadable. He shakes his head. "It doesn't matter, does it? My father's right—this is my duty; it's what Cillian would have wanted me to do. It doesn't mean I have to be happy about it."

He gets up to leave, but she finds her voice before he reaches the door. If he wants to sulk about his lot in life, she has plenty of ammunition to join him.

"Did it ever occur to you that this is my duty as well?" she asks, stopping him short. "Difficult as it may be for *you* to believe, I'm not exactly keen on marrying you—Cillian, either, for that matter. It has been my duty since I was only weeks old, so I will see it through. But it would be an awful lot easier if you didn't treat me like your enemy."

He pauses, one hand on the doorknob, though he doesn't look back at her. She waits for him to reply, but after a moment, he merely gives a grunt and continues through the door, closing it firmly behind him and leaving her alone.

Daphne leans back in her seat. She got under his skin—that's a start.

Beatriz

Beatriz isn't sure what wakes her up first—the pounding in her head or the voices murmuring outside her bedroom door. *Their* bedroom door, she remembers a second later, slitting her eyes open to find Prince Pasquale, blinking awake on the sofa, a gray silk quilt pulled up to his chin.

"There are people," she says, her voice coming out raw and groggy. "What do they want?"

She realizes after she says it that they still haven't spoken much more than a dozen words to each other, she and her new husband. The day before still feels like a hazy dream, not quite real, not quite her life. She half expected to wake up back in her childhood bed in Bessemia, to Sophronia's laugh or Daphne's off-key singing.

But here she is, a new bride in a cold bed with a husband who seems perplexed by her very existence.

Prince Pasquale looks at her that way now, like she's some sort of puzzle and he can't quite understand her question. When he does, though, he sits up straight and lets out a string of Cellarian words under his breath. She's not sure what they mean, exactly, but she'd imagine they're curses—not language her tutor thought to instruct her in.

He's on his feet in an instant, pacing the room and searching for something.

Outside, a male voice calls out. "Your Highness, have you risen yet?"

"Hopefully he has several times," another voice adds, followed by snickers.

"What do they want?" she asks him again, keeping her voice low even as her stomach is tying itself into knots.

"Proof," he whispers back. He crosses to a basket of fruit on the table near the door, picking up a bunch of red grapes, a pear, a banana, before putting them all back.

"Proof of?" she presses.

The prince's cheeks go red as he looks at her again. "Proof that we . . ." He trails off, glancing away. "Proof that the marriage was consummated."

Beatriz stares at him, agog. "I didn't think anyone participated in that antiquated tradition anymore."

Pasquale grimaces. "They didn't, not until a few months ago when my father decided to reinstate it," he says, holding up a strawberry. "Do you think this will work?"

She shakes her head. "Too pink," she tells him, getting out of the bed and pulling the comforter back. The sheets beneath are a pristine white. She turns toward the door, where more voices are joining in on the din. "Just a moment," she calls out, keeping her voice breathy and sleep-lined. "We aren't quite decent."

"I should hope not!" a man calls back.

Beatriz rolls her eyes at Pasquale, making him smile fleetingly before going back to the bowl of fruit. "Have you seen it before?" she asks him. "What these bedsheets should look like?"

He nods. "A couple of times. Beatriz . . ." He pauses, seeming to realize he's never said her name before. It sounds strange in his mouth, unsure and a bit frightened. "My father will be out there. If he realizes we didn't . . ."

He trails off, but he doesn't need to finish. Beatriz's mind is already a whirl of possibilities. Everyone will know that she's failed, that she couldn't manage to entice her husband. Her mother will find out, she's sure, and Beatriz cringes as she imagines her reaction. All that training, she'll say. All that time spent around courtesans, learning the art of seduction, and Beatriz couldn't even manage to seduce an awkward boy prince. Worse still, if the king knows the marriage hasn't been consummated, he'll have grounds to annul it, to send her back to Bessemia. It wouldn't be logical, but King Cesare rarely is. Beatriz's mother would never let her forget her failure then.

She shakes the thought from her mind and crosses to the mahogany desk in the corner, snatching a bejeweled letter opener and holding it up to her palm.

"If they want blood, we'll give them blood," she says to Prince Pasquale. "How much is there usually?"

He takes the letter opener from her before she can make the cut. "Not too much," he says. "It's a good idea, but if it's from your hand they'll notice."

She nods. "What do you propose, then?"

The prince props his left leg on the bed and holds the letter opener to the back of his calf with his other hand. "Rip a scrap of cotton from one of my tunics, would you? And find a pair of trousers?"

Beatriz nods, hurrying to the wardrobe; she finds a plain black tunic at the back and rips a strip of fabric from the hem. After a second of thought, she rips a second strip as well and grabs the first pair of trousers she sees.

When he makes a small cut on the side of his calf, about an inch long, she watches, both horrified and entranced. The prince lets out a low hiss of pain before passing her the clean handle of the bloodied letter opener and gathering the blossoming beads of blood on his fingers. He smears the blood on the middle of the bed, staining the white sheets crimson.

He does it twice more, until he's satisfied with the size of the stain, then takes the scrap of fabric Beatriz holds out and ties it around the cut, pulling on the trousers she passes him to hide it. She wraps the letter opener in the second strip of fabric and hides it in a desk drawer.

He starts toward the door, ready to let the crowd in. But something isn't right. She remembers her visits to the brothels, how the people who visited would look when they came in, pulled together and neat, and how they looked when they left.

"Wait," she hisses.

He pauses and looks back at her with a furrowed brow.

She steps toward him, hastily unbuttoning his tunic and rebuttoning it so a few buttons are askew. Reaching up, she runs her hands through his black hair, rumpling it.

"If we're going to do this," she tells him, releasing her

own hair from its braid and mussing it up, "we have to be convincing."

He nods and considers her for a moment before tugging the sleeve of her nightgown down so her right shoulder is bare.

"Good," she says, pinching her cheeks so they flush. She climbs back into the bed, careful not to touch the bloody spot before nodding to Pasquale to open the door.

Noblemen flood in—at least twenty, Beatriz would guess, led by the king himself. King Cesare is dressed in a red silk doublet, his dark brown hair oiled and slicked back, eyes bright and growing brighter when they land on Beatriz, who has pulled the covers up again, covering her bare legs and the bloodstain, though she's sure both will be revealed in a moment. She's not shy about her body, but she feels like she's supposed to be, so she plays the part.

"I hope you two had a happy wedding night," the king says, turning his gaze from her to his son.

Prince Pasquale withers a bit under his father's gaze but manages a nod. "We did, Father. Thank you."

The king looks him over, taking in his tousled hair, his misbuttoned shirt. He purses his lips. "Well then. Let's see it."

Pasquale nods, hurrying to Beatriz's side of the bed to help her up. When she takes hold of his arm, she feels it shake beneath her touch. She gives him what she hopes is a reassuring squeeze. As soon as she gets up, standing before the crowd of men clad in only her nightgown, a round of cheers and whistles goes up.

Beatriz has never been modest—Daphne has even called her shameless plenty of times—but this is different. Now she is on display, a thing to be consumed, and suddenly she doesn't feel shameless at all. Shame burns through her, hot and painful, and she has to fight the urge to cover herself.

Prince Pasquale must see this, because he steps in front of her, shielding her as best he can from the looks. He pulls back the duvet, baring the bloodstain for all to see. For a moment, no one speaks, and Beatriz holds her breath, waiting for someone to call it a fake, to realize their marriage is unconsummated, unverified.

After what feels like an eternity, though, the king claps his son on the shoulder and beams.

"Well done, my boy," he tells him. "I didn't think you had it in you. Of course, with a bride as lovely as this, how could you resist?"

Prince Pasquale manages a smile. "Thank you, Father."

"We'll leave you to it, then," the king says, looking at Beatriz again. His gaze makes her skin crawl. "I remember what it was to be young and newly wed."

When the king and his men have gone and it is only Beatriz and Pasquale alone in the room again, Beatriz sits down on the edge of the bed with a sigh of relief.

"It worked," Prince Pasquale says, mostly to himself, sounding like he doesn't quite believe it.

"It worked," she echoes, looking at her new husband. "But I don't understand why you wanted it to. You clearly have no desire to be married to me—now you're stuck," she adds.

He looks down at the floor, unable to meet her eyes.

"It's not that," he says slowly. "We just . . . we don't know each other, do we?"

"No," she agrees. "Though I never expected we would get that luxury. Pasquale—is it all right if I call you that?"

"You can call me Pas, if you like," he says. "Most people do."

"Pas, then. We might have tricked your father today, might have kept court gossip at bay for a few months. But we are young and healthy, and they will expect children to come soon," she says slowly. It's a bluff—Cellaria will fall and she will be back in Bessemia long before a child takes root in her womb; there are vials of herbs hidden away in her jewelry box to ensure just that; but she, too, needs the marriage to be consummated. Her mother was clear on that front. No one can ever doubt that this marriage is legitimate.

Pasquale doesn't respond for a moment, but his skin goes a shade paler.

"Pas," she says again, making him look at her. She holds his gaze the way the courtesans taught her, boldly and conspiratorially, like they are sharing a secret. He looks away almost immediately. "You don't want to bed me, do you?" she asks him.

"We barely know each other," he says again, cheeks going red.

"That doesn't matter. You want someone or you don't. And you don't want me," she says.

He doesn't respond for a moment, looking everywhere

but at her. "You're awfully blunt," he says finally. "Has anyone ever told you it's a bit off-putting?"

"Constantly," she says, shrugging a shoulder.

He doesn't say anything for a moment, but finally he sits down on the chaise, slumped over with his elbows on his knees, his head in his hands.

"It isn't you," he tells her. "Believe me, you are possibly the most beautiful girl I've ever seen, and everyone—*everyone*—has been telling me how lucky I am."

"What is it, then?" she asks him. "You prefer blondes? I've heard of girls using lemon juice to lighten their hair—"

"No, it isn't that," he says. He looks like he wants to say something but quickly thinks better of it and closes his mouth, biting his bottom lip so hard she's surprised he doesn't draw blood. He straightens up again, getting back to his feet. "You're right," he tells her. "We can't keep a charade like this up forever. We'll try soon. I just need time."

She nods. "It might help if you didn't discuss it like you're preparing to march into battle," she tells him with what she hopes is an encouraging smile. "From what I've heard, most people find it rather enjoyable."

He tries to smile back at her, but it doesn't quite reach his eyes. All of his smiles are like that, she realizes, fleeting things that are gone too quick to really see.

"I'll see you at breakfast, then, Beatriz."

"Triz," she tells him, making him stop short.

He turns to look at her, brow furrowed. "Pardon?"

"If I'm to call you Pas, you can call me Triz. My sisters are the only ones who do, but you are family now, I suppose."

He considers this for a moment before nodding. "I'll see you at breakfast, Triz."

Once she's dressed in a new gown of sapphire and gold brocade, Beatriz makes her way to the banquet hall for breakfast, trailed by her group of attendants. Her thoughts are a muddle of Pasquale's words and her mother's crushing expectations. If gossip about her cold marriage bed makes its way back to Bessemia, as she knows it will sooner or later if it's not taken care of, her mother will be irate.

Seduction is the thing Beatriz is supposed to excel at, more than either of her sisters. How can it be her downfall?

Pasquale said he would try, she reminds herself, but from what she's been made to understand, it isn't the sort of thing a person should have to try at. And the way he looked at her—like she was a frightful creature, or a goblet of poisoned wine . . . like a friend, maybe, once or twice. But never like a lover.

She wonders if her attendants can see it, the failure that crawls over her skin—if there is something in her eyes that gives away the fact that her virginity still clings to her, no longer an attribute that secured her value as a bride, but a sign that she is lacking as a wife.

Just outside the entrance to the banquet hall, Beatriz catches sight of Pasquale, standing with a young nobleman she vaguely recognizes, a boy with light brown hair and quick blue eyes that brighten as he laughs at something Pasquale says. But her gaze only lingers on the boy for a moment.

Pasquale, though, she can't take her eyes off. He is

smiling—truly smiling, not giving the fleeting ghost of a smile she's always seen him wear.

And the way he looks at the boy . . . she knows that look. It is the way she hoped he would look at her when they first met on the steps of the palace, or during their wedding ceremony, or even this morning when she asked him plainly if he wanted her.

The pieces fall into place in her mind and she understands.

Sophronia

Sophronia's first few days as Queen of Temarin pass in a blur. There are so many courtiers to meet, so many events to attend, so many tasks to oversee. She insists on interviewing her staff herself—she isn't foolish enough to believe she can keep spies out of her household altogether, but she's determined to at least be able to figure out who they work for. Then there are the dress fittings, where she is poked and prodded with needles and every last inch of her is measured.

Sophronia has always hated dress fittings—they make her hyperconscious of her figure, how much fuller it is than her sisters'. Now, in Temarin, she feels the eyes of the dressmaker and her assistants as they assess and measure her while she stands on a pedestal in her underthings. The seamstress shouts out numbers to be jotted down, and Sophronia feels each one like a dagger beneath her skin. She waits for the judgment, for the snide looks and the whispers, but instead, after what feels like an eternity, the seamstress fixes her with a frank look.

"You're quite lucky," she tells her. "Not many girls can pull off Temarin Yellow, but it will suit you quite well."

Sophronia blinks. "Are you certain?" she asks. Temarin Yellow is a bright shade, the color of a canary's wing. "Perhaps something darker would be more slimming?"

The seamstress scoffs. "You wish to appear smaller?" she asks, shaking her head. "You are a *queen*. Why shouldn't you take up every bit of space you deserve? No, I think you would thrive in color—Temarin Yellow, Varil Blue . . . I just got the most divine silk in from Cellaria the exact color of a pomegranate that would look spectacular on you. What do you think?"

Sophronia bites her lip and glances away from the dressmaker so the woman can't see how moved she is by a few words. *Why shouldn't you take up every bit of space you deserve?* The words echo in her mind, as if her memory is trying to etch them in stone.

"Whatever you think is best," she says.

The fitting takes most of the day, and when she returns to her room Sophronia is exhausted from looking at fabrics and trying on countless muslin mock-ups of dress cuts. Her spirits lift at the sight of an envelope on her bed. She picks it up immediately and the wax seal tells her it's from Beatriz. She breaks the seal and reads.

> *Dear Sophronia,*
>
> *I write this to you as a married woman, and I hope you find yourself similarly wed. Cellaria is beautiful. I wish I could send you some of their decadent cakes,*

but I fear they won't last the journey north. Write back to me soon.

Your sister,
Beatriz

Sophronia knows right away Beatriz's message is in code, if only because it sounds nothing like her. Before she can begin to decode it, though, a maid bustles in to remind her she's to have tea with the dowager queen and Duchess Bruna, who accompanied Sophronia on her journey. With a touch of annoyance, she slides the letter into her desk drawer to get back to later before following the maid out the door.

She hasn't seen much of Leopold in the three days since the wedding. With only a few weeks left before the weather begins to turn cold, he and his brothers and several of their friends have gone to the new royal hunting lodge in the Amivel Woods, the lodge her mother's spies reported Leopold had built after razing the village that once stood in its place. They still haven't consummated the marriage, and Sophronia finds she is both anxious and relieved about that fact.

In Leopold's absence, Queen Eugenia has taken Sophronia under her wing, bringing her to afternoon teas, evening musicales, and daily strolls in the garden during what the dowager queen likes to call *the gossip hour.*

Sophronia finds that her first impression of Queen Eugenia as unimpressive isn't entirely accurate. Eugenia wields her power differently than Sophronia's mother did, more quietly. She never raises her voice or loses her smile, and most of her battles are waged politely over tea, but they are battles she always wins. It's true that the majority of the court doesn't like her—Sophronia has seen the glares and heard a few whispers even in just the last few days—but they rely on her goodwill and everyone seems to know it.

Queen Eugenia has no trouble keeping the court operating smoothly even without Leopold. Many of the luncheons and teas they attend are thin excuses for the lords and ladies hosting them to ask favors that Sophronia suspects should be handled by the king. The Earl and Countess of Campary require a loan from the crown to rebuild the earl's summer home after it was set on fire by ruffians from a nearby village. Lord Nieves and Lord Treval need a judgment on where the line between their lands sits. Lady Whittem would like her husband's mistress banished from court.

No matter how large or small the grievance is, Queen Eugenia handles the matter, usually by throwing money at it.

Sophronia is curious to see what Duchess Bruna will ask of the dowager when they sit down for tea, and she's even more curious about how Queen Eugenia will handle it.

"Tell me, Your Majesty, how are you adjusting to life here in Temarin?" Duchess Bruna asks Sophronia, settling back in her chair as her maid—Violie, the girl from Bessemia—pours tea into three delicate porcelain cups painted with gold suns, the sigil of the Temarin royal family. Duchess Bruna is the late king's sister, a fact she enjoys reminding people of at every opportunity.

"Oh, quite well, I think," Sophronia tells her, lifting her cup to take a sip of tea. "Because I was betrothed to Leopold from infancy, my mother ensured I was raised in Temarinian customs as well as Bessemian ones. In a strange way, coming here almost feels like coming home. And please, you must call me Sophie. We are family now, aren't we?" she asks, offering Duchess Bruna a smile that could be called guileless if she hadn't spent countless hours before a mirror practicing it.

Duchess Bruna leans across the table to pat Sophronia's hand. "What a sweet girl you are, Sophie," she says. "And you must call me Aunt Bruna, just as Leopold does. You don't have any aunts or uncles in Bessemia, do you?"

"I'm afraid not," Sophronia says. "Both of my parents were only children."

"Well," Duchess Bruna says with a smirk, leaning back and glancing at Queen Eugenia. "So your mother *says,* though from what *I've* heard, no one even knows who her parents were. She could have siblings all over the continent and be none the wiser."

"Don't be beastly, Bruna," Queen Eugenia says. "Empress Margaraux is Sophronia's *mother* and the grandmother of my future grandchildren. I won't tolerate any rude remarks."

Duchess Bruna rolls her eyes and Queen Eugenia pretends not to notice, instead offering Sophronia a reassuring smile. Sophronia has heard far worse things about her mother over the years, but she's touched by the dowager queen's effort to protect her from them. She remembers what Queen Eugenia told her at the wedding—that when she was a young queen bride in a strange court, people had been cruel. Now she is ensuring that Sophronia has an easier time of it.

In sowing tensions, start with her. The empress's words come back to Sophronia, accompanied by a stab of guilt that she quickly pushes aside. Queen Eugenia has been kind to her, yes, but Sophronia's loyalty is to Bessemia alone.

"These cakes look wonderful, Aunt Bruna," Sophronia says. She picks up one of the thimble-sized cakes from the painted porcelain plate, holding it up to examine. It is delicately frosted to resemble a pink rose midbloom. When she takes a bite, it tastes like rose as well, along with a hint of something else. Pistachio, perhaps? She stops that train of thought. As her mother said whenever she found Sophronia hiding away in the kitchens with the pastry chef, baking is not a proper pastime for a princess. Even less so for a queen, she imagines.

"I had a letter from my sister Beatriz," Sophronia continues, thinking back on the letter she hasn't yet decoded, looking at Queen Eugenia. "She says the cakes in Cellaria are absolutely decadent. Are they like these?"

"Not at all," Queen Eugenia says without missing a beat. "Everything in Temarin is far superior to what one finds in Cellaria."

Duchess Bruna laughs. "And besides, the Cellarians treat using stardust as the gravest sin, so I'm not inclined to trust their expertise on decadence."

Queen Eugenia laughs as well, but Sophronia notices a flicker of tension in her mouth.

"Aunt Bruna and I had quite the adventure on our way into the city," Sophronia says, changing the subject. "We were set upon by a band of thieves."

"Yes, I heard," Queen Eugenia says with a heavy sigh. "Sadly not an uncommon occurrence these days."

"Ruffians," Duchess Bruna scoffs. "Luckily, we were near

enough to the meeting point that Leopold heard the commotion and came right away to have those horrid creatures taken away to prison."

"He did," Sophronia says, and though she doesn't mean to, her eyes dart to the side of the room where the servants stand and find Violie, only to see her own ambivalence mirrored in the maid's expression. She forces her gaze back to the dowager queen.

"I urged Leopold to show them mercy," she says carefully. "When the masks came off, they were only boys—around Gideon's and Reid's ages."

"You're very sweet, but they were *thieves,* Sophie," Queen Eugenia says.

Sophronia smiles softly. "Yes, that is what Leopold said as well. I'm sure you're right. I'm just so new to these things," she says, biting her lip before making her strike. "It does seem a bit . . . Cellarian, don't you think? To jail children over something so trivial? No one was hurt, after all. You could practically view it as a badly thought-out prank, if you were so inclined." She says it breezily, popping another tiny cake into her mouth and pretending not to notice the way Queen Eugenia's neck flushes or the way Duchess Bruna's eyes glint with gleeful malice. Sophronia would bet that by lunch the entire palace will be whispering that Queen Eugenia's policies *are* a bit Cellarian, aren't they?

"I'm sure you had thieves in Bessemia, Sophie," Queen Eugenia says, barely managing to hold on to her smile. "What is done with them there?"

Sophronia has to bite her tongue to stop herself from saying that in Bessemia, they keep their taxes low enough that no thieves would be so desperate as to attack a royal carriage. Instead, she shrugs. "It depends entirely on the circumstances," she says, which isn't strictly true, but she doubts the other women know that. "And if the victim of the crime does not wish to press charges, the matter is dropped."

She meets Queen Eugenia's gaze and holds it for a moment, not letting her expression shift from a bright, vapid smile. They could be discussing the weather rather than crime and punishment.

"Well, we are not in Bessemia," Queen Eugenia says, her voice sharpening at the edges in a way that makes Sophronia feel like a small child again, facing her mother's scolding. "And we are not in Cellaria, for that matter. We are in Temarin, where criminals are punished."

"Of course," Sophronia says easily. "As I said, I am so new to all of this. I hope you don't mind my asking questions."

"Not at all," Queen Eugenia says, though her tone makes it clear she minds Sophronia's questions a great deal, and even Duchess Bruna looks from one to the other of them uncomfortably.

"More tea?" she asks, motioning to Violie, who rushes forward to refill their cups. In her haste, some hot tea dribbles out of the teapot and onto Duchess Bruna's lap.

"Idiot!" Duchess Bruna screeches, leaping to her feet and slapping Violie so hard across the face that the sound echoes in the quiet room. Violie rears back, her hand flying up to her red cheek, but otherwise looks unsurprised.

"I'm so sorry, Your Grace," she mumbles.

"This gown is silk imported from the Alder mountains. Do you have any idea what it costs?"

"No, Your Grace," Violie says quietly. "But I'm certain I will be able to get the stain out."

"You'd better hope so—if not, the cost will come out of your pay!" the woman yells.

Sophronia doesn't know how much Violie's pay is, but she would guess it would take years for her to pay off the cost of the dress. When she catches Violie's gaze again, the girl's eyes are wide with fear and brimming with unshed tears as she hurries back to her corner, carrying the teapot in shaking hands.

Sophronia knows that look—she wore it often enough in Bessemia when she was the target of her mother's tempers, though her mother never struck her daughters. Sophronia forces herself back into conversation with Duchess Bruna and Queen Eugenia—the topic of which has turned to gossip about which noblewoman's husband was caught in a compromising position with his valet—but her mind is elsewhere.

As Sophronia and Queen Eugenia make their way back to the royal wing after tea, Queen Eugenia links their arms together and draws Sophronia close.

"I would appreciate it if you spoke more carefully," she says, her voice softer than Sophronia expects. She was dreading a thorough dressing down, which her mother would surely have given. Instead, Queen Eugenia sounds only concerned, not angry. "Duchess Bruna has always hated me. She tolerates me now because she relies on her proximity to the crown and the allowance that comes with it, but she is always looking for ammunition to use against me."

Sophronia frowns as if this hadn't occurred to her, as if she hadn't studied Duchess Bruna extensively over the years. "Oh, I didn't realize," she says. "What ammunition could she possibly have against you?"

Queen Eugenia smiles and pats Sophronia's arm. "Against *us,*" she amends. "Temarin does not like outsiders. Oh, they like you more because they haven't been at war with Bessemia since they won their independence from the Bessemian Empire, but make no mistake—they will always see you as an outsider."

Her words make sense. So much so that Sophronia suddenly feels ashamed of trying to undermine her. *Bessemia above all else,* she reminds herself, before changing tactics.

"I'm sorry," she says. "I just keep thinking about those boys—"

"Those thieves," Queen Eugenia corrects.

Sophronia makes a show of hesitating before she nods.

"You are too kind," Queen Eugenia says again. "But there's no need for your worry—I'm sure by now those boys are out on the streets once more, back to their families." She laughs at Sophronia's surprised expression. "What were you expecting, my dear? That we would put them to death? As you said, they were children, even if they were criminals."

That is exactly what Sophronia was expecting, and she manages a relieved smile. But all of her worries haven't abated. She can't forget the sound of Duchess Bruna's hand connecting with Violie's cheek, the red mark that was left in its wake, the tears in the girl's eyes.

"I'm beginning to understand what you meant when you spoke of your homesickness," she says, choosing her words carefully. "Not that I'm not enjoying Temarin—truly, I'm so happy here—but there are things I miss from Bessemia. I don't think I realized until I was speaking with Duchess Bruna's lady's maid. Did you know she's from Bessemia as well?"

"I thought I detected an accent," Queen Eugenia says, glancing sideways at her.

Sophronia shakes her head. "I know I'm far luckier than you were—I heard it said that you didn't even speak the language when you arrived. I learned Temarinian right alongside Bessemian growing up, so it's second nature for me. But still, it was nice to speak my mother tongue for a few moments with Violie. Especially since, as you said, I should try to distance myself from my homeland publicly. Do you think . . . Oh no, I couldn't ask." She glances away, the very picture of demure.

"Ask, Sophie," Queen Eugenia says.

"Just how angry do you think Bruna would be if I hired her lady's maid as my own?" she asks. "It's just . . . it would be nice, to have a bit of home around."

Queen Eugenia fixes her with a frank look. "You cannot save every maid with a cruel mistress."

"I know," she says quickly.

Queen Eugenia lets out a long exhale. "I imagine she'll

be a bit piqued, though I'd wager she only hired a Bessemian maid to endear herself to you, so she has no one to blame but herself. And, to be honest, I am petty enough to revel a bit in her irritation. Send her a gift—I know my sister-in-law is particularly fond of rubies—and I'm sure she'll forgive you fast enough."

Sophronia nods. "Thank you, Queen Eugenia."

The woman waves her words away. "We can't keep calling one another *Queen,* Sophie. It's dreadfully confusing. Call me Genia."

When Sophronia comes back to her room after dinner that evening, she finds Violie sitting beside the fire, one of Sophronia's new gowns laid over her lap and a needle in hand, though she isn't sewing. Her eyes are far away, staring into the fire, but when she hears Sophronia come in, she hurries to her feet and dips into a curtsy.

"Good evening, Your Majesty," she says.

"Good evening," Sophronia says, somewhat surprised. She had a maid deliver her request, along with a ruby bracelet from the royal jeweler, just after tea, but she didn't expect Violie to be switched into her household so quickly. Sophronia's eyes fall to the gown Violie is holding. She switches to Bessemian, not realizing until she begins speaking just how much she's missed it. "Was something wrong with it?"

Violie glances down at the dress and flushes. "No, not at all," she says. "I just . . . the maid who was demoted to make room for me keeps fluttering in and out, giving me dirty looks, and I wanted to stay busy but there was nothing to be done, so . . ." She trails off, and Sophronia smiles.

"So you're pretending to mend a brand-new gown?" she supplies. "Clever."

"Thank you," Violie says before hesitating. "For hiring me, I mean."

Sophronia nods. "It's nice to have someone from Bessemia about. It makes me feel a little less homesick. You must feel a little homesick too."

"A bit," Violie admits. "Mostly, I just miss my mother."

Sophronia wonders what that must be like. She thought she might miss the empress, but mostly, she just feels relieved not to see her every day.

"Oh," Violie says, laying the gown down over the arm of the chair. "King Leopold returned just a few moments ago and asked me to ask you to accompany him on a ride tomorrow afternoon. You have time, after lunch with Lady Enid and Countess Francesca and before the banquet to welcome Sir Diapollio."

"The Cellarian singer?" Sophronia asks, surprised, before she remembers he's arriving to sing a concert. "Oh yes, I'm quite looking forward to that. They say his voice is a gift from the stars. Tell Leopold I would love to join him for a ride. Was there anything else?"

"A letter and a package arrived for you," Violie says. "I left them on your desk—the package is from your sister in Friv and the letter is from your mother."

Sophronia smiles her thanks as she moves toward her desk, where Beatriz's letter is waiting as well, just out of sight. Both the box and the letter appear to have been tampered with already—apparently, her mother was right to be so concerned about codes and hidden messages.

"That will be all for now," Sophronia tells Violie as she takes a seat at her desk. "I'll ring if I need you."

Violie bobs a quick curtsy before slipping from the room, closing the door behind her. Sophronia glances from the box to the letter before deciding on the box first.

As she unties the ribbon and lifts the box up, a worry seizes her—Daphne couldn't have managed to steal King Bartholomew's seal already, could she have? Sophronia has barely begun to sow tensions between Cellaria and Temarin! Of course, Daphne very well could be that far ahead of her. *She* likely isn't losing time lobbying for mercy for thieves.

Still, when she lifts the box's lid and finds a book she lets out a sigh of relief. Even Daphne couldn't conceal something the size of a seal in a book so small. She opens the letter that accompanies it, scanning her sister's words.

Prince Cillian, dead. Not so surprising, really, given reports of his health, but Sophronia feels the shock of it all the same. Though Daphne, at least, seems to have recovered and kept her part of things in motion by betrothing herself to Prince Bairre.

Sophronia picks the book up, turning it over in her hands. She spots her sister's stitches on the spine immediately. She takes the letter opener and rips through them, finding another letter hidden there, this one sounding so much more like Daphne that it makes her heart ache and she thinks she might give anything to be with her sister now.

Her mother's letter looms far larger than its size, and

Sophronia can't bring herself to open it yet. Instead, she reaches into her desk and draws out Beatriz's letter, deciding to decode that first. The code work is a bit sloppy—coding has never been Beatriz's strong suit—but Sophronia knows her sister well enough to piece the message together. Apparently Beatriz hasn't yet consummated her marriage either, a fact that makes Sophronia feel a bit better about her own failure in that area.

She forces herself to set both letters and the book aside, picking up the envelope bearing her mother's seal and tearing it open. She scans the brief letter, knowing it is a farce from the salutation—*My dearest daughter.* Surely Sophronia has never been that. The rest is bland nonsense, congratulations on her nuptials, fond wishes for her future, tender words. But Sophronia's eyes catch on the last line. *Never doubt that my love for you is brighter than the burning sun.*

The burning sun is the clue. Sophronia lets out a long breath before lifting the letter to the lit candle on her desk, holding it just out of reach of the flame. The paper's surface darkens next to the heat and another message appears in the top margin, the letters a pale white.

Find Sir Diapollio to receive a little gift from me.

Daphne

When she invited Daphne to go shopping, Lady Cliona described Wallfrost Street as the fashion district, and Daphne expected something akin to Hapantoile's fashion district—entire blocks taken up by bright, clean storefronts and even more craftspeople selling wares from street carts, shouting their latest deals to lure customers over. Instead, Wallfrost Street is the length of a single Bessemian city block of stores, all neat and tidy but decidedly lacking in glamour.

"I don't see why this couldn't wait," Daphne says from atop her horse, glancing up at the gray sky. "It looks ready to start pouring rain at any moment."

Cliona lets out a snort beside her on her own horse. Four guards ride behind them, though they keep a polite distance. "You'd have better luck waiting for fire to freeze than for fine weather in Friv this time of year," she says.

"Still," Daphne says. "It isn't as though shopping will do me much good—I'm in mourning for Cillian."

"The king told my father that it would be appropriate for

you to set aside mourning gowns," Cliona says, shrugging. "You didn't really know him, after all, and it's better for Friv if you represent a bright future rather than a tragic past."

Daphne sees the logic in that, but as she realized during their journey north, Cliona is a terrible liar. And as any terrible liar would know, it is easier to skirt the truth than to try to break it.

"Why today, Cliona?" she asks, glancing sideways at her companion.

Cliona's ears turn red and she clears her throat.

"It's the queen," she says, her voice low, as if someone might overhear, though apart from the guards stationed three feet ahead of and behind them, there is no one else on the street. "She's been a bit . . . unwell."

Daphne hesitates, trying to decide just how much information to share in hopes of gaining some in return.

"She said something the other day, when Bairre and I were signing the new marriage contract," she says carefully. "Something about a curse the king had brought down on them. She seemed to blame him for Cillian's death. I don't see how that's possible. Prince Cillian died of illness. A mysterious one, certainly, but I don't see how that could be the king's fault."

Cliona bites her lip. "There's an old bit of gossip—poppycock, I assure you. They say that Bartholomew solicited the help of an empyrea during the last of the Clan Wars to win Friv for himself."

Daphne can't help but laugh. "Please," she says. "Even Nigellus couldn't manage a wish that large, and he's the greatest empyrea on the continent."

At that, Cliona's eyebrows arch high. "Is he? Says who?"

Daphne opens her mouth to answer but quickly closes it again. Everyone said it in Bessemia, she supposes, but no one ever offered any proof of it. Nigellus is simply notorious. But it occurs to her that another empyrea could claim that title and no one could very well prove it false.

"Star magic in Friv is . . . wilder than what you're used to," Cliona continues when Daphne doesn't respond. "Up in the north, when the aurora borealis is overhead, the power of empyreas goes erratic. Sometimes they get stronger, sometimes weaker, but it is impossible to predict."

"I hadn't heard that," Daphne admits, though as she says it, it occurs to her that she doesn't know much about empyreas at all. She knows about stardust, of course, and that empyreas are able to pull stars down from the sky to create bigger bursts of magic, but she understands it the same way she understands the sea—she knows what it is as a concept, but she's never seen it firsthand. "They say that there are far more starshowers there than anywhere else on the continent," she manages, desperate not to appear totally oblivious.

For a moment, Cliona looks wistful. "It's truly a sight to behold," she says. "Perhaps one day you'll see it yourself."

Daphne hopes not—if Friv is this cold in the south, she doesn't know how she would survive the north.

"And the stardust they bring tends to be more potent than anything you've used—I've seen it used to cure serious illnesses and make seeds take root in barren ground. It's even been used to get messages to people hundreds of miles away."

That piques Daphne's interest. "Really?" she asks skeptically.

Cliona nods. "I've never seen *that* done myself, only heard about it. They say the messenger and the target both need to be star-touched themselves in order for it to work."

Daphne files that bit of information away. She herself is star-touched, and so are her sisters. If she could talk to them . . . "So it's possible, then," she says, returning to the subject at hand. "The right empyrea, on the right night, making the right wish on the right star, could have won Friv for Bartholomew."

"That's the rumor," Cliona says carefully. "People like looking for an excuse for their failures. And if they can blame a woman, all the better. The empyrea they lay the blame on is a woman. Aurelia. I don't know about your Nigellus, but Aurelia is the greatest empyrea I've ever heard of, though no one's seen her since the war ended."

"Magic that big comes with a cost, depending on the size of the wish," Daphne says. "The only time I saw Nigellus use his power like that, he wished for the drought in Bessemia to end. It rained that very day, but he couldn't get out of bed for weeks afterward. A wish big enough to make Bartholomew king might well have killed her."

Cliona fixes Daphne with a meaningful look. "The stars exact a cost, yes, but Aurelia might not have been the one to pay it."

Daphne inhales sharply. "You think that's what killed Cillian? He wasn't even born yet—not even conceived yet."

Cliona shrugs. "But you could say Bartholomew paid a price all the same. That's the rumor. The queen seems to believe it, and the king thinks it best if she goes to visit her sister in the north for a few weeks. He thinks it will be easier to get her to leave the castle without you and Bairre about."

They pause in front of a sign that proclaims the shop to be Nattermore Dressmakers, and two of the guards disappear inside to inspect the space.

"Where is Bairre, then?" Daphne asks Cliona while they wait. "I assume he didn't get roped into a shopping expedition."

"No, he's hunting with my father and some other noblemen. He has a lot of favor to earn now that he's the heir," Cliona says.

The guards reemerge, one giving a nod that seems directed more at Cliona than at Daphne.

"Come on," Cliona says, pulling her toward the door. "I heard they just got lace in from Cellaria."

The tailor's shop is cramped but bright, lit by the storm-tinged sunlight shining through the large picture window and a half dozen oil lamps set on shelves and tables to lend light to the bolts of fabric that cover every available space. They line the walls, lean upright in corners—a few even rest on the single overstuffed sofa, yards of steel-gray velvet pouring onto the carpet below.

It is the opposite of the tailors in Bessemia, with their immaculate studios and plush chaises, their neatly organized catalogues of fabric samples, and the waifish, sharp-featured shopgirls who can sell you a new wardrobe or destroy your self-esteem with only a few loaded words. Daphne has a hard time imagining that anyone will be offering them champagne during their appointment today.

A petite, gray-haired woman with a wool shawl wrapped around her bony shoulders emerges from the back room, a cup of tea in one hand and a measuring tape in the other. When she sees Cliona and Daphne, her eyes narrow.

"You're late," she tells them.

"Apologies, Mrs. Nattermore," Cliona says, dipping into something that might be described as a curtsy, though the woman has no title and Cliona is the daughter of a duke.

Mrs. Nattermore barely spares Cliona a glance, instead turning her attention to Daphne, though as soon as she does, Daphne desperately wishes she would look anywhere else. Her scrutinizing gaze is so heavy that Daphne finds it difficult to breathe, though she forces herself to keep her back straight and her chin raised. She is a princess of Bessemia, the future queen of Friv—the future empress of this entire continent—and she refuses to cower before a dressmaker.

"So," Mrs. Nattermore says, the weight of an empire resting behind that single syllable. "You're our new princess, are you? You don't look like you'll last the winter."

Daphne opens her mouth to protest but quickly closes it again, forcing it into what she hopes is a pleasant smile.

"I'm in need of new dresses," she tells the woman.

"And a wedding gown," Cliona adds.

"I have a wedding gown," Daphne says, frowning. It's been hanging in her wardrobe since she arrived, deep green velvet with gold beaded flowers.

"You can't very well wear *that* now," Mrs. Nattermore

says. "Everyone will say it's cursed, bad luck. A shame, too—my fingers are still numb from all that beadwork."

"I'm . . . sorry?" Daphne says. She doesn't mean to apologize—knows there is nothing for her to apologize for. But the words are out of her mouth before she can stop them, the woman's steely eyes drawing them out of her practically against her will.

"No help for it now, I suppose. Cliona, draw the blinds. I have a few fabrics set aside. Diedre! Where is that girl?"

As Cliona draws the blinds, another girl slips into the room, this one close to Daphne's age, with coils of dark brown hair framing her pale face. In her arms she carries a stack of fabric bolts in varying shades of green, though none of them is the pure emerald of Daphne's original wedding gown.

Mrs. Nattermore ushers Daphne onto the platform and strips off her riding habit so quickly she doesn't even register it until she's standing in her chemise and Mrs. Nattermore's tape measure is wrapped around her shoulders, then her waist, her arm, her hips, measuring the distance from her shoulders to her waistline, from her waistline to her ankles. As the tailor goes, she shouts out numbers, and Diedre jots them down on a pad of paper with a stick of charcoal.

"Give me the first," Mrs. Nattermore says, and Diedre hurries to grab the top bolt off her pile, rushing it over to Mrs. Nattermore, who holds the free end of the fabric up to Daphne's face, her eyes narrowing.

"Too pale," she says, shaking her head. "It will wash her out. The bottle-green one, where is that?"

Diedre rushes to find another bolt, this one still light green, but a richer hue.

"Better," Diedre says with a nod before her eyes find Daphne's. "What do you think?" she asks.

Daphne glances at the three-paneled mirror, at her three reflections looking back at her.

This green is the color of grass in springtime. It makes her eyes look a bit brighter. She nods her approval.

"Cliona mentioned you had some Cellarian lace in? If we laid it over the bodice, in white perhaps?"

The words are barely out of her mouth before Cliona lets out a horrified cry and gives Daphne a warning look. Daphne is about to ask her what's wrong when Mrs. Nattermore speaks.

"Are you telling me how to do my job, Princess?" she asks, her voice icy.

"Oh no," Daphne says quickly. "Not at all, it was merely a suggestion. I do love Cellarian lace, after all."

"White is the color of death in Friv, Princess," Mrs. Nattermore continues. "We have one doomed prince already; would you doom another by wearing it on your wedding day?"

"No, of course not," Daphne says, startled. She's learned so many things about Friv, how could she have forgotten that? "I only thought—"

"Perhaps you'd best leave the thinking to me," the woman says curtly before turning to Diedre. "Take Cliona down to the cellar to show her the new velvets we got in—they should do nicely for the rest of the princess's wardrobe."

"Yes, Mrs. Nattermore," Diedre says, leading Cliona through the back door. As Cliona passes, she shoots Daphne a warning look. When the door closes behind Cliona, Mrs. Nattermore turns back to face Daphne.

The older woman sucks on her teeth, looking Daphne over from head to toe. "You want lace," she says slowly. "*Cellarian* lace. On your wedding day. Beyond the color, do you know what people will say? That your loyalty is not to Friv."

"It's only lace," Daphne says.

"Only lace," the dressmaker repeats, her voice dripping with disdain. "Most people in this country will never meet you, Princess. They will never hear you speak, never hear your wit—they say you're witty, though I can't say I believe it. All most people will know of you is what they *see*. What you think of as *only lace,* they will read as a message. What message would you like to send?"

The words work themselves under Daphne's skin, itching with shame. If her mother were here, she would be so disappointed. She raised Daphne better than this; she raised her to be thoughtful and deliberate, not to be swayed by something as useless as a scrap of lace.

"The original wedding dress you made," Daphne says, pushing the shame aside and forcing herself to meet Mrs. Nattermore's gaze. "It looked like armor—heavy, strong."

Mrs. Nattermore lifts an eyebrow and inclines her head in a nod. "A dress fit for the future queen of Friv," she says. "Not the delicate, frilly nonsense that is popular in Bessemia. Friv is not a delicate country, Princess. We have a bloody history—one that's barely history at all. We don't need a delicate princess. We need a princess who can survive the winter."

Daphne nods slowly. "Ermine, perhaps," she says after a moment. "As a trim."

Mrs. Nattermore considers it, her mouth pursing, though Daphne thinks she might be suppressing a smile. "Perhaps," she says. "Get dressed. I'll put the kettle on. You should warm your bones with a cup of tea before setting foot in that cold again."

When Daphne is dressed, she starts for the door the others went through, the one, she imagines, that leads to the kitchen, maybe the connection to Mrs. Nattermore's house. There she finds a kettle whistling on the stove but no sign of Mrs. Nattermore, Cliona, or Diedre, though the door to a set of stairs is slightly ajar, presumably leading down to the cellar the dressmaker mentioned.

They must be down there looking at the velvets still. Daphne pauses at the entrance, wondering if she should wait for them here, but she does want to see the velvets and make sure they don't pick out anything too drab for her.

She makes her way down the rickety stairs, following the sound of muffled voices, but when she reaches the basement, she can't stifle a gasp.

There are no velvets in the storeroom. Instead, every inch of space is stacked high with boxes and barrels, a few of them open, revealing their contents—rifles and pistols, all shining and new, and barrels upon barrels of what she can only guess is gunpowder. Enough weaponry to arm hundreds of people.

"Princess!" a voice cries out, startled, and Daphne turns to see Cliona, standing over one of the barrels, lid in hand, while behind her, Diedre holds a rifle in both hands, inspecting it.

Before Daphne can move, there is a creak on the stairs behind her and a cold, sharp knife comes to rest against her throat, just firmly enough that she feels the edge of it dig into her skin. All it would take is a bit of pressure and the blade would slice through her carotid artery, causing her to bleed out quickly. The thought of death looming so close should frighten Daphne, but instead she wonders if the placement of the knife is a lucky accident, or if this isn't the first time Mrs. Nattermore has held a knife to someone's throat.

"Well," Mrs. Nattermore says in Daphne's ear, her voice level. "I suppose the tea will have to wait."

Daphne

Daphne is forced into a chair, her arms bound with rope, Mrs. Nattermore all the while keeping the knife pressed to her throat. She feels the bite of its edge, though it hasn't broken the skin—not yet. She knows logically it is a likely outcome—this is not a situation any capable person would allow her to walk out of—but any fear that accompanies that knowledge feels far away, locked out of reach.

She won't die, she decides. She simply *won't*. She will do and say whatever it takes to walk out of this alive. After all, Bessemia needs her, and death doesn't frighten her nearly as much as the prospect of failing.

"I'll handle it," Mrs. Nattermore says to Cliona and Diedre, though her eyes rest on Daphne. The woman doesn't want to kill her, Daphne realizes, which isn't to say she won't, but the ambivalence is a tool to use. "Cliona and the guards will say they were attacked by rebels on the way back to the castle. Do we have all the guards?"

"Three out of four," Cliona says quietly. "There's a new one now; his family is loyal to the king."

"Then you'll say he valiantly gave his life trying to protect the princess."

Daphne remembers how the guards looked at Cliona, that nod that seemed directed just at her, as if to communicate something. Now she knows three things about these rebels: they're enemies of the king, Cliona's family is involved, and they are very well connected. If she lives through this, she'll have plenty of information for her mother.

Cliona falters, biting her lip before nodding. "Do it, then," she says.

The knife presses harder against Daphne's neck.

"You're operating under a flawed assumption," Daphne says, her voice coming out calm and level, though inside, her mind is churning. *Survive at any cost*, she reminds herself.

"Oh?" Mrs. Nattermore asks.

Daphne licks her lips, choosing her next words very carefully. She can't give away too much, but what will that matter if she's dead? She'll be no use to her mother or Bessemia then. Her mother has always said she could talk a snake into eating its own tail.

"That our desires don't overlap," she says carefully. It isn't a lie. They're working against the king, and so is she.

The three exchange looks. "There is no overlap," Mrs. Nattermore says, her voice brusque. "You want Friv united, or else you have no land to rule. We want a Friv with no king or queen, which means no princess, either."

Daphne smiles. Maybe the best way through this is honesty—as much honesty as she dares. Maybe she can make her way out of this not just with her life, but with a bit of progress to report to her mother. "I don't care for Friv," she tells them. "It's cold and coarse and I hate it here." The knife presses harder against her neck, and Daphne wonders if that was a little too much honesty. She changes course. "If you want it, you're welcome to it. All I want is to go home. You want to overthrow the monarchy? Wonderful. If you can manage it before my wedding, all the better. My mother will pay handsomely for my safe return, I'll go home, and Friv will be all yours. We can all get what we want."

"Is that meant to convince us?" Diedre asks scathingly. "We're here because we love our country. We are patriots."

"Then I'm assuming you don't want Friv and Bessemia to merge," Daphne says, looking from one to the other of them. She's shocked them, she can tell. Good. She was planning on waiting to sow that little lie until she had the king's seal to lend credence to it, but her mother has always said the best-laid plans are the most flexible. "That is the king's plan. My mother has no male heir. When Bairre and I marry, the integration of Bessemia and Friv will commence, and eventually, he and I will rule it together."

It is half true. Friv will be absorbed into Bessemia, along with Temarin and Cellaria, and Daphne will one day rule it all, but King Bartholomew knows nothing of this. Though if the rebels want to make him their villain, all the better.

"More reason to kill you," Cliona points out. "If you're dead, the alliance with Bessemia dies with you."

"If you kill me, you'll have a mess on your hands. All it will take is one person on Wallfrost Street who remembers me coming here with you, one person who sees only Cliona leave. And if King Bartholomew bartered Friv away once, he'll do it again. Killing me would be a short-term solution to a much larger problem. Perhaps, instead, I could be of some assistance."

It's a desperate ploy and she isn't quite sure what, exactly, she's getting into, but if she lives, what does it matter? There are few things Daphne wouldn't give for her life—in fact, nothing immediately comes to mind.

"You think we need you?" Mrs. Nattermore laughs. "There are rebels everywhere you look, Princess, loyal Frivians who see this king as the fraud he is, a power-hungry warlord who reached too far. There are rebels all over the highlands, ready to bring the clans back, ready to declare our independence if it means burning down the castle and everyone in it."

More information to file away in her next letter to her mother, though Daphne wonders how much the empress already knows. Their spies knew about rebellions in the highlands, noble families loyal to the king who were robbed in their carriages, threats that had been made against the crown, clandestine meetings held in basements not so different from this one. *Child's play,* her mother scoffed. *All words and bluster, no real action*. But here Daphne is, surrounded by weapons and enough gunpowder to level the city. If this doesn't count as real action, she can't imagine what would.

"You have support in the highlands," Daphne says, remembering the spies' reports. "But we aren't in the highlands, are we? Oh, you'll have support here as well, I'm sure. What would be the point of all these weapons if you didn't? But not enough."

For a moment, no one speaks.

"She isn't wrong," Cliona says, her voice quiet. "These weapons are all well and good, but they aren't going to be of any use if we don't have the manpower to get them into the castle, near the king."

"What would you suggest, then?" Mrs. Nattermore asks.

Daphne shrugs. "The king seems to have taken a liking to me," she says. "He's grieving a child, and here fate's delivered him a new one. I can use that. Not to mention the fact that I have unlimited access to the castle, including places even Cliona can't get into."

"Doubtful," Cliona says.

Daphne smirks. "So you've been alone in the king's study, then?"

Cliona's jaw tightens. "It's locked when he isn't there."

"Yes, I suppose that would stop some people," Daphne says.

Mrs. Nattermore stares at her for a long moment. "Who exactly *are* you?" she asks.

Daphne shakes her head. "There is plenty you aren't telling me," she says. "It's only fair I keep a few secrets for myself."

"What do you want, then?" Diedre asks, eyes narrow.

"Well, for one thing, I'd like you to drop the knife, Mrs. Nattermore. If you were going to use it, you would have by now, but it's terribly uncomfortable all the same."

There's a second of hesitation before Mrs. Nattermore drops her arm and the blade along with it. She crosses the room to stand with Diedre and Cliona, folding her arms over her chest.

"Any other terms?" Cliona asks.

Daphne holds her gaze and decides to press her luck. She thinks about the seal she's meant to steal from the king without his noticing. The impossible task her mother set her. But maybe not impossible—not if she has a little assistance.

"Stardust. I'd like some," Daphne says.

"Why not ask the king? He has plenty."

"If I ask the king, he'll ask questions. You won't," Daphne tells her.

The girl purses her lips before she nods. "Done."

"You do not make deals, Cliona. Your father does," Mrs. Nattermore says—another tidbit for Daphne to file away. She suspected Cliona's father is involved, but from the sound of it, he's their leader.

"When my father isn't present, I act in his stead," Cliona counters. "I'll explain the situation. If he disagrees with me, we can address it then, but for now, this is the best course of action. She's right—she's valuable alive and a risk dead."

"And if she tells the king about this the second she's back in the castle?" Diedre asks. "It's what I would do, if I were her."

"Well, let's hope she's smarter than you are," Cliona says, her eyes meeting Daphne's. "After all, we have our spies in the castle as well—including me. And she doesn't know where they are. The king's guards with their sharp swords, the chefs preparing her food, the royal empyrea who could make her life torture with the right wish. It could be anyone."

Daphne swallows but forces herself to hold Cliona's gaze. "We're understood," she says before smiling. "You see? There's no reason we can't get along."

Cliona takes the dagger from Mrs. Nattermore and cuts the rope tying Daphne to the chair.

"We've got appointments with the goldsmith and the cobbler. We can't have anyone getting suspicious, can we?"

Daphne gets to her feet, rubbing at her arms where the rope left red indents behind.

"Cliona," Mrs. Nattermore says when they approach the stairs. "If this goes poorly, your father will be very disappointed."

Mild as the words are, Daphne sees a real glint of fear in Cliona's eyes, the first time she's truly looked unnerved.

"It won't," she says through clenched teeth. She places a fist over her heart. "For Friv."

"For Friv," Mrs. Nattermore and Diedre echo, repeating the motion.

The rest of their shopping passes in a blur. As Daphne tries on dozens of necklaces and earrings and heeled slippers, she watches Cliona out of the corner of her eye. The spoiled socialite facade is back in place, but now Daphne can't look at her without also seeing the cold-eyed girl from the basement, examining a musket with a shrewd and determined gaze.

She should have seen it sooner, should have noticed that Cliona wasn't what she seemed. But then, Cliona didn't see her for what she was either—there is some comfort in that. And Daphne was able to seed rumors about the king's merging Friv and Bessemia—she thought she'd need the seal before she could manage that, but a whisper can travel even farther than a proclamation, and faster, too. *A broken country is a vulnerable one,* the empress likes to say. If Friv is fighting itself, it will be easier for Bessemia to overpower.

When they arrive back at the castle and pass their horses off to the stable hand, Cliona loops her arm through Daphne's, just as she did earlier, but this time the gesture feels more menacing. Daphne scans Cliona's hands for some kind of hidden weapon—a poisoned ring, a dagger the width of a quill—but there is nothing.

"There will be a missive in a few days," Cliona tells her. "Follow the instructions and you'll have your stardust."

"Instructions?" Daphne asks, dread pooling in her stomach.

At that, Cliona's smile sharpens into something else entirely. "You wanted to join our game, Princess. Let's see you play."

Beatriz

Even in Bessemia, Beatriz heard rumors of the beauty of the Cellarian sea garden, a swath of shoreline along the southern coast of the country, just outside the palace walls. At high tide, there is nothing to see, just the sandy beach and rolling waves—a sight still new to Beatriz, true, but nothing compared to what it becomes when the tide goes out.

It's like the sea is a blanket, pulled back to reveal bright thatches of plants that look more like a child's painting than any flowers Beatriz has ever seen. From far away, the shore looks like a jewel box, brimming with gemstones of every color and shape, but as she walks closer, it becomes all the more extraordinary. Some of the flowers have tendrils that reach out, licking at the sand in long, languid motions; others pick up and move at their leisure, sprouting spiky claws that snap at anyone who gets too close.

Beatriz's favorites, though, are the clusters of red blooms that unfurl slowly as time passes, each petal rolling down to reveal a vivid violet center. It isn't until she walks past the third one, though, that she notices the two black dots that seem to follow her every movement.

The flowers have *eyes.*

In Bessemia, her mother's gardens were the stuff of legend, carefully curated arrangements of the most beautiful flowers from all over the world. It was, Beatriz often thought as a child, like walking through a marzipan wonderland, beautiful and colorful and surreal, but static. Not sentient. Not like this.

She isn't the only one walking through the garden this afternoon, her satin slippers held aloft in one hand and her bare feet sinking slightly in the damp sand. There are many other courtiers she recognizes vaguely from the palace, couples walking arm in arm, laughing and splashing and enjoying the bright, warm day. It makes her miss her sisters more than ever—Sophronia would be fascinated by the garden, Daphne by the people. Beatriz tries to think of how she will describe it next time she writes to them but comes up short. It is utterly indescribable.

She casts an idle gaze around, scanning the faces of the others wandering through the sea garden, looking for one face in particular. She's seen sketches of Lord Savelle by her mother's spies but has yet to see anyone who matches them. She assumed he would be at the wedding, but she didn't see him there, either.

Not that you paid much attention to anything but the contents of your wineglass, a voice in her mind chides. It sounds like Daphne. Beatriz flinches. She knows she should be further along in her assignment by now, and she's already had to confess her failures in a letter to her mother. But she won't dwell on past mistakes—far better to fix them today. One of her servants mentioned, after a few carefully chosen, artfully blasé questions, that Lord Savelle enjoys strolling through the sea garden, so this seemed the best place to arrange their introduction.

Beatriz has it all planned—she will wander close to Lord Savelle, then stumble over a stone and pretend to turn her ankle. She considered actually turning it for the sake of authenticity, but there is no stardust to heal her quickly here. Lord Savelle will be obligated to escort her back to the palace—maybe even carry her. It will be only too easy to bat her eyelashes and thank him profusely for his help. She'll have him wrapped around her finger before they make it to the palace entrance, and it will be easy enough to use him to fuel a war with Temarin. The hardest part, it seems, is finding him.

But as she searches for Lord Savelle, she feels the gaze of the courtiers on her. The looks burn against her skin, but she tries to ignore them.

Are they wondering why she is here alone, and where her new husband is? She doesn't blame them. She's seen newlyweds before, how they are always at each other's side for at least a few weeks after their wedding, how oftentimes they rarely leave their rooms. She supposes she, too, would be wondering if something was amiss.

Pasquale has been nothing but polite, though in the few days since they wed he has still insisted on sleeping on the sofa in their room, only climbing in beside her a moment before the servants arrive in the morning, to keep them from whispering. It can't be comfortable—she always makes sure she stays awake later than him so she can put her drops in her eyes, and even in sleep he looks miserable. They don't speak any more about it, or about their first morning together. She doesn't mention the way she saw him looking at that boy.

Ambrose is his name, she found out later. No title, just Ambrose. The nephew and heir of a minor lord and Pasquale's favorite friend at court. From what she's gathered, they've been close since they were children, all but inseparable.

Beatriz tries to put it from her mind. After all, she doesn't know what she saw—Pasquale smiling? Why shouldn't he smile at his friend? In that moment, she thought she saw something pass between them, a look, an energy, but the more she thinks on it, the more she thinks she might have misinterpreted it. After all, a crown prince's preference for other men would have emerged in a rumor or two at least, but her mother's spies have never reported anything of the sort.

Perhaps it's only her pride, latching on to an easy excuse as to why he's shown so little interest in her. She knows there are men who prefer other men; in Bessemia there were a handful of lords and earls who were known to have male paramours. And it wasn't only men—there were women, too, who preferred other women. Back home, it was commonplace enough, and couples could marry regardless of gender, but beneath the thick veneer of lushness and sensuality, Cellaria is deeply prudish, not just devoted to the stars, but fearful of them. *The stars see all,* her tutor told her, *and*

Cellarians believe they judge and punish the sins they see. It was the opposite of what she'd grown up with in Bessemia, where the stars were not there to judge and punish, but to bless and reward. Yet she read Cellarian scriptures as part of her lessons, and she distantly remembers one of the many sins being something about men lying with men.

Of course, there were also proclamations against women showing their bare shoulders and people having affairs, and she's seen both of those things happen often enough in the last week without any kind of consequence from the stars or anyone. A country of hypocrites, as her tutor used to call it.

"Your Highness!" a high-pitched voice calls out behind her, and Beatriz turns toward it.

It takes her a moment to recognize the girl from her wedding—Pasquale's cousin. The fruit wine really went to Beatriz's head that night, and most of it is such a blur now. She can't quite remember the girl's name.

The girl is walking toward her, the train of her bright orange gown trailing over the wet sand, her slippers dangling from her fingertips. In the golden afternoon light, her blond hair almost glows, pulled into a long plait that dangles over her left shoulder.

A few steps behind her is her brother. Beatriz's mind was too fuzzy before to see him properly, but now that she is sober, she sees that he's handsome, with the same blond hair as his sister, though his face is far more angular, with a strong, square jaw, high cheekbones, and dark brown eyes. He's rolled his trousers up to his knees, like most of the men in the sea garden, and he's taken off his jacket as well, folding it over his arm, leaving him in a white tunic that is simple, though it looks well made.

"Hello," Beatriz says, lifting her hand to shield her eyes so that she can see them better. The other courtiers watch their approach, though they pretend not to. Many of the girls, in particular, let their gazes linger a little longer than necessary on the boy, not that Beatriz can hold that against them.

Shameless, Daphne's voice whispers through her mind.

"What brings the two of you out here?" Beatriz asks, hoping they'll call each other by name at some point so she doesn't have to admit she's forgotten them.

The girl shrugs. "It seemed a good day to get a bit of sun," she says with a bright smile. "The castle gets so stuffy sometimes."

"Not that it's much different here," the boy adds, glancing around at the courtiers milling about the sea garden. "But at least the air is a bit fresher."

The girl lets out a snort that draws several more disapproving stares. "For now, at least," she says. "We'll have to head indoors soon. It's a Burning Day."

Beatriz frowns. "Burning Day?"

The two exchange a look, but it's the girl who eventually answers.

"For the heretics," she says. "It happens once every fortnight. Anyone who's been found to be practicing magic, or breaking any number of other laws, is put to death."

And in Cellaria, burning is the preferred method of execution, Beatriz remembers from her studies, feeling her stomach sour. It is not lost on her that she wears a wish around her wrist at this very moment.

"I didn't realize it happened so often," she says, trying not to look as unsettled as she feels. *Every fortnight*. How many must be sentenced to death to make that necessary? "After all, magic has been outlawed since King Cesare took the throne, hasn't it? It isn't a new law, and people do know the punishment."

"Ah," the boy says, the corner of his mouth hitching up in a droll smile. "But desperate people do desperate things, and there are always rebels who think the law unfair."

"It's really nothing to concern yourself with," the girl adds, waving a hand. "But the smell does make the air rather unpleasant for a few hours afterward, so I would recommend heading indoors soon. Nicolo and I will escort you," she says, shooting a grin at her brother. Nico for short, Beatriz presumes, the name dimly familiar.

"Gisella is dramatic," Nicolo says. "You get used to the smell before too long."

Beatriz can't imagine she will ever get used to the smell of burning flesh, but she knows better than to say as much, lest she be thought sympathetic toward heretics. Instead, she forces a smile, looking from one of them to the other.

"Are you twins?" she asks.

"Technically, I'm five minutes older," Nico says.

Gisella rolls her eyes, giving her brother a sharp elbow in the side. "A fact he never lets me forget," she murmurs.

"I'm the same with my sisters," Beatriz admits, another pang of homesickness rippling through her. "We may be triplets, but I am still the eldest." She pauses, as if a thought is only just occurring to her. "I was actually hoping for word of them—I know they're heretics, but surely we should endeavor to keep our hearts open to all, even if we must prevent their rot from touching us. I sent a couple of letters, but it might take a while to hear back from them. I thought maybe I would ask the Temarinian ambassador for news—whether Sophronia's married yet, how she is adjusting, that sort of thing. Have you seen him?"

"Lord Savelle?" Gisella asks with a snort. "Oh, you won't find him here—he prefers his own company most days. I've heard he only visits the sea garden before dawn, when there is no one else around."

Beatriz's heart sinks and she has to stifle a groan at the prospect of having to drag herself out of bed before the sun.

"How is Pasquale?" Gisella asks. "He's been quite elusive, though I suppose most newlyweds are."

Well, wherever he's been hiding, it hasn't been with me, Beatriz thinks. Out loud, though, she takes a more neutral approach—perhaps this trip to the sea garden needn't be wasted.

"We're both finding marriage quite surreal," she says. It's the kind of truth she likes best, the kind that others can interpret however they like. "You must know Pasquale well, being cousins," she says.

"Oh, there are many of us cousins running about—a dozen, last I counted, not including King Leopold and his brothers in Temarin," Nicolo says, shaking his head. "But the Cellarian court isn't really a place for children—those of us raised here had no choice but to band together."

"Of course, Pas wasn't raised here at first," Gisella says.

"He came to live here when he was . . . what, thirteen or so? After . . ." She trails off, glancing at her brother, though Beatriz has a good idea of what comes next.

"After?" Beatriz prompts anyway, because though she knows the story, she doesn't know their version, and her mother has always told her that when it's repeated enough, gossip becomes its own truth.

"After Prince Pietro passed away," Nicolo says. "Before that, Pasquale lived in the south with his mother."

Beatriz pretends this is new information, though whispers of Queen Valencia made their way even to the Bessemian court. *The Mad Queen,* they called her. Beatriz heard a more factual telling of the queen's tragic suicide as part of her lessons, but it's the rumors that have stuck with her most over the years, even though most are too outrageous to be believed.

And as for Pietro's death . . . well, she remembers when news of *that* reached Bessemia and how, even at the age of twelve, she was certain her mother had had a hand in it. Beatriz was the only one of her sisters betrothed to a second son, but Pietro was already married and there was no help for that. Five stillborn children and a hunting accident later, though, and Pasquale was his father's heir. The empress had been either lucky or diabolical, and Beatriz has long understood things well enough to know it was the latter.

"Some people say they saw her walk into the sea one morning," Gisella says, lowering her voice, though there is no one close enough to hear now. "They thought she was going for a swim, I suppose. Her body washed up some hours later, stones in the pockets of her dress. Pasquale was never quite the same."

"I don't imagine anyone would be," Beatriz says, chewing on her bottom lip. Though she knew the bare bones of the story of Queen Valencia's death, hearing the more human details now digs beneath her skin. She thinks of her mysterious new husband, with his sad eyes and soft voice. She thought she knew him well, based on reports and gossip, but there are many things she doesn't know about Prince Pasquale.

Beatriz

That night, when Beatriz retires to their bedroom, she finds Pasquale already there, dressed in his nightshirt and standing beside the sofa, a pillow already in his hands. He looks up when she comes in, trying on a smile that doesn't quite reach his eyes.

"I heard you went to the sea garden today," he says. "Did you enjoy it?"

She doesn't answer him. Instead, she reaches behind her, fingers fumbling with the buttons of her gown. After a moment, she manages to undo enough of them that she can pull the dress off her shoulders, letting it fall to the ground in a pool of crimson brocade, leaving her standing before him in nothing but a thin white chemise that doesn't quite reach her knees.

Pasquale averts his eyes, his cheeks turning red.

"What are you—" he starts, but she doesn't give him a chance to finish the question. She crosses the room toward him and takes the pillow from his hands, tossing it aside. Taking his hands, she guides them to her waist, feeling them begin to shake.

"Triz," he says, his voice a warning.

She doesn't heed it. She rolls onto the tips of her toes and presses her mouth to his. She kisses him soundly, bringing her hands up to the back of his neck, anchoring him to her. To his credit, he does try to kiss her back, does try to respond to her touch as he must think he should. He does try, but when Beatriz reaches for the hem of her chemise, ready to remove that as well, his hands come to rest on hers, holding them still. He pulls back, looking at her with anguished eyes.

"I can't," he says.

Not *I won't*. Not *I don't want to*. But *I can't*.

She steps back from him, watching him carefully. "The boy," she says. "Ambrose."

Beatriz didn't know for certain before, but the second she says his name, the second Pasquale flinches and drops his gaze, she knows she's hit the truth of it.

She turns away from him, crossing to her wardrobe and finding a dressing gown. She pulls it over her chemise so that she doesn't feel so exposed. Her fingers shake as she pulls the sash tight around her waist, tying it into a bow.

"Does he know how you feel?" she asks.

She waits for him to deny it, to pretend he doesn't know what she's talking about. Instead, though, his eyes meet hers and he lets out an exhale, seeming to deflate as he does.

"No," he tells her, his voice barely louder than a whisper. "Or maybe he does. But I didn't tell him."

"He doesn't feel the same way," she says.

He shrugs, looking away. "There's no point in asking, is there? If anyone found out . . . I've seen people arrested for the feelings I have, Beatriz. My father's had them executed, and if you think he'd spare me that fate because I'm his son—"

"No, I don't think that," Beatriz interrupts.

Neither of them speaks for a moment, but the words linger and she can smell a faint scent that's worked its way indoors—the smell of smoke and fire and something else that she now knows is the smell of burning flesh. How easily they could both find their way into those flames.

She sits down at the edge of the bed, folding her arms over her stomach. "Does anyone else know?" she asks him.

He shakes his head. "Not a living soul."

"Then we keep it that way," she says.

Pasquale stares at her, mouth gaping open. "You . . . want to help me? Most think people like me are an abomination."

"The only thing abominable about you is your taste in shoes," she tells him, which makes him smile ever so slightly. For a second, she considers telling him about the wish on her wrist, but just because he has to trust her, that doesn't mean she can trust him. "Our fates are tied together now, Pas," she says instead. "If anyone finds out, it won't ruin only you. Our marriage will be annulled, and I could very well end up burning beside you for keeping your secret."

Pasquale swallows, staring down at his hands. "I know," he says quietly. "I'm sorry."

Something about his apology chafes her.

"You shouldn't apologize," she tells him. "I'm sorry that you're in this position, that you have to deny this part of yourself. I don't know how you do it."

He shakes his head. "What are we going to do, Triz?" he asks her.

"For starters, you can't keep sleeping on the sofa," she says. "If anyone happens to come in without warning, rumors will begin."

"But—" he starts.

"We'll only sleep," she says. "I don't think either of us will have a hard time keeping our hands to ourselves."

She means it as a joke, but his face turns red all the same.

"You were right before, though," he says. "It's only a matter of time before people start to talk."

She pauses for a moment, choosing her words carefully. There is no delicate way to ask the question, but she has to ask it anyway.

"I knew men like you in Bessemia," she says. "But there were others who were rumored to enjoy the company of both men and women. Might you . . ." She trails off.

He doesn't say anything for a moment but then shakes his head. "No," he says. "I can't imagine I could. I just . . . I don't think I work that way. I'm sorry."

Again, with apologies she doesn't want or need.

"We have time to figure it out, Pas. As long as we're in it together, we can figure it out."

He holds her gaze, unflinching, before nodding once. "Thank you, Triz."

The solemnness in his voice makes her uncomfortable. She shrugs off his gratitude.

"We're in it together," she says again. "Now come on, I'm sure your back is aching after a week on the sofa."

She crawls into the bed, making room for him to climb in beside her. The bed is so large that they don't come close to touching.

Beatriz tosses and turns for hours, but sleep doesn't claim her. It isn't that she's restless, not exactly. She feels strangely at peace now, not because a sword no longer dangles over her head, but because she knows it's there, because she can name it, because her mother taught her that it is better to know what one is up against than to believe there is safety in ignorance.

No, it is not her busy mind keeping her awake, it's her body. She feels as if it is the middle of the afternoon, as if she could go for a long walk in the sea garden or go for an hours-long horseback ride. She feels like she could climb a mountain, even.

She gets out of bed carefully, so as not to disturb Pasquale, and crosses to the cabinet by the door. There she finds a bottle of brandy and pours herself a glass, drinking it down in a single gulp. After a moment, she pours herself another. She paces the room, lit only by the moon and stars shining through the open window. After a few minutes of that, she returns to bed, tosses and turns some more, and goes back for another glass of brandy.

She becomes pleasantly tipsy, but no more tired. Instead, she feels the strange desire to run through the halls, knocking on doors and rousing the rest of the castle so that she isn't the only one awake. She even tries to wake up Pasquale, but he sleeps like the dead.

If Sophronia were here, she would tell Beatriz to try reading a book, and Beatriz would roll her eyes and call Sophronia boring, but she's just desperate enough to try it. She takes a book off the shelf at random and sits down on the chaise by the window.

The book, it turns out, is a record of the early years of the Celestian War, when King Cesare was new to the throne but already overzealous, determined to outlaw the use of stardust not just in Cellaria, but across the entire continent. It's a history Beatriz knows well, but reading just the first paragraph threatens to bore her to tears.

Her attention keeps drifting out the window, to the moon shining down and the constellations that surround it, moving across the sky at a slow and steady crawl. There is the Hermit's Cane, with its hooked top, thought to encourage seclusion and introspection. It has long been Beatriz's least-favorite sign because whenever it appeared, the entire Bessemian court became quiet and withdrawn. Balls were canceled. Tea parties postponed. The Hermit's Cane meant, to Beatriz, boredom.

There is the Queen's Chalice, with its gently curved goblet. Usually it foretells good fortune, but tonight it hangs upside down over Cellaria, a bad omen, though Beatriz has always thought that the zodiac, like most superstitions, gains its power from belief.

She wonders if Sophronia and Daphne can see the stars where they are; she wonders which constellations they can make out. Her eyes seek out one star in particular—she doesn't know why; it isn't particularly bright or large, just one of countless stars. It makes up one of the spokes of the

Wanderer's Wheel—a constellation meant to signal travel or, more broadly, change. If she believed in the stars, she might take it as an omen of her going home, and as unlikely as she knows that is, her heart clenches around the possibility.

She closes her eyes and thinks of her sisters as she last saw them, dressed in the fashions of their new homes, looking like strangers as they set off in their separate directions. She imagines walking back into the palace she grew up in, the familiar marble floors beneath her slippers, the paintings of her ancestors lining the walls, the scent of bergamot heavy in the air. It feels real—so real she swears she can feel the sharp edges of the crystal doorknob beneath her palm as she pushes open the door to the rooms she shared with her sisters. On the other side she can hear Sophronia's laugh and Daphne's low voice. Her heart lurches in her chest and she steps into the room, but there her fantasy fades and she is back in Cellaria, lonely and alone, with nothing but yearning to keep her company.

"I wish I could go home," she says, her eyes finding the star once more. Her voice comes out a whisper, but the words echo in her ears long after they leave her lips. The brandy finally takes hold, making her mind blurry and finally—*finally*—sleepy. More than sleepy, she feels drained, like every bit of energy, every thought, every feeling has been sapped from her. She closes the book, even that small movement a struggle, and leaves it on the chaise before climbing back into bed and falling into a deep and dreamless sleep.

Sophronia

Sophronia wears her new violet riding habit to meet Leopold in the stables. It's a gorgeous creation of sumptuous velvet with shiny gold buttons, yet she can't help but hear her mother's voice in her mind, telling her she looks like a grape. But when Leopold greets her with a broad grin and a quick kiss on the lips and tells her she looks beautiful, her mother's voice gets a little bit quieter. Despite herself, a flutter goes through her and she has to give herself a mental shake.

"How was your hunting trip?" she asks, forcing herself to think about the village Leopold razed to build his new lodge. According to reports from her mother's spies, the villagers were turned out of their homes without even the reimbursement necessary to relocate.

"Excellent, though I was sorry to abandon you so soon after our wedding," he says. "I thought you might like to explore the grounds, since you've been cooped up in the castle so long."

"You thought right," Sophronia says. "I don't think I ever realized how exhausting teas and luncheons could be."

"You were with my mother and her friends," he points out. "I think *exhausting* might be an understatement."

Sophronia laughs. The groom retrieves a stool for Sophronia to use to mount the horse, but Leopold waves him away, moving to stand behind her.

"Here, allow me," he murmurs in her ear, bracing his hands on her waist and lifting her up and into the saddle.

Sophronia feels herself flush—a trait her mother has long lamented her inability to control. As Leopold gets situated on his own horse, Sophronia's thoughts linger on her mother and the message she sent. She isn't surprised that her mother managed to rope the great Sir Diapollio into her plots, but she wonders if it has anything to do with Beatriz. Perhaps the singer will have word of her sister to share as well as whatever ominous gift he carries from the empress.

"Are you excited to see Sir Diapollio tonight?" she asks Leopold as they begin to walk their horses down the path, side by side.

He shrugs, giving her a bashful sideways glance. "His appeal is lost on me. He visits court to perform a few times a year, and I know most people—most women, I suppose—are enamored with him, but I don't understand why. He's a fine singer, I'll admit, but . . ." He trails off.

"I've heard he's quite handsome," Sophronia says, and Leopold laughs.

"Careful—there are those who would consider such faint praise a grievous insult to his beauty," he tells her. "Truth be told, I invite him for my mother. Hearing him sing in Cellarian brings her great comfort."

Sophronia nods, wondering if this is part of her mother's

gift—another weapon to use to undermine Eugenia. A weak one, if so. Everyone loves Sir Diapollio, Eugenia isn't alone in that. "Your mother has been very kind to me," Sophronia tells Leopold. "I know that she had a . . . difficult time when she arrived. She's determined that my experience will be better."

"Has it been?"

She gives a dramatic sigh. "Well, the palace is beautiful, and everyone I've met has been pleasant enough to me, and I'm *told* I have a handsome husband around here somewhere, though I must say I haven't seen much of him."

Leopold laughs. "Fair enough," he says, then hesitates before adding, "I might have to leave again soon. There have been some . . . skirmishes on the Cellarian border—nothing major, nothing sanctioned by me or my uncle Cesare. Our truce holds officially, but . . ."

"But the people on the border need reminding?" Sophronia guesses, her thoughts turning. The skirmishes are news to her, but they are hardly surprising. It's possible her mother even had a hand in them, though just as likely they came about organically. Tensions between Cellaria and Temarin haven't disappeared since the war's end, and especially near the border they tend to run a little higher. At least once a year, her mother's spies sent word that Temarinians had crossed into Cellaria to illegally sell stardust, or that Cellarians had crossed into Temarin to try to murder a local empyrea.

Leopold nods. "Nothing that would constitute breaking the truce with my uncle, but we'll parade the bulk of our armies along the border—call it a celebration of Temarinian strength, a reminder to our people that they have my protection."

"But it won't just be a reminder to Temarin," Sophronia says, understanding. "It'll serve to remind the Cellarians that you aren't to be trifled with."

"That *we* aren't to be trifled with," Leopold corrects with a crooked smile. "King Cesare got lucky in the Celestian War. He took my father by surprise and used the advantage he had by attacking by sea. We were unprepared—an embarrassing oversight, and my father spent years building up our naval forces to ensure that it wouldn't happen again. Should Cesare decide to test his luck, he'll be disappointed. But I'd rather it didn't come to that. I'd like to protect the alliance my parents created through me, not watch my uncle ruin it."

Sophronia knows about the Celestian War, how King Cesare sought to rid not just Cellaria but the entire continent of the empyreas and stardust he viewed as abominations, how he believed it to be his stars-blessed mission as king. She also knows how Leopold's father, King Carlisle, eventually agreed to a truce, arranged by Sophronia's father, that included Carlisle's marriage to Eugenia, Cesare's sister.

"They say Cesare's mad," Sophronia says. "Are you certain relying on his sense is the best course of action?"

Leopold shrugs. "My mother says it's our only course of action, apart from another war, which I don't want. She offered to go to Cellaria to reason with her brother, but given her personal connection, it didn't seem a wise idea." He winces. "It's a bit of a mess, really. Like trying to play chess with a toddler and just hoping he doesn't overturn the board in a tantrum. I'm sure my father would have known what to do, but I haven't the slightest idea."

Sophronia bites her lip. "Your father died suddenly, Leo. You became the youngest king in Temarin's history." She pauses, realizing he's given her the perfect opportunity. "Perhaps I could help," she adds. "I've never even set foot in Cellaria, and I've been studying my whole life to be queen of Temarin—I'm sure your mother is more than ready to enjoy a life of leisure as dowager queen."

He looks a little surprised but smiles. "I think that's a brilliant idea," he tells her.

Sophronia smiles back, a jolt of pleasure running through her. She realizes that part of her thought he would turn down her offer, that he might laugh at the thought of her being capable enough to do anything. It's what her mother would have done. But Leopold, for all of his many flaws, believes in her.

It shouldn't matter what he believes in, it shouldn't make her heart beat faster, it shouldn't let her forget, even for a second, who she is and why she is here. But it does, and that makes it dangerous.

She urges her horse to go faster, as if she can outpace her thoughts. "Come on," she says over her shoulder. "Let's race."

She hears Leopold make a noise that is half shock and half indignation before he presses his horse into a faster pace as well and the thunderous hoofbeats grow louder behind her.

The castle grounds blur past her, and she's aware that courtiers are milling about the gardens, watching them. She's riding too fast to make out much, but she can tell that the palace grounds are immaculately maintained, full of impossibly green grass, artfully pruned trees, and more flowers than she can possibly count. And when they leave the gardens behind and enter the sprawling woods, she's surprised that even the trees here look like they were designed by artists. There is nothing wild about the woods here—the setting could be plucked straight from an idyllic watercolor painting.

"Sophie!" Leopold calls behind her, closer than she expected.

"Catch me if you can!" she yells back, urging her horse to go faster.

"Sophie, wait!" Leopold calls, but Sophronia is enjoying herself too much to heed his words.

She can see a cliff's edge up ahead and decides that will be the finish line. As she approaches, she pulls her horse to a stop, looking out over the cliffside and realizing where they are.

The city of Kavelle is spread out below like a dirty blanket. After the splendor of the palace grounds, it's jarring to see it—crooked stone streets covered in grime, houses and shops that look like they might fall over in the face of a mild breeze, and more people than Sophronia has ever seen in one place. Surely too many people to fit in the city.

"Sophie," Leopold says behind her. "Come on, let's go home."

But Sophronia doesn't move. They're too far up to see any details, but she can tell even from this distance that Kavelle—Temarin's capital city—is struggling even more than she'd thought.

"What's going on there?" she asks, pointing to a particularly thick crowd of people in the middle of a city square.

"I don't know." He says it so quickly that she doesn't believe him.

"Then perhaps we should go see," she says, urging her horse along the cliffside until she sees a path that leads down to the city, blocked by an imposing gate and two guards.

"Sophie," he says again, following her. "Fine. It's an execution."

She stops her horse short and looks back at him. "An execution," she repeats. "Whose?"

He doesn't answer, and she urges her horse forward again until Leopold gives a sigh. "Just criminals."

That might have been answer enough, might have let her imagine he was talking about murderers or rapists, those whose crimes are punishable by death even in Bessemia. But he won't look at her, so Sophronia knows there is more he hasn't said.

"Criminals," she repeats. "What sort of criminals?"

He looks even more uncomfortable. "I believe most of them are thieves," he says, and something clicks into place.

"Would they include the thieves who attempted to rob my carriage?"

He lifts a shoulder in a shrug. "I assume so," he says. "Executions are held once a week for anyone arrested in that time."

Sophronia shakes her head. "Your mother said they'd been released, that they were home with their families."

As soon as she says it, she feels like the greatest fool. Eugenia told her a pleasant lie to soothe her, the way a parent would tell a child that a dead pet has been sent away to live in the country. The lie ruffles her that much more—she isn't a child to be condescended to, she is a queen.

"I discussed it with her," Leopold says. "We decided against making an exception."

The *we* doesn't fool Sophronia. Leopold would have spared the boys to make her happy, she's sure of this. Eugenia made this decision, and Leopold didn't have the strength to go against her.

Sophronia can't stand to look at him; instead she turns her gaze back toward the city and the gathered crowd. Now that he's said it, she can make out the vague outline of a scaffold, of ten figures standing below a beam, ropes around their necks.

"They're children," she says.

"They knew that what they were doing was wrong," Leopold says. "They knew the consequences. They did it anyway. If I showed mercy, it would only lead to more thievery—and the next victims might not be as lucky as you were."

More of his mother's words, she imagined. She thinks about the reports from the spies, how things have changed in Temarin in the year since Leopold took the throne. Raising taxes, removing people from their homes, executing every level of criminal—Sophronia thought them the actions of a careless, cruel king. She's had trouble reconciling that with the Leopold she knew, but now she suddenly understands. Leopold is none of those things—not careless, not cruel, not a king. Not really. He is a puppet, content to let his mother pull his strings, never questioning what she does with them.

In the distance, she hears the sound of the scaffold floor

falling away, the shouts of horror and glee from the spectators, but she doesn't hear the thieves at all—they die quietly, but they die all the same.

She turns back toward the scene in time to see several men dressed in black removing the bodies from the nooses and carrying them away. Seconds later, another ten figures are brought out, and Sophronia feels sick all over again.

"How many are there?" she asks.

Leopold doesn't answer for a moment. "I don't know," he admits. He reaches out to touch her arm, drawing her gaze toward his. It takes all of her self-control not to jerk away from him.

"Let's go home," he says.

Sophronia smiles, but she doesn't feel it. She smiles because she knows she should, because she knows that if her mother were here beside her, she would tell Sophronia to smile and flirt with her husband and wrap him as tightly around her finger as she can. She would tell Sophronia that the surest way to loosen Queen Eugenia's hold on Leopold is to establish her own.

And she needs that hold, she realizes. Not because of her mother's plans, not even for Bessemia's sake. For Temarin's.

That night, at Sir Diapollio's concert, Sophronia can't focus enough to enjoy the singer's talents. She knows he sings well and she can appreciate his good looks, even though he's several decades her senior. She can't enjoy Leopold's hand in hers, either, or the way he leans close to whisper in her ear as the night goes on. She has to force herself to laugh when he points out how all the ladies of the court hang on Sir Diapollio's every note. She has to force herself not to flinch away when he tells her she looks beautiful.

After what feels like an eternity, Sir Diapollio performs his final song and takes a great sweeping bow while Sophronia, Leopold, and the entire court applaud him.

"Can we go meet him?" Sophronia asks Leopold, offering him a bright smile that feels hollow, though he doesn't seem to notice.

"I should have known better than to invite him—even my own wife isn't safe from the famous Diapollio charms," he says, shaking his head. "Why don't you go on ahead—I need to have a quick word with Lord Fauntas first. But Diapollio should be recovering in the parlor on the left before the banquet," he adds, pointing the way for her.

They go their separate ways, and Sophronia hurries past the mingling crowd toward the door Leopold indicated, having to stop several times to gush over the concert with courtiers who pull her aside. When she finally reaches the door, it's ajar and she pushes it open, stepping into the dimly lit room.

"Sir Diapollio?" she asks.

There's a bit of mumbled Cellarian that Sophronia is fairly sure is a curse, then the rustling of silk and hasty footsteps. As her eyes adjust to the dark, she can make out two figures hurrying to distance themselves—little good that it does. Sophronia may still be an innocent, but she's spent enough time among the Bessemian courtesans to know exactly what she's interrupted.

"You didn't lock the door?" a familiar voice snaps at

Sir Diapollio, and Sophronia's body goes rigid. Eugenia steps out of the shadows, smoothing her hands over her wrinkled skirts. When she sees Sophronia, she stops short, her eyes going wide and her mouth gaping open, making her look, Sophronia thinks, a bit like a dying fish. She opens her mouth once, twice, three times, but words don't come out. Finally, she draws herself up a little straighter and walks past Sophronia, keeping her gaze leveled straight ahead and her chin high.

Sophronia turns her attention to Sir Diapollio, who doesn't look surprised at all at her interruption. Instead, he looks at her with knowing eyes and gives a small, mocking bow, and she understands.

"My mother's gift?" she asks, stepping farther into the room and closing the door behind her.

Sir Diapollio inclines his head. "She said you would know what to do with it."

Sophronia nods. She imagines herself going to Duchess Bruna, biting her lip, and confessing that she witnessed something but isn't sure whether she should say. *That* would pique Duchess Bruna's interest, and she would surely worm the whole encounter out of Sophronia before their tea had cooled. The entire castle would know in less than an hour's time, and Queen Eugenia would be ruined. Leopold would have no choice but to send her away from court, leaving a gaping wound in Temarin's power structure that Sophronia could quickly fill.

Still, Sophronia is disappointed that her mother's gift has nothing to do with Beatriz after all.

"Do you have any word of my sister Beatriz?" she asks.

Sir Diapollio's smile grows more lecherous. "A beauty, isn't she? I sang at her wedding. Everyone was enchanted by her—except the prince, of course."

"I've had letters from my sister that have told me far more than that," Sophronia says.

Sir Diapollio's expression shifts, the smile sliding off his face as he leans toward Sophronia, his voice dropping to a whisper even though they are the only ones in the room. "Of course. Siblings would exchange letters, wouldn't they? I know King Cesare and Queen Eugenia exchange plenty—I deliver them myself during our encounters."

Sophronia steps back from Sir Diapollio in surprise. "Letters?" she asks. "Another gift of my mother's?"

He shakes his head. "This gift, Your Majesty, is all mine, though it does come with a price."

"So not a gift, then," Sophronia says, though she knows that no matter the price, she'll pay it. *Secret letters between King Cesare and Eugenia*. Her mind is already a whirl of possibilities. Whatever they contain, she's sure her mother would tell her to do whatever necessary to secure them. But that thought raises a question.

"I'm surprised my mother wasn't interested in these letters as well," she says. It's possible he is trying to double-charge her, or perhaps the letters are forgeries and he thinks her more gullible than the empress.

Sir Diapollio smiles. "A man with my talent is limited by time, my dear. Already, my . . . charms are fading, and with them my audience. I decided long ago to accumulate secrets to sustain me. I sold your mother one, but now I find myself willing to part with another. For the right price. You see, Eugenia left in such a hurry, she forgot to ask me for her brother's latest missive." He reaches into the pocket of his jacket and pulls out a rolled letter with a red seal bearing the Cellarian royal sigil of the crescent moon.

"And how do I know the letter is authentic?" Sophronia asks. "The Cellarians don't use stardust seals. You could have written the letter yourself."

"You're cleverer than I expected," he says with a laugh. "But alas, I can't prove its validity. Yet I'm sure you can, once you read its contents. Consider it a compass, leading you in the direction of the truth."

"And how much will this compass cost me, considering it very well may be broken?" she asks.

"I rather like your ring," he says, his eyes dropping to her hand where it holds the letter. At first she thinks he means her wedding ring, but instead he's looking at the ring she wears on her smallest finger—a teardrop ruby set in a band of gold, studded with diamonds. It was part of the Temarinian royal jewels she inherited when she became queen, not something she'd part with under any normal circumstances, but she doesn't have a choice. Violie will notice its absence, but she can claim it fell off her finger without her noticing—small as it is, that will be a believable lie. She slides the ring off her finger and passes it to him, exchanging it for the letter.

"A pleasure doing business with you, Sophie," Sir Diapollio says, and Sophronia cringes at his use of her nickname. He doesn't notice. All of his attention is focused on the ring in his hand. "I'll give your regards to your sister when I see her next."

Sophronia barely hears him, already on her way out the door, desperate to get away from the singer as quickly as possible, shoving the folded letter into the top of her bodice as she goes.

Beatriz

Beatriz wakes up to someone shaking her shoulder none too gently. She tries to shove them away, a groan working its way past her lips, but it does no good—the shaking continues.

"Triz," a voice says, and somewhere past the skull-splitting headache, she recognizes it as Pasquale. "Wake up, my father needs to see you."

That gets Beatriz's attention. She forces herself to sit upright, her eyelids so heavy it takes all of her energy just to lift them. When she does, she sees Pasquale, already dressed and looking at her anxiously.

"I feel horrid," she tells him—the truth, even if it is entirely her own fault. How many glasses of brandy did she drink last night? Still, this feels like more than her usual postdrinking morning. Not only does her head feel like it's been split in two, but it's as if her blood has been replaced with lead. Every small movement costs her. "Can we postpone it?"

"No," he says, and somehow that single word sends a bolt of fear through her. She blinks, truly looking at Pasquale, and she sees that same fear echoed in him. "A servant girl was arrested with stardust in her possession," he says. "She's claiming she found it on our windowsill."

Beatriz tries to swallow, but her mouth feels like it's filled with cotton. There was no starshower last night—if Cellaria's drought of starfall had been broken, she would have seen it—and the only other way for stardust to appear is when an empyrea wishes on a star, pulling it down from the sky in the process. She saw Nigellus do it once, and though he hadn't appeared to do anything remarkable, she remembers the pile of stardust that appeared near him, glittering and gray and brimming with power.

Her stomach lurches and she feels like she might be sick. "I need water," she tells Pasquale, forcing her voice to come out level. "And then I'll get ready as quickly as I can."

He starts to leave and she climbs out of bed, even though every muscle in her body protests. Her mind is a whirl of panic and bewilderment. How did stardust get on her windowsill? Did someone put it there? Who? She thinks back to last night, when she drunkenly wished on a star in a fit of homesickness, though she pushes that thought from her mind as soon as it appears. She's no empyrea, after all, and if that wish had come true, wouldn't she be home right now? No, someone is trying to frame her.

"Triz?" Pasquale asks her tentatively. She turns toward him, eyebrows raised.

"You want to ask if I did it?" she says, her voice coming out sharper than she intends. She takes a deep breath, forcing herself to at least appear relaxed. "I didn't. Not everyone from outside Cellaria has the gifts of empyreas—only one in ten thousand or so has that power. Even if I were a heretic—which I'm not—I assure you, I'm utterly incapable of magic."

Pasquale nods and disappears from the room to fetch her water, but as Beatriz rings a bell that brings servants fluttering in to help her dress, she can't stop thinking about the words she spoke last night.

I wish I could go home. Idle words, really, an expression of longing, not a call for magic. That's all it was. It was only words, just a silly, magicless wish. And yes, she imagined herself home, felt for a moment that her imaginings were real, but that was the brandy, surely. Nothing more.

But no matter how many times she tells herself that, it doesn't untangle the twisted knot of her stomach.

The throne room is so packed full of courtiers that the guards escorting Beatriz and Pasquale have to push their way through the crowd to clear a path. The stifling heat caused by so many bodies crammed into such a small space heightens Beatriz's nausea, and she has to force herself to take deep, calming breaths to still her roiling stomach.

I'm never touching a drop of alcohol again, she tells herself, but as soon as she thinks the words, she knows they're a lie—she knows how seriously Cellaria takes charges of sorcery, knows too that King Cesare has become increasingly paranoid. If she makes it through this without being tied to a stake, she'll celebrate with an entire bottle of wine.

At least she knows how to hide how ill she feels. She did it often enough in Bessemia when her mother would summon her and her sisters at some ungodly hour—seeming always to know exactly which nights Beatriz had had one drink too many—for some lesson or other.

After her maids helped her get dressed, Beatriz managed a few minutes to herself to delve into her cosmetics case. She dabbed some tinted cream beneath her eyes, added a touch of rouge to her cheeks, and dusted her whole face with powder. She even added a couple of her drops to her eyes, though she'd used them before going to bed, as she always did.

It can't hurt, she tells herself now. If she's to stand before the king under charges of being an empyrea, she isn't about to chance her silver eyes showing themselves.

When they make it to the front of the room, Beatriz sees King Cesare sitting on his throne, his head propped up on his arm, reminding her of a bored child. When he sees them, he sits up slightly and waves a hand behind him.

Nicolo steps forward, a glass of red wine on a tray that he offers to the king, who takes a long sip before placing it back on the tray. Nicolo must be the king's cupbearer—in Bessemia it's a servant's job, but not so in Cellaria. Beatriz remembers one of the missives she and her mother received from their Cellarian spies: *King Cesare is never out of arm's reach of his goblet of wine, and his cupbearers are some of the hardest-working noblemen in the country. They are well rewarded after some time in service with a place on his council, estates—sometimes titles of their own. Most young lords, however, don't last long enough to reap the rewards.*

Beatriz files this information away in her mind and hopes she will have the chance to use it.

"Your Majesty," she says, dipping into a low curtsy before rising. She flashes him a beaming smile, as if she isn't quaking in her satin slippers. Beside her, Pasquale echoes her words and executes his own bow. "I understand there was some trouble with a servant this morning?" she says, tilting her head. "I assure you, Prince Pasquale and I will help in any way we can."

King Cesare's expression doesn't waver. His eyes cut to the left, where a girl no older than fourteen stands, flanked by guards, her wrists bound in iron manacles. She isn't crying, but Beatriz suspects that's only because she's cried herself out already—her face is red and her eyes are bloodshot.

"This servant girl claims she found stardust on your windowsill while cleaning this morning," King Cesare says, his voice indifferent even as his eyes spark with malice. "I would like to know how it got there."

"As would I, Your Majesty," Beatriz says, tearing her eyes away from the servant girl and looking back at King Cesare. She makes a show of hesitating, then biting her lip, as if she is debating her next words, when she has, in fact, been reciting this speech in her mind the entire time she has been dressing and making her way here. "Though I do have my suspicions. I must confess . . ." She trails off, giving a heavy sigh.

"Oh?" King Cesare says, sitting up straighter. "You would like to confess something, Princess Beatriz? I understand, coming as you do from a land like Bessemia, that it might be difficult to acquaint yourself with our customs. Confess, and I will show mercy." He doesn't even bother trying to make the words sound convincing. No doubt he believes *mercy* will constitute watching her burn.

"Your Majesty," Beatriz says. "I'm certain that you also find it odd that this stardust would simply appear on my windowsill like this, barely a week after I've arrived. I know that there are many in your court who disapprove of my marrying Pasquale, many who believe that I carry the same heathen stain as my mother and sisters. I'd hoped, in time, I would be able to prove them wrong, but I simply cannot wrap my mind around the fact that someone was so desperate to be rid of me that they would obtain stardust themselves and plant it on my windowsill. I cannot believe it."

"It is . . . unfathomable," King Cesare says.

"And yet, I must believe it's the truth," Beatriz says, offering another dramatic sigh. "What would the alternative be, Your Majesty? That I've come into your court, married your son and heir, as a scheming empyrea, set on destroying Cellaria with stardust and wishes?" She laughs, the sound loud and full, and a few courtiers join in, even as others glare at her. Even the king smiles, fleeting though his smile is. "Surely, you cannot believe that to be the case—if I *were* an empyrea, don't you think I would know better than to leave stardust around where anyone could find it? No, I believe it was planted, in an attempt to bring suspicion on me." Here, she affects a wounded look, letting her bottom lip tremble as she casts her gaze upward, as if to keep from crying. "It hurts me, Your Majesty, that there are those in your court who must hate me so much as to break your laws like this." She blinks quickly, letting a couple of artfully summoned tears trace down her cheeks.

Tears are a weapon, Beatriz's mother is fond of saying. *But they must be carefully wielded—too many and you are hysterical, too few and you will be overlooked. But the right amount . . . the right amount will make a man so uncomfortable he will do whatever is necessary to stop them.*

Beatriz seems to have hit the right balance. King Cesare shifts on his throne, casting a gaze around the room. He motions for his wine again, and Nicolo steps forward to offer him his cup, but this time, Nicolo's eyes meet Beatriz's. He doesn't seem discomfited by her tears, she notices, merely appraising. He offers her a small smile before taking the king's cup back and retreating behind the throne.

"Princess Beatriz," King Cesare says, leaning forward. "I hope you will accept my apology, and the court's apology as well. If you feel you have been . . . mistreated . . . well, that is no one's intent, I'm sure. If you should continue to feel that way, I pray you will tell me of your troubles so I can handle them," he adds before looking beyond her, to the crowd of courtiers. "Princess Beatriz is family. Should I get word that anyone is treating her ill, I will deal with you swiftly and harshly."

"Yes, Your Majesty," the courtiers murmur, almost in unison.

Beatriz is slightly taken aback by his reaction. She hoped to be believed, of course, but the speed with which King Cesare has gone from being ready to try her for sorcery to threatening his court on her behalf is enough to give her whiplash.

"Thank you, Your Majesty," Beatriz says, dipping into another low curtsy. When she rises again, she sees the servant girl still standing, shackled, between the guards. King Cesare's eyes follow her gaze.

"Never fear, Princess Beatriz, she will be sent to the dungeon to await the next Burning Day—we have no tolerance for heretics here," he says.

"Please, Your Majesty," the girl calls out. "Please, I didn't even know what it was—I only pocketed the dust because I thought it was pretty."

King Cesare ignores her, his eyes remaining on Beatriz, who is careful not to let her sympathy for the girl be seen. Though she would like nothing better than to ask King Cesare to show the girl mercy, she's heard enough stories from her mother's spies to know that all that will accomplish is Beatriz burning beside her. Pasquale must feel her waver, because he steps forward, placing a hand on her back.

"Thank you, Father," he says, bowing again to the king. "I hope that whoever is responsible for framing my wife is found soon and meets the same fate."

King Cesare nods, but he is already distracted, calling for more wine as the guards drag the crying servant girl away. Beatriz notes that *her* tears don't do her any good.

Beatriz clings to Pasquale's arm as he escorts her from the throne room, though she can feel it trembling beneath her grip. He guides her down the crowded hall and around the corner to an empty corridor. As soon as they are alone, Beatriz lets go of him and doubles over. She wants to retch but knows that nothing will come up. The nausea doesn't abate, though, even when she forces herself to take deep breaths. Through it all, she feels Pasquale's hand on her back, rubbing soothing circles.

"It's all right," he says, though he seems uneasy with this show of comfort.

"It isn't," Beatriz says, straightening up. She can't stop shaking all over. "I thought he was going to have me killed—on some level, I was certain of it."

She expects him to reassure her, to tell her she was never in any danger, but he doesn't. "I was too," he admits softly.

"And that girl!" she says, keeping her voice to a whisper in case anyone wanders by. "She's going to die for picking up a bit of sparkly dust."

Pasquale nods, glancing away. "She won't be the first, or the last. There was a boy just last month, the son of my former tutor, barely twelve—executed because one of his friends said he was talking about stardust. That's all it took, the word of a child, and he died for it. They killed his father, too, because he'd given the boy a book on the subject."

Beatriz feels sick all over again. She *knew* about Cellaria's intolerance for magic, about King Cesare's temper. But it is one thing to hear gossip and read reports, it is another thing to experience it firsthand.

"Did you . . . ," Pasquale starts, but then trails off. "Beatriz, you know my secret. If you have a secret as well, I hope you know that I'll protect it."

Beatriz almost wants to laugh at the thought. She has so many secrets, but none of them what he means. She is no empyrea, just a spy and saboteur here to bring his country to ruin. For a second, though, she wonders if he would protect that secret as well—he clearly has no love for his father or the way he rules Cellaria. And Beatriz's complicated feelings about her own mother aside, she can't deny that the empress would be a far better ruler than Cesare. When Cellaria is her domain, there will be no more Burning Days, no more children arrested for heresy, no more walking on eggshells to appease a mad king. Perhaps, if she told Pasquale all that, he would agree.

She shakes the thought from her mind. No. She doesn't *need* him to agree. She needs to do what she was sent here for, so she can return home as quickly as possible.

As if summoned by her thoughts, a man steps into the entrance to the corridor, a cautious expression on a face she knows right away from sketches.

"Apologies, Your Highnesses," Lord Savelle says, offering a bow. "I hope I'm not interrupting, but I wished to see if you were all right. That was quite an ordeal for you."

Beatriz forces a smile, wiping at her eyes to catch any tears that might have escaped. "Thank you, that's very kind," she says, pretending not to know exactly who he is. "I don't believe we've met, sir."

"Triz, this is Lord Savelle, the ambassador from Temarin. Lord Savelle, my wife, Princess Beatriz," Pasquale says.

Lord Savelle bows again. "A pleasure to make your acquaintance."

"The pleasure is all mine, Lord Savelle," Beatriz says with what might be her first true smile of the day. "I apologize for losing my composure—"

"No apology necessary, Princess," Lord Savelle says, waving her words away. "I've been in the Cellarian court for two decades now—I understand better than anyone what a . . . shock certain practices can be to a person. Which is why I sought to offer my compassion." He pauses. "I also bring word of your sister—Lady Gisella said you might welcome the news?"

"Sophie?" Beatriz asks, her heart rising into her throat. "Is she well?"

"Married," he says. "A day before you were, I believe. I'm told she and King Leopold are the very stuff of love ballads and poetry."

Beatriz smiles, though inside she hopes that Sophronia is keeping her wits about her. Still, her sister deserves a little happiness, if she can reach it. "I'm very glad to hear it." She pauses, as if an idea has only just occurred to her. "Please, you must join us for dinner soon so that Pasquale and I can show our gratitude."

Lord Savelle bows again. "I would be honored, Your Highness."

Perhaps, Beatriz thinks with a flutter of triumph, *home isn't so very far away after all.*

Daphne

Cliona's missive arrives just shy of midnight the day after their shopping trip, a note tied to the open window with black ribbon, fluttering in the slight breeze. Since Daphne's bedroom sits on the third floor, whoever left it would have had to scale the castle walls without being noticed—a feat even Daphne has to admit is impressive. The message inside is short, in hasty but delicate writing.

> *Steal your marriage contract. It's kept in the king's study, but you said that wasn't an issue.*

She isn't surprised Cliona wants to see the marriage contract—after Daphne told her that King Bartholomew and the empress were merging the countries, of course Cliona wants proof. Proof doesn't exist; there's no formal agreement, because the king would never willingly join his country to Bessemia. But Daphne can fix that easily enough. She might not be as good at forgeries as Sophronia, but she can certainly manage.

She pulls her dressing gown over her nightgown, tucking the missive into her pocket.

A thrill runs up her spine as she steps into the empty hallway with her candle, closing the door softly behind her. Dangerous as this may be, playing two sides and serving two agendas, she can't deny that a part of her enjoys the risk.

A week after Cillian's death, the castle has begun to come alive again, so she must be more careful than the last time she went sneaking about. Servants will be up, stoking fires and cleaning. The hallways near the kitchen in particular will be bustling.

When she reaches the office door, she sets down her candle, pulls the pins from her hair, and gets to work. Now that she's picked the lock once, the second time goes much quicker, and in just a few seconds, she's pushing the office door open and slipping inside.

She makes her way straight for the desk and begins rifling through the drawers, looking for the marriage contract. When she finds it, she sits down at King Bartholomew's desk and picks up his quill from its inkpot, flipping through with her free hand until she reaches the end.

> *This agreement is made in good faith and in the best interests of both Friv and Bessemia.*

It is easy enough for Daphne to change that period into a comma. She studies the rest of the handwriting, noticing the precise, unadorned script—easy to read and easy to imitate—but with a few markers to set it apart. The way the *a*'s and *o*'s slope slightly, how the *t*'s and *f*'s cross slightly higher than they should.

Once she's satisfied she can mimic the handwriting, she takes a deep, steadying breath and begins.

> *This agreement is made in good faith and in the best interests of both Friv and Bessemia, and the united country they will one day form, to be ruled by Prince Bairre and Princess Daphne upon the deaths of King Bartholomew and Empress Margaraux.*

It is a tight fit to squeeze in a couple of extra lines above the place where Daphne's mother and King Bartholomew signed and left their seals, but when Daphne replaces the quill in its pot and sits back to peruse the document, nothing looks amiss.

As she waits for the ink to dry, she considers Cliona's instruction to steal the contract. What if the king notices it's missing? That's cause for concern, but not Daphne's—if the king does notice, he won't blame her, so what does it matter? Her duty will be done.

Footsteps patter down the hall, and Daphne goes still for an instant before scrambling into motion. She touches the ink and finds it dry, so she rolls the contract up with Cliona's missive, tucks it into her pocket, and blows out her candle, shrouding the study in darkness.

The footsteps grow louder and louder—boots. Heavy ones. A guard? The steps sound regimented enough, evenly paced, rhythmic. Her mind spins with excuses, reasons for her presence in the king's office, but all of them sound suspicious, even to her own ears.

Just when the footsteps can't get any louder, they pass the office, fading away as they continue down the hall. Daphne releases a breath and sags against the desk. She waits until the footsteps have died away entirely before crossing quietly to the door and slipping back into the hall.

As soon as she's closed the door, though, the footsteps are back, coming toward her once more. Her fingers fumble with the hairpins, but there's no time to lock the door again. As the footsteps round the corner, she hastily shoves the hairpins back into her bun.

"Hello?" a voice calls out in the dark.

A familiar voice.

"Bairre?" she whispers.

The sound of a match striking, then flame as he lights a candle, illuminating his bewildered face. His overgrown chestnut hair is windblown and wilder than usual, in desperate need of a comb, but it suits him.

"Daphne," he says, the way he always says her name—as if the effort of being in her presence has already exhausted him. "What are you . . ." He trails off, looking at the door behind her. The crease in his brow deepens.

"I was trying to find the kitchens for a glass of water," she tells him before his thoughts can lead him further. She bites her lip, putting forth her best ingenue impression. "I thought maybe that led to a hallway, but it just seems to be a study of some kind. This castle is still such a maze, and it's hard to see much of anything in the dark." She holds up the extinguished candle and shrugs. "It went out a few minutes ago."

Bairre reaches behind her, trying the door to the king's office. It gives easily and swings open.

"That should be locked," he says, more to himself than her. For an instant, her heart goes still, but then he shakes his head. "The whole castle has been a bit distracted lately, I suppose."

"How did your hunting trip go?" she asks him, hoping to divert his attention from the unlocked door. He's been gone the last two days, since her shopping trip, hunting with the heads of some highland clans.

He frowns and lifts a shoulder in a shrug. "Well enough; we hunted. Got a few stags, even a boar."

"You weren't there to hunt, though," she says. "How did you get on with the rest of the party?"

"Why are you so concerned?" he asks, though the tension in his jaw gives away the answer.

She blinks. Why *is* she so concerned? She will be stuck with him once they're wed, she supposes. She'd expected that Cillian wouldn't live long into their marriage, but Bairre seems to be in perfect health. And once her mother leaves her the empire, Daphne imagines she'll run it herself while he . . . while he does what? She supposes she shouldn't care, but he will be her husband, so maybe she should. "Because the whole purpose of the trip was for them to see you as the crown prince and not the king's bastard, but I'm guessing that didn't work." She pauses, fixing him with a look. "Whether you like it or not, you're a prince."

"No one sees me that way," he says, shaking his head.

"Because *you* don't see yourself that way," she says. "My mother was a tailor's daughter and an emperor's mistress. No one wanted to see her as a ruler either, but she didn't give them a choice."

For a moment he doesn't say anything, but then he nods down the hall, back in the direction she came from. "It's that way."

She glances down the dark hallway, then back at him. "What is?" she asks.

His eyebrows lift. "The kitchens. I thought you were thirsty."

"I was," she says quickly. "I *am*. You just distracted me."

She starts off down the way he pointed, and he falls into step beside her. Though she won't admit it, she's grateful for the light he brings with him.

"There's a bell, you know," he says. "You can ring if you need anything."

"I did," she lies. "No one came."

He seems to accept that, and they continue to the kitchens in silence.

"You stay here," he tells her when they're just outside the door. "They know me, but the sight of the princess at this hour will get them flustered."

She nods. "Thank you."

He pauses for a second, eyeing her uncertainly. "Anything else?" he asks her. "Truffle cheese or spun-sugar pastries? Caviar?"

"I find caviar gauche, actually," she says with a bland smile. "Water will do."

"You sure you don't want pearl powder in it?" he continues, clearly enjoying this. "I hear your mother boils pearls in her tea to make her beautiful."

"Pearls don't boil," Daphne says before she can stop herself. "But they do dissolve in vinegar, under the right circumstances, and the effect makes for quite a show of wealth and power for an upstart queen dining with foreign dignitaries who are trying to undermine her. Perhaps there's a lesson there for you."

That wipes the smirk off his face, and he ducks into the kitchen without another word. When he appears a moment later, he presses the glass of water into her hands.

"You can find your way back?" he asks.

She nods, taking the glass from him and turning away without another word.

Back in her room alone, Daphne fishes the rolled-up marriage contract from her pocket. She crosses to the window and opens it, leaving the contract on the sill just where she found the missive, then shucks off her dressing gown and finally climbs into bed.

Exhausted as she is, she should fall asleep quickly, but instead her mind whirls over her conversation with Bairre. She tells herself she accomplished her goal: she distracted him—he never truly suspected what she was really doing in the king's study—but she didn't have to give him *advice*. What the court thinks of Bairre isn't her concern. Friv isn't her concern. Her concern is getting through the wedding, stealing the king's seal, and doing whatever else her mother demands of her. It would be better if Bairre liked her, but that's not likely to come about when she's insulting him.

So why did she do it?

Daphne falls asleep before she arrives at an answer.

She wakes at dawn to a draft coming in from the open window. She knows she closed that window the night before, and latched it for good measure. But now it's open and there, on her vanity, are another note and a small vial of shimmering powder.

The stardust.

She stumbles out of bed and crosses to the vanity, picking up the vial and turning it over in her hands. She sets it back down and picks up the letter, unfurling it and scanning it quickly. It's only four words, but they feel like a lead weight dropping into her stomach.

Well done. More soon.

Sophronia

Sophronia can't sleep. The moon is high in the sky, shining through her bedroom window and turning the gilded furniture silver and ghostly—appropriate, she thinks, as she's been feeling more ghost than girl the last few days. Ever since she caught the dowager queen with Sir Diapollio, Eugenia has been avoiding her altogether. There have been no more invitations to tea, no more walks in the garden catching up on gossip. When they are forced to be in the same room for banquets or balls, Eugenia won't even look her way. Which is just as well, since Sophronia wants to avoid Eugenia, too, after reading the letter her brother wrote her. The words still haunt her.

My dearest sister,

The news in your last letter is as welcome as you will be in Cellaria when you return home. We are close to being ready now—I daresay we could attack Temarin tomorrow and emerge victorious before the spring, but

I would like to make quicker work of it. I fear Temarin's defenses are still too strong to fall easily. A little more work on your end and they should crumble under the slightest breeze.

May the stars bless and guide you,
Cesare

Sophronia knows it's dangerous to operate under the assumption that the letter is real. Her mother has always stressed the importance of validating any information received and considering the trustworthiness of its source. Sophronia doesn't trust Sir Diapollio, so she isn't sure she can trust the letter, damning as it is.

But Sir Diapollio was right about one thing—she can verify its contents, though it's important she do so without raising any suspicions. And a queen from a foreign country, who has been on the throne for less time than the moon's cycle, demanding to see defense budgets would certainly raise suspicions.

She's spent the past two days trying to get information about castle budgets in more roundabout ways, but every time she's approached the subject of money at any of her luncheons or teas or dinners, the courtiers have been quick to change the subject; she can't pry more without again raising suspicions, so she's been forced to let it go.

She rolls over in bed to look at Leo, fast asleep on his back, one arm bent behind his head. In sleep, he looks like the boy she believed him to be, the one she imagined when she wrote him letters. He looks open and kind and soft. His mother's betrayal—if it's true—will devastate him.

One cannot be soft and wear a crown, her mother has told her on more than one occasion, whenever Sophronia has expressed any kind of moral misgivings during her lessons. *Or one will be crushed beneath its weight.*

There is some truth to that—not just for her mother, or Leopold, or Queen Eugenia, but for Sophronia, too. She can feel herself hardening. Perhaps her mother is right after all—to wield power, one must be sharp-edged, ready to draw blood.

She rolls away from Leopold and closes her eyes. She won't be sleeping tonight, she knows this. It's something that happens from time to time when her mind becomes too busy to trade its thoughts for dreams. Back in Bessemia, she would sometimes go down to the kitchens, where the pastry chef, Madame Devoné, would be up well before dawn mixing and rolling and baking her creations. She'd had few qualms about putting an inquisitive princess to work, teaching her how to fold batter to keep a cake light and roll layers of butter between dough to add flaky layers to pastries. The monotonous, repetitive actions had always helped calm Sophronia's mind.

It's a shame she can't do that now, she thinks, before catching herself. Why *can't* she do that now? She is the Queen of Temarin—the only person who outranks her is fast asleep beside her, and even if Leopold were awake, she knows he wouldn't tell her no.

Sophronia gets out of bed, finding her dressing gown

hanging in the wardrobe and tying it over her nightgown before slipping from the room and into the hallway.

It's strange to be in a kitchen again—and a strange kitchen at that. She'd grown familiar with the Bessemian palace kitchen. She knew where the grains were kept, how fresh the eggs were, that the oven was temperamental and always a few degrees hotter than it should be. This kitchen is a strange land, and it takes some time to acquaint herself with the landscape. The hour is somewhere between the night staff leaving and the early-morning staff arriving, so the kitchen is mostly quiet. The only other people around are a handful of servants cleaning.

When she asks one of them if it's all right if she takes up a corner, the servant girl stares at her with wide eyes, not responding except to drop into a clumsy curtsy, which Sophronia takes as assent.

She has barely managed to gather her ingredients before Violie appears, still dressed in her own nightgown, with her blond hair in a single long braid that coils over her shoulder. Sophronia can't quite manage to be surprised at her appearance—she'd guess that the second she arrived in the kitchen alone, one of the servants scurried off to find one of her maids. She's glad they found Violie, who could prove useful if Sophronia manages it right.

"How do you feel about cake?" Sophronia asks her.

Violie blinks at her with tired eyes. "It's three o'clock in the morning, Your Majesty," she says. "A bit early for cake, or late, I suppose."

"Don't be silly, it will be several hours before it's ready

to eat," Sophronia says, beginning to measure out the flour from a sack half as tall as she is. "Cake for breakfast."

Violie considers the question, leaning forward and bracing her elbows on the island counter. "In that case, I'm all for cake," she says. "Any reason in particular for this adventure?"

Sophronia shrugs. "Am I not allowed?" she asks, almost as a challenge.

"There's no rule against it—though that may be because no queen has ever set foot in this kitchen before," Violie says. "What can I do to help?"

They fall into an easy silence as Sophronia sets Violie up cracking eggs and measuring out milk. And as Sophronia begins to sift and whisk and fold everything together into a thick batter, her mind begins to calm enough that she forms a plan.

"How long have you been in Temarin, Violie?" she asks.

Violie seems somewhat surprised by the sudden question. "A year now, Your Majesty. I found work, briefly, in the kitchens, and then Duchess Bruna hired me just before King Carlisle passed away."

"So you've spent all of your time in the palace?" Sophronia asks.

"I've run errands in Kavelle, but yes, I've lived in the palace since I arrived," Violie says.

"You've still seen more of Temarin than I have," Sophronia says, shaking her head. "May I confess something, Violie?" she asks, lowering her voice. This is one of her mother's favorite tricks for gathering information—offer up a secret, not a real one, but something that gives the illusion of vulnerability. "I'm concerned for Temarin. The people seem unhappy—not within the palace, but in the city and, I'd wager, the rest of the country as well. From what I've gathered, they're hungry, and all we've done is increase their taxes. Tripled them, last I checked."

Violie blinks, looking surprised by Sophronia's frankness. "Yes," she says. "I believe that's accurate."

Sophronia shakes her head as if she's trying to rid herself of these unpleasant thoughts before continuing. "I'd heard this before I arrived, but as far as I can tell, the palace itself has made no cutbacks—the royal and noble classes seem to be doing as well as ever," she says. "I looked at the bill for my new wardrobe. It cost twenty thousand asters, not including shoes and jewelry. And if the gifts that have been sent to Leopold and me since our wedding are anything to go by, the rest of the nobles aren't hurting either, even the ones I believed to be in debt."

Violie says nothing, but she doesn't need to. Sophronia can see that she's troubled as well.

"Bessemia was not perfect, and I know plenty of our poor suffered there as well, but . . ." Sophronia trails off, shaking her head.

"If I may, Your Majesty," Violie says. "Do you remember . . . five years back now? Bessemia faced a hard winter followed by a cruel drought. The harvests were all pitiful."

Sophronia nods. She was eleven at the time, old enough to begin sitting in on her mother's council sessions. And it was impossible to forget how Nigellus had eventually used his power to end the drought.

"The effect of it rippled all over the country. No one was spending money, so no one was making money," Sophronia says.

"I don't know enough about the current situation," Violie says. "But I'd imagine it's something similar here. It happens. Economies rise and fall. The Bessemian economy rose again—flourished, even. I'm sure the Temarinian one will rise again as well."

Sophronia considers this as she pours the batter into the two prepared pans. Violie might be right, but if the letter is to be believed, there may be something more sinister at work. Sophronia glances at the large clock hanging above the stove. It's nearly dawn, which means the rest of the palace will be waking up soon.

"We cut taxes," Sophronia says, bringing the conversation back to her intended purpose.

Violie looks up at her, bewildered. "Pardon?"

"In Bessemia," Sophronia says, remembering how she and her sisters sat in on those meetings, how Beatriz was bored out of her mind and Daphne more focused on saying the right thing to impress the empress than on listening. Sophronia, though, was fascinated, reading through the proposed palace budget cuts and new tax laws until she'd all but committed them to memory. "My mother ordered that taxes should be cut. She also used money from the royal treasury to set up a fund to assist those who had lost their jobs or otherwise couldn't pay for necessities. She pressured every noble family to do the same. They weren't happy about it—they'd already given up a large share of the income they received from the taxes their estates took from the villages on their property—but she forced their hands. I remember my sisters' and my birthday that year—instead of the usual elaborate ball, we had a small tea party.

My mother said that if Bessemia was suffering, we were all suffering."

Violie looks at Sophronia, understanding lighting in her eyes. "And Bessemia recovered," she says. "By the next year, most everything was back to normal."

Sophronia nods. "I find myself curious, Violie, if similar measures have been taken in Temarin. But no one I've spoken to seems to know the first thing about taxes or budgets."

Violie bites her lip, looking uncertain. "Are you asking me to find those documents?" she asks.

Sophronia smiles. "We're both strangers here, Violie," she says. "But this is our home now—I think we both want what is best for it."

Sophronia hasn't said the words, but she knows Violie heard them.

"I'll see what I can do," Violie says.

"Excellent," Sophronia says, straightening up. "Queen Eugenia told me that she likes to rise before the sun to best seize the day. Will you please send her an invitation to have breakfast with me in my sitting room?"

"Will an invitation suffice?" Violie asks, raising her eyebrows. Clearly, Eugenia's avoidance of Sophronia hasn't gone unnoticed.

Sophronia purses her lips. "It can sound like an invitation, but see that she understands it's an order. From her queen."

Sophronia and Eugenia sit across from each other in Sophronia's sitting room, a round table between them set with cups of hot coffee and slices of cake. Neither has spoken since Eugenia arrived ten minutes ago, though both have finished their first cups of coffee and half of their cake. Sophronia meets Eugenia's gaze and gives her a placid smile, which only seems to bewilder the woman more.

Finally, Eugenia gives in and breaks the silence.

"This cake is divine, isn't it?" she says, trying for a conversational tone that might fool anyone else, but Sophronia hears the tension in her words. "The chef must be trying out a new recipe—is that cinnamon, do you think?"

"Cinnamon and blueberries, yes," Sophronia says as a servant steps forward with a fresh pot of coffee to refill their cups. Sophronia adds a cube of sugar to hers, but Eugenia leaves it black. "I made it, actually," Sophronia adds.

She expects Eugenia to be surprised, but she merely raises an eyebrow.

"Every queen has her hobbies," she says, shrugging. "I prefer gardening."

"Among other things," Sophronia says, keeping her voice light.

Eugenia's eyes narrow and she sets her fork down. "You did not see what you think you saw, Sophronia," she says firmly.

"It was quite dark," Sophronia agrees. "Perhaps I should tell Leopold what I think I saw—and heard—and ask for his opinion on what it meant?"

"Ah," Eugenia says, leaning back in her seat and eyeing Sophronia warily. "So that is where we are."

Sophronia feels a stab of guilt. She doesn't hold Eugenia's having a paramour against her—stars know her mother has had plenty of lovers. But if Sophronia is going to take power in Temarin, Eugenia will have to give hers up. And if Eugenia is truly plotting with her brother to overtake Temarin, well . . . Sophronia won't feel guilty about it at all.

Sophronia smiles and leans forward. "Friends keep secrets for each other, don't they? And I think we are friends."

"You are like the daughter I never had, Sophronia," Eugenia says, matching her smile, though there is ice behind it. "And I would hate for any of my . . . poor decisions . . . to reflect badly on you and Leopold, should they come to light."

"Oh, you needn't worry yourself about that, I'm sure we would manage," Sophronia says, shrugging. "But as I said, friends keep secrets. They also support each other, don't you think?"

"I suppose they do," Eugenia says slowly, lifting her coffee cup to her lips, though Sophronia notices that her hands shake slightly. It's strange, how powerful that makes her feel. It's alarming how much she enjoys it.

"Leopold has asked me to join in on his council meetings, to offer my thoughts and opinions on how Temarin is being run," Sophronia says. "I trust I can count on your support in those matters. It will take all of us together to make Temarin the best it can be. Don't you agree?"

Eugenia's jaw tightens, but she manages a smile and a curt nod.

"Wonderful," Sophronia says, beaming. She lifts her coffee cup for a toast. "To making Temarin strong and prosperous."

Beatriz

The evening Beatriz and Pasquale are meant to dine with Lord Savelle, Beatriz finds Pasquale in bed, clinging to an empty water basin with a sweat-sheened green pallor to his face. She pauses in the doorway and wonders whether she might have overdone it with the ravelroot in his afternoon tea—she wanted him too sick to attend dinner, not at death's door. But then, she's never had Daphne's gift for poisons.

"How are you feeling?" she asks, trying to ignore the guilt nagging at her. He looks miserable, and she did that to him. She needs time alone with Lord Savelle, she reminds herself. Still, the guilt doesn't recede completely.

"Oh, a little better, I think," Pasquale says, his voice hoarse. "I don't think I've vomited in the last quarter hour, so that's an improvement."

She lets out a small sigh of relief—if she'd gone too far with the ravelroot, he'd be vomiting more as time went on, not less.

"I feel terrible, abandoning you for the evening. Are you sure you don't mind if I go to dinner without you?"

He waves her concern away. "No, I know you wanted to hear more about Temarin and Sophronia—will you ask after Leopold as well? We've lost touch over the last couple of years, but he is my cousin."

"Of course," Beatriz says before biting her lip. "Would you like me to ask the servants for anything? Some bread, perhaps, now that your stomach's calmed?"

He nods slowly, though his grip on the basin tightens slightly at the mention of food. "Maybe in another hour or so? I don't want to get ahead of myself."

"Of course," she says, lingering by the door. Part of her wants to comfort him, the way he comforted her after she faced down his father in the throne room, but she isn't sure where to begin. Whenever she or her sisters were sick, her mother always kept them isolated, even from one another, to keep the disease from spreading. The isolation was usually worse than the illness itself. Should she approach his bedside? Rub his back, like he did for her? A small, foreign part of her wants to kiss his forehead for some reason she can't understand. Instead of doing any of those things, she stays by the door, her hand on the doorknob.

"Feel better," she says, with a small, strained smile. "I'll be back soon."

Though dinner is set up in the smaller dining room attached to Beatriz and Pasquale's rooms, *smaller* is a relative description. The table could hold at least a dozen people comfortably, and when Beatriz enters, she finds three places set at the far side, with Lord Savelle already seated to the left of the head. When he sees her enter, he rises to his feet and bows.

She waits for his gaze to sweep over her, and especially over the bare shoulders and décolletage her gown shows off so splendidly. She knows the rich violet color sets off her auburn hair, and she's carefully applied an arsenal of powders and creams to best complement her features. But Lord Savelle's eyes don't linger or leer the way other men's have. Stars, even when she's wearing her most demure dress, she can feel the king's lecherous gaze, watching her every move. Why is it, she wonders, that the two men she needs to ensnare are the two who don't show her the least bit of interest?

Well, she failed with Pasquale, there is no hope for that, but she refuses to fail here as well.

"Your Highness," Lord Savelle says. "Thank you again for the invitation."

"Thank you for joining us . . ." She pauses. "Well, *me,* at any rate. I'm afraid Prince Pasquale is a bit indisposed at the moment, but he sends his regrets and says we should carry on without him."

"I'm sorry to hear that," Lord Savelle says. When Beatriz takes the seat opposite him, he sits down as well. "I haven't been to this part of the palace before—it's stunning."

"You haven't?" Beatriz asks, frowning like she's surprised at that, when she actually could have guessed as much. From what she's heard, no one at court makes an effort to extend invitations to Lord Savelle, least of all the royal family. Pasquale seems to like him well enough, but then Pasquale isn't exactly known for hosting dinners or parties. If she hadn't suggested this dinner, it never would have occurred to him. "Well, I'm very glad you made it." She gestures for a servant standing near the door to bring wine, and once their glasses are full, she lifts hers and offers him her most beguiling smile.

"To you, Lord Savelle," she says. "And to the blossoming of new friendships."

A touch of color graces his cheeks, but he lifts his glass toward hers, sending a clink echoing through the otherwise quiet room.

"You flatter me, Your Highness, but thank you," he says before taking a sip of his wine. "I confess—I was surprised by your invitation."

"Oh?" Beatriz asks, raising an eyebrow. Idly, she traces a finger down the length of her neck while meeting his gaze—a trick she learned from a Bessemian courtesan who claimed it could lure a man to her from across a crowded ballroom. But if Lord Savelle takes any notice of the curve of her neck or the flirtatious look in her eyes, he gives no sign of it.

"Yes," he says. "I'm sure you haven't had the opportunity to notice yet, but I'm not very popular here at court."

"I can't imagine why," Beatriz says with another bright smile. "I see nothing about you that I don't like, Lord Savelle."

"Again, you are too kind, Your Highness—"

"Oh, you must call me Beatriz," she says, reaching across the table to place a hand on his arm. Lord Savelle doesn't jerk away from her, but he doesn't lean into the touch, either.

"Very well, Beatriz," he says, looking only slightly nonplussed. "But as I was saying, people have long memories. There are many here who haven't forgotten their . . . troubles with Temarin, who still see me as the enemy."

"That's silly," Beatriz says, retrieving her hand and masking her mounting frustration by taking another sip of wine. "The war has been over longer than I've been alive—surely no one holds a grudge *that* long."

"You are very young, Your—Beatriz, I mean," he says, shaking his head. He looks at her again, and this time it's plain that there is no attraction in his gaze. Beatriz is beginning to suspect that she could walk through the room stark naked and he would barely blink. The knowledge grates on her. This is what she was raised for—her beauty is supposed to be her best asset—and yet it has done her no good. "You remind me of someone, actually," he says, tilting his head to one side slightly as he watches her. "My daughter."

"Oh?" Beatriz asks, frowning as she sifts through everything she knows about Lord Savelle. "I didn't know you had any children."

"No, why would you?" he asks, shaking his head, and Beatriz wants to kick herself. "She was born about two years after I came here—her mother was my . . ." He trails off, looking at her warily. "She was my mistress," he says after a second. "I'm not terribly proud of how she came into the world, but I did give her my last name and all the privileges I could. She was raised in my household, given the same lessons any noble child had—truthfully, I spoiled her rotten. Fidelia was her name."

"Was?" Beatriz echoes, her stomach twisting. "What happened to her?"

At that, Lord Savelle lets out a sigh. "Nearly two years ago, she was brought before the king, just as you were. I believe in the deepest part of my soul that she was as innocent as you are, Beatriz, but she . . . lacked your charm, I suppose. King Cesare didn't believe her."

"Oh," Beatriz says. "That's why you came after me, to make sure I was all right."

Lord Savelle nods. "I thought he would kill me, too," he admits. "That is usually the way of the king's trials. But I suppose he didn't want to risk angering Temarin."

Beatriz bites her bottom lip, suddenly feeling like the worst sort of fool, showing up in a revealing gown with her coquettish tricks.

"I'm sorry," she tells him. "I can't begin to imagine what that must have been like. I'm not sure how you stayed—surely King Leopold would find a replacement for you, if you asked."

"I'm sure he would," Lord Savelle says, smiling slightly. "But as difficult as it is to be here sometimes, the idea of living somewhere she never did is . . . unfathomable to me."

Beatriz nods. "I suppose I understand that," she says. "Well, I am honored that you think I'm like her in any way. I will endeavor to earn that comparison, Lord Savelle."

When he offers her another small smile, Beatriz suddenly realizes how out of her depth she is. She knows how to play the part of the flirt, has been prepared to take that charade as far as necessary to meet her mother's aims. But this? Lord Savelle sees her the way a father sees a daughter, and that is a relationship she has no idea how to navigate.

Dinner doesn't last more than an hour, so when Beatriz comes back to the room she shares with Pasquale, she brings him a few pieces of warm bread on a plate. One of the servants offered to take it to him, but Beatriz insisted on doing it herself. Guilt over poisoning him—even if only slightly—still nags at her, and even though she knows the bread is a small thing, it's as much of an apology as she can muster.

When she steps into the bedroom, though, Pasquale isn't alone. Ambrose sits on the bottom corner of the bed, a book open in his lap, though he isn't paying attention to it. Instead, he and Pasquale are both laughing. Beatriz realizes she's never heard Pasquale laugh, *really* laugh, before. It's a nice sound.

"I hope I'm not interrupting," she says from the doorway.

Ambrose all but jumps off the bed, clutching the book in his hands tightly, while Pasquale sits up straighter, his cheeks turning bright red.

"Triz," Pasquale says, running a hand through his hair. He looks better, she notes, the green tint gone from his skin. "Sorry, you startled me . . . startled us. . . . Have you met Ambrose?"

Ambrose doesn't look at her as he takes a step in her direction, bowing low. "A pleasure to meet you, Your Highness."

"Oh, please," Beatriz says. "Call me Triz. I've heard so much about you from Pasquale, I feel I know you already."

Pasquale fixes her with a glare, but Ambrose only smiles uncertainly. "I came by because the library got a new shipment of books in from Friv and I wanted to bring one to Pas, but when he said he wasn't feeling well, I offered to read it to him."

"Oh?" Beatriz asks, crossing toward her vanity and unhooking her earbobs, then her necklace. "What book is it?"

"A volume of ghost stories collected from the highlands," Ambrose says. "What with the Clan Wars, apparently almost every square inch of Friv is a former battlefield of some kind."

"Beatriz's sister is in Friv," Pasquale adds, looking from one to the other of them with wary eyes. What does he think she's going to do, Beatriz wonders, tell Ambrose that Pasquale has feelings for him? Even if she did, it's clear to her after only minutes that those feelings aren't as unrequited as Pasquale believes. "Daphne, right?"

"Right," Beatriz says, turning back toward them. "Though, between us, I think Daphne's an awful lot scarier than any ghost."

They laugh like she's joking, though Beatriz isn't entirely certain she is. The thought sends a pang of longing through her—prickly as Daphne might be, Beatriz misses her terribly.

When his laughter subsides, Ambrose glances down at the book in his hands. "Well, I just wanted to leave this. It's getting late, so I should be going. Triz, it was a pleasure to meet you, finally. Pas, I hope you feel better."

"Oh, I will," Pasquale says. "If only so I can beat you in our chess match tomorrow afternoon."

Ambrose smiles. "Until then," he says, and departs.

When the door closes behind him, Beatriz collapses on the bed beside Pasquale, still dressed in her evening gown. "I can see why you like him," she says, glancing at Pasquale, who groans and throws an arm over his crimson face.

"Stop it," he tells her.

Beatriz smiles despite herself. For an instant, it almost feels normal—the way she felt with her sisters when they would pile together in one bed at the end of a long night of dancing, drinking, and flirting with boys they knew they could never do more than flirt with. Maybe kiss. Still, they gossiped about them, the ones they liked, the ones they thought liked them.

But it's not normal, she reminds herself. If it were, she would tell Pasquale that she's almost positive Ambrose is in love with him, too. But that knowledge won't do anyone any good—if anything, she tells herself, keeping that secret is the best thing she can do for Pasquale.

She rolls over on her side, propping her head up on her elbow.

"One day," she tells him, "we'll live in a better world."

It's the truth, she realizes. When her mother seizes Cellaria, the people will be ruled by Bessemian laws. Pasquale will be stripped of his titles, but she can't imagine he'd be much of a threat to her mother's reign. He might not even need to be exiled. There will be nothing to stop him from being with whomever he wants then.

"One day, we'll make one," Pasquale adds softly.

Beatriz's chest clenches so hard she thinks her heart actually hurts. She forces a smile before rolling away from him.

Daphne

Daphne finds King Bartholomew in the library. The vial of stardust is buried deep in the pocket of her wool skirt.

When the guards posted outside open the door and she steps into the library, she's momentarily stunned by the space. The rest of the castle betrays its newness—many walls are without decoration, some rooms are underfurnished, spaces simply don't look lived-in the way the centuries-old Bessemian palace does. The library, though, is something else entirely.

The room is two stories tall, with shelves that line each wall, full of more books than Daphne has ever seen in one place. So many books that it makes her dizzy trying to estimate how many there might be.

"Daphne," King Bartholomew says, rising from the armchair beside the roaring fire. The furniture in the room is sparse, like in the rest of the castle, but it's cozy—all overstuffed and upholstered in emerald-green velvet. When Daphne steps onto the rug spread out over the stone floors, her feet sink deep into the pile.

"I'm sorry to interrupt," she says, mustering a sheepish

smile. "I haven't seen the library yet, but I was hoping to find a book of poetry."

In truth, Daphne has no patience for poetry—that's Beatriz, who would sneak small leather-bound volumes out into the garden to read aloud in the shade of the trees. Daphne had liked listening to Beatriz's melodic voice reading from the books, but she'd never found much to enjoy in the words themselves. Pretty for pretty's sake, nothing of value for her.

The thought of Beatriz is soured by the last letter Daphne received from her sister, and the last line in particular.

> *It is somehow even hotter in Cellaria than I expected. I can't walk more than five minutes outdoors without sweating through my gown. I'm sure if you could you would pummel me all the way from freezing Friv for complaining, but I'm sure the cold suits you.*

It is nothing to get annoyed about, Daphne knows this, but the words still prickle against her skin, the insinuation that she herself is cold. Beatriz has said similar things before, often calling her a *cold, ruthless bitch*—always teasing, the same way Daphne would call Beatriz a *shameless harlot*—but the irritation lingers longer this time, in large part because Daphne is beginning to suspect that it's the truth. She hasn't shed a tear over Cillian, the sympathy she feels for his parents is perfunctory at best, and even when she had a knife to her throat and thought she might die, she found herself more annoyed than frightened. Perhaps Beatriz is right and her heart *is* as frozen as the Frivian highlands in midwinter.

She pushes her sister's letter to the back of her mind and focuses on the task at hand—another cold maneuver to take advantage of a grieving father.

King Bartholomew loves poetry—she remembers this from one of the many briefings she sat through with her mother's spies. He and Cillian both spent hours in the library, reading poetry. She assumed that the king would be here, mourning his son, so here she is.

And just as Daphne knew he would, the king smiles and gestures her closer, lifting up the book he's reading to show her the cover. She pretends surprise when she realizes it's a volume of poetry—Verity Bates, one of Beatriz's favorites as well. She'd even had Daphne translate a few volumes from the original Frivian for her to compare them to the official Bessemian translation. Daphne combs her memory for something she remembers.

"Oh, is that the one who wrote 'A Mood Black and Waning'?" she asks.

"You're familiar with Bates?" the king asks.

"She's one of my favorites," Daphne tells him, letting her smile broaden. "I find her use of color to indicate emotion so visceral."

The way he returns her smile tells her this was exactly the right thing to say. *Thank you, Beatriz, you shameless harlot.*

"I have quite a few volumes—on the shelves there," he says, motioning to a corner beside the window. "Please, help yourself to whatever you like."

"Thank you, that means so much," she tells him. With the first step of her plan complete, it's time for the second.

She starts toward the corner he indicated but stops short

halfway to unleash a sneeze so dramatic it sends a shudder through her entire body.

"Bless you, child," the king says, looking up from his book once more.

"Thank you, Your Majesty. I'm sorry, I think the Frivian air is taking some getting used to for me," she says before shivering for good measure.

"Well, it's no wonder, is it? Where on earth is your coat?" he asks, alarmed.

Daphne glances down at her day dress, the gray wool soft and warm enough that she would have been sweltering in Bessemia, but in Friv it's not nearly enough to ward off the chill. Contrary to Beatriz's dig, she does not like the cold at all.

"Oh," she says, faking a laugh. "I'm always forgetting it—in Bessemia we never have any need for coats indoors—" She breaks off, sneezing again, this time even more loudly.

The king's brow creases as he looks at her, the concern in his eyes so genuine that the slightest smidgen of guilt nags at her. She's come into the place that most reminds him of his dead son, and now she's faking an illness, which undoubtedly *also* reminds him of Cillian. She's playing on his grief, using it against him. If Sophronia were here, she would give Daphne that look of hers, the kind that reeked of disappointment and disapproval, the kind that would linger with Daphne for days and weeks after, eating at her.

But Sophronia's not here, so what little guilt Daphne feels slips away when King Bartholomew stands up and slips his jacket off, draping it over her shoulders.

"We've had enough illness in this family, Daphne," the

king says, his voice firm but kind. "You must take better care of yourself."

"Thank you, Your Majesty," Daphne says, dropping her gaze. Her fingers graze the seal through the pocket of the coat, and she tries her best to look chastened.

He goes back to his chair and his volume of poetry, but when she makes her way to the shelf, he speaks again.

"It's in volume two," he says, though his eyes are still on his book.

"What is?" she asks over her shoulder.

"'A Mood Black and Waning,'" he says. "It's part of the collection she wrote after her brother's passing. Cillian hated it, thought it was too dark and gloomy. Sometimes, though, there's something comforting about seeing your grief mirrored in another's. It helps us feel less alone."

Daphne tries to think of something to say to that, but no words seem good enough. After a second, he looks at her over the top of his book.

"He would have liked you," the king says.

Daphne swallows down her discomfort and tries to remember what Beatriz said about the poem.

"*A Mood Black and Waning* reminds me of my father, I suppose," she says. "I don't remember him, but sometimes I find myself missing him anyway."

It's another deception, another made-up vulnerability to endear her to a man she will eventually betray, but Daphne doesn't feel bad about it—not even when the king gives her a tender smile, the way she likes to think her own father might have smiled at her. Perhaps Beatriz is right and she is a cold, ruthless bitch after all.

She turns back to the shelves, pretending to scan them while she works through the next part of her plan, the bit she's truly dreading. She can't make her wish if he's here, and she doubts he'll let her leave with his coat—besides the seal, she can feel the heavy ring of keys in another pocket, the rolled-up bits of parchment crushed beneath them. The coat is full of all kinds of things he'll likely have need for.

So, if she can't leave with the coat, she'll have to get him to leave *her* in such a hurry he won't think about it.

She makes her way toward the library ladder, sliding it over to the poetry section and beginning to climb. She doesn't need to go too high—just a few rungs should be enough. When she's four feet off the ground, she takes a deep breath before rolling onto her tiptoes, pretending to reach for a book just an inch too far away.

Then she lets herself fall onto the carpeted stone below, holding out her left arm to break her fall. At least the agonized scream she lets out when her wrist snaps against the ground isn't fake. The pain jolts through her body, turning her vision white for an instant. When she opens her eyes, the king is beside her, holding her arm out. Even though she prepared for this, was ready for the pain, it still sends shock waves through her. As gentle as the king tries to be, she still lets out a cry when he touches her wrist.

"I think it's broken," he says, getting to his feet. "Don't move, Daphne, I'll send for a vial of stardust to fix it."

When King Bartholomew is at the door, she reaches with her right hand into the pocket of the coat, bringing out the seal and setting it on her lap before pulling out the bottled stardust as well. It takes some effort to unstopper it with

only one hand, while the other sends jolts of pain whenever she moves it, but she manages, pouring the glittering gray dust onto the skin of her injured hand.

"I wish this seal were doubled," she says, enunciating each word clearly.

Time turns to molasses, the air going still around her. When the sensation passes, there are suddenly two seals where before there was one.

She tucks the duplicate into the same pocket of the king's coat before picking up the original and the empty vial. The door opens and she hastily shoves them into her pocket, wincing in pain as she moves her injured hand.

When she looks up again, though, it isn't the king standing there, it's Bairre. The way he's staring at her, brow furrowed, mouth turned downward, eyes suspicious, tells her that he saw her with the seal.

"I fell," she tells him.

His expression doesn't change, but he holds up his hand, showing her the vial of stardust, identical to the one she just used.

"I saw my father talking to the guards, but I happened to have this on me," he says, then pauses. "What did you put in your pocket?"

"My pocket?" she asks, frowning. "Oh, when I fell, your father's seal fell out of the coat he lent me. I just tucked it back inside. It didn't look like it was hurt in the fall."

She reaches back into the coat pocket to pull out the duplicate seal as proof.

Bairre doesn't look entirely convinced. "I saw you put something into *your* pocket, though," he says.

Daphne ignores her thundering heart and lets out an annoyed sigh. "I know you don't like me, Bairre," she says, clenching her teeth in a not-entirely-fake pained way. "But if you'd like to accuse me of something, can you at least heal me first so I can properly defend myself without being distracted by pain?"

Bairre frowns, crossing the room and dropping down by her side. He unstoppers the vial and pours the stardust onto the back of his hand before taking hold of her broken wrist.

"Ow," she snaps.

He winces. "Sorry," he says, his voice soft. His touch is soft too—softer than she expected it would be, though the pads of his fingers are roughly callused.

"I wish these bones were set," he says before glancing at Daphne again. "Sorry," he tells her.

"For wha—" she starts before the pain in her wrist swells to an unbearable agony. She can *feel* the bones moving, feel them fusing together, and it hurts like nothing she's ever experienced.

After a moment, the pain fades, though it doesn't disappear completely. A sharp ache remains, throbbing beneath her skin, which has turned a mottled blackish blue.

"It still hurts," she says, looking down at her wrist. He's still holding it, his thumb resting against her pulse point.

"Yes, it will for a few days, more than likely—have you never been healed by stardust before?" he asks.

Daphne shakes her head. Beatriz and Sophronia both have plenty of times—Beatriz after being reckless and Sophronia after being clumsy—but Daphne has always been too cautious. Oh, she's had her fair share of scrapes and bruises, but those have always healed the natural way.

"Ah, well, healing something like a broken bone requires a lot of magic—often too much for stardust. The bones are set now, but it'll take another few days for it to heal entirely and for the pain to subside. I don't think a *thank you* would kill you."

Daphne jerks her hand away from him. "Thank you, Bairre," she says in a saccharine voice. "For following your father's orders, though not before calling me a thief."

He frowns. "I saw you put something inside your dress," he says. "If I'm wrong, I apologize, but—"

"If you want to see inside my dress so badly, you'll have to wait," she says, raising her eyebrows. "We aren't married yet."

A scarlet flush works its way over his cheeks. "That isn't what I meant—"

The door to the library opens again and the king comes in, holding a bundle of cloth in one hand.

"I could hear the bickering from outside the door," he says. "What is the matter?"

Daphne bites her bottom lip and flashes King Bartholomew her most innocent eyes. "Bairre thinks I stole something," she tells him. "But here, check your coat, everything is there, I promise." She shrugs off the coat, wincing as the sleeve goes over her wrist.

The king frowns. "I sent you in here to help the girl, Bairre, not interrogate her."

"Just check it," Bairre says, passing the coat to his father. "I saw her take something, I swear."

King Bartholomew sighs but takes the coat, feeling the

pockets. "Everything is here," he says to Bairre. "Now, apologize."

"But I saw—"

"Apologize," the king repeats, his voice firmer.

Bairre cringes but forces himself to meet Daphne's eyes. "I'm sorry," he tells her.

"I accept your apology," Daphne says with a smile she hopes is more magnanimous than smug. "And thank you so much for healing me, my prince."

He holds her gaze for a moment longer, searching for something, but she closes herself off, giving him nothing but a blank slate.

That afternoon, Daphne sits down at her desk with the king's seal, the letter he'd sent requesting her presence at tea, and a blank piece of parchment. The king's handwriting is more difficult to master than the writing on the marriage contract. Though it's neat enough, she can see his humble roots reflected in the drifting dots above the *i*'s and the tilting stems of the letters.

Once she has the hang of it, she begins to draft a letter from King Bartholomew to her mother.

Dear Margaraux,

I'm glad we could settle upon a new marriage contract for Daphne and Bairre—I know it was not the original match, but I wholeheartedly believe that they will one day be the right king and queen to lead a united Friv and Bessemia.

On that note, I've reason to believe there are rebels in Friv who are conspiring against that future and mean to move against us. I humbly ask that in the interest of our alliance, you assist in sending troops to put an end to it. Perhaps you could use your influence with Temarin as well, since their power in war is legendary and they, too, have a vested interest in our united future.

Your loyal ally,
Bartholomew, King of Friv

Daphne reads the letter again, wondering if perhaps she should specify what Temarin's interest is, but she decides it's better to let the imagination of the rebels run wild. This on its own will be enough to work Cliona and her group into a frenzy. Satisfied, she picks the seal up and holds it over the candle for a moment before pressing it to the paper, beside the forged signature, and pushes down, just as she saw the king do. When she lifts it, the wax seal is there, yellow with a spot of bruise purple in the middle.

That done, she wraps the king's seal in a thick wool scarf along with the sample of his handwriting. She hides the bundle in a box she brought with her from Bessemia—a plain wooden thing on the outside, but with a hidden compartment in the domed lid just big enough for her purposes. Then she fills the main compartment of the box with another wool scarf that she bought in town with Cliona, and a letter from her to Sophronia.

Sophronia

When Sophronia comes back to her sitting room after lunch, she finds Violie waiting with an armful of papers, looking quite pleased with herself.

"Please tell me that's not my correspondence," Sophronia says, eyeing the stack—there must be hundreds of papers there. She knows Beatriz is prone to rambling in her letters, but this seems like a new extreme.

"They're bills," Violie tells her, dropping them on the round table, which has been cleared since Sophronia's earlier coffee with Queen Eugenia. "I did a bit of asking around, but this was all I could access. It's only for your household, but I thought it might help."

"Did you look at them yet?" Sophronia asks. She knows she'll find no war chest funds noted alongside her dressmaker's bill, but Violie is right—it will be helpful. Especially since, until recently, Sophronia's household was Eugenia's.

Violie shakes her head. "No, Your Majesty. I'm afraid I can't read, so it would all be gibberish to me. But Mrs. Ladslow—she's the woman in charge of your accounting—assured me that all the relative documents are here."

"Oh," Sophronia says, cheeks reddening. "I'm sorry, I didn't mean—"

"No worries at all," Violie says. "Did you want to take a look at these? Or should I bring them back to Mrs. Ladslow?"

"No, I'll take a look," Sophronia says, sitting down at the table and reaching for the topmost piece of paper.

"Would you like any tea? Coffee?" Violie asks.

"No, but some help would be appreciated," Sophronia says, motioning to the seat across from her.

Violie hesitates. "As I said, I can't read."

"That's fine," Sophronia tells her. "I'll read aloud and we can pick our way through. You've been in Temarin longer than I have. I'm sure you have insights to add."

"If you say so, Your Majesty," Violie says.

"Sophie," Sophronia corrects. "You can save yourself some breath and I can stop expecting my mother to be standing behind me."

Violie smiles. "Sophie, then," she says.

"This one is for the brunch I hosted last week for Leopold's cousin's daughter's birthday," Sophronia says, scanning the sums. She reads the numbers three times to make sure they're right. "It cost ten thousand asters? I wasn't aware we were giving out stardust-coated gold nuggets as party favors."

Violie laughs. "You aren't far off, actually," she says. "The sparkling wine was imported from Cellaria. Five hundred asters a bottle, and the guests were quite thirsty. There were other costs, but I believe that was the biggest one."

"Who arranged the menu?" Sophronia asks. "I don't recall approving any of this."

"Queen Eugenia said you shouldn't be bothered with

such minuscule details, so she reused a menu from a previous brunch she hosted," Violie says.

Interesting, Sophronia thinks. Five hundred asters a bottle isn't unheard of for sparkling wine, but for a brunch? And the fact that it was imported from Cellaria piques Sophronia's curiosity. She wonders what else that money paid for.

"I remember that sparkling wine," she says after a moment. "Can you find the name of the vineyard? Since Eugenia is so fond of it, I might want to order a bottle for her birthday."

If Violie thinks it an odd request, she doesn't show it. "Of course, Your—Sophie, I mean."

Sophronia goes back to reading. She decides to break the stack of bills into groups—events, clothing, décor, food, and other. It quickly becomes clear that *other* is primarily made up of gifts to various courtiers. She recognizes the bill for the bracelet she had sent to Duchess Bruna when she hired Violie from her, one thousand asters, but there are others she has no knowledge of. In the last two weeks alone, she appears to have made gifts of everything from a prize Frivian stud horse to Lord Verimé to a summer estate on the southeastern border for the Croist family.

"I have yet to meet half of these people," she says to Violie. "Did Queen Eugenia arrange these gifts as well?"

Violie frowns. "If so, the request didn't come through me, though it's possible there is still some confusion between your household and hers. Perhaps the gifts were billed to you as a mistake."

Or Eugenia is using me to cover her tracks, Sophronia thinks. Not all of the gifts come from Cellaria, but Sophronia notices that all of the luxury items, like jewels, silks, wine, and apparently even horses, weren't bought in Temarin but imported from other countries, meaning the money spent didn't go into Temarin's economy at all. A coincidence, maybe, but the coincidences are piling up, and combined with Sir Diapollio's letter, a sinking suspicion has firmly taken root in Sophronia's gut.

It isn't proof, she reminds herself. She can't go to her mother with anything less than solid proof.

When she's halfway through the stack, she pauses, rubbing her temples to stave off the headache blooming behind her eyes.

"That bad?" Violie asks.

Sophronia doesn't say anything for a moment, instead leaning back in her chair and casting her gaze toward the ceiling. She can't tell Violie what she suspects of Eugenia, but there is another problem.

"My mother thought it was important to understand finances," she tells Violie. "Ever since my sisters and I turned ten, we managed our own accounts, paid our own bills. There were a few times when one of us overspent our allowance and she would refuse to give us more until the next month. Once, my sister Beatriz ran out of funds a week before the end of the month and had to eat off Daphne's and my plates, sneak her gowns off to the palace cleaners with ours, even do her own hair before parties." She shakes her head. "It must sound so frivolous."

Violie smiles. "It sounds like a lot of responsibility for children."

Sophronia bites her lip. "My sisters hated it, but truth be told, it was one of the only lessons from my mother that I enjoyed. It's a bit like a puzzle, and I've always enjoyed puzzles. Stars, if Leopold knew how to manage his own accounts, perhaps . . ." She trails off, remembering herself and remembering Violie, who is still more stranger than not. "Sorry," she says.

"Is it really so bad?" Violie asks, looking between the piles of papers now taking up the entirety of the table.

Sophronia makes a noncommittal noise in the back of her throat. "On its own? No. As much money as it is, if it were spread out from taxes across Temarin, it wouldn't cost too much. There's certainly plenty that I can cut—that I *will* cut going forward—but what concerns me is that I know this is just the start of it. If we were to look at more accounts, at Leopold's, at the dowager queen's and the princes', at those of every aristocrat who takes their living by taxing people who live in their territory . . . I'm worried that it will be more of the same and, put all together . . ."

"Worse, even, in some cases," Violie murmurs. When Sophronia raises an eyebrow, Violie shrugs. "When I worked for Duchess Bruna, it seemed she was always caught up in an effort to one-up her friends. If Lady Kester had a new gown embellished with a hundred diamonds, Duchess Bruna had to have one with two hundred. It was the same with parties, summer homes, carriages. And the men are even worse. Most of them lose thousands of asters in a single night gambling, and horse and hound trading is its own very expensive hobby. It's something I've noticed since I arrived—I'd always heard that war was an integral part of Temarin culture, but I suppose since they've had no war in decades, it's been replaced by sheer decadence."

"But it isn't their money," Sophronia says softly. "I can't request tax documents without stoking animosity from the court," she adds. "They'd think I was a foreigner meddling."

"Technically, you *are* a foreigner meddling," Violie says before catching herself and turning a shade paler. "Sorry, Your Majesty."

Sophronia laughs. "Why? You're right. But I'd rather not have my people think of me as their enemy." She pauses for a moment, but she knows what she has to do—she just doesn't like it. "Will you coordinate with Leopold's valet and see if we can find a time in our schedules for a picnic?"

Violie gets to her feet, smoothing out her gown. "I'll do that now," she says.

When she's gone, Sophronia casts another gaze at the piles of bills and picks up the next one.

It takes several days before Sophronia's and Leopold's schedules allow them time for a picnic, but the stars at least seem to be on her side, because the weather is perfect—sunny and bright, but crisp enough that she isn't sweltering in her heavy satin gown, this one a brilliant sapphire blue.

Leopold looks handsome, Sophronia can admit that. His

sage-green jacket brings out the color of his eyes, and in the sunlight, his bronze hair looks gilded.

"You're angry with me," he says, jerking her out of her thoughts. He says the words softly, though their guards keep even the nosiest courtiers far away.

Sophronia looks at him, ready to deny it and tell him that everything is just *fine,* but the second her eyes meet his she knows it will be fruitless. She *is* angry at him, and perhaps she should tell him as much.

"Yes," she says, holding his gaze. "I suppose I am."

He shakes his head. "If I could do it all over again, I would do everything differently," he tells her.

Some foolish corner of her heart lights. "You would?" she asks.

He nods. "I would have taken you another route that day. Around the north side of the palace, maybe."

That corner of her heart goes dark once more. "Oh," she says, turning away from him and looking instead at the silhouette of the palace. "I suppose I wouldn't be angry with you then, though only because I'd be too stupid to know that I should be. Would you rather I be stupid?"

Leopold lets out a long sigh. "That isn't what I meant, Sophie," he says.

"No?" she asks. "Those boys would still be dead, wouldn't they? And so would stars know how many others. Only my knowledge of it would be gone. Perhaps it's not too late—speak with your empyrea if you like, see if you can wish for a stupider wife."

"You're being ridiculous," he tells her. "That isn't even how wishes work."

"I *know* that," Sophronia snaps. "Because I'm *not* stupid, Leopold. I'm not angry with you because I *saw* the hangings. I'm angry that they happened at all."

For a long moment, he doesn't respond. "What would you have done?" he asks.

Sophronia hesitates. It doesn't matter what she would have done. She isn't meant to be a true queen, just a temporary one. Soon enough, Temarin will be under Bessemian rule—her mother's rule—and Leopold, his brothers, and his mother will be shipped off into exile in some distant place. None of this will have mattered.

Except it will. It will be another few weeks at least before Temarin and Cellaria go to war, months more before that war hobbles Temarin enough that her mother can claim it as her own. And that's not even counting whatever Eugenia may be up to. How many people will die—of starvation, of execution, of the cold itself once winter comes? It *is* important. And there is no reason Sophronia can't carry out her mother's orders *and* help the Temarinian people.

"You said Temarin's crime rate is at a high," she says. "Has it decreased at all since you imposed your stricter punishments?"

"They aren't *my* stricter punishments," he says. "My council decided—"

"The decree has *your* name on it," she interrupts. "Those executions happened on *your* orders. Not your mother's, not your council's, yours."

He grimaces but doesn't disagree. "No," he says. "The crime rate has even gone up in recent weeks. I just heard that the jail will have to have twice-weekly executions now because the cells are too full."

Sophronia nods. "So," she says. "All of those people—even *more* people—have decided that even though they very well might die for it, it's worth stealing. How desperate does a person have to be to make that choice, Leopold? Those boys were children. They should have been out playing with their friends, like your brothers do. Instead they decided to risk their lives stealing from people more fortunate than them. You should seek to understand why."

He doesn't speak for a moment, so she continues.

"It's a question I've been thinking a lot about," she admits, seeing her opening. "And I even took the liberty of looking over my household bills. I've spent well over five million asters, just in the two weeks since I arrived."

He frowns. "Is that . . . a lot?" he asks.

Sophronia forces herself not to roll her eyes. "Yes," she says. "Even one million asters would be enough to buy food for everyone in Kavelle for a month. I checked. And most of it went toward gifts for people I've never met, parties I never wanted to throw, services I never requested. Did you know that the curtains in our bedroom are steamed three times a day at a cost of a hundred asters a steam? Which is a lot," she adds, because he still looks confused. "I believe most of these payments are billed recurrently every week or month, left over from when it was your mother's household. It's an oversight, easy enough to fix, but I suspect we might find similar oversights in your own records, and the records of other households that the crown supports financially. Your mother, your aunt, your brothers, anyone else who relies on your kindness. *Our* kindness."

Leopold's brow furrows. "You wish to examine their accounts?" he asks. "I can't imagine they'll take kindly to you monitoring their spending."

"They don't have to know," Sophronia says, offering him a small smile. "Unless I find something truly alarming."

"I don't know, Sophie," Leopold says. "It's our money, and we can afford the luxuries our station demands."

"Our money," she repeats, staring at Leopold for a long moment as something clicks into place. "Leopold . . . where do you think our money comes from?" she asks.

He shrugs. "Never really thought much about it, to be honest, but I imagine it's in a vault somewhere, maybe beneath the palace?"

It takes all of her self-control not to shake him. "It comes from taxes, Leo," she says. "Every month, we collect taxes from the people for the privilege of living in our country. They send money to their landowners as well, whatever duke or count or earl owns the ground their house sits on. Almost every last aster in the palace comes from the pockets of the same people who are so desperate for money they are willing to risk their lives to steal it."

He stares at her as if she is speaking gibberish. He sits up a bit straighter, his brow deeply furrowed. "Are you sure?" he asks.

"Yes."

"I had no idea," he murmurs. Silence stretches out between them, Leopold deep in thought and Sophronia watching him. It's possible, she thinks, that he is not cruel, merely oblivious. She isn't sure if that's better or worse.

"Leopold, can you request the latest tax laws from around the country?" she asks him.

He nods. "I'll ask about it today," he says.

"I'd also like to take you up on your offer to join in on your council meetings," she says. "When is the next one?"

Beatriz

Beatriz finds Gisella in a compromising position—her back pressed against the wall of a dimly lit corridor, her arms snaked around the neck of a handsome boy Beatriz vaguely recognizes as the son of an earl.

When Gisella hears her clear her throat, she tears her mouth away from the boy's and blinks at Beatriz as if coming out of a daze. She doesn't appear at all embarrassed by the circumstances, instead offering Beatriz a bright smile, her red lip paint smeared.

Beatriz immediately likes her even more.

You don't need to like her, her mother's voice whispers through her mind, but Beatriz ignores it, just as she always tries to ignore her mother's voice, with mixed results.

"Your Highness," Gisella says, shoving the boy's shoulder away and dipping into a brief curtsy.

She might not be embarrassed, but the boy is, his face turning as red as Gisella's lips as he hastily falls into a deep bow.

"Lady Gisella," Beatriz says, trying to stifle a smirk. "Might I have a word?"

The boy bows again, stammering out an apology Beatriz doesn't pay attention to. Gisella links her arm through hers and throws the boy a brilliant smile.

"I'm sure I'll see you again soon, Lord Elio," she says before following Beatriz down the hall.

"Your lip paint," Beatriz tells her.

"Oh," she says, pulling a silver compact mirror from the pocket of her gown and opening it, examining her reflection and running a finger around the line of her lips, cleaning up the red smears. "Thank you."

"I'm sorry to interrupt, it seemed to be going well," Beatriz says. "Pas said you were looking for a husband—it looks like you found a handsome one."

"Yes, well, if I don't find one soon, my father will pick one for me, and I certainly don't want that," Gisella tells her, rolling her eyes. "Elio is wealthy enough to appease my father but young and handsome enough that it doesn't seem like a total chore. Besides, he's so frightened of me I doubt he would deny me my freedom. I could do a lot worse."

It occurs to Beatriz that Gisella could do a lot better than a boy who's terrified of her, but she can't deny there is some logic there. And she can't even bring herself to pity the other girl her choices—she still has more than Beatriz does.

"I wanted to thank you," she tells Gisella. "For sending Lord Savelle my way. I was finally able to make his acquaintance and learn news of my sister."

And, she doesn't add, now that she's made his acquaintance it has become easy to maintain it. She has taken to joining him on his morning walks in the sea garden. The first couple of mornings, it was difficult to force herself out of bed, but she quickly began to look forward to the walks. They don't talk often, but the silence is comfortable and the conversations they do share are refreshing to Beatriz after all the false friendliness of the Cellarian courtiers. He's told her, quite honestly, about his early years in Cellaria, the adjustments he had to make, the resentment he's felt. He's told her about Temarin, a land she knows she might one day see, though it will look quite different under her mother's rule by then. He's told her about his daughter, too—little things, like her favorite color and how she had a terrible singing voice but he misses the sound of it. He's shared himself so freely that Beatriz can tell he's been lonely, but she belatedly realizes she enjoys their morning strolls so much because she's lonely too.

"Oh?" Gisella asks. "How is the little heretic?" Beatriz must give her an alarmed look, because Gisella laughs. "That is what you called her, isn't it? Both of them, even."

"Yes, of course," Beatriz says, laughing as well. "She's well. Madly in love with her new husband, apparently."

"Don't sound so jealous. You and Pasquale seem to be getting along well," Gisella points out before pausing. "He can be a difficult person to know—the court has said some . . . unkind things—but I do think you're good for him. He needs a little boldness."

"Thank you," Beatriz says, though she isn't entirely certain any of that was a compliment. "What . . . what has the court been saying?"

Gisella gives her an embarrassed smile. "Oh, I shouldn't

have said that. It's nothing, really. Everyone gets so bored here when winter starts to close in, they have to amuse themselves somehow, I suppose."

"What, exactly, Gisella?" Beatriz asks again. Gisella's eyes go wide and Beatriz gives her arm a reassuring squeeze. "I'm not angry, certainly not at you. But I'd like to know what lies I have to combat—I'm sure you'd want the same in my position."

Gisella purses her lips, considering it. "I'm sure I would," she admits after a second. "It's really nothing, Your Highness. Pasquale is just . . . so quiet. Most people don't know the first thing about him—when a mystery is that large, speculation is bound to arise."

"What sort of speculation?" Beatriz asks, trying to smother her rising panic over what exactly they could be speculating about and how close it might hit to the truth.

Gisella bites her lip. "People are wondering if he's as mad as his mother was," she says quietly. When Beatriz doesn't speak, she hurries on. "It's easy enough to fix, really. Bring him with you the next time you visit the sea garden, make sure he doesn't hide in the corner at the next banquet. I love my cousin," she says. "And I'm sure everyone else would come to love him too, if only they knew him."

Beatriz nods slowly. It doesn't matter, really, whether anyone *likes* Pasquale. In a couple of months, if everything goes to plan, he won't be the crown prince anymore. These rumors will be insignificant. It will be better, even, for Pasquale if he doesn't have support, if Beatriz's mother doesn't see him as a threat. But still, it is such an easy thing. "I'll see what I can do."

"Ladies!" A voice booms behind them, and Gisella briefly closes her eyes and gives a sharp inhale, her grip on Beatriz's arm tightening. But then her expression clears and she pastes a broad smile on her face. Beatriz manages to do the same as they turn toward the voice.

King Cesare strides toward them, a gaggle of courtiers around him, all dressed in an array of vibrant silks and jewels. Beatriz barely makes out Nicolo trailing behind them, carrying the king's wine goblet, but when he sees them, his eyebrows arch. He and Gisella seem to have a silent conversation—a realization that sends a pang of sadness through Beatriz. She remembers doing the same thing with her sisters.

"Lady Gisella," the king says. "Princess Beatriz. You both look especially beautiful today, don't they?" he says, glancing around at his entourage, who are all quick to nod and agree with him.

Beatriz feels his gaze trace over her body, lingering on her breasts. Her gown isn't particularly revealing—it might even be one of her more demure dresses—but suddenly she feels naked. It takes all her self-control not to cross her arms over her chest.

"Your Majesty," Gisella says, dropping into a sweeping curtsy, with Beatriz half a heartbeat behind her. "It's a fine day today, isn't it? I was just saying to Princess Beatriz that we should take in the air at the sea garden. She said she had a bit of a headache—isn't that right, Princess?"

Beatriz hasn't the slightest idea what she's talking about, but she decides to play along. "I do," she tells the king with a sheepish smile. "The air here in Cellaria is so much fresher than in Bessemia, but I believe I'm still adjusting to the change in altitudes."

"Oh, no need for that," King Cesare says, waving her words away. "You know what always cures a headache? A cup of wine. Nicolo! Give the princess some wine."

Nicolo looks flustered. "Your Majesty, I only have your goblet and—"

"No arguments!" King Cesare barks.

Just as Nicolo steps forward, his brow furrowed, Beatriz offers the king a smile. "That is very kind, Your Majesty, though I'm afraid wine seems to have the opposite effect on me," she says, silently adding *like most people.*

There are a few gasps from his entourage, and one woman begins fanning herself vigorously with her silk fan. Even Gisella gives another sharp inhale.

"You refuse your king?" King Cesare asks, his voice dropping, all traces of joviality gone.

"No," Beatriz says quickly. "No, of course not, Your Majesty. It's only that I would hate to inconvenience you."

"Would I have offered if it inconvenienced me?" he asks, his eyes boring into her so deeply that she feels his gaze in her very bones.

Beatriz has never thought of herself as someone easily intimidated. Stars, she has always been the one of her sisters who is willing to speak up against their mother. Even when the empress was at her strictest, even when she put them through grueling lessons or inflicted her most nightmarish punishments, Beatriz never truly feared her mother. But there is a small part of her now that fears King Cesare. Her mother is logical if nothing else, and predictable because of it. King Cesare is neither. So Beatriz accepts the goblet Nicolo offers her and takes a small, closemouthed sip, struggling not to cringe as she does. The knowledge that she's put her mouth where his mouth has been makes her feel sick, but when she lowers the goblet, she forces a smile.

"Thank you, Your Majesty. You were right—it was very refreshing," she says, passing the goblet back to Nicolo.

"There, you see? You must remember, Princess Beatriz, your king is correct in all things. Aren't I?" he says, and again, his entourage is quick to agree. Beatriz suspects he could proclaim the sky green and they would fall all over themselves to tell him how brilliant he was. "Come, let us walk."

Before Beatriz knows what's happening, King Cesare has her arm linked in his, his other hand resting atop that arm so that she feels well and truly trapped. She glances behind her to see Gisella looking at her with wide eyes as she falls in with the rest of the king's entourage, but Beatriz knows Gisella won't help her—she can't even be upset about that. After all, what help can Gisella, or anyone, give her? The king has already come close once to having her executed. She can't tempt him into it a second time. So she forces herself to keep smiling as King Cesare escorts her down the long hallway.

"Tell me, Princess Beatriz," he says, loudly enough that his entire entourage can hear him. "How are you finding married life? A girl like you is certainly made for it, I'm sure."

The courtiers erupt into giggles. Beatriz keeps her eyes

trained straight ahead, but she can feel King Cesare's gaze focused down the front of her dress. Bile rises up in her throat, but she forces it down.

"Oh yes," she says as pleasantly as she can manage. "Prince Pasquale and I are very happy. I'm so grateful to Your Majesty and my own mother for arranging the marriage. He is truly everything a girl could hope for in a husband—you must be so proud of him."

Beatriz hopes that by talking about Pasquale, she will remind him that she is his daughter now and he should stop ogling her breasts, but it seems to have the opposite effect. If anything, his leer intensifies.

"Of course you would think so, having never been with a real man," King Cesare says, to more laughter from his entourage. Beatriz never knew she could find the sound of laughter so grating, but it's beginning to make the headache Gisella made up feel all too real. "Should you be so inclined, we can always remedy that, Beatriz. I'm sure Pasquale wouldn't mind." He slides his hand over her arm, a gesture that seems to leave a trail of slime in its wake. She could take a dozen baths and still feel it on her.

"Oh, I don't . . ." She trails off. She's always been an excellent flirt, better than Daphne or Sophronia, but suddenly she feels like she's been thrown into some new game she doesn't understand, one with life-and-death stakes where she has to balance on the thinnest tightrope.

Something bumps into her back, and suddenly she feels liquid soaking through her skirt.

"Apologies, Your Highness," Nicolo says.

Beatriz glances behind her to find that he's spilled wine on her gown, making a deep red stain against the aquamarine silk. She's so relieved she wants to sob—she'll have to go back to her rooms to change now. A quick glance at Nicolo tells her that he knows this as well, that he spilled wine on her intentionally.

"You bumbling fool!" King Cesare roars, snatching the goblet off the floor and hurling it at Nicolo's head. The gilded rim glances off his temple and his hand flies up to cover it, but not before Beatriz sees the trickle of blood.

"Apologies, Your Majesty," Nicolo says, bowing deeply. "Allow me to fetch you a new goblet of wine—and I can escort the princess back to her rooms so she can change into something clean."

"Yes, do," the king snaps, letting go of Beatriz's arm. She's so glad to be rid of his hands on her that she stumbles as she walks toward Nicolo, and he puts a hand on her elbow to steady her. "I'll see you again soon, Princess," the king calls after her as she and Nicolo make their way down the hallway, Gisella hurrying behind them.

"Thank you," Beatriz says to Nicolo when they round the corner and are out of sight and earshot of King Cesare and his entourage. Gisella has managed to catch up with them and now falls in on Beatriz's other side.

"He's gotten worse lately," Gisella says, keeping her voice to a whisper even though they're the only ones in the hallway. Beatriz can't blame her for being paranoid—any word against the king could translate to treason. "He's always . . . liked younger women," she says carefully.

"Children, really," Nicolo points out. "Lady Emilia's handmaiden was only fourteen. Still, I'd have thought his son's wife would be off-limits."

Beatriz thought as much as well, even after he groped her on their first meeting. She thought he was all bawdy talk and inappropriate comments. Even after he'd leered at her while inspecting her bedsheets after her wedding—she'd felt uncomfortable, certainly, but never unsafe. She felt unsafe today, despite being surrounded by people who could have spoken up, could have helped her. But only Nicolo had, and paid a high cost for it.

"Let me see your head," Beatriz says, stopping in the middle of the hallway and pulling Nicolo to a stop beside her.

"Trust me, it isn't the first time he's thrown something at me," Nicolo says, trying out a laugh that rings false.

"His temper's been getting worse as well," Gisella says, peering over Beatriz's shoulder as she eyes the wound on Nicolo's temple. It's a shallow cut, and it should heal with only a bandage. In Bessemia, an injury like that wouldn't even warrant the use of stardust to heal it.

"I'm sure we can find bandages in my chambers," Beatriz tells him, tearing one of several ruffles off the sleeve of her gown. She presses it to the wound, then brings his hand up to hold it in place. "Keep that on it until we get there, unless you want to stain your shirt."

"Instead of just ruin your gown?" he asks, though he does as she says.

Beatriz snorts. "Please. If my maids can remove a wine stain, they can mend a sleeve," she says before hesitating.

"You keep saying he's getting worse," she says. "What do you mean?"

Nicolo and Gisella exchange another look, have another wordless conversation, though this one Beatriz can surmise the gist of well enough.

"If you think I would betray your confidence—" she begins.

"It isn't that," Gisella says, shaking her head. "But it's a difficult question to answer. He's always been . . . temperamental."

Beatriz nods—that much she knew. Reports of King Cesare's volatile moods were common when she was in Bessemia; she expected them. But they're worse than she'd thought. It almost seems as though King Cesare has no inhibitions whatsoever—perhaps unsurprising given that he always seems to have a goblet of wine nearby. When Beatriz says as much to Nicolo and Gigi, they exchange another look.

"I may have started diluting his wine, along with the other cupbearers," Nicolo admits. "We started off a little at a time so he wouldn't notice, but by now his wine is roughly half grape juice."

"When did you start diluting the wine?" Beatriz asks, frowning.

Nicolo shrugs. "It must have been about six months ago? I suppose his behavior started becoming more erratic just before then."

Which would have been in the spring. Beatriz thinks back to the reports her mother received from her Cellarian spies around then—she remembers the usual scandals, affairs with younger women, a temper tantrum or two. She remembers a story about King Cesare stripping off his shirt in the middle of his birthday banquet because he proclaimed the room too hot. From someone else it would have been alarming behavior, but from King Cesare, it was more of the same.

But it's possible some of the king's behavior went unreported, Beatriz tells herself, before another thought occurs to her. It's also possible that her mother didn't share those reports with her. It's a ridiculous thought—Beatriz might have plenty of her own reservations about her mother, but keeping that information from Beatriz wouldn't help either of them. Yet her mother also hadn't told her about Lord Savelle's daughter, even though the information would have helped her. It's possible her mother didn't know about that, either, though it's doubtful. The empress is playing her own game, Beatriz knows this better than her sisters, and there must be a reason for it.

They come to a stop outside the door to her chambers. "Come in, I'll look at your wound."

Nicolo nods before glancing down at the empty goblet he carries. Gisella follows his gaze.

"I'll go down to the kitchens to refill it," she says, taking the goblet from him. "We don't want to risk the king's temper if you dawdle."

Beatriz leads Nicolo into the small parlor off the entrance to her rooms, where she finds a maid cleaning the fireplace. The maid stands up when they enter and drops to a curtsy.

"Daniella," Beatriz says. "Lord Nicolo tripped up the stairs and cut his face. Will you send for a physician?"

Daniella's eyes dart to Nicolo, to the cut he's covering with the scrap of lace. "Of course, Your Highness," she says, bobbing another quick curtsy before hurrying out the door.

Nicolo fixes Beatriz with a glare. "I don't need a physician," he grumbles. "And if I'm not back with more wine soon, the king will have my head."

Beatriz isn't entirely sure that's an exaggeration. "I know," she says, rolling her eyes. "But how else was I supposed to explain bringing a boy, alone, back to my rooms when my husband is not home, if not by a medical emergency?" she asks.

Nicolo clears his throat, glancing away from her. "Fair enough, but I can't stay and wait for a physician," he says.

"I *know,*" she says again, gesturing to a high-backed chair next to the fire. "Sit there, I'll be right back."

He follows her direction and she slips from the parlor into the bedroom, returning a moment later with a clean strip of linen torn from one of Pasquale's nightshirts, a bowl of water, and a clean washcloth. She feels Nicolo's eyes on her as she approaches him, wary but curious.

"Do you know what you're doing?" he asks her. When she glares at him, he holds his hands up in mock surrender. "I'm only saying, I wouldn't expect a princess to know how to treat a wound. Besides, back in Bessemia, don't you have vials of stardust lying around, ready to heal every splinter and scratch?"

Beatriz gives a snort as she dips the washcloth into the

water and brings it up to the gash on Nicolo's temple. "I never used stardust, remember?"

"Ah yes, because you were horrified by Bessemia's sacrilegious ways," he says, amusement coloring his voice.

"Besides," she interrupts. "I know how to clean a wound because my sister Sophronia can be clumsy and our mother would always give her the worst lectures whenever she hurt herself. It was easier for me to take care of things."

It's a half-truth—the wounds were usually caused during their training. Sophronia was hopeless with a dagger and stabbed herself a handful of times while practicing. But the empress's ire was real enough, though it would often go further than lectures. Once, when Sophronia dropped her dagger mid–sparring match, the empress made her stand out in the snow barefoot for half an hour.

"Sophronia's the one in Temarin?" Nicolo asks.

Beatriz nods. "It's a funny thing, with the three of us. I love my sisters equally, but I think I like Sophronia more. Daphne is so much like our mother, in good ways and bad. But Sophronia's softer. She has always needed me."

He nods slowly, meeting her gaze. "It's always easier to love people who need us than people we need, I think. Being needed makes one powerful. Needing, though, makes one vulnerable."

Beatriz considers this as she dabs at his wound with the cloth, making sure to clean it thoroughly. "I suppose I see some truth to that," she says before pausing. "Thank you, for helping me get away from him."

She doesn't have to specify which *him* she means. Nicolo's frown deepens.

"You should try to avoid him if you aren't with Pasquale," he says.

Beatriz has to laugh. "I'm his daughter now," she says, though she still feels King Cesare's hand on her arm, feels his gaze burning a hole in her gown, as if he were looking right through it. "He might say some things, but he would never go further, surely."

"He has a tendency to fixate on girls," Nicolo says, dropping his voice. "And when he does, he becomes . . . single-minded in the pursuit. He took a liking to Lord Enzo's daughter a few months back—Lord Enzo sent her to a Sisterhood in the mountains to keep her away from him. A few days later, the king had her back at court. A few days after that, she was in his bed."

Beatriz's stomach plummets. "Willingly?" she asks.

Nicolo fixes her with a level look. "You've seen what he does to those who refuse him," he says. "I think it depends on your definition of *willing*."

Beatriz swallows. "I appreciate the warning," she says, feeling nauseated, though she isn't quite sure why. She's been raised for this, hasn't she? Brought up to be aware of how men view her, how to use their interest in her against them. Trained to flirt with and seduce powerful men to serve her purposes.

Pasquale doesn't want her. Neither does Lord Savelle. What does it matter if King Cesare does? She knows that if she wrote to her mother about his attentions, the empress would tell her to encourage them, to use them to sow more chaos in the Cellarian court. It would be so easy, wouldn't it? To use his attraction to her to make him look even more unstable, to be able to whisper in his ear and drive him to war with Temarin when the time comes?

Yes, she knows exactly what her mother would tell her to do, if she were here. But she isn't, and Beatriz knows that this is a line she cannot cross, a part of herself she cannot give up.

"I don't mean to frighten you," Nicolo says softly.

"You didn't," she says, forcing a smile. "I can handle myself, I promise."

"I believe that," he says slowly, looking up at her.

Beatriz lowers the washcloth, his gaze catching hers and holding it.

There, she thinks. *That* is the way she hoped Pasquale would look at her—it's the way she expected Lord Savelle to look at her. It isn't, however, the way King Cesare looks at her. Nicolo doesn't look at her like she's a thing to possess, but rather simply like she's a girl he desires. It occurs to Beatriz then that there is nothing simple about it.

She quickly covers his wound with the dry cloth, applying pressure to it and trying to ignore the fluttering in her belly.

Shameless, Daphne's voice whispers through her mind, though she tries to ignore it. Inconvenient as it is, she has to admit that the feeling is a pleasant one. She isn't foolish enough to act on it, but she can appreciate it at least. Doesn't she deserve that?

The door to the parlor opens and Gisella comes in, holding a fresh goblet of wine. Her eyes dart from Beatriz to Nicolo for a moment, though if she's alarmed at their closeness, she doesn't show it.

"Here, keep pressure on it," Beatriz tells him, bringing his left hand up to cover the cloth. "The bleeding isn't too bad—give it a few minutes and I'm sure it'll stop."

Nicolo clears his throat. "Yes, thank you," he says, getting back to his feet. "And thanks, Gigi," he adds hastily, grabbing the goblet of wine from her and hurrying out the door.

When he's gone, Gisella looks at Beatriz with raised eyebrows. "What did you do to him, threaten to set him on fire?" she asks. "I've never seen him move that fast before."

"I think it's the threat of the king's temper," Beatriz points out, though she isn't convinced.

Gisella rolls her eyes. "He's been the king's cupbearer for almost a full year now—here's hoping not for much longer. The one he replaced now sits on the king's council, you know."

"It seems a dangerous ladder to try to climb," Beatriz says.

Gisella shrugs. "Perhaps, but that's what makes it so fun," she says with a grin. "Oh! Before I forget—I intercepted a messenger on my way here. There was a letter for you."

Gisella reaches into the pocket of her gown and pulls out a cream envelope, sealed with yellow wax dotted with violet.

Beatriz's stomach sours even as she reaches out to take it. The letter is from her mother.

Sophronia

Not even five minutes into her first council meeting, Sophronia is sure of one thing: Leopold has no hand at all in running Temarin. She knew he was uninvolved with most things, but now she doubts he's ever made a decision as king that wasn't whispered in his ear first. He might wear the crown. He might even believe he is in charge, and if his council members were asked, they would surely agree with him, but her mother was right: Queen Eugenia runs Temarin from the coastline to the Bessemian border, with the help of the other council members, Lord Verning and Lord Covier, whose primary function seems to be to agree with whatever she says.

"We've received word from Lord Savelle," Lord Verning says after introductions are made. He glances at Sophronia. "That is our ambassador stationed in the Cellarian court, Your Majesty," he adds, in the same tone one would use when explaining something to a small child. Sophronia forces a grateful smile, as if she didn't already know this and hadn't had a letter from Beatriz just this morning detailing her habit of morning strolls with Lord Savelle. It doesn't sound like the seduction their mother planned, but Beatriz has always been one to handle things her own way.

Lord Verning clears his throat before continuing. "He expressed concerns for King Cesare's . . . health."

"Is my brother ill?" Queen Eugenia asks, tilting her head. Sophronia studies her as casually as she can, searching for any indication of undue concern, but Eugenia betrays nothing that suggests she's been in contact with him. She might as well be hearing news about a casual acquaintance instead of her sibling.

"Not so much ill as . . . temperamental," Lord Verning says carefully.

"That is not news," Queen Eugenia says with a laugh. "Cesare has always been temperamental."

"Yes, but more recently he's taken to jailing and executing any person who disagrees with him. I believe the Duke of Dorinthe was the most recent casualty of his temper," Lord Verning says.

Queen Eugenia's eyebrows rise. "He had a duke executed?" she asks.

"Indeed. Lord Savelle also mentioned that he has been behaving inappropriately toward his new daughter-in-law."

"Beatriz?" Sophronia can't help but ask. It's the first thing she's said during the meeting, and she'd been resolved to hold her tongue and listen, but the mention of her sister makes it impossible. She knows that Beatriz can handle herself, but still, the thought of her sister having to contend with a lecherous and possibly mad king makes her feel sick.

"Well, he'd hardly be the first king to try to seduce a young bride away from her husband," Lord Covier points out.

"From what Lord Savelle says, Princess Beatriz has proven quite adept at rebuffing him. But his attentions have been . . . public."

"He's making an ass of himself," Queen Eugenia surmises.

"He's losing the respect of his court," Lord Verning says. "There have been rumblings of coups from families close to the throne, but no one can agree on who they would support to replace him."

"Why wouldn't Pasquale?" Leopold asks, echoing Sophronia's own thoughts. "He is the crown prince."

"Prince Pasquale has no allies of his own at court," Lord Verning says. "And there are many families hungry for power who wouldn't think twice of climbing over him to take it."

Oh, be careful, Triz, Sophronia thinks, though she knows her sister would laugh off her concern. And with good reason. If anyone can woo the Cellarian courtiers to her side, it's Beatriz.

"He has a friend in Temarin," Leopold announces. "He's my cousin, his wife and mine are sisters. If it comes to it, we will give them whatever support we can."

Sophronia glances sideways at him, surprised by the passion in the declaration. When the time comes to declare war on Cellaria, she doubts she'll have trouble convincing Leopold to do it.

Lord Verning exchanges a look with Queen Eugenia, so quick that Sophronia almost misses it. Could it be that he's involved in Eugenia's plot with Cellaria as well? Before she can ponder that possibility further, Lord Verning turns back to Leopold with a bland smile.

“Of course, Your Majesty, we will keep you apprised of the situation.”

“Good,” Leopold says before glancing at Sophronia. “The queen and I would like to discuss the palace’s finances,” he announces.

“Oh?” Lord Covier asks, sitting up and flipping through the stack of papers in front of him. “Ah yes, it looks like we are prepared to increase taxes two percent next month to increase the palace treasury, though we can also increase Kavelle’s city taxes if you would like more—”

“No,” Leopold interrupts, his eyes widening. “No, the opposite, in fact. We’ve been discussing the possibility of trimming palace expenses so that we can *cut* taxes.”

Lord Covier, Lord Verning, and Queen Eugenia exchange looks.

“I don’t understand, Your Majesty,” Lord Covier says, leaning forward. “You wish to be less affluent?”

Leopold frowns, looking to Sophronia for help, so she jumps in.

“We have become aware of the plight many of the commoners in Temarin are facing,” she says. “They can barely afford the taxes they are paying now. After looking over the accounts for the royal family, we’ve spent over thirty million asters so far this month alone. Many of our people can’t afford to put food on their tables. Why should we take what little money they have to buy ourselves diamonds?”

“Diamonds?” Queen Eugenia asks with a laugh. “Surely we didn’t spend thirty million asters on diamonds, Sophronia.”

“No,” Sophronia allows, looking down at the stack of papers she brought with her, containing highlights of the account documents she and Leopold have spent the last few nights going over. "No, it looks like diamonds and other jewels cost three million this month. Various parties and celebrations totaled ten million—"

"Well, the wedding was a large expense," Lord Covier interrupts.

"My dowry paid for the wedding," Sophronia tells him. "It wasn't included in my calculations. Shall we talk about the gifts?"

"What gifts?" Queen Eugenia asks.

Sophronia searches her papers again. "There was the one-million-aster hunting lodge you bought for Lord Haverill, the six-hundred-thousand-aster necklace you gave Lady Reves, and the"—Sophronia feigns a squint for added drama, though she knows exactly what she's looking at—"solid gold tennis racket that you had made for Sir Eldrick that cost a particularly magnanimous nine hundred thousand asters."

Queen Eugenia's gaze hardens, but she meets Sophronia's stare. "I like to think that generosity toward friends is a positive trait, Sophie."

Friends, Sophronia thinks. Eugenia has no friends at court. Which makes the extravagant gifts all the more perplexing.

"Perhaps it would be *more* generous if any of that money was spent in Temarin," Sophronia replies. "But the lodge is just across the Bessemian border, the necklace came from Cellaria, and the tennis racket was custom-made in Friv. I'm sure their economies are very grateful for your generosity."

Queen Eugenia purses her lips like she's tasted something

sour. "I can't help but feel quite targeted here," she says, her voice tight.

"Apologies, Genia," Sophronia says with a blinding smile before turning toward the man to her left. "Lord Covier, I understand you raised taxes on your domain more than ten percent over the last year? Shall we delve into the impressive gambling debts you've racked up that your tenants are paying for?"

Beside her, Leopold gives a snort of laughter that he tries to disguise as a cough, while Lord Covier turns a curious shade of puce.

"You are oversimplifying matters, Your Majesty," Lord Verning says. "Many other factors contribute to the decision to raise taxes. Infrastructure costs, the salaries of those paid by the crown . . . our war treasury, should we ever need it. It's far more complicated than you might realize."

"Do you think so?" Sophronia asks, furrowing her brow and shuffling her papers to bring another to the front. "Because I have the numbers for all of those things you mentioned, as well as Temarin's budgets for several other necessary aspects of running a country. Shall we go over them one by one? I'm particularly interested in this one, which shows that significant amounts of money have actually been *withdrawn* from Temarin's war chest, without any indication of what was done with that money."

She watches Eugenia closely as she pushes the piece of paper to the center of the table so they can see it clearly, the relevant sections underlined by Sophronia herself when Leopold handed them to her last night. It was worse than Sophronia had imagined—when King Carlisle died, Temarin's war chest totaled over five billion asters. Now it totals less than fifty million. Barely enough to pay for food rations for their troops for two months, certainly not enough to pay for weaponry or build up defenses. And if Cellaria attacks by sea like they did in the Celestian War, Temarin will not be able to afford to use the fleet Leopold's father spent so much time and money assembling. They are, as of now, defenseless.

And there it is—the flash of fear on Eugenia's face. Not fear at the situation or what it means, but the fear of someone who has been caught. It isn't guilt, not quite, but it's close. She quickly smooths it over with a smile.

"A misunderstanding, I'm sure," she says, picking up the piece of paper to take a closer look. "I'll have a word with our accountants about it, but I'm sure there's a perfectly reasonable explanation for the withdrawals. After all, Temarin hasn't had need of its war chest in two decades, and as you said, we are in the middle of a financial crisis. Perhaps it was decided that the money would be more useful elsewhere."

"By whom, exactly?" Leopold asks. Sophronia realizes she's never heard him angry before, not even last night when she explained exactly what the documents meant. He's angry now, though, his voice quiet and steady but his eyes blazing. "Because the document shows that those withdrawals were made after my father's death, but I certainly never signed off on them."

An uneasy silence falls over the table, only broken when Queen Eugenia leans across the table to take hold of her son's hand. "Oh, Leo," she says with a soft smile. "Your father would be so proud to see you take control of things, but darling, you must remember that he trusted Lord Covier, Lord Verning, and me to help you rule. Sometimes we had to make some small decisions in your absence—it is our duty to you and to Temarin. It was your father's final wish."

Sophronia sees the moment Leopold begins to soften and doubt the numbers he's seen with his own eyes. She braces herself for his reversal, but instead he shakes his head.

"My father's final wish was for me to be king," he says. "I don't think I have been a good one so far, but I will be. And I intend to start by finding out exactly what happened to the war chest and replenishing it immediately." He pulls his hand from his mother's and leans back in his seat. "We can go through the accounts item by item if you like, but I will be lowering Temarin's countrywide taxes by half next month, and Kavelle's city taxes as well."

The three council members splutter. "Your Majesty, that number is far too great," Lord Covier says. "Perhaps we can work toward it in time, but one percent might be a more reasonable—"

"Half," Leopold repeats. "Sophronia and I have gone over our accounts and there will be some sacrifices to make, but I assure you it is doable and necessary, given the damage our careless spending has wrought on our subjects over the last year. In addition, I would like to make it known that no nobleman's regional taxes can exceed ten percent of a commoner's income."

It's a plan he and Sophronia came to together, after going over the accounts—a number small enough so that the people may recover their losses from past months while allowing them to also live and save for the future, but large enough to cover necessities and begin rebuilding the war chest in case those funds cannot be recovered. Hearing Leopold lay out the plan in his clear voice, with a steady gaze that betrays no weakness, is enough to make her swoon a bit.

"It is too much, Your Majesty," Lord Verning says, shaking his head. "Your court will be devastated by the loss of their income."

"It is one of the perks of being of noble birth," Lord Covier adds. "You understand that, Your Majesty. What is the point of being king if you cannot live in luxury?"

Leopold frowns. "My father might have died before he could teach me much about being a king," he says. "But he made sure I knew that it was a duty, not a gift. That duty is to the people of Temarin, and it is not one that can be ignored."

"Eugenia," Lord Covier says. "Surely you can help explain why this is a terrible idea?"

Queen Eugenia opens her mouth but quickly closes it again when she catches Sophronia's eye. Though Sophronia doesn't speak so much as a word of threat, Queen Eugenia hears it all the same, and for the barest instant, she looks like she'd like nothing better than to launch herself across the table and strangle Sophronia with her bare hands. Instead, she forces a smile and turns to her son.

"Of course, darling," she says. "It is a brilliant plan and I'm sure Temarin will be very grateful to you for it."

That night, Sophronia tells Violie all about the meeting while Violie helps her out of her dress and into her nightgown and plaits her hair. Sophronia skips over certain bits that Violie doesn't need to know—like how she'd blackmailed Queen Eugenia into agreeing with her or that her suspicions about Eugenia conspiring with her brother have been all but confirmed—but she doesn't see the harm in telling Violie the rest. If Violie hadn't given her the first batch of household bills, she might never have known how bad things in Temarin were.

"You should have seen Leopold," Sophronia tells her. "He was magnificent. I barely recognized him."

"It sounds like you were quite magnificent yourself, Sophie," Violie says, securing Sophronia's plait with a scrap of yellow ribbon.

Sophronia blushes, but she knows Violie's right—she *was* magnificent. She stood her ground against three of the most powerful people in Temarin; she held them responsible for their actions, pushed for a solution they hated, and even blackmailed a queen to see it done. She can't help but remember all the times she folded before her mother at the slightest hint of conflict. She'd never been able to stand up for herself.

But this wasn't about standing up for herself, she realizes. It was about standing up for others, for the people of Temarin who didn't have the power to stand up for themselves. She did that, and she feels proud of herself for it.

"The empress won't be pleased, I'd bet," Violie says, drawing Sophronia out of her thoughts.

She frowns, catching Violie's eye in the large gilded mirror.

"The empress?" she asks slowly. "What does my mother have to do with anything?"

Violie blinks twice before shaking her head. "Sorry, I

meant Queen Eugenia. Old habit, I suppose," she says with a laugh. "Empresses, queens, it gets a bit confusing sometimes. Why are there different names for the same position, anyway?"

"Oh," Sophronia says, somewhat surprised. She's heard the story so much growing up that it's ingrained in her mind, but even though Violie grew up mere miles away from Sophronia, it was an entirely different world. "Well, about five centuries ago, the Bessemian Empire included the whole continent—Temarin, Cellaria, and Friv as well. A few wars later, lands were surrendered, independences won, and Bessemia became the small but proud nation it is today, but the title remains. As you said, old habits."

Violie smiles. "Well, what I meant was that Queen Eugenia couldn't have been pleased. She sent her maid to request a meeting with you tomorrow morning, though *request* might be too mild a word," she says.

"Oh," Sophronia says, her stomach sinking, though she isn't surprised. Eugenia doesn't strike her as the type to go down without a fight. "What did you tell her?"

"That your schedule was quite busy and you couldn't possibly fit in a meeting with her for three days at least," Violie says with a wink. "It seemed smart to give her some time to let her anger go from a boil to a simmer."

"And it reminds her that she is no longer queen," Sophronia says. "Brilliantly done, Violie."

It's Violie's turn to blush. "I think you might be rubbing off on me, Sophie."

When Sophronia says her good-nights to Violie and slips through the door that connects her dressing room to the bedroom she shares with Leopold, he's already in bed, sitting up against a pile of pillows with a book open on his lap. When he hears her come in, he looks up, his eyes bright.

"Do you know about tariffs?" he asks her.

Sophronia can't help but smile. He's taken to reading everything he can get his hands on over the last few days, constantly peppering her with questions about tax codes and economic theories. To her mind, they're silly questions—things she studied years ago that seem like child's play—but Leopold is enraptured by all of it. She catches sight of a stack of books on his bedside table with pages marked by bits of parchment.

"What about tariffs?" she asks, climbing into bed beside him.

"Well, apparently, if someone—say Lord Friscan—were to buy a horse from Friv instead of a perfectly fine horse from Temarin, we could impose a fee for him to import it. It looks like Temarin had tariffs in place until about fifty years ago, but they were repealed. What if we put them back into place? It would encourage the wealthy to put their money into Temarin's economy."

Sophronia doubts his mother will approve of *that*.

"I think that's a brilliant idea," she says. "Lord Friscan might disagree, though," she adds.

Leopold waves a dismissive hand. "If Lord Friscan wishes to buy yet another horse from outside Temarin for his already-overflowing prize stables, he can shoulder the cost."

"The cost that will be paid to us," Sophronia points out.

"Ah, yes, but I had a thought about that," he says, putting his book aside and reaching for another, flipping through until he finds the right place. "A public fund," he says. "We had one about two hundred years back, during the Great Famine. My many-times-great-grandfather allotted treasury funds to establish the donation of food and necessities to those who couldn't afford them. We could bring it back and—"

Sophronia cuts him off with a kiss, taking both of them by surprise. When she pulls back, they're both blushing.

"What . . . what was that for?" he asks. "Not that I'm complaining, but . . ."

But she hasn't initiated any kind of physical contact since the hangings, and every time he's touched her, she's had to force herself not to recoil. She thought she'd done a good job of hiding it, but apparently not.

She shrugs. "All that talk of tariffs and philanthropy is very attractive," she says.

"I'll remember that," he laughs, then sobers. He puts both books on the nightstand and turns toward her. "If I could go back, Sophie, I'd do it all differently. When my father died so suddenly and his council swept in and said they would handle everything, I . . . was relieved. I was fifteen and I didn't want my life to change. I wasn't ready to be king and I knew it. I was glad to have an excuse not to take on the responsibility, glad that someone else would. If I could go back, *that's* what I would change. The state Temarin is in now is my fault."

Sophronia sees how much it hurts him to say those last words, sees the truth of them hit him square in the chest. She doesn't know if she's forgiven him for it, doesn't know if she'll ever be able to look at him without seeing those bodies hanging from the gallows, but she also understands that they had very different upbringings. He was a boy who wasn't prepared to be king, and the blame for that isn't his alone.

"We can't change what's past," she tells him, placing her palm against his cheek. "But I trust that you'll change the future."

"*We'll* change the future," he tells her, kissing her again, and she's glad he can't see her face, sure the myriad of lies she's told are suddenly etched onto it. When he pulls back, she's managed to school her features into a smile.

Leopold falls asleep with his arm around her waist, and she can feel his deep, even breaths soft against her neck. She can't sleep, though.

We'll change the future. She hears Leopold's words again and again in her mind, and she begins to imagine what that future might look like, if her mother's plan didn't exist. She sees them side by side on the Temarinian throne, sees them older and wiser, riding through a cleaner, happier Kavelle, where the people cheer their names; sees them leading council meetings together, like they did today, but with advisors who respect them. She sees them ruling, together, for the rest of their lives, and she knows they could do it. She knows it deep in her bones.

The only thing she doesn't know is how that future and the one her mother's been plotting for can coexist.

The next morning, Sophronia sits down to write her mother a letter she likely should have written immediately after her conversation with Sir Diapollio. She needed proof that the message from King Cesare was legitimate, she tells herself, but she knows that isn't the whole truth. She was afraid to tell her mother that Eugenia and Cesare were plotting to take Temarin out of her grasp. She was afraid her mother would find some way to twist it into being Sophronia's fault.

But she has not only confirmed those suspicions but started undermining Eugenia's plans, and she knows her mother cannot find fault with her now—she might even be proud, though that feels like too much to hope for.

Still, Sophronia is proud of herself, and that feels like enough.

She details the events of the last week in full, including the letter from Cesare to Eugenia word for word, then tells her mother the steps she is taking to undo the damage Eugenia has done. She knows her mother wants Temarin to fall, but on their terms, not Eugenia and Cesare's. If Cellaria manages to get control of Temarin, Bessemia will have a hard time conquering both.

Feeling quite pleased with herself, Sophronia uses the Hartley Obfuscation to code the message into a bland and boring letter about the Temarinian weather and gives it to Violie to deliver to Bessemia.

Daphne

When the empress summoned the princesses to the archery field for a lesson a month before their sixteenth birthday, Daphne was thrilled. Ever since she'd first picked up a bow at the age of eight, after her mother's spies learned that Prince Cillian loved archery, she'd felt like it was a part of her. She would spend most afternoons on the field, with the string pulled taut and the feathered tail of the arrow brushing her cheek before she let it soar through the air. Few things were as satisfying as the sound of the arrow's point piercing the target.

But her mother wasn't waiting for them alone. With her was a group of five young men Daphne recognized right away—archers. She'd seen them compete at the last tournament, though none of them had made it to the semifinals. All of them had been, in Daphne's opinion, entirely average.

"Your lucky day, looks like," Beatriz said, looping her arm through Daphne's and giving her a quick grin before her eyes darted over the boys. "Though it might be mine, too," she adds thoughtfully.

"If you make it through the day without flirting, I'll give

you my new shoes. Those lavender heeled slippers with the bows you were coveting," Daphne told her, mostly because she knew Beatriz would fail horribly, though it would be fun to watch her try to control herself.

"Those shoes are gorgeous, but I don't want them *that* badly," Beatriz said with a laugh.

"Add my new hat to the pot," Sophronia said from Beatriz's other side, sharing a conspiratorial look with Daphne.

Beatriz scowled at Sophronia, but she was fighting a smile. "Throw that violet day dress in and you've got a deal," she said.

Sophronia looked at Daphne with raised eyebrows and an amused smile. "Deal," she said. "But the second you bat your eyelashes or drop any kind of innuendo, *we* get to borrow whatever we like from your wardrobe for a month."

"Two months," Daphne corrected.

Beatriz pursed her lips. "Fine," she said. "But it's a moot point anyway. I can behave myself."

When they reached the empress, she greeted her daughters with her usual tight-lipped smile.

"I thought we would have a little fun today, my doves," she said. "Let's have an archery competition, shall we?"

Her eyes lingered on Daphne as she spoke, and Daphne stood a little straighter, trying to hide her own smile. Beatriz always flourished in their seduction lessons, while Sophronia did best with coding and bookwork. Daphne's skills were usually strongest in lockpicking and poisons, but those talents weren't quite as showy. Winning an archery tournament, though—that would certainly impress her mother.

They were paired off then, and Daphne easily defeated her first opponent. Sophronia and Beatriz advanced as well, though neither came as close to the bull's-eye as Daphne had managed. In the next round, she beat Beatriz without even trying, while Sophronia lost gracefully to the last of the men.

He had better aim than Daphne expected, though his arrow had a habit of veering left.

"All right," the empress said with a gracious smile that managed to not show teeth. "Our last round. Sir Aldric, you first."

Sir Aldric stepped forward and lifted his bow. His right shoulder was too high, Daphne thought. He needed to relax it before he—

As soon as she thought it, he released the arrow and it predictably veered off, just barely landing on the target.

Daphne smothered a smile as she stepped forward and aimed her arrow. This would be easier than she expected, but that didn't mean she wasn't going to show off.

She narrowed her eyes on the target, took a deep breath, and let her arrow fly.

It landed smack in the middle, a perfect bull's-eye.

She spun toward her sisters, no longer bothering to hide the grin spreading over her face. Beatriz and Sophronia both cheered, rushing toward her and throwing their arms around her in a flurry of silk and ruffles and lace. When they pulled apart, though, Daphne's eyes searched for her mother, longing to see her approval.

Instead, her mother's expression was stony as ever, the corners of her mouth pulled into a frown.

"Sir Aldric," she said, turning toward the man. "Tell me, how did this outcome make you feel?"

For a moment, Sir Aldric looked surprised at the question. He glanced at Daphne, then back at the empress. "There are many tournaments, Your Majesty, one cannot expect to win them all. The princess has a good arm and a good eye."

"That wasn't what I asked," the empress said, her frown deepening. "How did the outcome make you feel?"

Sir Aldric shrugged, considering the answer. "No man likes to lose, I'll admit."

"Of course not," the empress said, looking at Daphne, even as she continued to address Sir Aldric. "My daughter bested you—quite soundly, I might add. What do you think of her?"

"As I said, she has an admirable talent," he said carefully.

"She does," the empress said—exactly what Daphne longed to hear, but not in that voice, not said like a curse. Daphne held her breath, waiting for the other shoe to drop. "But you don't love her for it, do you?"

At that, Sir Aldric looked even more bewildered, and Daphne wanted to sink into the ground beneath her feet. Just moments ago, she had been proud and victorious; now she had never felt more like a failure.

"She doesn't entice you," the empress continued, pacing toward Daphne. "You have no desire to impress her, to woo her. You don't want her in your bed."

The words landed like punches. Sophronia steadied Daphne with a hand on her arm, giving her a reassuring squeeze, but Daphne barely felt it. All of her focus was on her mother, whom she had managed to disappoint once more, this time by succeeding.

"No," Sir Aldric said after a moment. "I suppose not, Your Majesty."

"Thank you, Sir Aldric," the empress said. "And the rest of you. You may leave us now."

As the men filed away, the air went still and silent.

"It was a tournament," Beatriz said when they were gone. "Daphne won. What's wrong with that?"

"There is only one tournament, only one prize," the empress said, her eyes still on Daphne. "If you hope to control your princes, you must remember to be what they want you to be. And no man wants a woman who emasculates him."

Daphne frowned, trying to wrap her mind around the lesson—and it was a lesson. Things with her mother always were. But this . . . The empress had spent years grooming them, training them, making them the best they could be. Now she wanted them to be less impressive, to dull themselves to protect a fragile ego?

"Sir Aldric is a sore loser," Beatriz continued, shaking her head. "All men aren't like that."

"If you believe that, you're more naïve than I thought," the empress scoffed. "And you forget—these aren't men we're discussing. They're princes—spoiled boys who are used to getting everything they want. If you don't understand your opponent, you've already lost. Do you understand, Daphne?"

Daphne looked up at her mother and forced herself to nod. "I understand, Mother."

In the week since Daphne's theft of the king's seal, she's begun to spend more time exploring the castle grounds. It started with the stables, and the stable hands there are always quick to saddle a horse for her.

Her morning rides are refreshing—she hadn't realized how much she had missed riding until she started again. And it has allowed her to explore more of the grounds—the thicket of woods to the north, the meadow to the south. In her mind, it doesn't compare to Bessemia. The trees are mostly skeletal, and even though it's only fall, there is already a thick blanket of snow covering the ground. But fresh air is fresh air, and Daphne will take it however she can get it. Her happiest discovery on these rides has been the eastern field, set up with large straw targets, not so different from the ones she used to use for archery practice.

When she got back to the castle after that discovery, she asked a maid for a bow and arrows, and a set appeared at the foot of her bed that evening, polished and new, carved from wood so dark it was nearly black. It was different from the one she'd left back home—stiffer, less accustomed to her grip—but the second she got onto the field and lifted the bow in her arms, pulling the string back, part of her felt comfortable for the first time since she'd come to Friv.

It's been months since she's shot an arrow, not since that lesson of her mother's, which left her embarrassed, furious, and brimming with something she could only describe as shame. She was so out of practice she didn't even hit the target the first few times. But as the days pass, it slowly comes back to her, and she remembers why she loves it, the feeling of the bow pulled taut in her hands, the flex of the muscles in her arms and back, making her feel strong and capable and sure. The feeling of releasing the arrow, like letting out a heavy sigh.

Just a few days after she started practicing, and she's already getting back to where she was before. Her arrows usually find the target now, and they are making their way closer and closer to the bull's-eye. It feels good, to see her progress, to feel like she has proven something, even if there is no one else around to see it.

She nocks a new arrow and lifts her bow again, focusing on the bull's-eye. She takes a deep, steadying breath and—

"Drop your shoulder."

She spins toward the voice, in the process accidentally releasing the arrow and sending it just past Bairre's left ear.

He doesn't flinch, instead keeping his eyes on her and merely raising an eyebrow.

"If you're hoping to kill me, you need to work on your aim."

"If I were hoping to kill you," she tells him, nocking another arrow, "poison would be far less conspicuous. Less messy, too."

She turns back toward the target and aims again. After a second, she realizes Bairre was right—her shoulder is so tense it's almost touching her ear. She forces herself to relax it before letting the arrow fly.

It isn't a bull's-eye, but it's solidly in the smallest ring around it. She drops the bow to her side and turns back to Bairre.

"Did you come out here to accuse me of theft again?" she asks him.

"I apologized for that," he says, shaking his head.

"Only because your father made you," Daphne points out.

He doesn't deny it. Instead he reaches behind him to draw his own bow, carved from the same dark wood as hers.

"Mind if I join you?" he asks.

Daphne shrugs. "It's a big field, plenty of room for us both," she says before mentally kicking herself. If her mother were here, she would chide her for her sharp tone—she needs Bairre to like her, to desire her. As it is, they can't have a conversation that lasts longer than a few minutes without insulting each other.

He moves to the target next to her, lifting his bow and pulling an arrow from the quiver behind his back. She watches him for a moment before forcing herself to speak.

"I didn't know you enjoyed archery," she says. "I've heard Friv has some of the best tournaments in the world. Have you competed?"

He looks at her, surprised, before shaking his head. "It's just a hobby for me," he says. "Cillian was in a class of his own, though, so we would practice together sometimes. There's something . . . relaxing about it."

She's surprised to hear her own thoughts spill from his lips. "It's hard to feel stressed after shooting pointed weapons at a target," she agrees.

"Especially when you can picture that target as my face?" he asks.

She opens her mouth to deny it, but when she looks at him, she's surprised to find he's almost smiling at her. It's too wry at the corners to be a true smile, but it's the closest she's seen from him.

"Well, whatever helps," she tells him before nocking another arrow.

This time, though, she hears her mother's voice in her mind. *There is only one tournament, only one prize.* As badly as she wants to prove to Bairre that she can hold her own, she needs him to like her more, and that means dulling herself.

It kills her to do it, but she lets her arrow go wide. It lands at the outer edge of the target with a thwack that Daphne feels in her soul. It's a game, she reminds herself, a means to an end, but still the mortification of failing rakes over her skin like hot nails.

"Rotten luck," he says, nocking his own arrow and taking aim at the target.

His form is terrible—his elbow is too low and his stance is too narrow. The effort of firing the arrow alone will be enough to knock him off-balance.

"Wait," she says with a sigh before approaching. She lifts his back elbow so it doesn't sag and send the arrow high. "Now square your hips."

"What?" he asks, glancing back at her over his shoulder, brow furrowed.

She nudges his front foot wider, then, feeling heat rise to her cheeks, she sets her hands on his hips, adjusting him so his entire torso is directed at the target.

"There," she says, dropping her hands away quickly. "Try now."

His gaze lingers on her a second longer, skeptical and uncertain, before he looks back at the target. He aims and releases the arrow. It lands just inches from the bull's-eye. For a moment, he just stares at the arrow in shock.

"How did you do that?" he asks her.

She shrugs. "I had a good teacher in Bessemia," she says.

"Right," he says, clearing his throat. "Your turn, then."

Daphne's smile is strained as she takes aim once more, this time letting the arrow go early so it doesn't even make it to the target, instead burying itself in the grass two feet short.

"Not your day, is it?" he asks.

She bristles but shoves her pride down. "Apparently not."

Daphne waits for him to nock his next arrow, but instead he just stares at her, his expression even more perplexed than usual.

"If I didn't know better, I'd say you were trying to shoot poorly," he says.

"Then you know less than I thought," she says. "My wrist is still a bit sore from my fall."

It's a lie, but a believable one.

"May I?" he asks, holding his hand out.

Daphne places her left hand in his, letting him unbutton the leather glove and peel it back from the pale skin of her wrist. He turns it over in his hand, brushing his thumb over her pulse, making her heartbeat pick up. She wants to pull away from him, to tug her glove back over her skin before he can do that again, but she doesn't. Instead she remembers her training and takes a step closer to him, looking up and biting her lip.

"How does it look?" she asks him.

"Still a bit bruised," he says. "You should rest it a couple of days longer."

"I should," she agrees with the small, secret smile she had to spend weeks perfecting in the mirror. "But I've never been terribly good at resting."

He smiles back, but after a moment—far too soon—he looks away and drops her hand.

"Cillian always said you were clever," he tells her. "He said your letters were some of the wittiest things he'd ever read—and he read a lot, so you can take that as a high compliment."

The words sit like tar in the pit of her stomach. She doesn't want to think about the dead prince, the one she wrote letters to by candlelight, the one she can't even mourn.

"Oh?" she forces herself to say. "And do you agree?"

He laughs, but he sounds vaguely uncomfortable. "Maybe too clever for your own good. Tell me, would you have let Cillian win at archery as well? Or is it because I'm so terrible at it?"

Daphne goes still. "I didn't realize it was a matter of winning or losing," she says. "I thought we were only practicing."

"Really?" he asks, raising his eyebrows. "Because the look in your eyes says otherwise. And you flinch as soon as you fire the arrow—almost like you know exactly where it will go. So is it pity? Or false flattery? Because I think I've had enough of both in the last couple of weeks."

That gives her pause, and for a moment, she only looks at him, getting a glimpse beyond the furrowed brow and angry jawline and the resentment in his eyes. For the first time, he looks like a boy who lost his brother and had his life turned upside down in a single moment.

"I'm sorry," she says, and this time there is no sarcasm in her voice. "I didn't . . . shall we go again?"

He hesitates for a second before nodding and nocking another arrow.

This time, his form is better. She can tell he's checking himself for the corrections she made last time, though a part of her still wants the excuse to place a hand on his shoulder or hip—anywhere, really. Stars above, she's becoming as shameless as Beatriz!

When he releases the arrow, it grazes the bull's-eye, landing just outside.

"Well done," she says, meaning it.

"Better than I usually do," he admits. "The elbow adjustment helped."

"You're welcome," Daphne says before taking her own stance and raising her bow.

She runs through her inner checklist, making sure her shoulders are dropped, her elbow in place, her hips squared. She takes aim and releases the arrow, sending it flying into a perfect bull's-eye.

When she catches sight of Bairre's expression, she has a second of panic. His expression is unreadable, and she's reminded of how Sir Aldric looked when she beat him, how he told her mother he found her unattractive because of it. For a second, she worries that her pride has ruined any feelings Bairre might have had—if they ever existed; worries that she's killed her mother's plans thoroughly.

But then something in his face shifts and he almost smiles.

"Impressive," he says. "You might even have given Cillian a challenge. He would have been mad about you. He already was, just through letters, but in person he wouldn't have stood a chance."

Daphne glances away before she forces herself to meet his gaze.

"And you?" she asks him. "Do you stand a chance?"

Bairre holds her gaze for a moment before looking away, his jaw flexing.

"I'll let you be," he says after a moment. "I didn't mean to interrupt."

She opens her mouth to tell him he's not interrupting, to ask him to stay, but he's already walking back to the castle, the answer to her question still locked away.

Sophronia

Sophronia dunks a miniature sponge cake into her cup of coffee and takes a bite without looking up from the page she's been studying for the better part of an hour. The new draft of the updated tax code is a dense beast of a document—Sophronia suspects intentionally—and she's found error after error. Does Lord Covier believe that if he drowns the important information in unnecessary words, she will miss it?

Actually, she wouldn't be surprised if that's exactly what he believes.

She sets her coffee and cake down and picks up her quill, circling a particularly verbose sentence that rambles on long enough to take up half the page.

"What good will announcing lower taxes do if the people don't understand a word of the new policy?" she grumbles aloud.

Leopold glances up at her from the other side of the sitting room, hunched over a piece of parchment with his own quill in hand.

"Perhaps it's an issue of the language barrier?" he asks.

She shoots him an annoyed look. "I guarantee you, Leopold, my Temarinian vocabulary is larger than that of many villagers. How many do you think will know the meaning of *verisimilitude*?"

He frowns. "Did Covier throw that in there? *I* don't even know what it means."

"Neither does he, apparently, since he used it incorrectly," Sophronia says, striking through that sentence altogether. "One would almost think he's *hoping* no one understands a word of this. We should really think about replacing him and Verning," she adds. She knows better than to even suggest he replace his mother, and besides, it is handier to keep Eugenia close. Sophronia hasn't received a response from her own mother yet, and she's sure the empress will have ideas of her own for how to keep Eugenia from ruining their plans.

"Let's get through this afternoon first," Leopold says.

This afternoon, they are to go down to Kavelle along with Eugenia and Leopold's brothers to announce the lowered taxes. It's something she's both excited about and dreading, and she knows Leopold is anxious as well. He's been tweaking his speech all morning, and he's eaten nearly the entire plate of sponge cakes she made.

"You're giving good news," she reminds him. "They'll be cheering your name by the time you're through."

There's a knock on the sitting room door, and without waiting for an answer, Eugenia bustles in. Her eyes fall on Leopold first and she greets him with a broad, warm smile, but when she notices Sophronia it dies on her face.

"Oh, you're both here," she says. "How nice."

"Actually," Leopold says, glancing at the clock hanging above the marble mantel, "I'm late to meet Gideon and Reid—I told them I would walk them through everything today. Is it all right if I bring the rest of the cakes with me? Might help calm their nerves."

"Yes, *their* nerves," Sophronia teases.

Leopold kisses her cheek. "Are you done with that?" he asks, nodding toward her papers. "I can drop them off with Covier on my way."

"Just about," Sophronia says, striking through another sentence and passing the pile to Leopold. "Tell him it needs to be simpler—language that even children can understand. We don't want anything misinterpreted."

"I'll tell him," Leopold says. As he passes his mother on the way out, he stops to give her a quick kiss on the cheek as well.

"Not *too* many sweets for your brothers!" Eugenia calls after him, but the door shuts before she finishes. She sighs and turns back to Sophronia, and Sophronia can see the instant the facade falls and Eugenia goes from being a doting mother to being an adversary.

"Sophie," she says, inclining her head.

"Genia," Sophronia replies, matching the woman's cold smile. "Today should be quite exciting—Leopold's nervous, though. I couldn't believe it when he told me he'd never given a speech in Kavelle before! One would think he'd be a familiar face to the people he rules over."

Eugenia doesn't respond for a moment. Instead, she tilts her head to one side and looks Sophronia over with a critical eye. "It won't work, you know," she says.

Sophronia frowns. "Lowering taxes? I don't see why it wouldn't, but we can go over the figures again if you like—"

"They'll never love you," Eugenia interrupts, coming to sit across from Sophronia and pouring herself a cup of coffee as if they're discussing the latest fashions. "Oh, Leopold might be enamored at the moment, but we'll see how quickly he tires of you once you've actually let him between your legs—don't insult me by lying, servants talk, you know that."

Sophronia, who had indeed been about to lie, closes her mouth again.

"And Temarin," Eugenia continues, clicking her tongue. "If the hearts of kings are fickle, Temarin's heart is downright tempestuous, especially toward foreigners."

Something in her words digs beneath Sophronia's skin, nettling her. It's the bitterness in her voice, but more than that, the hatred. She's heard Eugenia speak of Temarin with wariness before, but never with this level of vitriol. It occurs to Sophronia that this is the real Eugenia, the one plotting with her brother to conquer a country she hates. And if she is letting Sophronia see past all her illusions, it means she knows the game is up.

"I'm not you," Sophronia tells her.

Eugenia laughs. "No, you are not," she agrees. "That's just it. My husband never loved me, neither did this stars-forsaken country, but the true difference between us, Sophie, is that I never needed them to. You're so desperate to be loved that you would slit your own throat to endear yourself to vultures."

Sophronia is careful not to show how deep the words

cut. She suspects that they hurt worse because there is some truth to them.

"Oh, you don't need to worry for me, Genia," Sophronia tells her with a smile she doesn't even try to pass off as genuine. "I assure you I'm quite adept at recognizing vultures for *exactly* what they are."

Violie helps Sophronia dress for their trip to Kavelle, the two of them debating which dress will be best suited to the occasion—nothing ostentatious, which rules out the vast majority of her wardrobe, but still something regal and strong. Finally, they settle on a plain velvet gown in a deep plum, with only the barest touch of silver embroidery on the bodice. They forgo all jewelry except a tiara, though even that is the simplest one she owns, made of thin, spindly silver and studded with pearls.

"You are quite unfashionable," Violie proclaims, tucking the end of Sophronia's braid up in a simple bun and securing it with a pin. "But still every inch a queen."

Sophronia snorts. "Honestly? I prefer this," she admits, examining her reflection in the mirror. "Can you ask the other maids to start working on the rest of my wardrobe? Strip away all the jewels and embellishments. The entire court is bound to be upset with me, and I'd like to lead by example. And . . . ," she says, biting her lip and thinking about the conversation she had with Eugenia. She wouldn't be surprised if Eugenia had another card up her sleeve, and if she is getting desperate she will be all the more dangerous for it. Sophronia was sure enough of her suspicions to share them with her mother, but she needs to be ready with incontrovertible proof in case she needs to reveal Eugenia's treason to Leopold. "Did you ever find out about the sparkling wine from the brunch? Where it came from?" she asks.

Violie blinks. "I'm afraid I've run into a bit of a mystery there. I asked the kitchen staff—they said it was from the Cosella vineyard in the south of Cellaria."

"No mystery there," Sophronia says. "The best sparkling wines come from that area."

Violie nods, biting her lip. "But they couldn't provide an address. Eventually, I found an address for another vineyard in the area, the one the palace usually orders sparkling wine from. They haven't heard of any vineyard with the name Cosella."

Sophronia frowns. "That is curious," she says. "If they're charging so much per bottle, one would think they had a reputation."

"As I said, a mystery," Violie says.

"I'll write to my sister," Sophronia says. "Perhaps they serve the wine at the palace there."

"Perhaps," Violie says before pursing her lips. "It's an awful lot of trouble over a bottle of sparkling wine, isn't it?"

Sophronia shakes her head, giving Violie an embarrassed smile. "A quirk of mine, I'm afraid. Once I set my mind to a mystery, I can't rest till I see it solved. For my own edification."

Before Violie can respond, a maid pokes her head into the room. "Your Majesty, Duchess Bruna is here to see you—"

Duchess Bruna doesn't wait for the maid to finish,

elbowing past her and into Sophronia's dressing room, her face nearly the color of Sophronia's purple gown.

"Aunt Bruna," Sophronia says, offering her a pleasant smile. "I'm running late, but we can speak this evening, perhaps—"

"That Cellarian *bitch* cut my allowance!" Duchess Bruna erupts. "Can you *believe* the nerve? She has *always* hated me, Sophie, but this is a new low. You must put a stop to it right away."

Sophronia glances at Violie and dismisses her with a nod before turning back to Bruna.

"Actually, Aunt Bruna," she begins, as gently as possible, "that wasn't Eugenia's decision—it was mine, and Leopold's."

Bruna stares at Sophronia as if she's just started speaking Frivian. "I am the sister of the late king, Sophie," she says, her voice cold. "It is utterly thoughtless to treat me this way. That money is what I am owed."

Sophronia lets out a long sigh, glancing at the clock hanging on the wall. "Unfortunately, Aunt Bruna, Temarin's finances are quite in shambles—you aren't the only one being affected. The entire royal family will be cutting spending, Leopold and I more than anyone. I'm hopeful it will only need to be a temporary measure, until Temarin gets back on its feet, but it is a necessary one."

Bruna shakes her head, her jaw clenched. "This is . . . illegal," she bites out.

Sophronia has to bite her own lip to keep from laughing—that will surely upset the duchess more. "I assure you, it isn't. We will all have to make sacrifices, Aunt Bruna. Do you need help going over your books to make the necessary adjustments?" she asks.

"Of *course* I do," Duchess Bruna snaps, though Sophronia's relieved to see that her face has returned to a more natural shade. "You took the only maid of mine with legible handwriting, you know."

Sophronia frowns, certain she must have misunderstood. "Violie?"

"The rest of them all write like writhing chickens—how is it a Bessemian peasant girl has better Temarinian writing than those born and raised here?"

Bruna seems to be talking more to herself than Sophronia, but Sophronia turns the question over in her mind. How indeed?—especially because Violie told her she didn't know how to read.

Sophronia counts twenty guards that escort their carriages from the palace entrance to the gates. A platform has been set up just on the other side. There are two carriages, the first carrying Sophronia and Leopold, the second carrying Eugenia, Gideon, and Reid.

The sound of the crowd greets them even before the carriage pulls to a stop beside the gates.

"Ready?" Sophronia asks Leopold.

He hesitates, pulling the curtains slightly aside so he can see what awaits them. "It's a lot more people than I've spoken to at court," he says.

"You'll do fine," she tells him. "Everyone loves good news."

He nods, turning back toward her. "A kiss for luck?" he says with a grin.

Sophronia laughs and leans across the carriage to kiss him quickly on the lips, trying to ignore Eugenia's words echoing in her mind: *We'll see how quickly he tires of you once you've actually let him between your legs.* She forces a smile. "Let's not keep them waiting."

He raps his knuckles against the window and a guard opens the door, helping them out of the carriage and into the bright afternoon sun. Sophronia takes Leopold's proffered arm and they make their way toward the towering gates that lead to Kavelle. Just through the golden curlicues, Sophronia can see a crowd of people gathered. Leopold was right—there are more people than she can count waiting to hear him speak.

A wall of guards guides them through the gates and up onto the platform, and Sophronia gives Leopold's arm one last squeeze of reassurance before letting go and stepping back to stand beside his mother and brothers. The noise from the crowd is deafening, but she can't tell if it's made up of cheers or curses. Both, perhaps. But when Leopold clears his throat and lifts a hand, the crowd falls silent.

For a long moment, he freezes, staring out at the crowd. Though she can't see his face, Sophronia notes the tension in his shoulders, how they hitch up toward his ears. He doesn't appear to be breathing.

"Good afternoon, good people of Kavelle," he says before clearing his throat again. "I know that Temarin has been facing difficult times, and nowhere is that more clear than here in the capital, but as your king, I will be doing everything in my power to see us through this."

"Horseshit!" a man cries out from the middle of the crowd. Sophronia's eyes find him quickly, as do the guards making their way through the crowd. When one of them grabs the man's arm roughly, Leopold holds his hand up again.

"Release him, please," he says, and after a second of confusion, the guard does as he's told. Even the man looks bewildered.

"I have been . . . lax in my duties since taking the throne, and I can't blame you for not believing me, but I assure you I'm in earnest. Starting next month, the taxes you owe will be halved."

There are whispers at that, a swell of quiet voices that buzz through the space until they nearly drown Leopold out altogether. "We will also be setting up a food distribution system through which those in need will be able to pick up rations, free of cost."

There is more murmuring at that. Sophronia scans the crowd, trying to discern whether the people are pleased or not, and her eyes snag on a familiar face. There, near the front of the crowd, is Violie. It isn't surprising—there are other palace servants she recognizes dimly, come to hear news that affects them as much as anyone—but the surprising thing is that Violie isn't alone. A boy of about eighteen stands just behind her left shoulder, whispering something in her ear that seems to annoy Violie. She frowns and she says something back—something, Sophronia thinks, that appears unpleasant. A lovers' quarrel, perhaps. Another secret Violie has been keeping.

Sophronia takes note of the boy's face—sharp angles and dark brown eyes, black hair in need of a cut, skin gold from the sun, a pale white scar across his left cheek. Violie catches her watching and turns a shade pinker before offering her a smile. Sophronia forces herself to return it before turning her attention back to Leopold.

"Temarin has faced troubled times before, and we have always come out the other side of them—stronger and united," he says.

There is a smattering of applause—some of it even seems genuine, but it isn't enough to cover the jeers. Certainly not loud enough to cover up the woman screaming "Liar!" at the top of her lungs as she pushes her way to the front of the crowd. She is slight in stature, with wiry gray hair pulled back from her face and partly covered by a dusty blue kerchief. Her wrinkled face is bright red from the effort of yelling, but her eyes are determined and focused on Leopold.

The guards in the crowd start moving toward her, but again, Leopold raises his hand to stop them, allowing her to come to the platform.

"How many won't come out the other side of this, *Your Majesty*?" she demands, her voice dripping with derision. "How many of our sons have been killed for stealing to survive, all the while you've been stealing from *us* to fill your coffers? How many parents have starved so that their children are fed? My own daughter died in labor because she couldn't afford to pay for a doctor after your men took her last penny in taxes. How many others have stories like hers?"

The crowd close enough to hear her nods, and Sophronia wonders just how many of them have lost people they loved because of Leopold's naïveté. It is one thing to understand the cost in terms of ink and paper, but another to see it reflected in the eyes of so many people.

Leopold must feel it as well, because he has no answer for the woman. Sophronia isn't sure she does either, but before she knows what she's doing, she's stepping up beside Leopold, placing her hand on his arm.

"We're sorry to hear about your losses—about all of your losses," she says, surprised at how clear and level her voice comes out. "King Leopold and I will do everything we can to—"

Before she can finish, someone in the crowd throws a stone—a small thing, the size of a fat grape—and it strikes her cheek. It surprises her more than anything, but when she lifts her fingers to her face, they come away bloody.

"Sophie!" Leopold exclaims, pulling her behind him as more stones begin to join the first.

"Seems only fair," a man near the front yells, throwing a larger stone that hits Leopold square in the shoulder, knocking him back a step, "to repay death with death!"

"Get back to the gates," Leopold says to her as guards begin to close in around them and the crowd becomes more agitated. He keeps hold of her hand as they hurry toward Eugenia and the princes. When they meet, Sophronia grabs hold of Reid's hand and the five of them huddle together. Another stone hits Sophronia's hip, a third smacks the back of her head hard enough that she sees stars, but she forces herself to ignore the throbbing pain and keep moving, putting her arm around Reid's shoulders to shield the boy from the attacks.

The guards form a tight circle around them, but the barrier doesn't hold—before they are even off the platform, three guards have fallen, one stabbed with a dagger, one clobbered over the head, and a third dragged down into the crowd. Sophronia's heart thunders in her chest as the people get closer, shouting curses and threats and Temarinian words she doesn't recognize but that don't sound positive. Someone grabs hold of her gown, tearing the hem. Another person pulls at Leopold's arm, knocking him off-balance before a guard pushes them away.

They are nearly to the gate when Reid is torn away from her, one moment standing beside her, the next gone altogether, her hand suddenly empty.

"Reid!" Sophronia screams, but the guards are already pushing them through the gate, the iron bars slamming closed as soon as they're through, but even the gate isn't enough to stop the crowd. They reach through the bars, throw stones, shout.

"Reid," she says, pulling Leopold to face her.

"You're bleeding," he says, looking dazed. He's been hit as well, a streak of blood marring his temple. "What about Reid?" he asks, frowning. "Where is he?"

"The crowd pulled him away from me," she says, panicked tears stinging at her eyes. "He's gone!"

Leopold lets out a curse and lets go of her, turning away to summon the guards.

"Find him," he says, his voice cracking. "Now."

The guards draw their swords and slip back into the angry crowd.

"Leopold," Eugenia says, hurrying toward him, her eyes red with tears. "Where is he? What happened?" she demands. "I saw him just seconds ago and then . . ." She swings her gaze to Sophronia. "You."

"The crowd," Sophronia says weakly, the guilt of it already outweighing any kind of logic. "They grabbed him—I tried to hold on but—"

"This was *your* idea," Eugenia seethes, stepping toward Sophronia until they are inches apart. She expects Eugenia to strike her, but before she can, Leopold shoulders his way between them.

"Enough," he says, his voice firm. "If you're giving blame, I'll take the lion's share," he tells his mother, running a hand through his hair that comes away streaked with blood.

"Your Majesty," a guard says, approaching. "You're wounded—Queen Sophronia is too. You should be looked at."

"I'm fine," Leopold snaps. "But take Sophie, and my mother, and Gideon."

For the first time, Sophronia glances at Leopold's other brother. Gideon looks to be unharmed, but his face is pale and his eyes wide. He looks so much younger than his fourteen years.

"I'll stay," Sophronia says, slipping her hand into Leopold's. "I'm fine too."

It's only partly true—the back of her head is throbbing and should likely be looked at—but she's certainly as fine as Leopold is. If he isn't getting help, she isn't either.

"Your Majesty! Your Majesty!" a voice at the gates cries, and after a second, the guards part enough that Sophronia can see Reid, frightened but unharmed, with a stranger's hands on his shoulders. Or rather, not entirely a stranger. Sophronia recognizes him as the boy Violie was speaking with earlier, with the scar across his cheek. "I have him, he's not been hurt."

The guards open the gate and both Reid and the boy come through, Reid immediately running into Eugenia's arms, sobbing.

"You have my gratitude," Leopold says to the stranger, holding a hand out. "I was afraid . . ." He shakes his head. "Thank you . . . what's your name?"

"Ansel, Your Majesty," the boy says, bowing his head and taking hold of Leopold's hand, shaking it. "And no thanks is necessary—anyone would have done the same."

Leopold glances behind him, at the gates where the angry crowd can still be seen and heard. "I don't believe that's true," he says.

"Tell me, Ansel," Sophronia says, finding her voice. "I thought I saw you with my maid, Violie. Is she safe?"

"I believe so, Your Majesty," he says. "I saw her and some of the other palace maids slip back through the gates just before everything went sideways. From what I gathered, about half the crowd came armed and ready for a fight. I told Violie to get the others safe and then tried to warn the guards, but it was too late." He shakes his head. "I'm sorry, if I'd been faster—"

"No apologies necessary, Ansel," Leopold says. "You did all you could and more. My brother is alive because of you.

You must dine with us, please, so we can show our thanks. Next week? I'll have someone give you details."

Ansel smiles and bows again. "If you insist, Your Majesty, I would be honored."

As the guards usher Sophronia and Leopold toward the palace, she glances back at Ansel, who simply waves, but it does little to assuage her gnawing suspicion. If she can't trust Violie, she certainly doesn't trust him. She isn't sure she can truly trust anyone.

It's nearly an hour before Sophronia gets back to her rooms, her muscles aching and her whole body exhausted, though any physical wounds have been mended with a few pinches of stardust from the court empyrea. She wanted to stay while he tended to Leopold's head injury, but Leopold, the empyrea, and the royal physician all insisted she needed rest.

Though as soon as she sees Violie sitting by the roaring fire, she knows rest will have to wait awhile longer.

"You're back," Sophronia says as she toes off her slippers and removes her gloves. "I heard you made it back safely, but I'm glad to see it with my own eyes."

Sophronia realizes as she says the words that they aren't a lie. Maybe she's a fool for it—her mother would certainly say so—but no matter who Violie really is, who she is reporting to, Sophronia is glad she's safe.

Violie shakes her head. "I was never in any real danger," she says. "How are *you*?"

Sophronia can still feel the dull ache from where the stone struck the back of her head. The doctor said she would be fine, but the shock remains. Someone *hit* her. Someone, some stranger, hates her so much that they want her dead. Many someones, she supposes, if the jeers of the crowd were anything to go by. The thought of it makes her sick, but she forces a smile.

"I'll live," she says. "Leopold's wound was worse—he's still being looked at." She pauses. "Reid went missing, swept away by the crowd."

Violie's eyes widen. "He's just a child—is he all right?"

"He is," Sophronia says, watching her expression carefully. "All thanks to your friend."

Violie frowns, her brow furrowing. "My friend?" she asks.

"Ansel, I believe his name was," Sophronia says. "I saw you speaking with him just a moment before the riot broke out."

A faint spark of recognition flickers in Violie's eyes. "Oh, him," she says. "I'd never met him before; he just started talking to me—flirting, more like. I wasn't interested and told him as much. That's all."

Sophronia tilts her head, choosing her next words carefully. It won't do to let Violie know of her suspicions, but she'd like some answers. "He said he told you and the other palace servants that the riot was about to happen, that you should hurry back here."

Violie hesitates just long enough that Sophronia can see her reshaping her story—it's subtle, a flicker behind the eyes, something Sophronia wouldn't know to look for if she didn't know how to do it herself.

"Of course he said that," Violie says with a light laugh. "Some boys, Sophie, enjoy playing the role of hero—saving the prince wasn't enough praise for him, I suppose. He had to claim to save a gaggle of servant girls as well."

It's a good lie, Sophronia has to admit, but it's a lie all the same.

"How *did* you know to hurry back here, then? Did someone else tell you about the riot?"

Violie sighs and offers Sophronia a small, tight smile. "I'm no stranger to the shifting tempers of mobs," she says. "I saw it often enough in Bessemia."

Sophronia frowns. "There were mobs in Bessemia?"

"Not like that," Violie says quickly, then hesitates. "My mother was—*is*—a courtesan. Sometimes the men who came to the pleasure house she worked at would get angry with the girls, sometimes a group of our neighbors would gather to try to 'remove the stain of sin from our streets,' as they said. They didn't often turn violent, mind you, but I suppose I learned to recognize the signs of when they would, so that I could go for help. There's a shift in the energy. I felt it in that crowd, so I gathered the other servants and we made our way back. We'd barely got to the servants' entrance when that man threw the first stone."

Sophronia regards her as she speaks, noting every slight arch of her eyebrows, every flare of her nostrils, every shift in the inflection of her voice. She wonders where Violie learned to lie so well, or if it is simply a natural talent.

"Well, I'm glad you're safe," Sophronia tells her, letting it drop. "I'd like to get some rest—it's been a trying day."

“Of course,” Violie says, crossing to the wardrobe to find one of Sophronia’s nightgowns. In a few short, quiet moments, Violie helps her change and brushes her hair, Sophronia all the while watching her face in the vanity mirror.

Who is this girl? And, more importantly, who does she work for? Sophronia’s mother seems a plausible option, though again Sophronia thinks it’s a bit too obvious for her to send a Bessemian servant as a spy. Duchess Bruna is another possibility, though Violie helped Sophronia work explicitly against the duchess’s interest. The other possibility that comes to mind is Eugenia, though that wouldn’t make sense either.

“Oh,” Violie says, jerking Sophronia out of her thoughts. “Before I forget, there was a letter for you, from your mother.”

Sophronia’s heart speeds up, but she tries to appear uninterested. “Oh? I suppose I’ll take a look before bed.”

Sophronia waits until Violie heads off to sleep before she opens the letter, sitting up against her pillows as she unfolds it and scans her mother’s words. The letter isn’t in code, she notes, and there is no sign it has been tampered with, which raises more questions.

What you’re telling me is that Eugenia has done a better job of destabilizing Temarin than you have. Leave her to me. It seems you are having problems with the simplest of orders, so let me be plain: I don’t care about Temarin’s finances; I don’t care about

Temarin's peasants, and therefore you don't either. Do not delude yourself into believing you are a real queen, my dear. The role doesn't suit.

Sophronia immediately crumples the letter in her palm, not needing to read it a second time—the words will be scalded into her memory for a long while to come.

It isn't the cruelty that gets to her—*that* she's used to from her mother. It isn't even the insinuation that the empress is watching Sophronia, that she has someone close enough to her to deliver a message that made it to her unopened. Sophronia knows her mother well enough to expect both of those things. No, the thing that hits her the hardest is the quashing of hope that leaves Sophronia feeling like a fool for daring to hope in the first place.

Maybe her mother is right, maybe she is softhearted and weak.

The thing is, though, Sophronia doesn't feel weak. For the first time in her life, her mother's disapproval doesn't feel lethal. *The role doesn't suit,* her mother wrote, about Sophronia being queen. But these past days, that hasn't felt like the truth.

Sophronia drops her mother's letter into the cup of hot tea Violie left on her bedside table, watching the words melt away until they are illegible. Satisfying as it feels for the moment, Sophronia knows she can't silence the empress that easily.

Beatriz

Stardust.

That is the gift Beatriz's mother has sent her, hidden away in the false bottom of a small bejeweled music box along with a note:

> *Your time has come. Hide it on Lord Savelle. When he is discovered with it, Cesare's council will urge him to show mercy and send Savelle back to Temarin in order to avoid war. I trust you'll be able to convince him otherwise. Act quickly, I would hate for you to be caught with it instead, my dove.*

Beatriz can't bring herself to be surprised, really. In the two days that have followed the gift's arrival, she has realized this was, in many ways, inevitable. The empress wouldn't have told Beatriz to get close to Lord Savelle without a reason, and there is no surer way to start a war than by executing a country's ambassador.

Still, for two days Beatriz has skipped her routine of taking morning walks in the sea garden with Lord Savelle, knowing that every moment the stardust remains in her possession, her own life is at risk. Her mother threatened as much—and Beatriz has no illusions that the final line of her mother's letter is anything but a threat. She tells herself she is hesitating so that she can think up a plan, that she is waiting for the right moment, but that isn't the whole truth of it.

Today, though, Beatriz forces herself up with the sun. She makes her way out to the sea garden and finds it deserted, apart from one lone figure standing out amid the brightly colored water plants, his back to her and his hands buried in his pockets.

Beatriz approaches Lord Savelle, each step feeling heavier than the last. When she reaches the wet sand, she takes her shoes off, holding them in her hand as she walks the rest of the way.

"Ah, Princess," Lord Savelle says, turning toward her and looking mildly surprised. "I thought you'd grown bored with me."

"I could never," Beatriz says with a smile. "But I've had trouble sleeping the last few nights and was in no mood for company this early." It's not entirely a lie. Since she read her mother's letter two days ago, her thoughts have been keeping her up, though she hasn't felt that strange restlessness again since the night before she was summoned by the king.

"I confess I'm glad. I was beginning to worry about you," Lord Savelle tells her.

That makes Beatriz uncomfortable, though she can't quite say why. She isn't sure anyone has ever worried about her before. Her sisters, perhaps, but no more than she worries about them. She doubts her mother has worried about her, personally.

Lord Savelle turns his gaze to the horizon where the sun is just beginning to crest. "Many parts of Cellaria have lost their charm for me, you know—this alone never has."

Beatriz stands beside him as they watch the sun rise in silence, casting the sky and sea in shades of oranges and pinks.

"I used to bring Fidelia out with me to watch the sunrise," he tells her after a moment. Beatriz glances at him, frowning slightly. He's mentioned Fidelia quite a bit on these walks, but he's never told her that. "It was our ritual. She had trouble sleeping too," he adds, looking at Beatriz. "Usually after this, she would manage to sleep—sometimes until noon, but I never had the heart to force her up earlier."

"You were a good father," Beatriz tells him. She might not have any experience with fathers, but she certainly can't imagine going to her mother when she couldn't sleep—Empress Margaraux prizes her eight hours of sleep above most things, her daughters included.

"I was, I suppose . . . until I wasn't," he says, his smile turning sad. "It's a difficult thing, Princess, for a parent to be unable to protect their child."

Beatriz is aware of the vial of stardust in her pocket. She knows what she needs to do—pretend to lose her footing and then, when he reaches out to steady her, drop the vial into his pocket. It can be done in a matter of seconds. But she is frozen in place.

"I don't remember my father," she tells him instead. "He

died when I was only a few days old. Rumor has it that he never even held me, or my sisters, because he was so disappointed we weren't sons."

Lord Savelle looks at her, surprised. Beatriz is surprised at herself as well—those three sentences might just be more than she's ever said about her father before.

"I don't believe your daughter's death was your fault," she continues, glancing away and back toward the sun. "If there had been a way for you to protect her, I'm sure you would have found it."

For a moment, Lord Savelle doesn't say anything. Finally, he lets out a long breath. "Thank you, Princess."

"I told you, call me Beatriz," she says with a soft smile.

He smiles back but doesn't acknowledge her words. "I received a letter from King Leopold last night," he says. "Your sister is safe, but there was a riot in the city. The royal family was attacked by a mob of angry peasants."

Beatriz looks at him in alarm. "But Sophronia is safe?" she repeats, echoing his words.

"She was struck in the back of the head with a stone, apparently. Here, such an injury could have been serious, but I'm told the royal empyrea used stardust to heal her quickly. She's fine."

"Thank the stars," Beatriz murmurs.

"Tell me, Princess—" Lord Savelle begins.

"Beatriz," she reminds him, but he only smiles before continuing.

"Do your sisters have difficulty sleeping at night as well?" he asks.

Beatriz blinks. "Sorry?" she asks.

"You said you had difficulty sleeping at night," he reminds her. "I was wondering if your sisters were the same."

"No," Beatriz says after a moment. "Well, sometimes Sophronia, but she always says it's because her mind feels too busy, even when she's exhausted to her core. For me, it's different. Night falls and I don't feel tired at all, but sometimes I feel I could sleep an entire day away."

"More often lately?" he presses.

Beatriz considers it. "I suppose so," she says, forcing a laugh. "My body hasn't quite adjusted to Cellaria yet—it's bright out longer here, you know. There's less night to sleep through."

Lord Savelle makes a noncommittal noise in the back of his throat. "As I said, my daughter had similar troubles," he says. "Will you come see me if it gets worse?"

Beatriz frowns. "Worse?" she asks.

"I used to have an herbal blend of tea made for Fidelia—perhaps it will help you as well," he says with a shrug.

Beatriz's frown deepens. "Why?" she asks before she can stop herself.

"Because I'd have hoped someone would have done it for her," he says simply. "And because I believe your father would want someone to look after you."

From everything Beatriz has heard about her father, she doesn't believe that, but she can't bring herself to correct him.

The palace's clock tower begins to chime.

"Ah, I should be getting back," Lord Savelle says. "I have

a breakfast meeting with the king's council to update them about Temarin's affairs."

He turns to start walking back to the castle, and Beatriz feels her chance slipping away.

"Wait!" she says.

He turns back toward her, eyebrows raised. He's close enough that she can still do it, just as she planned—just a little stumble. He'll catch her. She'll slip the vial of stardust into his pocket. It should be easy.

But it isn't. Suddenly, it feels like an impossible task.

"Thank you," she says instead.

Lord Savelle gives her a quick nod before heading back toward the palace.

Beatriz tries to put Lord Savelle and his discomfiting concern for her well-being out of her thoughts. She'll go back down to the sea garden tomorrow morning, she tells herself, and this time she'll do what she must. Every time she tells herself this, though, she believes it a little bit less. Especially because, as dusk begins to fall, she finds herself getting that familiar tingling in her body, that alertness that tells her she won't be sleeping again tonight.

If that's going to be the case, she's determined that she won't be bored, and that she'll keep others up with her as long as possible. Which is why she invites Pasquale, Ambrose, Gisella, and Nicolo to an impromptu dinner on the beach. It turns into a lavish affair, for an outdoor meal, with a silk blanket laid out over the sand, big enough to fit thrice as many people comfortably. The palace chefs have prepared a basket of roasted pheasant, rolls of bread, carrots and parsnips, and tiny pies that fit in the palm of a hand, each stuffed with berries. And, of course, Gisella has managed to secure plenty of wine.

Dinner is consumed quickly enough, the five of them devouring the offerings, but the wine lasts a bit longer. When the moon is high in the sky, Beatriz can feel the energy of the party waning, and Pasquale begins fidgeting beside her. She knows it's only a matter of time before he suggests turning in.

Which is how Beatriz finds herself explaining the rules of a Bessemian drinking game, Confessions and Bluffs. She played it often over the last couple of years at balls and parties, though she's never been able to play it with her sisters—it's a terribly uninteresting game to play with people you know inside and out, after all. But she doesn't know these people, except perhaps Pasquale, and sometimes she thinks even he seems more mystery than not.

She tells herself that she suggests it for fun, to get to know her new friends better, but she knows that isn't the entire truth. Her mother didn't raise her to do things for fun, and she certainly didn't raise her to make friends. Confessions and Bluffs is a good way to gather information.

"It goes like this," she tells them, sitting cross-legged on the blanket, her veridian skirt spread around her in a circle of frothy silk. The wine bottle she holds in her hands is half empty, but there are several more to go. "I'll go first and confess something—it has to be something interesting, no boring facts about what desserts you prefer or the names of your childhood pets—and you lot will decide if the confession is the truth or if I'm bluffing. For each person who gets it right, I take a drink, but if you get it wrong, you drink. Simple, no?"

"Deceptively simple," Nicolo says from where he sits to her left, his long legs stretched out in front of him and his hands behind him so that his face is tilted up toward the sky. Beatriz tries not to notice how close his leg is to hers, but she'd have an easier time ignoring a flame held to the palm of her hand.

"Dangerously simple," Gisella adds, her voice a low purr in the night. She hugs her legs to her chest, her chin resting on top of her knees. Her blond hair is unbound from its usual style and hangs in loose waves around her shoulders.

Beatriz winks at her. "Aren't all the best drinking games dangerously simple?" she asks. "I'll go first so you can see how it's done. Once, at a ball in Bessemia, I ran through the gardens in my chemise on a dare."

The four of them exchange looks, but Pasquale is the first one to speak.

"Truth," he says. "I don't think you're one to turn down a dare."

After a second of contemplation, Gisella and Ambrose agree with Pasquale, but Nicolo frowns.

"Bluff," he says finally.

Beatriz purses her lips, and after a second she lifts the bottle to her lips for one drink before passing it to Pas, who looks surprised.

"The three of you lose," she says, nodding at Gisella and Ambrose as well.

Pasquale laughs, but he takes a drink before passing it to Ambrose. "I thought for sure that sounded like something you would do," he says.

Beatriz shrugs, leaning back on her hands. "It almost was," she says. "But the actual dare was to run through the gardens in my corset. My sister didn't think I'd go through with it, but as you said, I never turn down a dare."

"How did you know she was bluffing?" Pas asks Nicolo, shaking his head.

Nicolo shrugs. "Just lucky, I guess."

"And now it's your turn," Beatriz tells him. "What will your confession be?"

Nicolo holds her gaze as he takes the bottle of wine from his sister, and she realizes that the words sounded more flirtatious than they should have. Not that anyone else seems to have heard it, but then again, that's how Beatriz talks to everyone.

"You know the court treasurer?" Nicolo asks, leaning forward and tearing his gaze away from Beatriz to look at the others. "Lord Nodreno?"

"Vile man," Gisella says, wrinkling her nose. "I caught him trying to accost a serving girl once. He stopped when he saw me, but I doubt it was the first or the last time."

"That's the one," Nicolo says. "He was opposing a motion my father was trying to get before the king, so I . . . slipped some herbs into his midday glass of wine. It didn't do anything serious, but it did render him unable to get more than a foot from the privy for the next few hours, and he missed the council meeting."

Gisella gives a very loud, unladylike snort. "I don't know if that's true, but I hope it is, so I'm going to believe you."

Pasquale considers it for a moment, and Beatriz can practically see the gears turning in his mind, no doubt weighing the morality of the move as well as the believability of it. "What herbs?" he asks after a second.

Nicolo glances at Beatriz. "Are questions allowed?" he asks her.

She inclines her head. "Any good bluffer knows how to defend their lies. I'll allow it."

Nicolo turns his attention back to Pasquale. "Bichterwood leaves and helve."

Pasquale frowns. "Bluff," he says.

Ambrose leans forward. "Pas knows his herbs," he says. "I'm with him on this one. Beatriz?"

Beatriz chews on her bottom lip and regards Nicolo thoughtfully. "Truth," she says after a moment.

Nicolo smiles before taking two quick drinks from the bottle and passing it across the blanket to Pasquale.

"No," Pasquale says, but he takes the bottle. "Bichterwood and helve wouldn't cause that."

"They wouldn't—they were to mask the flavor of the sylxen root," Nicolo says.

"But you didn't say—"

"He didn't have to," Beatriz says, impressed despite herself. "He wasn't obligated to tell you the whole truth in the follow-up questions."

Pasquale groans and takes his drink before passing it to Ambrose, who frowns at Nicolo and Beatriz before taking his drink. "You two are far too good at this. It isn't fair," he says, wiping the red stain from his lips.

"It's a drinking game—it's not meant to be fair, it's meant to make you drink," Gisella says, taking the bottle from his hands. "My turn now. I've never kissed anyone."

Beatriz has to smother a laugh, having seen firsthand that Gisella is telling a bald-faced lie. But she holds her tongue, letting the others answer first so as not to ruin the game. The others pronounce Gisella a liar immediately and she grins, taking four drinks.

"Fine," she says with a loud sigh. "I suppose that one was a bit easy. Pas? Ambrose?" she asks, holding the bottle toward them.

Ambrose takes it first, his fingertips tapping at the glass while he thinks about his confession. Even before he speaks, though, Beatriz knows whatever he says will be the truth. She doesn't think Ambrose is capable of lying about anything. The realization makes her vaguely uneasy. After all, she knows what to expect from liars, but earnestness is another matter entirely.

"I don't know how to swim," he says finally.

For a second, Beatriz is tempted to tell him it's not a scandalous-enough confession. But as she looks at Ambrose, she feels her heart soften slightly. He is not someone made for scandals, so perhaps not being able to swim is enough.

"Truth," she says.

"Is it in the rules that we can toss him in the ocean to test?" Gisella asks her.

Everyone laughs except for Ambrose, whose eyes widen before he realizes she's only joking.

"Never mind," Gisella says, waving a dismissive hand. "That gave me my answer. Truth."

After a second of thought, Pasquale and Nicolo vote truth as well, and with a strained smile, Ambrose takes four quick drinks from the bottle of wine.

"I'm not good at this, I'm afraid," he says, passing it to Pasquale.

"Depends on the objective," Pasquale says with a grin. "You and Gigi are tied for having the most to drink—some might say you're winning."

It's hard to tell in the moonlight, but Beatriz could swear a light flush works over Ambrose's skin.

Pasquale holds the bottle of wine in one hand, leaning back on the other elbow and staring up at the sky for a second before shaking his head.

"I don't want to be king," he says finally.

A beat of silence follows his words before Gisella laughs.

"*Everyone* wants to be king," she says. "Bluff."

Ambrose and Nicolo agree with her assessment, both casting their votes for bluff, but Beatriz hesitates. He's never said those exact words to her, but she feels certain he's spoken around them, leaving the outline of a truth. Pasquale doesn't want to be king—he doesn't even want to be a prince.

"Truth," she says softly.

Pasquale meets her gaze over the smoldering fire and she sees his surprise there, and an instant of vulnerability before he seals it away behind a grin and shakes his head. "Of course it's a bluff. Like Gigi said—who doesn't want to be king?"

He takes three drinks before passing the bottle to Beatriz so that she can take her drink as well.

For a second, she considers calling him out on the confession. She knows liars, after all, and the lie Pasquale just told was so palpable, so glaringly obvious, that she's surprised no one else caught it. But perhaps they don't want to see it. Nothing good will come of her pushing the matter, so she forces a smile and takes her drink without complaint.

"You were doing so well, Triz," Gisella says, shaking her head. "But I suppose Nico won that round, didn't he?"

"I didn't realize there were winners or losers," Nicolo says. "And like Pas said—I don't feel like much of a winner, being the most sober one here. Pass the bottle, would you, Triz?"

She does, and for a second their fingers brush and he lingers, or maybe she lingers. She isn't sure, but she knows it goes on a heartbeat longer than it should before the contact is broken. She knows that she regrets the loss of it when it is.

Ambrose is the first to call it a night, just after the clock tower strikes midnight, citing the need to be up early the next day. Gisella follows half an hour after that, saying she needs her beauty sleep. Pasquale makes it until nearly two in the morning before he begins drifting off on the beach and Beatriz has to insist he goes to bed, promising to join him soon.

Then it is only Beatriz and Nicolo, passing the last bottle of wine between them until they run out of things to talk about and just sit together in silence.

"It is late," Beatriz says finally. "Will you walk me back to my rooms?"

Nicolo nods and gets to his feet, holding a hand out to help her stand. She's unsteady on her feet—after all the wine it's hardly surprising—but Nicolo keeps his hand around hers. Even when she finds her footing, he doesn't let go for another few seconds, and when he does, Beatriz wishes he'd held on longer.

They start back toward the palace, walking side by side.

"I'm sure Pas is missing you," Nicolo says when silence stretches out between them.

Beatriz gives a snort of laughter before she catches herself and offers him a sheepish smile. "I'll admit, it's nice to have a few hours apart," she says, shaking her head. "No one tells you that when you get married, you never have a moment alone. I thought being a triplet was one thing, but at least I slept in my own room, my own bed."

She realizes how bitter she sounds and quickly amends her remarks before he can see the truth of her marriage. "I love Pasquale, truly, but it's nice to have a moment with just my thoughts."

"I'm sure they're fascinating," Nicolo tells her with a small smile.

Beatriz hesitates, eyeing him in the moonlight, the way his face is cast in high relief. He is all sharp angles and dark eyes and full lips. Handsome.

Sophronia always liked to say Beatriz made poor decisions in the presence of handsome faces. If she were here, she might tell Beatriz to let him walk away, because he is a dangerous sort of handsome.

But Sophronia is not here to talk sense. Silence falls over them as they make their way back into the now-quiet palace—even the servants seem to be asleep, and not another soul is around. It's almost eerie, given the life and energy usually flooding the palace halls, but it's also peaceful.

"Are you still missing them? Your sisters?" Nicolo asks, jerking her out of her thoughts.

"Wouldn't you miss Gigi?" she asks.

"Sometimes, I'm sure," he says. "But also, sometimes I probably wouldn't."

Beatriz bites her lip. "I used to crave a little distance, you know," she admits. "When we were growing up, I would get so annoyed. They were always so close. Sometimes it felt like they were smothering me. I couldn't wait until I was old enough to leave and come here and see all manner of new and exciting things."

"And now?" he asks.

She considers the question carefully, aware that even if she likes Nico, she can't trust him. He is a social-climbing boy, determined to win the king's favor. She suspects he would sell her out if he had the chance, and even though she respects him for that, she certainly isn't about to be that chance.

"I miss them—of course I do—but Cellaria is a heady daydream of a place. It's everything I imagined growing up. I always wanted to see more of the world."

He laughs. "It's funny—I have as well, but nothing seems more exotic than Bessemia. To me, Cellaria is boring. Give me mild weather and dry air and glittering white palaces. It sounds like a fairy tale."

"It is," she says, smiling softly before shaking her head. "There are so many places I'd like to see if I could—Friv and Temarin and the eastern isles, not to mention all of the places beyond that, places we don't even have names for."

He doesn't say anything for a moment, and she worries that she's said too much, been too open, that she's frightened him somehow.

"Sometimes," he says finally, "I feel like I'm so hungry for the world that I would swallow it up whole if I could."

Beatriz's mouth stretches into a grin. "You'd have to share it with me," she says. "Half and half."

He glances sideways at her, a wide smile tugging at his lips as well. And in that look, Beatriz feels like he sees her entirely, every inch of her inside and out. They're walking through the royal wing now, both nodding at the guards posted outside the entrance, though even those guards seem half asleep and barely spare them a second look.

"Half and half," he agrees.

They come to a stop outside the door to the rooms she shares with Pasquale, but neither of them makes a move to leave. On the opposite wall, the large windows have been left open so the moon and stars cast the hall in an ethereal glow.

She wants him to kiss her—she wishes for it so badly that she thinks she might sacrifice just about anything for the feel of his lips against hers.

"I wish you would kiss me."

She doesn't realize she's spoken the words out loud until she sees the surprise play over his face. But then he takes a step closer to her and reaches his hand up to her cheek, the tips of his fingers so light against her skin that she barely feels them.

"I hoped you would say that," he says, the words more breath than voice.

"We shouldn't," she tells him, though even as she says it, she's tilting her face toward his.

"We shouldn't," he agrees. "But I hoped and you wished and here we are."

The kiss is inevitable. As soon as his lips brush over hers, she realizes there was never any avoiding it. They've been careening toward this moment since he kissed her hand at her wedding. Trying to pretend otherwise was a fool's game, and now that it's happening, now that his arms are around her waist and her hands are in his hair and the kiss has no end in sight, she can't remember why she tried to resist it.

The courtesan Sabine's words whisper through her mind. *If you can become what they want you to be, they'll burn the world down in your name.*

But in this moment, Nicolo just seems to want her. She doesn't have to become anyone, just to be herself. And that feels like a whole different kind of power. One she would drown in if she could.

When they break apart, though, and her eyes meet his, a realization shudders through her. He wants her, yes, but she wants him as well. Just as much. And her mother and the courtesans never told her how to navigate that.

"I'm sorry, I shouldn't have . . ." Nico trails off, and Beatriz gets the feeling he wants to kiss her again. This time, though, his sense wins out and he turns away from her, hurrying back down the hall and leaving her alone.

She turns to go into her rooms, but when her hand is on the doorknob, she catches sight of something glittering on the stone floor beneath her feet. She crouches down, reaching out to touch it, and the pads of her fingers come away glittering as well. Her stomach plummets.

What was it she said? *I wish you would kiss me.* Simple-enough words, a common-enough phrase. No real power in it.

But in the light of the stars, she wished and it came true, and now there is stardust on the floor where she stood and a sharp pain already beginning in the space between her eyes, like a postdrinking headache, but so much worse. Like the morning Pasquale shook her awake to tell her that the king wanted to speak with her because stardust had been found on her windowsill. On a night just like this one, when she couldn't sleep.

Beatriz goes toward one of the narrow windows that line the hallway, peering out at the night sky. There is the Dancing Bear, making its way across the sky. There is the Thorned Rose. And there are the Lovers' Hands, clasped directly overhead, but something about them is not quite right. It takes her a moment to find it, but when she does, the world shifts beneath her feet: a star is missing from the thumb of one of the hands.

She stumbles back from the window, a dozen excuses rising to her mind. Someone else could have pulled the star down, couldn't they have? And whoever left the stardust on her windowsill before might have left it outside her bedroom door now, another ploy to frame her. The headache coming on could just be a headache, caused by too much wine. There are a dozen excuses, but she knows she is lying to herself.

She made a wish and brought a star down from the sky. And it isn't the first time. She thinks back to before, when she wished on a star in the Wanderer's Wheel. Then, she wished to go home, and that didn't come true. But wishes work in mysterious ways, don't they? And it was soon after that wish that she met Lord Savelle, the key to her returning home.

Lord Savelle. He asked about her sleepless nights, seemed particularly interested in them because his daughter had suffered the same affliction. What was it he said? *I believe in the deepest part of my soul that she was as innocent as you are.* She'd taken that to mean that he'd thought them both innocent, but maybe he'd meant the opposite. That he knew his daughter was an empyrea and that Beatriz is as well.

And is she? It seems impossible, utterly unfathomable, but here she stands with the proof of it on her fingers and in the sky. One person in ten thousand has the potential to bring down the stars, only a fraction of them ever manage to control it, and yet here she is, somehow. Two things become very clear to Beatriz. First, she needs to get out of Cellaria as quickly as she can, before her power is discovered, and second, Lord Savelle's knowledge makes him a threat.

She scoops the rest of the stardust off the floor and brings it into her apartments, trying to ignore her blossoming headache. Wishing for Nicolo to kiss her was a small wish—certainly no bigger than her wish to go home—so she suspects the effect on her will be the same. Already, she can feel a headache blossoming. She needs to act now. A low fire is burning in the bedroom, and she casts a glance at Pasquale, who is fast asleep, before throwing the stardust into the fire and watching it burn. Then she retrieves the vial her mother sent her from its place in her cosmetics kit, along with a few pots of pigments and creams. She sits down at her vanity and gets to work.

Beatriz never thought of herself as a coward, but as she sneaks into Lord Savelle's rooms just after sunrise, while he is out in the sea garden, she realizes she just might be one. She knows she can't plant the stardust on him in person—if she tries, she will lose her nerve like she did last time. Which led her to cake her face in enough creams and powders that she looks like a woman at least three times her age. In her plainest gray dress, she manages to pass for a maid, if no one looks too closely.

In her disguise—with a hunched-over walk to match, because Beatriz does nothing by halves—she gains entrance to Lord Savelle's rooms with ease. There are fewer guards than outside the royal wing, she notices, and with servants beginning to tend to their chores, she blends in easily enough.

Perhaps it *is* cowardly, she thinks as she places the vial of stardust in one of Lord Savelle's boots, but she would rather be a living coward than a dead hero.

She leaves his rooms as quickly as she came in and wanders the halls outside until she comes across a guard. She lets herself bump into him, as if by accident.

"Watch where you're going," he snaps at her.

"Oh!" she says, pretending to be flustered. "I'm so sorry, sir, I find myself distracted."

The guard doesn't take the bait, as Beatriz thinks he might have if she still looked like herself—he's perfectly happy to ignore a woman past middle age.

"Sir, please," she says before hesitating and biting her lip. "Do you know what stardust looks like?" she asks, dropping her voice to a whisper.

That gets his attention, and his eyes snap to her as if truly seeing her for the first time. "Why do you want to know?"

She pretends to hesitate again. "I think I might have seen some in the Lord Ambassador to Temarin's rooms. There was a small vial of some kind of silver dust—"

"Where?" he interrupts, standing up straighter.

"Tucked away in one of his boots. In the wardrobe, a tall black pair."

The words are barely out of Beatriz's mouth before the guard is hurrying past her, toward the rooms she just came from.

When she gets back to her own rooms, Beatriz suddenly feels so exhausted, her head pounding and every muscle aching, that sleep claims her as soon as she climbs into bed beside Pasquale. She doesn't wake again until dusk, and by the time she does, Lord Savelle's arrest is all anyone is speaking of.

Daphne

Daphne finds Cliona in the woods outside the palace, sitting with her back against a tree trunk with a book open on her knee and a half-eaten apple in her hand. When she hears Daphne approach on horseback, she looks up, unsurprised.

"Were you followed?" Cliona asks through a mouthful of apple.

Daphne rolls her eyes and dismounts, keeping hold of the horse's reins. Her usual mare, Mánot, hurt her ankle, and the horse the stable hand saddled for her instead isn't as well trained. It was all she could do to keep her saddle on the ride here.

"Of course not," she says. "The king believes the castle grounds are safe and says I don't need a guard as long as I stay within the bounds."

"Good," Cliona says, closing her book and getting to her feet. "My father was impressed with you."

Daphne has to bite her tongue to keep from giving a sarcastic response about how much she values Cliona's father's opinion. *Remember to keep your enemies close, my dove—and the enemies of our enemies all the closer,* the empress wrote, in response to Daphne's weekly update, telling her about the rebels and their frustrations with King Bartholomew.

They won't succeed, but if Daphne can keep their anger stoked, they'll be able to weaken Bartholomew's hold on Friv and make it easier for Margaraux to eventually seize it.

"You weren't lying about the marriage contract," Cliona says, her voice soft.

Daphne shakes her head. "In fact . . ." She breaks off, reaching into her pocket to draw out the forged letter from the king to her mother, complete with his seal. She passes it to Cliona. "I was arranging to have something sent to my sister when I spotted this on the postmaster's desk, along with some other correspondence. I grabbed it when his back was turned."

"Well done," Cliona says, sounding impressed. She opens the letter and scans it, the furrow in her brow deepening. "You read it?" she asks, glancing at Daphne, who makes a show of hesitating before she nods.

"Bartholomew knows about your little rebellion. He's readying for a war," Daphne says.

Cliona merely lifts a shoulder in a shrug. "Then we'll give him one."

Daphne raises her eyebrows. As much as Cliona's reaction will suit her mother's goal of destabilizing Bartholomew's rule, she's surprised at how quickly the other girl jumped at it. "You think it will be so easy?" she asks, wondering if perhaps she has been underestimating the power the rebels have, if it is something her mother should be concerned about. "That letter says he's soliciting help not just from Bessemia, but from Temarin as well."

"And?" Cliona says. "The rebellion has the majority of the highlands."

Or perhaps the rebels have exactly as much power as Daphne thought, and Cliona is simply a fool. She is comparing a puddle to the sea. It's hardly surprising—Friv prides itself on staying separate and secluded, on acting as if the rest of the world doesn't exist. No one at court talks about what's going on in Temarin or Bessemia or Cellaria—she knows, she's asked around, trying to learn what her sisters and mother are up to, but with no luck. While Daphne studied the entire continent growing up, she would be surprised if Cliona even knows what the capital cities are called, let alone Temarin's reputation as a brutal war power.

"Bartholomew might know about the rebellion, but he doesn't know about you," Cliona says. "You're in a position to help us—you stole this letter, but when he doesn't receive a response, Bartholomew will write her again. You could get to her first, convince her not to send troops."

Daphne laughs. "Why exactly should I do anything more to help you?" she asks. She will, of course, since it furthers her mother's goals as well, but she's interested to see what Cliona will offer her.

"You do us another favor, you get more stardust."

It takes all of Daphne's self-control not to grin. "How much?" she asks.

"A vial," Cliona says. "For now."

"And all I have to do is write to my mother?" Daphne asks.

"Well, I'm not going to trust your word on that alone," Cliona says, rolling her eyes. "I'll write the letter, you can copy it and sign it, and then I'll give it to the postmaster for you. And one more thing—I'd like you to dance," she says, a slow grin spreading across her face.

Daphne blinks. "Pardon me?"

"At your betrothal banquet tomorrow night," Cliona says. "The king invited the heads of the highland clans to attend. Some are on our side, others are loyal to the king, but there are a handful we believe may be amenable to joining the rebellion. Three in particular."

"You think I can turn them in a single night?" Daphne asks, raising her eyebrows. "I'm flattered, truly, but I think you overestimate my skills."

"I don't think I do," Cliona says. "And you won't try to turn them, just tell me, in your opinion, if you believe it's *possible* to turn them."

Daphne pretends to consider it for a full minute. She knows that her loyalty is being tested more than anyone else's. "What are the names?" she asks.

"I'll leave you a list with the letter you'll copy—word for word," Cliona says.

"Anything else?" Daphne asks, even though she's already gathering her horse's reins.

"Just a general reminder that we're watching, we're everywhere, don't do anything stupid," Cliona says.

"Yes, yes, trust me, I'm terrified," Daphne says. She

moves to step into the stirrup and mount her horse, but as soon as she shifts her weight, the girth snaps and the saddle slides off, knocking Daphne flat on her back, the air fleeing from her lungs. She looks up just in time to see black hooves reared up over her and hears the horse let out a hair-raising shriek. Instinct takes over and she turns her face away, closing her eyes tight and waiting for the inevitable impact. Instead, Cliona's hands grab her arm and yank her out of the way with surprising strength.

The horse's front hooves hit the ground where she was lying a mere instant before, and then he's off, running into the woods.

Daphne sits up, wincing as she does. "No need for the literal demonstration," she snaps at Cliona. "I believed your threats already."

"You think I was behind that?" Cliona asks, looking so angry that Daphne believes she's innocent. "It was an accident."

Daphne shakes her head, looking at the discarded saddle lying beside her. She takes hold of the girth and holds it up for Cliona to see—the leather is cut clean through three-quarters of the way, the rest roughly ripped.

"Not an accident," Daphne says, standing up on shaky legs. "The stable hand said my usual mare turned her ankle, but, come to think of it, I didn't recognize the man."

"And you didn't find that suspicious?" Cliona asks.

"Not until now," Daphne admits, frowning. "It isn't as if I've been here long enough to know all the stable hands. I wasn't exactly expecting an assassination attempt."

"*Assassination attempt* sounds awfully dramatic," Cliona says.

"I'm sorry, I was just nearly trampled to death by a horse," Daphne says. "What, exactly, would you call that?"

Cliona rolls her eyes. "You aren't asking the right question," she says. "Who wants you dead, Princess?"

"Apart from you?" Daphne asks.

"If I wanted you dead, I wouldn't have saved you—you're welcome for that, by the way," Cliona retorts.

It's a solid point. "Then I don't know," Daphne says. "But I'm certainly going to find out."

She reaches down and collects the broken saddle, hefting it over her shoulder and starting into the woods, back in the direction of the castle.

"A little gratitude wouldn't kill you," Cliona calls after her.

"Maybe not, but one near-death experience was enough for me and I'd rather not risk it," Daphne shouts over her shoulder.

For a brief moment, Daphne considers alerting the king to the attempt on her life, but she dismisses the idea immediately. He would never give her a moment without guards again, and that would make it impossible to carry out any new orders her mother sends her. And besides, tampering with her saddle? If someone truly wants her dead, they'll have to try harder than that.

When she gets back to the stable, she looks around for the stable hand who saddled up the horse this morning, but he's nowhere to be found. Instead, there is Mánot in her stall, with no sign of a turned ankle, and one of the stable hands she does recognize.

"Gavriel," she says, smiling when she sees him brushing down another horse. "It looks like Mánot is feeling better."

"Better, Your Highness?" he asks, frowning.

"Yes, the stable hand this morning said she turned her ankle. I'm afraid I didn't catch his name."

"It's only been me this morning," he says, his frown deepening. "Ian is home sick today, so I've been busier than usual—you say someone else helped you?"

Daphne holds on to her smile, trying to read Gavriel's expression, but if he had anything to do with her damaged girth, he's a better liar than she is, which she doubts.

"Yes, it must have been another servant trying to help," she says, waving a hand dismissively. "But he did saddle up a different horse for me—taller than Mánot, chestnut, black mane?"

At that, Gavriel's face goes ashen. "Vrain?" he asks. "But he isn't fit to ride. He only just arrived as a betrothal gift. Excellent bloodlines, but wild."

"A gift for me?" Daphne asks. Gavriel nods. "From whom?"

"King Bartholomew," he says before looking away, his cheeks reddening. "Apologies, Your Highness, I believe it was meant as a surprise."

Daphne smiles, even though her mind is turning this over, trying to fit the pieces together. "Oh, I won't tell him," she promises. "However, on our ride he did get away from me.

I stopped to adjust the saddle and . . . well, I hope he didn't get far."

"I'll send scouts out right away," Gavriel tells her. "We're lucky that's all it was—Vrain has thrown the last few trainers who have tried to ride him."

"Yes," Daphne says. "Very lucky indeed."

That night, Daphne finds the list and letter Cliona promised her. She decides to tackle the letter to her mother first, reading over what Cliona drafted for her.

My dear Mother,

I hope you are well. I write to you because I fear King Bartholomew has not left the war behind him—he sees enemies everywhere, always talking about rebel factions plotting against him. He even mentioned writing to you to request troops! I know that he was a great hero in his time, but I beg you to ignore his pleas. There is no one plotting against him—everyone I have met has been wonderful to me, and they all seem to look forward to Prince Bairre's and my rule.

Daphne

It sounds nothing like a letter Daphne would send her mother, but that's just as well—the empress will know it's a fake as soon as she sees it. Daphne writes it out verbatim in her own hand, adding only a closing, *May the stars shine upon you and Bessemia,* before turning the piece of parchment over and finding the jar of ink hidden in the back of her desk drawer. She begins to write the real message.

Dear Mama,

Ignore this, it is a ruse. I have it all well in hand with our rebel friends. More soon.

Daphne

When she's done, the ink dries to invisibility. It will stay that way until her mother dusts it with the ink's accompanying powder—an invention of Nigellus's that uses stardust, indicated by Daphne's closing on the false letter.

She sets that aside and unfolds the list of names. All three are familiar to her by name only.

Lord Ian Maives, Cliona has written. Daphne mentally adds *queen's brother-in-law, close friend of king.*

There is no possibility of Lord Maives's siding with the rebels, and Daphne suspects Cliona included him as part of her test, to see if Daphne's information is good. She moves on to the next name.

Lord Rufus Cadringal

There's one that could go either way. The new Lord Cadringal is barely older than Daphne, with five younger siblings. His father died suddenly, and Daphne would wager the boy is lost and impressionable.

The third name on the list gives Daphne pause.

Haimish Talmadge

Not a lord—not yet, at least, but Daphne knows that his father was one of King Bartholomew's most loyal generals during the war. It's how he went from being the third son of a blacksmith to the lord of one of the most prosperous parts of Friv. If it were Lord Talmadge's name on Cliona's list, Daphne would dismiss it without another thought, but it isn't, and she realizes she doesn't know much about Haimish Talmadge at all.

She supposes it's time to change that.

Sophronia

The package Daphne sent has been thoroughly examined, as Violie explains to Sophronia, apologizing for its delay in reaching her. But however thoroughly the palace staff might have searched it, they didn't discover King Bartholomew's seal and a sample of his writing hidden in the false bottom. Daphne has done her duty, and once Beatriz does hers, it will be Sophronia's turn, though in the meantime she hides the entire box in the back of her wardrobe. Part of her hopes Beatriz makes her move soon so she can see her sisters again, but she's surprised to realize that a part of her is dreading it. Though the harsh words from her mother's letter echo in her mind, reminding her that *queen* is not a role she is meant to fill, Sophronia knows she could be a good one in Temarin, and what's more, Leopold is on his way to becoming a good king as well, now that he's trying.

Temarin is a broken land—in part, at least, due to him—but Sophronia knows that they can fix it. After seeing firsthand how the people have been suffering, she finds she isn't eager to turn the responsibility or the crown over to her mother. The crown feels like *hers*.

The riot was a step backward, but in hindsight, Sophronia knows that they should never have organized a speech in the first place.

"We wanted credit," she told Leopold the night after the riot, when they'd gone to bed, both of them exhausted and contemplative.

"We tried to help," he said, shaking his head. "They didn't want it."

"We could have halved their taxes and said nothing, let our actions speak for us," she said. "But we didn't. Because we wanted credit, we wanted approval. But Leo, we can't take that without taking blame as well. And blame for the bad far outweighs the good we've tried to do to counteract it."

"But we're *trying*," he told her, sounding alarmingly close to a child—though perhaps it wasn't so alarming at all. In many ways, Leopold is more of a child than Sophronia ever has been. "Don't they appreciate that we're trying?"

"We wanted credit for trying," she said with a heavy sigh. "But after so much betrayal, so much hurt, so much death—why should they give us credit for doing the bare minimum to clean up a mess we made ourselves?"

Leopold didn't say anything for a moment. "So how do we change their minds?" he asked her.

"I don't know," she admitted. "But I suppose we start by acknowledging that we may not be able to, that the damage done might be unfixable. And then we keep trying to fix it anyway. Not for the glory of it, but because it's right."

Leopold didn't say anything for so long that Sophronia

thought he might have fallen asleep. Just as she was about to drift off, though, he spoke again.

"You keep saying *we*," he said. "It wasn't *we*. It was me. I'm sorry that you were hurt because of me."

Sophronia rolled toward him so that they lay face to face. The moonlight pouring through the window cast a silver sheen over his face, turning it spectral. He looked older than he had the day before, like he'd lived a lifetime in just the last few hours. "We're in this together, Leo," she told him softly.

She thinks about that now, when she is alone in her room—the perfect opportunity to take out the seal so she can forge a letter in King Bartholomew's handwriting, drawing him as well into the imminent war. Her mother has always said it's good to be prepared, and Sophronia is sure Beatriz will have Cellaria frothing for war any day now. She should get the letter done, so it can be ready to deliver when the time comes. She should do as her mother said and not worry about Eugenia and her plots, should let her do even more to weaken Bessemia. She shouldn't care if Eugenia drives it into the ground. She should do what her mother told her to do.

Instead, she encodes a letter to Beatriz, asking about the origin of the Cellarian wine the queen has been spending millions of asters on, then rings for a servant to send it out with the day's mail.

The only good thing that comes from having dinner with Ansel is that Eugenia is even more distrustful of him than Sophronia. Every time he slurps his soup or uses the wrong fork, she flinches like he's physically struck her—not that Ansel notices. He's too busy charming the princes with stories of his time as a fisherman's apprentice sailing the Vixania Ocean.

"I heard there are sea monsters in those waters!" Reid says, his eyes growing wide.

Ansel scoffs. "That's what the Frivian sailors would have you believe—so that they get to keep all the fish for themselves," he says. "The worst monster I met on those trips was my captain. He snored like an angry bear and was quick with his fists."

"He *hit* you?" Gideon asks.

Eugenia jumps in, the glare she shoots at Ansel making the room feel chillier. "That is not appropriate conversation for the dinner table."

"Apologies," Ansel says, offering a sheepish smile that doesn't quite match the mirth in his eyes.

"Are you still a fisherman?" Leopold asks, using his knife and fork to cut a bite of steak. The way he holds the gold cutlery, the way he knows exactly how to cut his food, even the way he chews it, marks him as a king. Leopold likely doesn't even realize he's doing it, but Ansel does. He holds his own cutlery with clumsy hands, and if Sophronia had to guess, she'd say he's never eaten steak before.

"No, Your Majesty," he says. "We mostly caught firetail—a good, moderately priced fish—but over the past year, it's become too expensive for the lower classes to afford, and it isn't fine enough for nobility like yourselves. The captain let most of us go."

Leopold glances at Sophronia, and though she's glad

to see the discomfort in his eyes, the urge to *do something,* she's too wary of the messenger. Ansel has been polite since he arrived for dinner, and it's possible that his speaking with Violie was a coincidence, but Sophronia doesn't trust him. She's learned to listen to her instincts.

"What do you do now, then?" Sophronia asks, reaching for her wine goblet and taking a small sip, keeping an eye on Ansel all the while.

Ansel holds her gaze. "Odd jobs, mostly," he says, shrugging. "I suppose the last one I did was scrubbing down the gallows after hangings."

He says the words conversationally enough, but Sophronia has to suppress a shudder. Eugenia, however, suppresses nothing.

"That's *enough,*" she snaps, dabbing her mouth daintily with her napkin, her expression queasy. "It is poor form to discuss such unpleasantness while we are dining."

Sophronia can't help but roll her eyes. Eugenia can block out the mention of the *unpleasantness* all she likes, but she had an active hand in causing it. And if she forgets it, Sophronia will gladly remind her.

"Oh, Genia," she says, biting her lip. "You look unwell—I know how guilty you must feel. Would you like to lie down?" she asks.

Leopold gives her a warning look—still loyal to his mother. It's why Sophronia needs Beatriz to confirm her suspicions about the vineyard. He won't believe his mother capable of treason and treachery without proof.

"I'm fine," Eugenia bites out.

"I'm glad to hear it," Sophronia says, before turning

back to Ansel. "Did you spend much time in Friv while you worked on the ship? Or Bessemia, perhaps?"

Ansel glances from Sophronia to the still-glaring Eugenia. "I can't say I did—I only worked on the ship for a year, and as the newest member of the crew, I was never allowed off when we docked. I've never set foot on soil that wasn't Temarinian."

Sophronia nods and nibbles at her dinner roll. She wishes Daphne were here—Daphne could lure information out of anyone, their mother's always said so. She could ask them about the weather and by the end of the conversation, somehow know their darkest secrets. Sophronia, on the other hand, isn't even sure Ansel is his real name, let alone who he has ties to.

"We can find a job for you," Leopold says suddenly, looking quite pleased with himself. "Somewhere in the palace, perhaps? Do you have any skills besides fishing?"

The last thing Sophronia wants is for Ansel to be lurking around the palace, but she holds her tongue for now.

"That's too kind of you, Your Majesty," Ansel says, shaking his head.

"It isn't kind enough," Leopold says. "You likely saved my brother's life," he adds, glancing at Reid, who sinks down in his chair, his ears going red.

"Well, I appreciate it all the same," Ansel says before pausing. "I'm good with horses. Is there an opening in the stables?"

Leopold smiles. "I'll speak to the stable manager myself tomorrow morning," he says.

"Leopold, I really don't think—" Eugenia begins, but

she's interrupted by the dining room door opening and a flustered messenger hurrying in. He manages a quick bow.

"Your Majesty, Your Majesty," he says to Leopold and Sophronia in turn. "We've just received worrisome news from Cellaria. Our ambassador, Lord Savelle, has been arrested for sorcery—they say they're going to execute him."

The rest of the table—even Eugenia—is shocked, but Sophronia isn't surprised by the news. She sees her mother's plot coming together in this, sees an unavoidable war on the horizon. A war she is supposed to shove Temarin into. Daphne did her duty, now Beatriz has done hers. It's Sophronia's turn at last.

In the wake of the messenger's announcement, everyone leaps into action. Servants are sent to find Lord Covier and Lord Verning, the princes are sent back to their rooms, and Sophronia, Leopold, and Eugenia are brought to the council chambers. It isn't until they are near the door that Sophronia notices that Ansel is still with them.

"I'm sorry our dinner was cut short, Ansel, but if you come back tomorrow we can get you situated in the stables," she tells him, hoping he takes the words as the dismissal they are.

Ansel glances at Leopold. "Actually, Your Majesties, I was hoping I might join you."

Eugenia lets out a loud snort she makes no effort to disguise. "Why in the name of the stars should you?" she asks. "This is a matter of great national importance, and you are . . . a failed fisherman's apprentice," she says.

"Mother," Leopold says, giving her a warning look before turning back to Ansel. "But I'm afraid she's right."

"All due respect, Your Majesty, but you are making decisions that affect the entire country, while only consulting with a very narrow segment of it. Perhaps the voice of someone less privileged by birth would be welcome?"

Sophronia wants to argue that point, but she knows it's a valid one. Her mother has several members of Bessemia's merchant class on her council and has always said that different viewpoints can be helpful. Sophronia just doesn't want *Ansel*'s viewpoint. Leopold's brow furrows for a moment and he glances uncertainly at his mother, then Sophronia.

"Leopold," Eugenia says. "You can't possibly be considering this."

"He has a point," Leopold says. "We're discussing the possibility of war here, Mother. A war that will mainly affect those outside the palace walls. If I want to create a better Temarin, I need to hear from those who live in the heart of it. He stays." With that, Leopold strides into the room and sinks into the chair at the head of the great oak table

"Thank you, Your Majesty," Ansel says, bowing his head before following Leopold into the room and taking the seat to his left—the seat that usually belongs to Eugenia. With a clenched jaw and a murderous look in her eyes, Eugenia takes the one next to Ansel, while Sophronia takes her usual chair at Leopold's right.

Seconds later, Lord Covier and Lord Verning arrive, taking two of the remaining seats at the table. They both spare Ansel a bemused look but don't question his presence. Instead, Lord Covier clears his throat and begins.

"According to our sources, Lord Savelle was arrested a few days ago—they found a vial of stardust among his things, and they say he acquired it because he's an empyrea who used star magic in order to harm King Cesare," he says. "There has never been any evidence that Savelle is an empyrea, and as to the stardust . . . well, he knew that giving up magic would be required of him when he took his post. He's held it for two decades without even a hint of an issue, that unfortunate business with his bastard aside. I find it difficult to believe that has suddenly changed."

Eugenia jumps in. "As I said before, Cesare has always been mercurial, and we had word that he was becoming increasingly paranoid. These charges are at best a figment of his imagination, at worst a flimsy excuse to force us into another war. And if he wants a war, we can give him one."

"With what money, Eugenia?" Sophronia asks before she can stop herself. This may be her mother's plan, but it is Eugenia's as well, and she knows better than anyone how ill-equipped Temarin is. They couldn't win a snowball fight.

"We will find money," Eugenia says, as if that much can simply be dug out of a parlor sofa. "If they execute Savelle, they are declaring war. We have no choice but to defend ourselves and our countrymen."

"Your countrymen will be those who shoulder the cost and the burden," Ansel says, leaning forward. "During the last war with Cellaria, I hadn't been born yet, but I heard stories from my parents—they said their taxes went up significantly. Some months they even doubled."

"Surely you aren't implying that there is a price you are

unwilling to pay for our country . . . ," Lord Covier begins. Then he frowns. "Who are you?"

Leopold makes quick, distracted introductions, and Lord Covier and Lord Verning exchange contemptuous glances.

"Your Majesty—Temarin can't afford a war," Ansel says again. "The people are already suffering."

Leopold frowns. "How much money does a war cost?" he asks, glancing around the table.

"Well . . . er . . . that's a complicated question," Lord Verning says, clearing his throat.

"Then let's uncomplicate it," Leopold says. "Tell me the average cost per month of the last war with Cellaria, as well as a detailed look at where the money to pay for it came from. How much from the treasury, how much from taxes, how much from other sources."

Lord Verning blinks. "I don't have that information on me, Your Majesty."

"Then go find it," Leopold says, grumbling the words more than speaking them as he rakes a hand through his hair. Lord Verning hesitates for a few seconds before pushing back from the table and hurrying from the room, casting a bewildered glance back at Leopold over his shoulder.

"And where is the Cellarian ambassador?" Leopold continues. "I want a guard put on him at all times."

"You wish to make Lord Fiorelli a prisoner?" Lord Covier asks, glancing at Eugenia uncertainly.

"Lord Fiorelli may prove to be the only bargaining chip we have, and I'm not about to let him slip back to Cellaria when he hears about this mess," Leopold says, looking at one of the guards standing by the door. "Go, put one of your men on him."

The guard gives a quick bow before leaving.

"Sympathetic as I am to the matter of cost, Ansel," Leopold says, turning back toward him, "there are bigger factors at stake—King Cesare is planning on killing my ambassador. My mother is right—that is an act of war in and of itself. Who's to say he won't be pushing at Temarin's borders next? And then there is the personal aspect," he adds.

"Yes, in regard to Princess Beatriz . . . ," Lord Covier says, looking down at the papers in front of him. Sophronia's heart gives a stutter. Beatriz is fine, she has to be. "There were some reports from our spies that Lord Savelle and Princess Beatriz had grown . . . close. They've dined together alone and had taken to walking together in the sea garden when no one was about. One of our spies speculates that that closeness might be the real reason for his imprisonment."

Sophronia struggles to keep her face impassive, though she knows there is truth to that rumor. Beatriz told her so herself—she said she'd enjoyed their walks together, even liked the man. *She still betrayed him, though,* Sophronia thinks, *because that was her assignment*.

Just as Sophronia's assignment is to push Leopold to declaring war. Once she forges an alliance between Friv and Temarin with King Bartholomew's seal, Friv will fall in right behind it, entering a war that will leave all three countries so vulnerable that Bessemian forces could conquer them without much of a struggle.

Sophronia understood this in the abstract, when she viewed it playing out like pieces on a chessboard, cold marble figures falling one by one, but now that she's here, she's seen the personal cost behind it, how this war won't just devastate Temarin's security and economy but will kill its people—both in battle and from starvation.

Yes, her mother will be there to pick up the pieces; yes, she will eventually rebuild the country; yes, it might eventually become stronger as a result. But how many Temarinians won't survive to see it?

The thought shouldn't bother her. *Bessemia above all.* But even though the crown she wears is a hollow one, even though she has only been playing the role of queen, she can't help but feel that these are *her* people. That she will be failing them.

Lord Covier continues, oblivious to Sophronia's churning mind. "As I mentioned in our last meeting, there are plenty of scheming nobles looking to have Pasquale disinherited—I believe they'll use Princess Beatriz's ties to Savelle against her, and against Prince Pasquale as well. I'm in agreement with your mother. If we strike early, strike *now,* we will be able to catch them by surprise. We can work with the prince and princess to have King Cesare deposed and put them on the throne instead, before they lose any more support. Everyone wins."

Everyone won't win, Sophronia thinks. Maybe if Eugenia hadn't depleted Temarin's war chest, if the empress weren't waiting to declare her own war once Temarin was wounded, maybe Lord Covier's plan would have merit. Sophronia knows that when all is said and done, the only one who will win is the empress. Sophronia thought she would win with her, alongside Daphne and Beatriz—and isn't that what winning looks like? The three of them together again, home again. Her sisters will be so surprised when they reunite, Sophronia thinks—she's gotten quite good at standing up for herself, they won't even recognize her. Maybe she won't recognize them, either.

That is what winning looks like, what it has always looked like. But it doesn't feel like winning now, not when she understands the cost.

"Sophie?" Leopold asks, drawing her out of her thoughts. "You've been unusually quiet. What are you thinking?"

Sophronia looks up at him and immediately wishes she hadn't. His expression is open, his eyes utterly guileless. He trusts her, wants her help, and she knows without a hint of doubt that the advice she is supposed to give him will ruin him. Will ruin Temarin. She might not like Ansel, but he's right—Temarin can't afford this war. And the people who will suffer the worst will be the people most vulnerable. All so that her mother can claim a crown—*another* crown—and more land, more power.

She used to think Temarin would be better off under her mother's rule, and maybe once that was true, but now? Leopold might not be perfect, but he's trying. He cares. And Sophronia knows that together, they can pull Temarin out of the hole it has sunk into. She knows they can make it better, even better than her mother could, if only because they won't have to break it first.

Sophronia knows the answer she is supposed to give. She imagines herself saying it. *You should declare war.* Four words. Not even her words, really, but ones that have been scripted for her since before she took her first breath. Words she has always been destined to say.

"Ansel is right," she says instead. "Temarin can't afford a war—going into it will destroy us."

Leopold frowns. "Even if not doing it puts Pasquale and Beatriz in danger?" he asks.

Sophronia swallows. "Beatriz can take care of herself," she says, hoping that it's true. "Temarin can't."

Beatriz

Beatriz tries to ignore the persistent guilt that nags at her, but it becomes her constant companion during the days after Lord Savelle's arrest. It follows her to tea in the palace solarium with Gisella. It walks beside her when she strolls through the sea garden with Pasquale. It even lies next to her in bed, keeping her awake for hours and haunting her dreams when she does manage to sleep.

He won't be executed, not yet. King Cesare seems to be engaged in a staring contest with Temarin, knowing that executing their ambassador would be an act of war, but tempted to risk it nonetheless.

The letter Beatriz finds from her mother, tucked into the petals of a dried rose she sent, doesn't help matters.

You have set up your dominoes, my dove. All that's left to do is knock the first down. See to it that no mercy is shown to Lord Savelle.

The empress has been patient for nearly two decades, but now her patience is running thin. Beatriz knows how easy it would be to convince the king to execute Lord Savelle; she imagines herself doing it over breakfast with the king and Pasquale—how she might affect a melodramatic sigh and let slip how unsafe Lord Savelle makes her feel, how he tried to convince her to use magic but how she, of course, resisted him. Anything to stoke King Cesare's righteous fury against the man, anything to make war with Temarin seem worth it.

But instead she holds her tongue and eats her poached eggs and lets King Cesare ramble on about sacrilegious Temarinians, which courtiers he suspects are plotting against him today, and whether or not someone is trying to assassinate him. This last one, at least, is a new paranoia.

"Who would want to kill you, Your Majesty?" Beatriz asks, giving him her most charming smile. She hasn't forgotten about his wandering hands or leering gaze, though he seems to keep both to himself when Pasquale is around, at least.

But rather than returning her smile, King Cesare only glowers at her. "I can think of two people who would stand to gain quite a lot by killing me," he says coldly.

Beatriz exchanges a glance with Pasquale before she forces herself to laugh. There is nothing funny about being accused of trying to murder a king, but Beatriz is aware of the guards standing at the door, of the servants bustling in and out to distribute and collect plates. She knows that if she doesn't play it off as a joke, that rumor will grow legs, and that is the last thing she needs.

"You're too funny, Your Majesty," she says. "Truly, nothing would make us happier than if you were to live forever—ruling seems like a terrible chore. I much prefer being a princess to a queen. All of the glamour, none of the responsibility. Isn't that right, Pas?"

Pasquale nods, but he lacks her ability to think quickly under pressure. Stars bless him, though, he tries his best. "I can't imagine anyone would want to kill you, Father," he says, though he keeps glancing at her as if taking instruction. "Why, without you, Cellaria would surely cease to exist."

It might be laying it on a bit heavy, but King Cesare gives a snort before reaching for his wine again, looking at least somewhat appeased.

"You're damn right, Pasquale," he says before finishing off the glass and gesturing for his cupbearer to bring him more—not Nicolo, Beatriz notes with a mixture of relief and disappointment, but another boy. This one, she remembers, is some third cousin once removed of Pasquale's.

"My bitch of a sister in Temarin keeps writing me about Savelle," the king says once his glass has been refilled. "Wants me to grant him mercy, at least so she says."

Here's Beatriz's chance—the perfect opening to push him to execute Lord Savelle—but confusion swarms her. She received Sophronia's letter the day after Lord Savelle was arrested, telling her about Cesare and Eugenia plotting together to seize Temarin and asking about a wine label. Beatriz hadn't thought much of it—it seemed likely to be a moot point anyway, with war looming so close. But if Cesare and Eugenia are plotting together, the king's outburst doesn't make sense. Wouldn't they be coordinating better? It's possible, of course, that King Cesare's memory is faltering, but if he possesses the faculties to plot a siege, he can't be that far gone, can he?

And the wine label—Beatriz has had her fair share of wine in Cellaria, but none of it has been from *Cosella,* and a few casual inquiries to the servants have yielded only confusion.

"What do you mean?" Beatriz asks now, wondering if Sophronia might be receiving faulty information.

King Cesare waves a hand and laughs, his dark mood of only seconds ago suddenly forgotten. That isn't unusual these days either—his black moods are like Cellarian rainstorms: brutal, but fleeting.

"Eugenia must think me an idiot," he says. "Telling me she wishes I would release Savelle so he could return to Temarin, all the while reminding me of the reasons I should just burn him and be done with it. I'm beginning to suspect she wants me to kill him."

That makes Beatriz frown. If they are conspiring together to start a war, why would Eugenia put up the pretense of telling him not to execute Savelle? And what's more, why would she have to try to convince him of anything at all? If Cesare really did want a war with Temarin, like Sophronia thinks, why wouldn't he have executed Lord Savelle straightaway?

"Perhaps she is simply goading you," Beatriz offers, though the wheels of her mind are still spinning. "That is what siblings do, isn't it? I know my sisters and I always took great joy in trying to get a rise out of one another. Perhaps she simply doesn't realize the gravity of the situation."

"And you do?" King Cesare asks her, a mocking note to his voice. "Tell me about the gravity of the situation, Beatriz."

She can feel his mood darkening again, and even if she couldn't, the look Pasquale sends her is warning enough.

"Well," she begins, feeling like she is walking on a rotting bridge—one false step will send her plummeting. But she hears her mother's words echo in her mind. *You have set up your dominoes, my dove. All that's left to do is knock the first down.*

"It just seems like a very serious thing," she says. "The ambassador of a foreign country, coming into your lands—your home, even—with such disrespect. It isn't as if he simply spoke out of turn or didn't show you the proper deference, Your Majesty—he flouted what many would call Cellaria's most serious law. He didn't only disrespect you, he disrespected the stars. Is that not a serious thing?"

She feels like the entire room is holding its breath—not only her and Pasqual, but the servants and guards as well. Even the air itself seems particularly still.

"You are quite right, Beatriz—almost as intelligent as you are beautiful," the king says, and Beatriz lets out a breath. Then, suddenly, King Cesare slams his palm against the table, the sound of it echoing through the room and making everyone jump. "Lord Savelle's offense cannot stand—he will be executed at the next burning. If Temarin wants to bring war to our door, let them. We'll be ready."

Beatriz should feel relieved—she's done everything she was meant to do. She has set up her dominoes and knocked the first one down. All that's left to do is watch Cellaria tumble. She should feel relieved—proud, even—but all she feels is dread and guilt.

❧❦☙

"Are you all right?" Pasquale asks her as they head back to their rooms after breakfast.

"Fine," she says, shaking her head. "I just . . . never believed he would do it, I suppose. Which is foolish, I know, but . . ."

"You and Lord Savelle have spent some time together," he says. "You like him. But if you'd said anything else, you know you very well might have ended up executed beside him."

Beatriz hesitates before nodding. "He said I reminded him of his daughter," she admits.

Recognition flashes in Pasquale's eyes. "I remember Fidelia," he says. "I saw it, you know."

Beatriz frowns. "Her death?" she asks. There are plenty of people who enjoy watching the burnings, people who make an event of it, with parties before and after. But Pasquale hasn't struck her as the type.

"Oh no, not that," Pasquale says, looking away and lowering his voice. "I saw her . . . you know . . . use magic."

Beatriz nearly stops walking. "You did?" she asks. "What . . . what did she do?"

"It was the night of the summer solstice," Pasquale tells her. "She was a year or so older than me, and, well, you know my father and his attentions."

Beatriz barely suppresses a shudder, but Pasquale must notice it, because he continues.

"He tried to lead her away from the party, but she didn't

want to go—I saw it, I'm sure plenty of other people saw it too, but no one did anything. I wanted to, Triz, but I froze. I couldn't even move. She said something—I don't know what, but I saw her lips move and her eyes were casting around wildly, looking for help. Looking for the stars, I think now, calling on them. Then everything happened quickly. A candle blew over even though there wasn't any wind. A fight broke out in another corner of the ballroom. A tree outside crashed through a window. Any one thing might have been a coincidence, but all together?" He shakes his head. "*I wish you'd let me go*. That's what she said, I think. My father never said as much, he just called her an empyrea and had her executed, but I think that's what she must have said. She wanted his hands off her badly enough that she brought a star down—you can see it missing, from the Hero's Heart. And it worked. He let her go—if only so the guards could arrest her."

Beatriz swallows, unable to speak. Fidelia knew what she was doing, she tells herself. It was a choice, one she understood the consequences of.

The king's words still nag at Beatriz from earlier, conflicting with Sophronia's. Beatriz knows she should let them go, that they don't matter anymore, but she can't.

"Pas, have you heard of the Cosella vineyard?" she asks him.

He frowns. "Cosella?" he repeats, shaking his head. "It sounds vaguely familiar, but I don't think it would be familiar to me if it is a vineyard. Why?"

"It's nothing," she says, giving his arm a squeeze. "It doesn't matter."

That night, King Cesare throws an impromptu banquet—a celebration, he says, though with him that can mean any number of things, many of them bad. Still, she and Pasquale dress up for the occasion, as they're expected to, and sit in their appointed seats in the banquet hall, just to the right of the king. As Beatriz looks around the crowded room, she notes that most people look somewhat confused by the gathering as well, though no one seems keen to question a party.

When glasses of wine are served, the king takes his from Nicolo—who seems to go out of his way to avoid Beatriz's gaze—and stands. A hush falls over the room, and King Cesare clears his throat.

"As you may know, we discovered a heretic in our midst," he says, prompting some jeers. "There was some question of what was to be done with Lord Savelle—execution would have been a foregone conclusion for anyone else, but I was told I must consider the consequences of such a decision. Surely, executing an ambassador will bring the Temarinians to our borders in force, frothing at the mouth for blood and war. There are many on my council who wish to avoid that, even if it means allowing Cellarian laws to be broken in my own court."

King Cesare pauses, his gaze falling on Beatriz. She feels the rest of the crowd follow his look, feels the eyes of the entire room on her.

"But as the . . . divinely alluring Princess Beatriz said," he begins, and Beatriz has to fight to suppress a gag, "there can be no mercy for heretics. The stars would see Lord Savelle burned for his sacrilegious behavior."

These words are met with overwhelming applause, giving Beatriz the opportunity to lean toward Pasquale and ask through a pasted-on smile, "Did I say that?"

"I don't believe so, no," Pasquale replies, sounding more tired than confused. Though Beatriz hasn't known the king nearly as long as Pasquale has, she feels a bit tired of all of this as well—of feeling like she's walking a tightrope, of having her words twisted, of never knowing which side of the king they will be subjected to tonight.

Guilt threatens to drown Beatriz again, but a small part of her is relieved as well, like her own armor has grown another layer. Who would accuse her of using magic now, with the king himself making her out to be the stars' most devout defender?

Then again, she thinks, casting King Cesare a sideways glance, she is the furthest thing from safe. All she can do is hope the king's affection for her doesn't lessen—or grow, for that matter. Walking a tightrope indeed.

Pasquale, Nicolo, and Gisella have all said that he wasn't always this way, that he's grown worse over the years, and she knows that oftentimes people's minds can begin to go before their bodies do, but King Cesare is only in his fifties. It can't be aging, and if it were some sort of malady, surely someone would have diagnosed him.

When the applause dies down, Beatriz sees the king reaching for his glass of wine again. Her eyes follow the wineglass—refilled so many times tonight she's already lost count. Nicolo mentioned that the cupbearers had taken to diluting the wine. As soon as she thinks it, another thought occurs to her: if she wanted to poison the king, his wine would be an excellent means—he's never far from the stuff, and she would never have to handle it herself. So long as the bottle was poisoned, the culprit could be untraceable. Perhaps when Nico and the cupbearers diluted the wine they were actually diluting a poison, decaying his mind instead of killing him outright.

It's what I would do doesn't mean anything, Beatriz knows this. But something about the notion won't let her go, and her mother has always told her and her sisters to trust their instincts. She only wishes she knew more about poisons, but she's never been as good with them as Daphne, and with something like this, she isn't inclined to take chances.

She eyes the wineglass as King Cesare passes it back to Nicolo.

"So I say: death to the heretic who dared worm his way into my home, and death to any Temarinian who seeks to avenge him. And lo and behold," the king continues, reaching into his pocket to remove a cream-colored envelope, with a theatrical flourish. Beatriz is close enough to make out the vague shape of the seal—a sun, cast in yellow wax, with a spot of violet in the center to mark it as royal. "It seems my young nephew is foolish enough to declare war before I've even spilled blood! Well, if King Leopold seeks to make war with us, we'll teach that boy a thing or two about what war means. To Cellaria!" he cries out, lifting his glass again. The rest of the court follows suit, echoing his toast, and Beatriz goes through the motions as well, even as her mind is spinning.

War with Temarin, just as her mother has designed, just as she and Sophronia have put into action. Vaguely, she wonders what Daphne is up to in Friv, but she can't waste her thoughts there—whatever it is, she's sure Daphne is making their mother proud. Just as Beatriz herself has, just as Sophronia must have if she's convinced Leopold to declare war. Her thoughts drift to Lord Savelle, his death warrant signed now, but she forces herself to ignore him. Soon Cellaria will fall and Bessemia will claim its pieces. Soon Beatriz will get to go home.

Her false smile feels somewhat more real as she lifts the wine goblet to her lips and takes a sip.

Beatriz supposes it doesn't actually matter whether someone is poisoning King Cesare or not, whether he actually has been conspiring with his sister or not—Cellaria will likely be under her mother's control long before this possible poisoner succeeds. It shouldn't matter . . . but Beatriz's curiosity gets the better of her. At the end of the banquet, she tells Pasquale to go back to their rooms without her because she's left her shawl in the banquet hall. Of course Pasquale doesn't notice she wasn't wearing one to begin with—he might not even know what a shawl is.

It's an easy enough thing after that to wait around a corner until she hears King Cesare's booming voice coming toward her. She steps out at just the right moment, walking straight into him.

"Oh!" she says, looking up at King Cesare with wide eyes. "I'm so sorry, Your Majesty, I was thinking about how wonderful your speech was and I got a bit distracted," she says with a bright smile.

Behind him, his usual entourage of simpering courtiers fusses over him—as if Beatriz's bumping into him might have caused him serious bodily harm. He waves them away impatiently, keeping his gaze on her. Beatriz has to force herself not to recoil from his leer and hold on to her smile.

"It was a wonderful speech, wasn't it?" he says, looking pleased with himself.

"Yes, indeed," Beatriz says, before breaking off into a little cough. "Oh, I'm sorry, my throat's just a bit dry—"

"Nico!" King Cesare says, holding his hand out for the goblet.

Nicolo looks at her with a furrowed brow but passes the goblet to the king, who passes it to Beatriz. She'll explain it to Nicolo after, she thinks, once she knows for sure.

Beatriz takes the wine, then frowns as if a thought has just occurred to her. "Oh, if I am getting sick, the *last* thing I would want is to make Your Majesty ill as well," she says, glancing back at the courtiers, all carrying their own goblets. One woman—Duchess Lehey—holds it off-kilter, a sign that it has no contents she is worried about spilling.

"Duchess Lehey—might I take your cup? You look to be finished," she says.

"I . . . of course, Your Highness," the woman says, though she doesn't appear happy about it. But when the king gestures for her to hurry up, she quickly passes the goblet to Beatriz, who pours a small amount of the king's wine into the empty goblet. She pretends to take a sip of the wine and smiles at the king.

"Thank you, Your Majesty. It is quite refreshing."

As soon as she gets back to her rooms, she says a quick hello to Pasquale, distractedly reading a book, and goes to her dressing room, where she finds a small glass vial in the false bottom of her jewelry box. She transfers the wine from the goblet into the vial and begins to pen a letter to Daphne.

Sophronia

Leopold leads Sophronia through the labyrinthine palace hallways, which she still hasn't quite figured out how to navigate herself, even after almost a month here. They climb so many winding staircases that her leg muscles scream in pain and her breath goes short.

"Just a bit farther," he says over his shoulder, though he, too, seems winded.

Sophronia grimaces at him but steels herself and continues to follow him up, up, up, until finally, he pushes open a wooden door and leads her into a small room, lit only by the afternoon sun pouring through a single wide window.

The room is circular and possibly the smallest chamber she's seen in the palace—if she and Leopold were to hold hands, they could each touch an opposite wall easily. It's also empty of any furniture, with only a threadbare, color-leached rug spread over the stone floor.

"It's the highest guard tower in the kingdom," he tells her, answering the question she hasn't asked. "Not much of a use for it since the war with Cellaria ended, but it's got the best view."

He tugs her toward the open window and gestures. When Sophronia looks out, she can't help but gasp at the sight that awaits. It feels like all of Temarin is spread out before her, stretching all the way to the horizon. Everything is so small she suddenly feels like a child playing with toy figures again. She can barely make out the dots that must be people below, clustered together in the crowded streets of Kavelle.

"They look like ants," she says, her voice full of wonder. "And they all look the same. You can't tell from all the way up here who is a commoner and who is a duke."

"I doubt there are any dukes who dare to wander around Kavelle," Leopold says, his voice low. He's standing behind her, his head just over her shoulder, so close she can feel his breath against her cheek as he speaks.

Sophronia points to a particularly thick cluster of dots in one of the squares. It must be hundreds of people. "What's going on there?"

"Ah. That's what I wanted to show you," he says, sounding quite pleased with himself. "Do you remember when we spoke about the possibility of a public fund? In theory, it would take some time for the tariffs that would pay for it to be put into place, but I decided to get a head start. You cut a significant amount of money from the palace budget for the month, and I managed to . . . encourage many of the noble families at court to donate—"

"Encourage?" Sophronia asks, glancing back at him over her shoulder with a raised eyebrow.

"With significant pressure," he admits with a halfheartedly sheepish smile. "I may have very vaguely threatened a few of them with stripping their titles or taking away various estates.

I told Aunt Bruna I'd been considering making her my new ambassador to Cellaria—a very exalted position, mind you."

"Never mind the fact that their king is mad, magic is outlawed, and they've imprisoned the last ambassador we sent them," Sophronia says, biting her lip to keep from laughing. She can only imagine how Bruna took that offer.

"She was . . . less than enthused," he admits. "Gave me three hundred thousand asters to change my mind. I didn't even know she possessed that much money, considering how she's always asking for an increase in her allowance."

"I'd wager she has far more than that if she was willing to part with it so quickly," Sophronia points out. "How much did you raise altogether?"

"Nearly two million," he says, looking a bit smug. "Enough to budget for five food depositories throughout Temarin—just like that one," he says, directing Sophronia's attention back out the window to the gathered crowd. "In the five biggest cities now, but I'm hopeful soon we'll be able to expand the program into smaller towns and villages."

"How does it work?" she asks.

"Every morning, a line will form, and everyone will take a set amount of rations depending on the number of people in their household—a collection of produce, meat, and grains procured from local Temarinian farmers."

Sophronia glances back at Leopold. "And how is that going?" she asks.

He shrugs. "It's a work in progress. We first opened yesterday morning, and it was chaos—no one was keen to form a neat and orderly line. But when it became clear that it was the only way they'd receive food, things calmed down a bit.

There's some conflict now about how to verify that people are taking only what they need. I heard word that there were some who took extra rations and tried to sell them to those who missed out, at an astronomical markup. It isn't a perfect system, but we're working on it."

Sophronia feels a smile tug at her lips. "Look at you," she says.

His cheeks flush, but he's smiling too. "Yes, well, it turns out I have a knack for this. No one is more surprised than I am," he says before pointing once again to the square, where several larger shapes move toward the shop. It takes a second for her to realize what they are.

"Wagons?" she asks, frowning.

"Indeed. Carrying fresh game. Ansel introduced me to a group of unemployed workers from various backgrounds. Their skill sets differ, but it turns out with a bit of training from my kitchen staff, they're all quite capable of putting together a decent stew."

Sophronia watches the wagons approach. "There are so many," she says, glancing back at him. "Where did you find so much game?"

"I issued a challenge," he says, practically beaming. "It's the end of the week, the court gentlemen tend to want to hunt. So I said that whoever ended up with the most weight by three o'clock would win a prize. They were all quite motivated."

"How did you convince them to donate their quarry?" she asks.

He shrugs. "Technically, it isn't their quarry. It was caught on the palace grounds, so it belongs to me. Or, rather, it belongs to us. And besides, I allowed them to keep the pelts and they know where their next meals are coming from, so no one had any complaints."

"And the prize?" she asks. "As you said, they seem to have been quite motivated. And since money is so tight—"

"The prize cost us nothing," he says. "But I thought we might use your late-night kitchen excursions—they were quite interested in the possibility of serving a cake baked by the queen at their next party."

"Oh, I like that idea," Sophronia says with a grin.

"I thought you might," he says before his expression wavers. "What do you think of the rest of it?" he asks, almost tentatively, as if he's afraid of her answer.

Sophronia steps closer to him and lifts her hand to cup his cheek. "I think it's brilliant—*you're* brilliant," she says.

He covers her hand with his and sighs. "Thank you for telling me not to declare war on Cellaria. You and Ansel were right. I hate that things got as bad as they did," he says. "I don't know how . . ." He trails off, shaking his head. "That's not true. I know exactly how."

"Your father died suddenly," Sophronia says. "He was young and healthy, no one expected him to fall off his horse—"

"Yet you were plenty prepared. Even though you aren't even in line to inherit your mother's throne, she prepared you," he points out.

Sophronia bites her lip to keep from blurting out the truth—that she was prepared for something else entirely. Something she has now gone against. She still can't believe she's done it, but she has, and she is not foolish enough to believe there won't be consequences.

"My father never prepared me to be king," he continues. "I don't think he believed I was capable of it."

"If he saw you as a child, Leo, it's because that's what you were," she says softly. "He set you up with a council—"

"My mother put together the council," he interrupts. "It turns out, my father couldn't even do that much."

Sophronia frowns. "She said your father personally asked Covier and Verning to guide you," she says. More than that, Eugenia blamed King Carlisle for their incompetence.

Leopold shrugs. "I thought so too. I suppose she was trying to protect me from the truth of my father's antipathy. But Covier let the truth slip this morning—she brought him and Verning in after my father died. I know they're lacking, but my mother's like me. She never had to be political either—I'm not surprised she didn't know better."

Sophronia doesn't say anything, the gears of her mind turning. She's already had suspicions that Covier and Verning are working toward Eugenia's aims, but to what end? How would giving Temarin over to Cellarian rule serve them?

"But you were right," Leopold says, drawing her out of her thoughts. "The past can't be changed. Only the future. I want a new council, one with you and Ansel—maybe someone from the merchant class as well?"

Sophronia is careful to school her expression into something neutral at the mention of giving Ansel so much power. She supposes he's the first commoner Leopold has ever had a conversation with, and she has to admit Ansel has wormed his way close to Leopold brilliantly, saving his brother and standing up to Leopold just enough to seem brave and bold. Of course Leopold is naïve enough to fall for it, but Sophronia isn't.

"And my brothers," Leopold continues. "I want to ensure that I don't make the mistakes my father did. And as of now, Gideon is next in line for the throne. If something were to happen to me, I'd want him to be prepared."

"I think that's a fine idea," Sophronia says, smoothing her thumb over his cheekbone. "Though Gideon won't be next in line forever," she adds.

Leopold shakes his head. "There's no pressure on that count, Sophie," he says, stooping to press his forehead against hers. "I meant what I said on our wedding night. There's no rush. And I know I've broken your trust."

Sophronia doesn't speak for a moment. He isn't wrong—his actions hurt her as well as Temarin. The boy she knew from letters wasn't the boy she met, the boy she married. He isn't perfect—but he's *trying.*

Her mother warned her about losing her heart to him, but the prospect of not doing so seems ludicrous now, not because she's forsaken her mother, not because she has no more plots or plans against him, but because she realizes she's already in love with him. She doesn't know when it happened or what their future holds. All she knows is that what's between them now is so much stronger than a perfect figment of ink and paper. It's real.

She tilts her head up and catches his lips in a kiss that she feels all the way to her toes. She could kiss him like this every day for the rest of their lives, she realizes. The idea makes her giddy. She pulls back a fraction of an inch and grins at him.

"Why don't we retire for the evening?" she asks.

Leopold's brow furrows in confusion. "It isn't even dinnertime—are you tired?" he asks.

Sophronia holds his gaze and shakes her head. "No," she says, kissing him again. "I'm not tired at all."

Sophronia and Leopold have nearly made it back to their room, hand in hand, when they hear shouting coming from down the corridor. Leopold glances at Sophie, frowning.

"I know that voice," he says, pulling her down the corridor toward the shouts. Sophronia follows, though she'd like nothing better than to drag Leopold into their rooms and close out the rest of the world for a few hours. She knows that voice too, and she knows deep in her gut that nothing good will come of this.

They round the corner to find Ansel being held by two palace guards, struggling. When he sees Leopold, he struggles harder.

"You liar!" he shouts. The guard holding his right arm reaches for his sword, but Leopold holds up a hand.

"Stop," he says to the guards. "Let him go."

The guards exchange a look but do as he says. Ansel looks just as confused as they do, shrugging off their hands, though he makes no move toward Leopold and Sophronia.

"What are you talking about?" Leopold asks him, keeping his voice level and calm.

Ansel frowns, glancing between him and Sophronia.

"You're joking," he says, but when Leopold doesn't respond, he stands up a little straighter. "You declared war on Cellaria, after you said you wouldn't. It's all anyone in Kavelle is talking about."

"Then it's a rumor without a foundation," Leopold says, shaking his head. "You were there when I made my decision to avoid it. Nothing's changed."

One of the guards clears his throat. "With all due respect, Your Majesty, I was one of the guards who posted notices of the war in town this morning. The palace is recruiting soldiers as we speak."

Bewildered, Leopold glances at Sophronia, who lets out a low exhale.

"Your mother," she says, quietly enough that the others can't hear her. "She went behind our backs."

Leopold shakes his head. "She wouldn't. Covier or Verning, maybe—"

"Covier and Verning couldn't buckle their own shoes without guidance—your mother's guidance, specifically. She wanted a war, and when you didn't give in, she went around you," Sophronia says. The rest of it rises to her lips—the letter from Cesare, how Eugenia has spent the year since Leopold took the throne draining Temarin's war chest, how she has quietly been plotting against him and the whole country—but she holds her tongue. This is not the place, not when they have an audience. Still, the words she does say shock him.

She looks at the guards and Ansel.

"We aren't going to war," she tells them. "There was a . . . miscommunication. We'll be sorting it out now."

"It's too late for that," a new voice says from behind them. Sophronia and Leopold turn to find Eugenia approaching, vivid violet silk skirt billowing around her. She doesn't look smug, Sophronia realizes. Which is a surprise—after all, she got what she's been working toward for at least a year.

"I hope you had nothing to do with this, Mother," Leopold says, his voice low.

"Me?" Eugenia asks, raising her eyebrows. "*I* didn't send a declaration of war to Cellaria."

"Neither did I!" Leopold snaps.

"And yet one apparently arrived. I understand that it was signed by you," Eugenia says.

"Signatures can be falsified," Sophronia says. She should know—she was meant to falsify King Bartholomew's signature to force Friv into the war as well, though a signature is nothing on its own.

"From what my spies in the Cellarian court tell me, the letter was also sealed," Eugenia adds, as if reading Sophronia's mind. "Marked with a drop of blood."

"Not *my* blood," Leopold says.

Eugenia shrugs. "An empyrea would have been able to clear that up easily enough," she says.

"But sorcery is illegal in Cellaria," Sophronia finishes, understanding dawning on her, "so they would never know. And they had a signature, Leopold's seal marked with blood that was allegedly his, and a mad, paranoid king on the throne who will take any excuse he can get to reignite the Celestian War."

This has her mother's fingerprints on it, but Sophronia can't see how they got there.

Eugenia nods slowly, unable to smother a smile. "Which means we are now at war with Cellaria, whether you like it or not."

Leopold shakes his head. "I'll tell them it was a mistake," he says.

Eugenia looks toward Sophronia, and Sophronia sees that *now* she looks smug.

"You can't," Sophronia tells Leopold, dread pooling in her stomach. "That kind of back-and-forth will lose you all credibility with your people. And Cellaria won't believe it was a mistake. We can refuse to go to war with them, but they'll still come at us."

It's a brilliant move, backing Temarin into a corner. Eugenia claims she didn't do it, and Sophronia believes her. She knows her mother's work when she sees it, and with a sinking feeling, she realizes she knows exactly how her mother carried it out, and who helped her do it. Without a word, she pushes past Eugenia, leaving Leopold, the guards, and Ansel behind as she hurries to her rooms. She dimly hears Leopold calling her name, but she ignores him. She runs through her sitting room, into her bedroom, and to the wardrobe where she hid King Bartholomew's seal.

There, in the box Daphne sent, she finds her sister's letter and the sample of King Bartholomew's handwriting. But the seal containing his blood is gone.

Friv's sigil is the Northern Star—different from Temarin's blazing sun, but Sophronia imagines them both in her mind, sees how, if it were her, she would take a needle to the seal's wax before it hardened, shifting the star's points into sun's rays. If someone looked closely they might be able to see the difference, but why would they look at all? Not when it was Leopold's name on the letter, Leopold's signature, providing news that King Cesare must have expected and been working toward for so long.

It's exactly what Sophronia would have done. But she didn't. Which means someone else did.

Sophronia finds Violie in the small room next to Sophronia's that she was given when she became her lady's maid. Sophronia doesn't knock, surprising Violie and causing her to jump up from her place on her bed, where she was sitting with an open book on her lap. A book Violie told Sophronia she couldn't read.

But Violie doesn't seem to remember that, or else she's hoping Sophronia doesn't, because she holds the book in front of her and smiles.

"Sophie," she says. "I'm sorry—did you have need of me? I thought you were with the king."

Sophronia's eyes go to the book, then back to Violie. "I want you gone," she says, her voice as calm as it is cold. "Now. You can have a few moments to pack your things and then I'll have guards escort you out of the palace."

Violie takes a step toward her, but Sophronia stops her with a raised hand.

"Sophie," Violie begins.

"It's *Your Majesty,*" Sophronia tells her. "I trust you'll find your way back to Bessemia on your own. And when you see my mother, give her my regards. I hope whatever she offered you was worth it."

Sophronia turns and starts back toward the door. When her hand is on the knob, Violie speaks, her voice soft.

"My mother's life," she says.

Sophronia glances back over her shoulder. "What?"

"It's what she offered me," Violie says. "My mother is ill—the physician said she had Vexis."

Sophronia winces. Vexis is a disease of the brain, and though no one knows what causes it, as it progresses, the sufferer's mind fractures. The past becomes the present, the present becomes the past; oftentimes people don't know who they are or recognize the faces of their closest friends and family. It is almost always fatal, and there is only one cure.

"We couldn't afford stardust, and it isn't a sure thing anyway," Violie says. "I thought that if I was going to steal stardust, I'd better get my hands on the strongest kind I could. So I broke into Nigellus's laboratory at the palace. I was caught immediately," she says with a bitter laugh. "I knew I probably would be. I just . . . didn't care. I thought I'd be taken to prison, but imagine my shock when I was brought to the empress instead."

"And she offered to cure your mother in exchange for what? Spying on me? Are there more of you, watching my sisters?" Sophronia says.

"No, only me," Violie says, and she sounds ashamed, though that does little to soothe Sophronia's ire. "You were the weak link, she said, the only one she couldn't rely on. I was only supposed to watch you, to make sure you stayed on your path."

"You're the one who helped lead me off it," Sophronia says. "You gave me those budgets."

"Because you asked," Violie counters. "What was I supposed to do, refuse you? I thought once your mother told you to drop it, you would—"

"But I didn't," Sophronia says.

Violie exhales, slumping down. "No," she says. "So your mother asked me to do one more thing before she cured my mother. Find the seal she said was in your possession, forge a note in King Leopold's hand, and declare war on Cellaria. It was such a small thing—I managed it in a few minutes."

"How?" Sophronia asks. "How did you manage to forge his signature?"

"The same way you would have, I imagine," Violie says. "I was in your mother's employ for two years before I came here—many of the lessons you were given, I had as well. Forgery, lock-picking, disguises."

"And you can read," Sophronia says, nodding toward the book.

Violie offers her a rueful smile. "No one suspects an uneducated servant," she says. "You were so busy trying to save me that you never thought . . ." She trails off, biting her lip. "I am sorry. I didn't want to do it. I had no choice."

Sophronia tightens her grip on the doorknob.

"You had a choice, Violie," she says. "You traded your mother's life for millions of Temarinians who won't survive this war, won't survive my mother's siege. Who will die in battle or from starvation or disease. You saved your mother, but how many mothers did you kill?"

Violie blanches, but she holds her ground. "I'm sorry," she repeats, but Sophronia knows that if she could, she'd do it all over again, exactly the same.

"Guards will be here in half an hour to escort you out," Sophronia tells her, pulling the door open and stepping through. "If I ever see you again, I'll have you arrested." With that, she shuts the door with a slam.

There is one last hope, she thinks. She returns to her room, sits down at her desk, and begins writing to her sisters.

Daphne

Daphne is just putting her satin slippers on when a maid walks in, holding a small box. "From your sister," she says, and when Daphne raises an eyebrow, she quickly adds "Princess Beatriz."

Daphne tries to appear pleased, but she's already running late for her engagement ball, and Cliona's list of names is weighing heavily on her mind. Whatever Beatriz wants—and Daphne knows her sister well enough to be sure she wants something—Daphne doesn't have time for it right now.

"Thank you," she tells the maid, taking the box from her. "Will you fetch my wrap? It's particularly chilly this evening."

When the maid goes to the wardrobe, Daphne opens the box to find a letter and a small vial of what appears to be red wine. The package doesn't appear to have been tampered with, but that doesn't surprise Daphne—Friv is a bit more lax in their security than Bessemia. She guesses that because it is a new monarchy, they haven't yet learned to see enemies around every corner. Daphne supposes it makes things easier for her, though it also led to that assassination attempt.

She pushes the thought aside and opens the letter.

Dearest Daphne,

I came across a Cellarian cure for migraines and wanted to pass it along to you—I know yours cause you such trouble when they come about. The king himself swears by this mixture, though I haven't the slightest idea what is in it. Of course, I wouldn't be surprised if you puzzled out the recipe. I'm happy to send you more if you need any.

Your sister,
Beatriz

Daphne searches for a sign of what code the letter is in, but none appears. She rolls her eyes. Just like Beatriz to forgo coding the letter—she was never as gifted at it as Sophronia and Daphne. Daphne reads it again, picking out the lies in an effort to see the truth.

First, Daphne has never suffered a migraine in her life, and to the best of her knowledge, the king of Cellaria doesn't suffer from them either. Surely that would have been mentioned in the spy reports.

I wouldn't be surprised if you puzzled out the recipe. That's it, then. The king is drinking whatever's in the vial, and Beatriz wants to know what it is. A couple of logical steps have been skipped, she knows, but she knows her sisters even better. Sometimes they don't need logic. In Bessemia, they would often have conversations without any words at all. It's comforting to know that even with all these miles between them, some things haven't changed, but Daphne's irritation outweighs that. She has plenty on her own plate without doing Beatriz's work as well. She puts the vial into the drawer of her desk and tosses the letter into the fire.

She has a rebellion to infiltrate, she thinks, letting her maid drape the ermine wrap over her shoulders. Beatriz is just going to have to figure it out for herself.

The Frivian castle has been quiet as a crypt since Daphne arrived, but she hadn't realized just how quiet it has been until she steps into the banquet hall where her betrothal ball is being held. The large room is packed full with groups from the twelve visiting highland noble families, six lowland noble families, and every castle-dwelling noble who had been observing the mandated monthlong mourning period.

Daphne has heard that Friv is a wild, unrefined place, but she hasn't fully understood what that meant until now, when she finds herself enveloped by the overwhelming smells of ale and roasted meat and the sounds of countless conversations, all loud and some conducted in accents so strong she can't begin to pick apart the words.

The large room is packed with bodies, most of them far taller than any Bessemian, all dressed in wool and velvet. The men all look in desperate need of a haircut, the women wear few jewels. Daphne spent most of her life learning about Frivian customs and celebrations, but it is another thing entirely to find herself thrown into the center of them.

She's careful to school her expression into a polite smile and hide any hint of her distaste as she scans the room, looking for a familiar face.

"Ah, Daphne!" a voice calls. Daphne follows it and finds King Bartholomew standing near the center of the room, with Bairre as well as two men she does not recognize. When she goes to join them, the king makes quick introductions.

"Lord Ian Maives and Lord Vance Panlington," he says.

Daphne curtsies toward each man in turn. She has all but eliminated Lord Maives already from Cliona's list, but it is still good to put a face to his name, and Lord Panlington must be Cliona's father.

"It was very kind of you to send Lady Cliona to accompany me on my journey to Friv," she tells him, offering up her most charming smile. "We became the fastest of friends."

She watches his expression carefully—Mrs. Nattermore implied he was the head of the rebels, so he must know about what happened at the dressmaker's and her own involvement now, but Daphne also wonders if he knows something about the assassination attempt on her. She believed Cliona when she swore she wasn't involved, but it is possible Lord Panlington didn't wish to entangle his daughter in such nasty business.

But if Lord Panlington knows anything about her at all, he doesn't give it away. Instead, he bows low and kisses her gloved hand.

"I'm very glad to hear it, Your Highness," he says.

Finally, she turns toward Bairre. She hasn't seen much of him over the last week, not since they met on the archery fields. He's been holed up in meetings with his father, trying to make up for missing a lifetime of princely training and elbow-rubbing in a few short days.

He cleans up quite well, dressed in midnight-blue velvet that fits him better than anything else she's seen him wear—she wonders if it's the first thing he's owned that was made specifically for him. His hair is brushed, though still overgrown. Daphne finds that she's relieved he didn't cut it. It suits him.

"Prince Bairre," she says, curtsying again.

Bairre bows in turn and mumbles something that sounds like her name. He's nervous, she realizes, and she can't blame him. Daphne has been trained for events like these, to smile and mingle and make a favorable impression. Bairre has been raised to linger on the outskirts, watching but not participating. He must be miserable.

"The children should start the dancing, Bartholomew," Lord Maives says, clapping the king on his shoulder.

If anyone dared touch her mother like that, Daphne reckons they would lose that hand, but Bartholomew only smiles.

"Of course," he says, lifting his goblet high in the air. In seconds, everyone falls silent. When he speaks again, his voice is booming, loud enough to reach the farthest corners of the room. "I won't drone on and keep you from eating, drinking, and merriment," he says, gazing around the room. Daphne looks as well, searching for the slightest hints of resentment. She finds plenty, but Bartholomew gives no indication that he notices. "It has been a difficult time for my family and for our country, but I hope that today marks the turning of a corner for all of us. I hope that you will join me in welcoming Princess Daphne to Friv and to my family, and join me in wishing her and my son, Prince Bairre, a star-blessed union. To Daphne and Bairre."

"To Daphne and Bairre," the crowd echoes, raising their own goblets toward her and Bairre. With everyone's attention on her, she decides to give them a show. She slips her hand into Bairre's and flashes him an adoring smile. For an instant, he's shocked, but then he returns it, somewhat warily.

"A dance!" Bartholomew calls out, and from the corner, a quartet picks up their instruments and begins to play. She recognizes it as a carrundel and lets out a quiet groan. Bairre hears it and glances at her, eyebrows raised.

"I'm not very good at this one," she admits. She was taught the traditional Frivian dances alongside Bessemian ones, but her feet never took to them the same way. She found them rough and erratic, with none of the softness and grace of the ones that played out in Bessemian ballrooms.

"Then I suppose you'll have to follow my lead," he says, lifting their joined hands to walk her out to where a small space has opened up in the center of the room.

"If you step on my toes," she tells him, through a smile that is all for show, "be assured I will seek my revenge."

"I would expect nothing less," he replies. He shifts their joined hands so that their fingers are entwined and settles his other hand on her waist. She places her hand on his shoulder, feeling the firm muscle beneath his velvet jacket.

He steps toward her, and at the same time, she steps toward him, the result the clash of his chin with her forehead.

"Ow," she says, lifting her hand off his shoulder to rub her head.

"I step forward first, you step back," he tells her, brow furrowed in concentration.

"Why is your chin so sharp?" she asks with a scowl. She'd never noticed how pointed it was before, but now she feels certain it's left a permanent dent in her forehead.

"You're the one with the head hard as marble," he volleys back. "Here, follow me."

He says it like it's easy, but in reality, for every two steps he takes, Daphne is lucky if she manages one without tripping over her feet. In Bessemia, she was considered a good dancer, though not as graceful as Sophronia or as spirited as Beatriz, but Frivian dances are a whole other beast.

She stumbles, she falters, and she steps on Bairre's toes every few seconds—though he never once complains. Luckily, as soon as they begin, other couples join them, so she doesn't feel that her failure is quite so much on display. And after a time, she begins to enjoy herself, the quick beat of the music working beneath her skin, her steps becoming more confident, Bairre's hand on her back like an anchor. When he releases her waist to send her twirling across the dance floor, she can't hold back the wild, unrestrained squeal of joy that rips its way from her chest.

When the song reaches its crescendo, Daphne is out of breath and smiling so broadly her cheeks ache. Bairre is smiling too, a truer smile than she's ever seen on him. She decides she likes it—it is a smile she cannot help but return. Though the song ends, his hand still rests on her waist, steady and sure and warm through her velvet gown.

"You're a better dancer than I thought you'd be," she tells him, making no move to step out of his arms even as the couples around them break apart.

With the spell of the music waning, the placid mask begins to fall back into place. "Yes, well, even bastards are given lessons," he says, dropping his hands from her waist.

She takes a step back, her own hands falling to her sides. "Don't put words in my mouth," she says. "I was trying to pay you a compliment."

"Your Highness," a voice cuts in, and Daphne turns to see a young man of around twenty approaching, his dark hair swept back from his face and secured with a leather tie, highlighting his knife-sharp features. "I was wondering if I might have the honor of a dance with Princess Daphne."

Bairre tears his gaze away from Daphne, shrugging. "You would have to ask it of her, Haimish," he says before turning on his heel and walking away.

Haimish, Daphne thinks, smiling at the man and accepting his hand. The third name from Cliona's list. She knows she should focus on him, but she can't keep her eyes from following Bairre as he walks across the dance floor, shoulders hunched and ready to slip back into the shadows. But he is no longer a bastard, so no one lets him, their eyes following his every move. Daphne almost pities him.

"A dance, then, Princess?" Haimish asks, drawing her attention back to him. She pastes on a bright smile.

"I would like nothing more," she says before biting her lip. "But I'm afraid I turned my ankle during the last dance. I'm sure it's fine," she says when his eyes widen in concern.

"But I think it might be best if I sit down for a bit, to be sure."

"Of course," he says, offering her his arm. Daphne takes it and lets herself be helped to the far wall, where some seats have been set up. He helps her sit and then turns to go.

"Wait!" she says. When he turns back toward her, she dons a sheepish smile. "Will you sit with me for a bit? I'm afraid I don't know many people here."

"You don't know me, either," he points out, but he sits down beside her nonetheless.

"Then we will have to change that, won't we?" she asks. "Haimish, was it?"

He nods. "My father is Lord Talmadge."

Daphne affects a brighter smile. "Oh, him I know, at least by reputation," she says, watching Haimish's face carefully. "His skills in the last of the Clan Wars is legendary—even in Bessemia, they sang ballads about him."

"Truly?" Haimish asks, looking at her with raised eyebrows.

"Oh yes," she says. "In Bessemia, we haven't had any war in centuries—the people were always hungry for tales of valiant heroes from other lands, fighting for their country."

There it is—a scoff he can't quite hold back, though he does manage to catch himself rolling his eyes.

"What is it?" she asks, still all wide eyes and empty smiles. "You don't think he was a hero?"

"I think war is a more complicated thing than you might imagine, having only heard tales and ballads," he says, his eyes traveling across the ballroom.

She registers the condescending note in his voice but ignores it. He's not wrong—she doesn't know about war the same way Frivians do.

"And you?" she asks him. "You don't look old enough to remember the last Clan War."

He smiles, though his eyes are still on the crowd. "I was two when Bartholomew was crowned king," he says. "Though there are those who say the war never really ended. There are those who believe that war is as much a part of Friv as the soil, trees, and snow."

Daphne glances sideways at him, a question on her lips, but then she sees that his roving gaze has settled, and she follows it to where Cliona is standing beside Bairre, her head bent toward his as she murmurs something that makes him smile—not really smile, the way he did on the archery fields or even just a moment ago, but it still ignites something ugly in the pit of Daphne's stomach, though she's sure Cliona is only exploiting their friendship for the sake of the rebellion. It shouldn't bother her that Cliona is manipulating him—stars know she's doing the same—but a strange, foreign part of her feels protective of Bairre. No one could call him naïve, she doubts any royal bastard is, but he hasn't learned yet that everyone wants something of him.

"Cliona said they've been friends since they were children. Cillian, too," Daphne says to Haimish, in an effort to veer away from that troubling line of thought. "I'm glad they have each other to rely on in their grief."

As soon as she says the words, she wonders how true they are. Bairre loved his brother, she knows that, but Cliona? If she's been actively working against the royal family, that included Cillian. And the disease that killed him was one that eluded every physician who examined him. She knows firsthand that Frivians aren't shy about assassination attempts. What if the rebels were responsible for Cillian's death? And what would that mean now for Bairre? Maybe she's right to be protective of him. After all, their betrothal is the only thing keeping Friv within her mother's grasp, and Bartholomew doesn't have any other bastard sons lying about, as far as she knows.

"He was a good person, Prince Cillian," Haimish says, drawing her out of her thoughts. He tries to hide it, but she sees how his eyes keep going to Cliona in the crowd, as if drawn there by some invisible force.

"Yes, I believe he was," Daphne says, then pauses. She chooses her next words carefully. "Bairre is a good person too. If anything were to happen to him, it would be disastrous."

That gets his attention. He looks at her and raises his eyebrows, appearing bemused. "Your devotion to Prince Bairre is touching, Your Highness."

"Is it?" Daphne asks, tilting her head. "And here I was thinking the same of your devotion to Cliona."

Haimish goes rigid—Daphne doubts he even breathes. The only change in him is a flush that begins to work its way up his neck.

"Why, you've barely been able to stop looking at her all night. And she seems to be doing everything possible *not* to look at you. Which of your parents disapproves? I'd wager it's her father. I've heard he's very protective of her, and then there's the matter of your loyal war hero father. Is that why you joined the rebellion? To prove you're more than your father's son?"

Haimish is quiet for a few more seconds, but then he surprises Daphne by smiling. "Something like that, I suppose," he says. "How did you figure it out?"

She shrugs. "You underestimated me and got sloppy," she says. "It was actually quite easy. Why would Cliona put you on my list? She must know your loyalty better than anyone."

Haimish rubs the back of his neck. "We had a bet. I lost."

"So it's all a game to you, then," Daphne says, rolling her eyes. "Believe it or not, I do have better things to do."

"Relax," he says with a snort. "It's not *all* a game. Think of me as a test. Well done. The other two names are genuine."

"Well, I doubt you can win over Lord Maives. He's even closer to the king than your father is, not to mention the fact that he's the queen's brother-in-law. Trying would be foolish."

Haimish makes a noncommittal noise in the back of his throat, and Daphne forces herself not to roll her eyes. If he wants to try to turn Lord Maives, let him.

"And Rufus Cadringal?" he presses.

Daphne notes that Haimish doesn't use Cadringal's title. Lord Cadringal has only come into it recently, but she wonders if he and Haimish are familiar enough that it's a difficult habit to break.

"Going by what I already know, I think it's possible he'll turn. But I haven't met him yet, so it's difficult to say for certain," Daphne says, scanning the crowd. "Do you see him?"

"Unfortunately, they had some carriage issues and were

delayed. I heard they sent a messenger ahead to say they would be arriving before dawn."

"That is unfortunate," Daphne agrees, the wheels in her head turning. Across the banquet hall, Bairre says something to Cliona before slipping away, outside the main doors. "Thank you for keeping me company, Haimish. If you don't mind, I need to have a word with my fiancé."

She finds Bairre leaning against the stone wall outside the banquet hall beside a lit sconce, his sharp-boned face thrown into high relief by the flickering flame. More than ever, he looks half feral, but when his eyes find hers, there's a flash of softness—so quick she can't be sure it ever existed at all.

"Are you hiding out here?" she asks him. "The highlanders don't seem so bad, boisterous as they might be."

He shakes his head, a smile flickering at his lips. "I just needed a minute," he says. "What did you think of Haimish?" he asks her.

Daphne rolls her eyes to show how trying she found him, and Bairre barks out a laugh. "Fair enough," he says.

"He did mention that one of the families—the Cadringals—was delayed. I thought we might take them hunting tomorrow as a way of making up for it," she says.

"The Cadringals?" Bairre asks, his eyes lighting. "I haven't seen Rufus since . . . well, since we both had different titles, I suppose."

"Since you both lost loved ones," she adds.

He nods, glancing away. "It's not necessary, you know."

"What?" Daphne asks.

"Trying to charm him," Bairre says, shrugging. "The Cadringals were among the first families to swear fealty to my father, and Rufus was friends with both Cillian and me. We took lessons together whenever he was at court. He never treated me different than Cillian. If there's anyone whose loyalty I can depend on, it's him."

Daphne considers this, adding it to the information she's already gathered about Rufus Cadringal, along with what she's gathered about Bairre as well—beneath the gruff exterior, there's so much he doesn't understand about his new position. If someone is trying to kill her, if someone already succeeded in killing Cillian, he very well may have a target on his back as well, and at the moment he's an easy mark. She leans against the wall across from him.

"A strong ruler knows not to depend upon anyone's loyalty, Bairre," she says softly. He doesn't know that Cliona is working against his family, after all. He doesn't know about Daphne herself. His ignorance of her motives is a boon, but if he looks around the faces of the Friv courtiers and sees no enemies, it very well might get him killed. She feels certain her mother would see that as Daphne's fault.

He shakes his head, not speaking for a moment.

"How do you do it?" he asks finally.

She frowns. "Do what?"

He shrugs. "Look at everyone around you and see how you can use them, how they can betray you. You and my father both, talking about the people in that room like their value can be tabulated on a sheet of paper, what they're worth to the crown and to Friv. I always thought he was mercenary about it, but you might be even more so."

Daphne watches him for a moment, trying to concoct a response. The courtesans in Bessemia taught her that the key to seduction was understanding what a man wanted and becoming that thing. But what does Bairre want her to be? Apologetic for her nature? Or is he truly in awe of it? That's the challenge with Bairre—she never knows *what* he wants from her. So she decides to give him the truth for once.

"Unlike you, unlike your father even, I was raised to wear a crown from the moment I was born," she says slowly. "You, on the other hand, were meant to lurk in the background, on the periphery. Maybe Cillian would have given you some kind of position on his council, given you a title, even, but you would never have had real power. And the thing you learn quickly when you have real power is that everyone, on some level, wants to take it from you. Oh, they might never act on it, might never even admit it to themselves, but they all want what you have. And that makes them easy to understand, easy to handle, but always, *always,* dangerous. Every single person in that room, Bairre, would stab us in the back if they thought they could get away with it."

He considers this for a moment before his full mouth curls into a smirk. "And here they call you charming," he says dryly.

"You don't want me to be charming. You want me to be honest," she tells him. He doesn't deny it. "So here's the truth—everyone wants power."

"That's just it," he says, leaning his head back against the stone. "I don't. I was perfectly happy in Cillian's shadow, perfectly happy as the bastard brother."

Daphne stares at him for a moment, her eyes tracing

the lines of his face, the tension in his jaw, the flare of his nostrils.

"You're a liar," she says, pushing off the wall and coming to stand in front of him.

"Pardon?" he says, his eyes meeting hers.

She waves her hand at him. "All of this—the sulking, the bitterness. It isn't resentment, it's guilt. Because you weren't happy in your brother's shadow, because you desperately wanted all of this. And now you have everything you wanted, and your brother is dead."

Bairre stares at her, speechless, with such an intense loathing in his eyes that it knocks the breath from her lungs.

"You don't know me," he says.

"No," she agrees. "No one really does, I'd imagine." She pauses, something inside her breaking open. She knows what it is to be jealous of siblings: she's spent her life envious of Beatriz's confidence, of Sophie's effortless kindness. Though the mere thought of them leaves her winded. If anything were to happen to them, she doesn't know what she'd do.

"You didn't kill him," she says, her voice softening. "If envy alone were enough to kill, there would be no one left in the world. Maybe he *was* the one born for this, maybe he would have been a better prince, but he's dead and you aren't. You can skulk around feeling sorry for yourself, or you can fill that role in a way that would make him proud. That's up to you."

For a long moment, he doesn't say anything, his eyes downcast. Finally, he looks at her again, his expression one of a pure, naked vulnerability that makes something in her chest crack.

"I don't know how," he says quietly.

She takes a step closer to him, holding out a hand. She tells herself it's part of her plan to earn his trust, to seduce him, part of a long game. Deep down she knows it isn't the whole truth. "Well, as you pointed out, I do. So tomorrow, we will go hunting with Lord Cadringal and I will help you act like the prince you're meant to be."

He looks at her hand for a moment, as if it might be holding a knife, before eventually taking it in his. She can feel the rough calluses of his palm against hers. It isn't as unpleasant as it should be.

Beatriz

Beatriz reads Sophronia's letter so many times she knows it by heart, but the words never quite make sense.

I couldn't go through with our plan. I know Mama will think me weak for it, but I believe you'll at least understand. It wasn't right, and it wasn't worth the cost. I couldn't do it.

But it seems Mama knows me too well and she's taken that choice from me. I'm sure by now you've received Leopold's declaration of war. It's a fake, but that won't matter. My only hope is if you release Lord Savelle and send him home. I have no right to ask this of you, I know that, but I think deep in your heart you know this is wrong as well.

I don't think either of us stands a chance against Mama, not on our own, but if we work together—if by some miracle of the stars Daphne works with us—I think we have a chance to break Mama's hold. Freeing Lord Savelle is the first step, and I promise you, I will stand by you no matter the consequences.

I love you and I trust you and I miss you.

Parts of it aren't surprising—their mother has always called Sophronia soft, though Beatriz thinks *sensitive* might be a better word. Either way, it isn't a quality that serves a Bessemian princess well, and the empress has done everything she can to harden Sophronia. It has never quite worked.

No, what surprises Beatriz is the strength in Sophronia's words. Not just the guilt or the hand-wringing over whether what they're doing is right—that, Beatriz might have expected from her sister. But action? That Sophronia has actually stood up and refused their mother? That is unfathomable from the girl Beatriz knew.

But of course that rebellion has been for nothing—Sophronia should have anticipated as much. All their lives, their mother has been a step ahead of them, always seeming to see everything and know everything. But then, Beatriz supposes she has always been the one pushing back, the one rebelling.

I think deep in your heart you know this is wrong as well. Those words linger in Beatriz's mind, long after she burns the letter in her fireplace and readies herself for bed. Does she know it's wrong? Yes, she's been plagued by guilt over framing Lord Savelle; yes, she's been haunted by thoughts of him imprisoned, of him burned, because of her. But it's an ugly necessity, isn't it? A way to save her own life, yes, but also a way to save Cellaria—to save other people like her and

Lord Savelle's daughter and all of the others who have been or will be executed for acting against Cellaria's strict laws. Beatriz might not agree with her mother about much, but she believes that Cellaria will be better off under her rule. Isn't that worth the cost of one man's life?

Beatriz isn't sure anymore.

"You look troubled," Pasquale says, coming into the room from the parlor, still dressed for dinner. He's been dining with his uncle—Gisella and Nico's father—as well as some other members of the royal council. By his expression, she doubts it went well.

"So do you," she points out. "I wish I could have gone with you."

"Believe me, I do too, but they were very insistent about talking to me alone. They might have suspected you'd manage to charm a few of them over to our side," he says with a wry smile.

"Our side?" Beatriz asks. "Have we taken sides?"

"I think there's something seriously wrong with my father. I think that war with Temarin is the last thing anyone needs. Our truce has been good for both of our countries—it's imperative that it holds. They disagree. My uncle, specifically, seems determined to go to war. So I suppose there are sides now," Pasquale says, collapsing into bed beside her. "I know my father, Triz. I know his moods. I know his temper. But this is something else. He's sick. I know it, and I think they know it too but they can't admit it."

"Of course not," Beatriz says with a snort. "Their power is reliant on his. It's why no one tells him no."

Beatriz suddenly wonders if her mother is responsible for the king's worsening condition. She wouldn't put it past her, and a mad king would serve her purposes. It would be easier to gain the loyalties of the hostile country if she liberated them from such a tyrant. *I think deep in your heart you know this is wrong as well.* Sophronia's words echo in Beatriz's mind again.

"Do you want to be king?" Beatriz asks. Though they are alone in the room, she still lowers her voice.

Pasquale looks at her with a furrowed brow. "What sort of question is that?" he asks.

Beatriz remembers the game on the beach, how he said he was lying about not wanting to be king, how Beatriz knew it was actually the truth.

"I think you would be a good one," Beatriz says softly. "Maybe not the one your father was, even in his prime, but a fair one. A just one. You could create a better Cellaria."

Pasquale's frown deepens. "We aren't talking about that," he says, more firmly than necessary.

Beatriz looks at him, at the boy she married knowing she would eventually betray him. The husband who is nothing like what she expected, nothing like what she hoped, but somehow the friend she needed.

"We are talking about that," she says, holding his gaze. "That's exactly what we're talking about. Your father is unwell. He's making bad decisions for Cellaria. The only way this ends well is with you on the throne. So I'm asking you, is that what you want?"

Pasquale lets out a long exhale. He looks away from her,

but when his gaze returns, she remembers how she thought he looked when they met, like a frightened puppy. Now, though, she thinks the puppy might have teeth. "I never thought I did. I still don't. But I think it's what I need to do, or rather what's needed of me. And with you by my side, the prospect seems less frightening."

Beatriz nods slowly, a plan taking shape. A wild plan, an impossible plan, maybe, but the only chance to help her sister. *Stars damn you, Sophie. You and your blasted conscience.* She looks at the boy whose life she has bound irrevocably to hers, and a brittle smile forms on her lips.

"Well then," she says. "I suppose we'll have to stage a coup."

Trust is not something that comes easy to Beatriz. Her mother has never encouraged it, not even between her and her sisters, though that at least was inevitable. But she, Daphne, and Sophronia have never had friends—anytime they grew close to others their age, their mother did something to wreck the blooming friendship. Beatriz remembers when she was eight and she began to make friends with the daughter of an earl who shared her love of both fashion and theater, and how the girl's family soon moved away from court, to their country estate, and Beatriz never heard from her again. Though it seemed like a cruel twist of fate at the time, Beatriz sees her mother's fingerprints clearly now, on that incident and so many others like it.

Trust no one but me, their mother has always seemed to say, even if she's never said the words exactly. The lesson has been learned nonetheless. Beatriz and her sisters don't have friends, they don't have confidantes, they only have themselves, and their mother.

I love you and I trust you and I miss you, Sophronia said in her letter, and it's those words that Beatriz repeats again and again in her mind as she and Pasquale sit in their parlor and wait for their guests to arrive. She *does* trust Sophronia, maybe more than anyone—certainly more than Daphne, who Beatriz is fairly certain will never say a bad word about their mother, let alone act against her. In that, Beatriz knows Sophronia is mistaken, but that is a problem for another day.

She trusts Pasquale, too, she thinks as they watch the door. In part, it's a mercenary trust; they have no choice but to put their trust in each other, at least for now. But that isn't it, not entirely. She trusts him because he's Pasquale, and from the moment they were thrust together, their fates were forged.

And when Gisella and Nicolo step into the room with Ambrose at their heels, Beatriz realizes she trusts them as well, in part because she has little choice, but also because they're her friends. Maybe, with Ambrose most of all, it's a tangential trust—Pasquale trusts him, so Beatriz does as well. But Gisella and Nicolo trusted her enough to warn her about the king's proclivities—Nico even risked his own safety to protect her from them.

When they're all seated around the roaring fireplace, Beatriz and Pasquale exchange a look. They didn't talk this part over, but Beatriz knows she'll have to take the reins. She looks around at the other three and clears her throat.

"King Cesare is unstable," she says. "We all know that, don't we?"

Ambrose looks uncertain, while Gisella and Nicolo have one of their wordless conversations, but no one disagrees. After a moment, all three nod. Beatriz considers mentioning that she believes someone has been poisoning his wine, that it might have proven fatal if Nicolo and the others hadn't been diluting it, but she holds her tongue. She'll wait until she hears back from Daphne before saying anything for certain.

"If he continues to go unchecked, he will bring ruin to Cellaria," Beatriz says. "This war with Temarin will only be the beginning."

"Temarin declared war on us," Ambrose says, his voice soft. "It hardly seems avoidable now."

Beatriz bites her lip. "I had word from my sister, Sophronia—the declaration is a forgery. She and Leopold have no desire for a fight with us, just as we should have no desire for a fight with them. We're family, in more ways than one. It's in both Cellaria's and Temarin's best interests to maintain the truce."

Beatriz takes a deep, fortifying breath before continuing. "Once Lord Savelle is executed, there will be no turning back, no stopping this war." *No stopping my mother from claiming both broken countries as her own,* she adds silently. Because that is what she is doing in supporting Sophronia. Beatriz has never shied away from rebelling against their mother before, but those were little rebellions, meaningless rebellions, done for show and little more. This, though, there is no coming back from. Beatriz knows this, but frightening as it might be to break with the empress, turning her back on Sophronia isn't a possibility. She steels herself and continues. "If King Cesare wishes to damn us all by crossing that line, it is up to us to stop him."

Nico glances around at each of them in turn. "We're talking treason here," he says.

"Nico," Gisella starts.

"I'm not passing judgment," he says quickly. "I just want to be very clear. What we're discussing is treason. People burn for this."

"People are burning for a lot less these days," Beatriz says.

Nicolo levels her with a look. "That's not funny."

"No, it isn't," she agrees, holding his gaze. "Do you think it's right? Burning people for using magic?"

She finds that she desperately wants to know what he says—not just to know if he will stand with them, but to know what he would think if he knew the truth about her. Would he look at her any differently? Would he happily watch her burn? She doesn't think so, but she can't be sure.

"Not even using magic," Pasquale puts in. "We all know that the evidence presented against most of them is flimsy."

Beatriz waves his words away. "But beyond that," she says. "When we spoke of it before, Gigi and Nico, you didn't seem to think it sacrilegious so much as scandalous. Pas, you've never expressed the same level of hate I've heard from others. If Lord Savelle is guilty of what the king has accused him of, do you think he should die for it?"

For a moment, none of them says anything, but to Beatriz's surprise it is Ambrose who speaks first.

"It's a lot of power for a person to have," he says quietly. "But I've read many books—far too many, more than likely, and a good many of them illegal here, I'll admit. I've read stories of terrible things empyreas have done with that power, but also the good things. The great things. The miracles." He hesitates, looking around at the others with some degree of mistrust. Beatriz can't blame him. The words he's saying could get him killed. But he continues. "No, I think if Lord Savelle has the power to bring the stars down from the sky, to bend them to his will, that perhaps we should consider that the stars have seen fit to bless him. If that's the case, would killing him then count as sacrilege?"

It's a wordy answer, and more of a theological debate than Beatriz can quite wrap her head around, but as far as she understands it, Ambrose doesn't wish her dead, and that is good enough for her. She glances at the others.

"I'm not sure about all of that," Gisella says, looking at Beatriz. "But I'd be lying if I said I hadn't wished on a few stars myself, just to see if I had the gift. You have, too, Nico, don't pretend you haven't."

Nicolo scowls at his sister before looking at Beatriz. "She's right. I have," he admits. "I'd imagine most people have, even in Cellaria. It's not something a person should burn for."

Beatriz feels somewhat validated, even though it isn't as much of an affirmation as she'd like to hear. It's enough, she supposes. She turns toward Pasquale, who meets her gaze with surprising steadiness.

"I've known my father's laws were wrong for a long time, but I think about Lord Savelle's daughter often. She didn't deserve to die for what she did. I wish I could have done something to help her then, but I'll certainly help her father now."

Nicolo looks from Pasquale to Beatriz. "So?" he asks. "What do you have in mind?"

Beatriz glances at Pasquale. This is the part of the plan he thought was lunacy, but he's willing to trust her. She hopes the others are as well.

"We're going to break Lord Savelle out of prison and send him back to Temarin."

Beatriz

Beatriz dips a fluffy angled brush into a pot of powder just a shade darker than Gisella's skin, brushing it just below her cheekbones. In the bright light of her bedroom, Gisella looks like a performer in one of the farces the king has put on every so often—her face has been painted and powdered so much that she doesn't look like herself any longer. She looks a good twenty years older, with bushy eyebrows, heavy-lidded eyes, and hollowed-out cheeks.

"I don't see why you couldn't have made me prettier," Gisella complains, eyeing herself in the gilded vanity mirror. "A bit of rouge on the cheeks—a little tint on the lips, maybe."

"Because," Beatriz says, trading the angled brush for the biggest, fluffiest one she has and dipping that into a pot of translucent powder—*Think of it as a seal, to finish off any illusion*, the Bessemian Mistress of Disguises, Madame Curioux, told her. "People notice beautiful girls—you know that as well as I do. But they tend to ignore and forget plain women. Or, better yet, women above a certain age. And tonight, we want to be ignored and forgotten."

It's been two days since Nicolo, Gisella, and Ambrose agreed to help Beatriz and Pasquale break Lord Savelle out of the dungeon. Pasquale wanted to wait longer, to plan better, but with the king's unpredictable moods, Beatriz doesn't want to risk him moving Lord Savelle's execution date up.

Gisella lets out a dramatic sigh. "Fine," she says, looking at her reflection again and frowning. "Though I could have done without this reminder of my own mortality. Do you really think I'll have this many wrinkles?"

Before Beatriz can answer, Nicolo gives a snort from his place, lounging on the chaise. "Gigi, we're about to commit treason. If we live long enough for you to get wrinkles, consider yourself lucky."

Gisella rolls her eyes. "Ever the optimist."

"I am wondering, though," Nicolo says, glancing at Beatriz. "Exactly how did a Bessemian princess become so accomplished with cosmetics? Surely you had a maid to apply them for you if you wanted."

Beatriz knew this question was bound to come up, and she has a response ready. "My sisters and I used to like sneaking out of the castle from time to time to visit a tavern down in the city. It was nice to sometimes spend a night with people who didn't know who we were."

It isn't a complete lie—Beatriz did use her talents with a cosmetic brush on several occasions for such a purpose—it just wasn't the original reason for her studies with Madame Curioux. But Nicolo seems to accept the answer readily enough.

"I still don't see why the two of you have to do this bit alone," he says. "It's the most dangerous part."

"Because people underestimate women, Nico," Gisella says. "They won't think we're capable of breaking a man out of prison. Are you disappointed you don't get to have any fun?"

He snorts again. "Trust me—playing lookout sounds like exactly the right level of fun for me tonight."

Gisella opens her mouth to issue some scathing retort, Beatriz is sure, but she interrupts with a smile. "You're all done, Gigi," she says, setting the brush down. "Do you mind checking on Pasquale and Ambrose while I disguise Nico? They should have gotten back by now."

Gisella raises her eyebrows at Beatriz but gets to her feet. "Fine," she says. "But do try not to add adultery to our list of crimes tonight, will you?" she says over her shoulder when she reaches the door. She's gone before either of them can respond.

Nicolo's cheeks flush red and he doesn't look at Beatriz as he makes his way toward her, sitting down on the vanity bench his sister just vacated. "I didn't tell her anything," he mutters under his breath.

"I didn't assume you had," Beatriz says, focusing on the jarred pigments in front of her. He and Gisella have almost the exact same skin tone, so she can reuse the same colors, which will make things simpler. "My sisters always used to know if I'd kissed anyone," she admits. "It was like I had a sign hanging around my neck."

"Did you . . . kiss a lot of people, then?" he asks.

Beatriz glances at him. If she didn't know better, she might think he sounds jealous, but considering that she's married, the boys she kissed before are the least of their problems.

"A few," she says with a shrug, dipping her brush into a slightly darker shade. She won't need to do as much work on him as she did on Gisella—just enough that anyone who might recognize him won't. She'll add a few wrinkles to age him, darken the circles under his eyes, maybe shade his nose to alter its shape. "For as long as I could remember, I knew I was going to marry Pasquale, and I knew I had to be a virgin when I did, but even in Cellaria, there's nothing that says I couldn't kiss anyone. I suppose I thought of it as practice."

He stays perfectly still as she begins to paint and powder his face.

"I never thanked you," she says after a moment. "I know you're nervous about this, and I don't blame you for that. Pasquale and I have asked a lot of you. I'm grateful for your help."

He shakes his head. "Don't thank me, Triz," he says. "Really. It's nothing."

"It's treason," she reminds him. "You said as much yourself. Not many would risk death for another person, even if that person is their cousin—"

"I didn't offer for Pasquale," he interrupts, his voice strained. "Don't misunderstand—I would never have betrayed his confidence, but I didn't offer my help for him. I offered it for you."

Beatriz becomes even more aware of how close they are—close enough that the scent of him invades her senses: clean cotton, apples, and something else that is just Nicolo. She remembers how it felt when he kissed her in the corridor. She wonders if he'll do it again now. It would be inadvisable, but she wants it more than she ever imagined she could.

She focuses on her paints, dipping a smaller brush into a bluish-violet powder. "Look up," she says, without thinking or preparing herself for what will happen when he does, when their eyes meet and lock and the wanting grows so strong Beatriz thinks she might drown in it. She swallows and lightly brushes the color beneath his eyes, exaggerating the faint shadows that are already there.

"It's all the more noble," she says, forcing her voice to come out light and teasing. "To risk so much for someone you barely even know."

"I'm not noble," he says, his voice sharp-edged enough to fend off any argument. "If you had any idea what was going through my mind, Triz, you'd know there's nothing noble about me."

Beatriz picks up another brush, smoothing out the edges of some of the wrinkles she's given him. He should look ridiculous like this, with his painted-on wrinkles and the violet half circles beneath his eyes. He *does* look ridiculous, Beatriz tells herself. It's just that she wants to kiss him anyway, consequences be damned.

"Perhaps, then," she says slowly, setting the brush aside, "we should just be ignoble together."

Try as she might, Beatriz can't quite banish thoughts of her mother from her mind. Even here, standing a hairsbreadth from a boy she should not be alone with, she imagines her mother's disapproval. A hundred miles away, and Beatriz can imagine her mother's narrowed gaze, her flared nostrils. She can hear her mother's scalding voice in her ear.

Even you wouldn't be such a fool as to go losing your heart, Beatriz. I didn't raise you to flutter about with one of your own pawns so shamelessly. Just when I think you can't disappoint me more, you find new depths to explore.

The voice shouldn't get under her skin—especially not now that she's decided to wreck the rest of her mother's plans to help her sister. But it does. Beatriz isn't sure there will ever come a time where her mother's voice doesn't follow her, offering up opinions she doesn't want or need.

Beatriz tells herself that she kisses Nicolo because she wants to, because she's wanted to kiss him again ever since the last time. She tells herself she kisses him because she wants him and he wants her and nothing else matters—just the press of lips and the touch of tongues and Nicolo's strong, sure hands brushing over the small of her back, pulling her down onto his lap.

It's the truth, but it isn't the whole truth. She also kisses him because she knows she shouldn't, because it will upset her mother if she ever finds out, because, as Sophronia once pointed out, all her mother has to do to convince Beatriz to jump off a cliff is to tell her not to do it.

The door opens and Beatriz and Nicolo break apart, Beatriz standing up and stepping out of Nicolo's arms quicker than a bolt of lightning flashing across the sky. But not, she realizes when Gisella gives her a knowing look, quickly enough.

"It seems no one can keep their hands to themselves these days," Gisella mutters, stepping into the room, followed a beat later by Pasquale and Ambrose, both of whom flush at her words.

What exactly have they gotten into, Beatriz wonders, though a part of her is happy for Pas, dangerous as it might be. Perhaps it should alarm her that Gisella has apparently just witnessed both her and Pasquale kissing other people, but it doesn't. They're all committing treason together—there's the promise of mutually assured destruction in that.

Hastily, Beatriz grabs the powder brush and dusts some translucent powder over Nico's face. "There," she says quickly. "Done. Ambrose, Pas, did you get the clothes?"

Pasquale nods, his ears still red, as he drops a bundle of clothes in varying shades of gray on top of the bed. "It's laundry day, so we grabbed a few things off the drying lines. Nearly got caught but didn't."

"Then let's get dressed," Beatriz says, eyeing the servants' garb. "If the guards change at midnight we only have an hour to get down there."

The plan, if it can even really be called that, is a simple one.

Ambrose and Pasquale ready Ambrose's family's boat, currently docked at the city port rather than the one reserved for royalty and nobility. It's a small boat, but one Ambrose has sailed on his own many times to visit his family's estate on the northern coast near the Temarin border. He told his uncle he would be doing just that so no one will think his absence for the next few weeks strange while he ferries Lord Savelle to the safety of Temarinian soil. It will be a longer trip than Ambrose has taken before, but he feels confident he can manage it.

Nicolo is the lookout, playing the part of a servant sweeping the hallway outside the palace dungeon. If he sees anyone who shouldn't be there, he's supposed to waylay them however he can.

Gisella and Beatriz, dressed and made up like middle-aged servants, bring dinner and wine for the guards—a duty Beatriz relieved two young serving girls of by demanding in her most princess-like tone that they forget whatever else they had to do and organize Pasquale's bookshelves right this moment.

But as Beatriz and Gisella lower the trays they carry before the two guards standing watch over the dungeon cells, the knot in Beatriz's stomach refuses to loosen. So much can go wrong, she knows, and if it does? It isn't only her life on the line anymore. It's Pasquale's and Gisella's and Nicolo's and Ambrose's. The thought makes her feel sick, but she forces herself to hold on to her bland smile and make pleasant small talk about the weather with the guards until both men drain their wine goblets. Mere seconds later, they are both slumped over, heads lolling and eyes closed.

"Do you think we gave them too much?" Gisella asks, biting her lip, though she doesn't sound too concerned.

Beatriz checks both men's pulses. "They're fine," she says. "Just sleeping. It should last half an hour, but if they wake up sooner—"

"I know," Gisella says, shooting her a quick grin. "I'll express my concern and tell them you ran for help and then very subtly . . ." She trails off, holding up Beatriz's poison ring, with its hidden needle. "And when we're through with this, you must tell me where I can get one of these."

"When we're through with this," Beatriz echoes, taking

the ring of keys from its peg beside the guards. Now she has thirty minutes—preferably closer to twenty to be safe—to figure out which of the fifty or so keys will unlock Lord Savelle's cell.

Beatriz hurries down the hall, away from Gisella, sparing each cell a glance only to confirm that Lord Savelle isn't inside. Most of them are empty—the main prison is down in the city, and both are mostly cleared out every two weeks on Burning Day—but a few are occupied by servants or minor courtiers who angered the king in some way or other. A few call out to her as she passes, but she ignores them, aware of the heavy key ring she holds and how quickly twenty minutes can pass.

She almost hurries right past Lord Savelle's cell, coming to a sharp stop when she recognizes his light brown hair in the moonlight coming through the small window above him. Stripped of his usual fine clothes and dressed in the same threadbare dull gray outfit the rest of the prisoners wear, he looks like a stranger.

"Lord Savelle," she whispers, stepping up to the bars and beginning with the first key.

Lord Savelle blinks at her. It takes a moment for him to see through her disguise. "Your Highness?" he asks. "What are you . . . ?" He trails off when his eyes fall to her fingers, trying the first key, then the second, and he gets his answer. "Why?" he asks instead.

Beatriz doesn't answer at first, trying a third and then a fourth key, to no avail. She's played tonight's events countless times in her head during the past day, running over every little thing that could go wrong and smoothing them all out. She never did figure out what to say to him, though. She decides to tell him the truth—she feels she owes him that at least.

"Because we both know that if one of us should be imprisoned for using magic, it should be me," she says, her voice a whisper in the darkness, an admission she has never before spoken aloud. It's much harder to ignore once she says the words. It's also impossible to take them back.

Lord Savelle isn't surprised, though. Of course he isn't. She thought he might have guessed, but now she knows for sure.

"I was worried you would tell someone that you suspected me," Beatriz says, focusing on the lock so she doesn't have to look at him. "So when the opportunity came to . . . remove you, I took it. I'm sorry."

She doesn't tell him the rest of it, about her mother's plan, though she's tempted to.

For a long moment, Lord Savelle doesn't reply. Beatriz manages to try six keys in that time, none of them the right one.

"I can't say I fault you for that, Beatriz," he says softly. "If my daughter could have lied to save herself—even if it meant pushing the blame on another . . . stars help me, I wish she had."

Beatriz was ready for fury and condemnation, expected him to react as her mother would have. But if she'd had a thousand years to guess, she couldn't have imagined him forgiving her. In her bewilderment, her fingers fumble with one of the keys and she drops them, letting out a curse. She picks the ring up. She isn't sure which key she tried last, so she has to start again.

She considers telling him the rest. He must assume the stardust she planted in his room was stardust she created herself—he can't know her mother had anything to do with it. This, she finds, is a secret she can't surrender. It's too big, too much a part of herself. Once it's gone, she isn't sure what will remain.

"My friend has a boat," she says instead, leaving another wrong key in the lock so she can reach into her satchel and pull out another servant's cloak, pushing it through the bars to him. "Put this on," she adds before going back to the keys.

How much time has gone by since she left Gisella? Five minutes? Ten? She isn't sure.

"A boat?" he echoes.

"To take you to Temarin," she explains. "It's the only way to save you—and to prevent a war."

At that, Lord Savelle gives a surprised laugh. "War might be a bit extreme," he says. "Only a mad king or an idiot would . . ." He trails off.

"King Cesare hardly seems sane, does he?" she asks. "And though I've heard enough about King Leopold to question his intelligence, my sister tells me the declaration of war he sent was a forgery. If we can get you back to Temarin, it might be enough to prevent the war from happening. But we have to hurry."

Lord Savelle doesn't need to be told twice. In a few quick motions, he throws the cloak over his shoulders. It's long enough to mostly cover his prison clothes, and it's dark enough out that no one should look too closely at him. Beatriz tries a few more keys, but the door stays locked. Her heart is beginning to pound loudly in her ears, drowning out every other thought.

"Are you coming too?" he asks her.

Beatriz looks up, surprised, and almost drops the keys again. "What?" she asks.

"To Temarin," he says. "Surely you don't mean to stay here."

She blinks. The thought had never occurred to her, though now that he's said it, she wonders if it should have.

"Beatriz, if you stay here, they will find out what you are, sooner or later," he says slowly. "And they will kill you for it."

Beatriz frowns, trying another key, then another. "It isn't that simple," she says, thinking of Pasquale and Gisella and Nicolo. She doesn't want to leave them, to abandon them to the whims of a mercurial king. "I think someone is poisoning the king, causing his madness. I can't prove it yet, but when I do—"

"Ah," he says, looking at her with appraising eyes. "I'm merely the first part of your plan, then. You mean to make yourself a queen."

Beatriz bites her lip, shame heating her face. Daphne always said she was shameless—if Beatriz sees her again, she'll delight in telling her sister she was wrong.

"You can't deny, Cellaria will be a far better place with Pas and me on the throne," she says. "We could change things, fix things."

It occurs to her as she says it that it's what her mother

has always said—the same justification she gives for all of her ugly deeds. *It's not the same,* Beatriz tells herself, but she doesn't quite believe it. And then there is the threat her mother now poses—Beatriz knows she won't let go of her dream of a united empire without a fight. But if Beatriz and Sophronia form an alliance, they might stand a chance. A small, optimistic part of her imagines Daphne joining them, though she doubts that possibility. Beatriz loves her sister, but she knows that Daphne is the empress's creature, through and through.

"Cellaria would be a far better place with a pig on the throne," Lord Savelle says, and, more out of habit than true fear, Beatriz casts a glance around to make sure no one else heard that. Lord Savelle notices and laughs. "I'm already due to be executed, Beatriz. There isn't much point in holding my tongue."

Beatriz reaches the last key on the ring, but that doesn't work either. She frowns. Did she miss one? Perhaps the lock stuck and she should have tried harder? There isn't time to try them all again—the guards will be waking up any moment now, and if Gisella doesn't manage to subdue them both on her own . . . she pushes the thought from her mind. She will not let her friend pay for her mistake.

As if summoned by her thoughts, she hears the sound of heavy boots pounding against the stone floors, coming toward her. She lets out a string of words that were decidedly *not* a part of her Cellarian lessons.

"Leave me," Lord Savelle tells her, his eyes somber. "Perhaps if you hide somewhere, they'll think—"

He breaks off when Beatriz drops the keys, her fingers going to the bracelet around her wrist. *Use them wisely,* her mother said. *Break the crystal and make your wish.* But Beatriz knows that if her mother could see her now, *wise* is the last thing she would call her. Beatriz doesn't care. She drops the bracelet to the ground.

"Find my sister," she tells Lord Savelle. "Tell her I sent you. Tell her . . . tell her I tried."

Lord Savelle opens his mouth to say something, his brow creased in confusion, but Beatriz doesn't give him a chance. "I wish Lord Savelle could make his way safely to the docks, and on to Temarin."

"Beatriz—" Lord Savelle begins, but before he can say more, lightning strikes out of a clear sky, hitting the stone wall of the dungeon and creating a crack in the narrow space of Lord Savelle's cell, just wide enough for him to slip through. Shouts go up from the other prisoners, and the rhythm of the approaching footsteps grows faster—several sets, she thinks. "*Go,*" she tells Lord Savelle. "Or they'll kill us both. There's a boat waiting in the city harbor. Run."

Lord Savelle hesitates only a second, but he must hear the boots as well, know how close they are, know that there is nowhere for Beatriz to hide. He gives her one quick nod before forcing his way through the crack in the wall and disappearing from sight.

A mere heartbeat later and the guards round the corner and come into sight. Beatriz turns to meet them, forcing herself to appear calm despite her racing pulse. She holds her hands up to show that she is unarmed.

One guard steps forward, a golden stripe on the sleeve of his jacket marking his higher rank. His eyes widen slightly as he takes in the empty cell with the hole in its wall, and Beatriz with stardust at her feet. His eyes scan her face, and she feels him searching through the layers of cosmetics, though he seems already to know what he will find.

"Your Highness," he says, his voice not wavering even when she meets his gaze with a challenge. "You're under arrest for treason."

She doesn't protest as the guard takes hold of her arm while another binds her wrists. All she can do is hope that the others are safe, that Ambrose and Lord Savelle got away, that maybe Pasquale decided to join them—he's surely safer there than here.

But as the guards lead her down the hallway toward the entrance, she hears the guard's words again. *You're under arrest for treason.* Not for breaking a man out of prison, not for using magic—though she's sure the latter at least will be added to her charges—but for treason. For plotting against the king.

Only four people know of her treason, the four who participated in it with her. By the time they reach the dungeon's entrance, Beatriz isn't quite surprised to see Gisella and Nicolo standing near the door, their heads bent together as they speak in whispers. Both of them look up as the guards lead her past, and Nicolo, at least, has the grace to look away, too ashamed to meet her gaze. Gisella doesn't. Her dark brown eyes hold Beatriz's, unflinching and unapologetic. She lifts one shoulder in a shrug, and it is all Beatriz can do not to launch herself at the other girl and strike her however she can. Even with her hands bound, she'd bet she could manage to hurt her. Not enough, though.

So she looks away from both of them and focuses her gaze forward, keeping her head held high and her mouth closed, and goes to meet her fate.

Daphne

Daphne sits before the fire in her room, the letter from Sophronia in her hand. She's read it once but can't bring herself to read it again. *I need your help, Daph,* Sophronia has written, outlining how everything has gone sideways in Temarin—how Sophronia has tipped everything sideways by going against the empress's plan. *You must have seen how wrong she is now, how wrong we are to do her bidding.*

It's ludicrous to Daphne, who has seen nothing of the sort. What she has seen is that Friv is a wild land, in need of a stronger hand than King Bartholomew possesses. She can't understand why Sophronia couldn't simply do as she was told. Daphne did her duty, she stole King Bartholomew's seal, had a knife pressed to her throat, ingratiated herself with rebels she's fairly certain want her dead—Daphne has gone above and beyond what she was instructed to do. Sophronia couldn't even manage to forge a simple letter, to lead the king who is supposedly madly in love with her into war.

And what about Bairre, a voice whispers in her mind,

though she is quick to quiet it. What about Bairre? He doesn't want to rule, he said so himself. In some ways, she'll be doing him a favor.

I cannot depend on your sisters, the empress told Daphne shortly before they left to meet their destinies. *Sophronia is weak and Beatriz is flighty. You, my dove, are the one I can depend upon, and the only one I trust to rule in my stead when I'm gone.*

Daphne considers sending the letter on to their mother so that she can deal with whatever problems Sophronia has caused, but she hesitates. It sounds like the empress already has the situation in hand, and Daphne doesn't want to get Sophronia in any more trouble with their mother, no matter how angry she is. But she can't write back to Sophronia either, certainly can't offer her any kind of help. She feels only a quick pang of guilt as she tosses Sophronia's letter into the fire before getting to her feet and calling for a maid to help her change into her riding habit.

"You must remember never to promise anything—not even the asters in your pocket. I know you and Lord Cadringal are friends, but things have changed. You're both now responsible for many more people than just yourselves," Daphne tells Bairre while they wait for the Cadringals to meet them at the border of the castle's hunting grounds. Lord Cadringal and his five siblings arrived an hour before dawn, so the hunt has been arranged for the afternoon, giving them plenty of time to rest and recuperate from the trying trip. Daphne struggles to push Sophronia and her letter from her mind, to ignore the guilt nagging at her. It occurs to her that the advice she's giving to Bairre applies to her as well—she loves her sister dearly, but if Sophronia has diverged from their path, Daphne cannot follow her. Her mother is depending on her. Sophronia will come around, she tells herself. She'll realize her error and their mother will forgive it, eventually.

She shakes Sophronia out of her thoughts and focuses on Bairre, who is frowning at her, an expression she's grown familiar with and even become somewhat fond of. He's been pacing for the last few minutes, his hands clasped behind his back. "You don't know Rufus—he won't ask anything of me."

Daphne knows she should feel annoyed with him, but she's surprised by the hint of jealousy that pricks her, that he seems to genuinely believe that. Maybe he was right about her. Maybe she is mercenary, but only because she's had to be. Sophronia's voice barges into her thoughts again—*I need your help, Daph*—but again Daphne pushes her out.

"I can guarantee you that before the hunt is over, he'll pester you to talk to your father about lowering his region's taxes," she tells Bairre.

Bairre considers this. "I don't see why we couldn't," he says. "I've been hearing stories about how this past winter was more difficult than anticipated. A lot of the highland clans are struggling."

They're more than struggling, Daphne thinks. *They're plotting.*

"Just don't make promises you won't be able to keep," she says, her thoughts straying again to her sister. Sophronia promised loyalty to their mother, she promised to do as she was told. Those promises have been broken now, and though Daphne pities her, she's also angry at Sophronia. How difficult could it have been to just follow orders?

"Daphne?" Bairre says, looking at her strangely.

She shakes her head, trying once again to clear Sophronia from her mind, though she feels her lingering in the corners like cobwebs. "Sorry, what did you say?"

"Are you all right?" he asks, frowning. "You seem out of sorts."

"I'm fine," she says, with a tight smile. "I didn't sleep well last night, I suppose."

Bairre opens his mouth to reply and she suspects he will push her on that flimsy excuse, but his eyes catch on something over her shoulder. His expression shifts and he raises his hand in a wave. Daphne turns to follow his gaze and sees a group of six coming toward them—all with the same bright red hair. She counts three girls and three boys, the oldest of whom must be Rufus. She knows that he and Bairre are the same age, but as he comes closer she realizes he must tower over Bairre by nearly a foot, and over her nearly double that.

"Rufus," Bairre says, holding a hand out toward him, but Rufus ignores it and crushes Bairre in a hug instead.

"Good to see you, Bairre," he says when they pull apart, his highland accent so thick that Daphne can barely dissect the words. "I was so sorry to hear about Cillian."

"I was sorry to hear about your father as well," Bairre replies.

Rufus nods his thanks before turning to Daphne. "And

you must be the charming Princess Daphne we've heard so much about over the years," he says, taking her proffered hand and kissing the back of it before releasing it and straightening up. "Might I present my sisters, Liana, Della, Zenia. And my brothers, Verne and Teddy," he continues, nodding to each in turn.

"Theodore, now," the youngest boy, Teddy, insists.

"Right," Rufus says with a smirk. "Theodore. You lot remember Bairre—*Prince* Bairre. And this is his bride-to-be, Princess Daphne."

The cluster of siblings bow their heads toward her and Bairre.

"Your Highnesses," they murmur.

Daphne smiles in response. "Now then," she says. "Shall we hunt?"

The bow feels good in Daphne's hands. The second she lets her first arrow fly, hitting a fat pheasant midflight, she feels a strange peace settle over her. Everything else might be a muddled mess, but this she knows.

"Good shot, Princess," Rufus says over his shoulder with an appraising smile.

"Daphne," she tells him, reaching behind her to pull another arrow from the sling. "It's only fair, Rufus."

"Daphne it is," Rufus says, turning toward Bairre. "Quite a markswoman, isn't she?"

"Indeed," Bairre replies, his eyes scanning the woods around them for any sign of movement. "Daphne is all kinds of deadly."

The way he says it, Daphne isn't sure whether he means it as a compliment or an insult. She decides to take it as a compliment.

"Do you hunt often, Rufus?" she asks. "I've heard the game up north is even more plentiful."

She still isn't sure of him, at least not in regard to whether he's sympathetic to the rebels. His affection for Bairre seems genuine, but Daphne knows that it's quite possible for a person to smile at you one moment and stab you in the back the next.

"Our deer grow to nearly twice the size of the ones here," he tells her. "Though they've been scarce the last few months."

"Hush," Rufus's middle sister, Della, says. She glares at them over her shoulder. "You'll scare away the game."

"She's very serious, Della is," Rufus says to Daphne, his voice a somber whisper. Still, his sister hears and shoots him another glare. "You have sisters as well, don't you?" he asks Daphne.

"Yes, two," Daphne says, keeping her voice quiet as she searches the woods for any hint of movement. The mention of her sisters feels like a knife in her chest, though she tries not to show it.

"Older or younger?" Rufus asks.

She glances at him, surprised. No one has ever asked her that question before, she realizes. Everyone has always known her, and her sisters, as a unit almost. "We're triplets," she tells him. "Though, technically, I'm the middle one. Beatriz is the oldest, Sophronia is the youngest, though only by a few minutes each."

I need your help, Daph. The voice echoes in Daphne's mind no matter how she tries to drown it out.

"You must miss them," Rufus says, oblivious to her thoughts. "Though I admit, there are plenty of times I'd like to put a few hundred miles between me and my siblings."

Liana is the only one of his siblings to hear this, and she fixes him with a glare.

"How are you finding being a new lord?" Daphne asks, changing the subject. If she doesn't get the topic away from her sisters, she thinks she'll go mad. She needs to focus on the task at hand and gather information for Cliona. "I'm sure it's a lot of responsibility to have taken on so suddenly."

Rufus winces. "It's a position I was raised for, though I never thought it would be so soon," he says, then pauses. "And it has been a difficult year, even before my father passed. Our crops didn't produce their usual amount, and as I said, the population of deer and other game seems to have gone down. Our people are struggling."

Daphne catches Bairre's gaze and lifts a shoulder just an inch in a shrug, as if to say *I told you so*.

"I'm sorry to hear that," Daphne says.

Rufus waits for a moment to see if she'll say more, offer anything, but when he realizes she won't—she *can't*—he shrugs. "Friv is a stubborn country, Daphne. We've survived worse, I'm sure we'll survive this."

He doesn't sound sure, though. Daphne doesn't doubt that if Cliona's father were to approach him, if he were to promise Rufus things that Bairre and Daphne can't, Rufus would have to consider his offer. Taking even more allies away from Bartholomew will further her mother's goals as well.

"Can we stop for some water?" Zenia interrupts, pouting. She's the youngest, only ten. She carries her bow by the string, hanging at her side in a way that makes Daphne cringe. She hasn't fired an arrow all afternoon and seems perfectly content with that.

"We haven't seen any deer yet," Verne says. "We should get at least one before we pause."

"We would have gotten more than that if the rest of you would *hush,*" Della says.

Of Rufus's siblings, Della is Daphne's favorite. It must be middle-sister camaraderie.

"Zenia's right," Bairre says with a sigh. "Let's take five minutes, and then we'll try awhile longer."

Della scowls but drops her bow, sticking the arrow she'd nocked back into her quiver.

Liana opens the satchel she carries, drawing out several skins of water and passing them out. When she hands Daphne hers, she doesn't look at her.

"Tell me, Daphne, are your sisters as much of a pain as mine are?" Rufus asks, causing Liana to throw his waterskin at him, nearly hitting him in the face with it.

"Oh, absolutely," Daphne says, unscrewing the top to the waterskin. "Once, Beatriz got so angry with me, she went into my room and emptied my entire wardrobe onto the lawn outside my window. It was quite a surprise when I returned from the bath."

And my other sister decided to throw a decade and a half

of careful planning away the first chance she got, she adds silently.

Everyone laughs, even sullen Liana. Satisfied, Daphne lifts the waterskin to her lips and takes a deep drink. After walking and riding for an hour, the water is cool and refreshing. She takes another drink, but before she can finish it off, there's the snap of a twig to her left and she freezes, the skin halfway to her lips.

There, in the middle of the lush forest, is the most beautiful stag Daphne has ever seen. There were deer aplenty in Bessemia, but they were lithe things, more sinew than meat. This stag is easily twice the size of those creatures, towering all the higher because of the antlers crowning his head. He's a handsome creature, and he hasn't seen them yet, has somehow missed their chatter. He grazes on, head bent low over a patch of grass.

Slowly, Daphne lowers her waterskin, setting it softly on the ground at her feet before reaching for an arrow and nocking it.

"What—" Verne starts, looking at her with bewildered eyes before Rufus claps a hand over his mouth, nodding toward the stag. The others follow his gaze, but no one moves to draw an arrow.

This one is all Daphne's.

She draws the arrow back, keeping her eyes on the stag and, specifically, on the long stretch of his neck. The muscles in her arm tighten and strain, but she forces herself to take a deep breath, to focus on the stag and nothing else.

Then she releases the arrow, sending it whirring through the air with a soft whistle.

It misses by a yard, finding the trunk of a tree behind the stag. At the sound, the animal straightens up, its eyes finding Daphne. For a second, it stares at her, unmoving, before taking off into the woods.

Della and Rufus are ready, giving chase with their siblings at their heels, but Daphne's feet are anchored to the ground. They feel so heavy suddenly. Her whole body feels heavy. The bow falls to her side and her head spins.

"Daphne?" Bairre asks. "Are you all right?"

"Fine," she says, too quickly. She shakes her head to try to clear it, but that only makes him look at her more strangely. "Why do you ask?"

"Because you shouldn't have missed that stag," he says before pausing. "And you look ready to keel over any second."

"Don't be ridiculous," she says, though she has to force the words through the fog descending on her mind. Why is she so tired? She wasn't a second ago, but now all she wants is to find a soft patch of ground somewhere and lie down, just for a moment.

"I'm fine," she tries to tell him, but the words don't make it out of her mouth before her knees suddenly buckle and her mind goes quiet and black. The last thing she's aware of is Bairre's arms catching her before she hits the ground.

Daphne

Consciousness slips through Daphne's fingers like smoke, but every so often she grasps enough to open her eyes. Every time she does, she isn't alone. Bairre sits in a chair beside her bed; sometimes he is upright, hands knitted in his lap, brow furrowed. Other times he is sprawled out with his head back and eyes closed, his chest rising and falling in long, even breaths. In those moments, he could be a stranger, his expression smooth and peaceful and open. In those moments, her fogged-over, feverish mind wonders what it would be like to touch his cheek, to run her fingers through his messy hair, to press her lips to his.

Once, she opens her eyes to find him watching her, his silver eyes resting on hers.

"Why are you here?" she asks him. Her voice comes out raspy, and he's quick to pass her a glass of water from the table beside him.

She doesn't drink from it, instead staring at its contents.

"It's been tested," he says, reading her wary expression. "You remember what happened?"

Daphne frowns, taking a small sip of the water, then another. She doesn't fully trust him, but her thirst wins out over her sense. In a few seconds, she drains the glass, passing it back to him. He pulls a rope hanging beside him. Far away, she hears the tinny ring of a bell.

"Vaguely," she says. Her voice still sounds rough, but her throat hurts a bit less. She leans back against the pillow. "The waterskin—it was poisoned."

The thought is a thorn beneath her skin—how disappointed her mother would be, especially after the lessons Daphne and her sisters have been given in detecting and concocting poisons of their own. Especially considering Daphne has always excelled at those lessons. Her failure to recognize the fact that she was being poisoned is an embarrassment.

He nods. "My father is having everyone questioned, trying to ascertain who is responsible."

"I'd imagine it's the same people who were responsible before," she says.

It's only when he looks at her with alarm that she realizes she's spoken out loud. She cringes and sits up a little straighter.

"What do you mean *before*? Someone else poisoned you?" he asks.

"No," she says quickly. She pauses, searching for a plausible lie, but nothing comes. Her mind feels clouded with fog, nothing visible except what's directly before her—in this case, the truth. "But last week, the girth of my saddle was damaged and I nearly ended up trampled."

Bairre lets out a long exhale. "Perhaps you simply fell."

She glares at him. "I assure you I didn't. You can ask Cliona, she was there."

Stars above, what was *in* that poison? Truth serum? She closes her eyes for a moment and opens them again. "Don't tell your father. It isn't as big an issue as it seems, they failed both times."

"And you're content to let them try a third?" he snaps.

Daphne opens her mouth, then closes it again, swallowing her words. She knows he's right, but she can't help but feel that the attempts on her life mark *her* as a failure. Like she's vulnerable and therefore weak. The thought of anyone knowing fills her with shame.

"If they try a third time, they'll fail a third time," she says.

"The only reason they failed this time is because you *happened* to spot that deer before finishing the water. The physician said a few more sips and we wouldn't be having this conversation."

Daphne suddenly feels nauseated, any retort she could have given stolen away by the knowledge of how close she came to death.

Daphne remembers the girl who passed it to her, Rufus's oldest sister, Liana. She remembers that the girl wouldn't look at her. Her mother's words come back to her. *Men say poison is a woman's weapon. They say it like an insult because they think it cowardly, but poison is clean, it's covert. It is so much easier to control the effects of a poison than it is the tip of a blade in the heat of combat. It is easy to get away with and, if used correctly, impossible to trace. Poison is a woman's weapon because it is a smart weapon.*

"Liana," she says slowly. "She didn't seem to like me."

Bairre lets out a long breath. "Zenia confessed."

Zenia. Daphne remembers the youngest girl, her hair still hanging in two plaits on either side of her round, freckled face. She couldn't be more than ten years old.

"I thought you said your father was still trying to find the person responsible," Daphne says.

"Zenia was only following orders. She didn't know what the poison would do. All she had to do was empty a vial they gave her into your water. Someone offered her a wish so powerful it would bring her father back from the dead. That someone is the person we're trying to find."

"A wish can't do that," Daphne says.

"No, but she was desperate enough to believe it might be," he says. He runs a hand through his hair. His eyes are tired—whatever sleep he's managed to get, it hasn't been enough. "She's being held in her family's rooms until it can be decided what to do with her. Rufus has been begging for mercy, of course."

"Of course," Daphne says. She tries to sit up, but pain ricochets through her body and her arms collapse.

"Careful," Bairre says, leaning forward. He reaches out like he wants to touch her but thinks better of it and lets his hand fall back to his side.

"She's a child," Daphne says, ignoring him. "She didn't know what she was doing."

"She tried to kill you," Bairre says, his eyes sparking with something she can't quite put a name to.

"If someone told you they could bring back Cillian, you would have done the same, I would bet."

He shakes his head. "You said it yourself—it isn't possible."

"But if you thought it was, if there were even the slightest chance," she says, "there's nothing you wouldn't have done."

He doesn't deny it.

"Keep her under watch," Daphne says. "Question her as thoroughly as possible to find who put her up to it. Then let her brother discipline her as he sees fit."

Bairre looks ready to protest when there is a knock at the door.

"Come in," Bairre says, and a servant enters, holding a pitcher of water on his tray. He moves to pour it into the glass Bairre holds, but he stops him.

"You drink it first," Bairre says.

The man pauses, his face turning a shade paler.

"Your Highness—"

"A necessary precaution," Bairre says with a smile that might as well be strung with barbed wire. "You understand. I'm sure there's nothing to fear."

The servant swallows before taking a sip from the side of the pitcher. Satisfied, Bairre holds out Daphne's glass and lets him fill it before setting the tray on the table.

"Will . . . will there be anything else?" the servant asks, his voice wavering.

"Not at the moment," Bairre says, passing the glass back to Daphne. "Thank you."

The servant scurries away, closing the door behind him.

Daphne takes a sip from the refreshed water glass, watching Bairre over the rim of it.

"Why are you here?" she asks him again.

He frowns at her. "Someone tried to poison you, remember?"

She shakes her head. "Why aren't you out there interrogating the rest of the castle?"

"My father is handling that," he says.

"Still, your time would be better spent helping him than playing nursemaid to me," she says.

He shakes his head. "Zenia didn't make that poison herself, it wasn't her plot. Which means someone—maybe many someones—still want you dead. I wasn't going to leave you alone, at their mercy, even before I knew about the other attempt."

"There are guards," she points out.

"I'm not sure I trust them, either," he says. Daphne remembers her trip to the dressmaker, how three out of the four guards who accompanied them were on the side of the rebels, according to Cliona. Bairre isn't wrong to have suspicions. "How are you feeling?"

"My head feels like it's been cleaved in two," she tells him. "And I'm so cold. But it also feels like my whole body is on fire."

Bairre leans forward, touching her forehead with the back of his hand. "You're still burning up," he says. "You should try to sleep more."

He takes a cloth from the table beside him and dabs it along her brow, her cheeks, down her neck. It comes away damp with sweat. This close, she can see the tiredness in his eyes, how pallid his skin is.

"How long has it been?" she asks.

"A day," he answers.

Daphne blinks her surprise away. A whole day, gone. "You need sleep too," she says.

"I'm fine," he tells her. "I'm not the one who was poisoned."

"No," she agrees. "But for some reason you've been sitting there for an entire day, taking care of me. Whatever sleep you've found in that chair couldn't have been comfortable."

"It's a small chair," he admits. "But I'm fine. You need sleep."

She holds his gaze as she finishes the second glass of water. "I won't sleep if you don't," she tells him.

"You can't be serious," he says, raising his eyebrows.

She pats the space beside her in the large bed. "You don't want to call my bluff," she tells him. "Come on, there is plenty of room and I don't want to hear you complaining about your aching back tomorrow."

"It's not proper," he tells her.

She laughs, but it comes out weak. Already, she can feel her mind growing fuzzy again, sleep clawing at her. "I didn't think you cared much about that," she says. "Besides, we're betrothed, and I can't imagine you'll have trouble keeping your hands to yourself. I must look a fright."

"That's an understatement," he says with a belabored sigh, pushing up from the chair and sliding onto the bed beside her, though he stays on top of the covers. "You look an inch from death."

Daphne tries to give him a shove, but her arm is so heavy and weak it has no effect.

"Just sleep," he tells her, rolling onto his side to face her, his cheek against the pillow.

She should sleep—exhaustion is ready to pull her under any second—but instead she lets her eyes scan his face, tracing his sharp cheekbones and the long, dark eyelashes fanned over them. His jawline is dotted in stubble. After a second, he opens his eyes again, meeting hers with a quiet intensity that makes it impossible for her to look away.

"I'm glad you aren't, you know," he says softly.

"Aren't what?" she asks.

"Dead," he says.

She pulls the blankets tighter around her, hugging herself to ward off the cold. "Are you?" she asks. "I thought it would be a relief—you said it yourself. You never asked for this, for me."

"You didn't ask for me, either," he reminds her. "You didn't ask for Cillian, or to come to Friv in the first place, you were just thrown into all of it. You didn't ask for any of this."

You didn't ask for any of this.

It's the first time it's occurred to her that she didn't. She never protested, never fought it, but she didn't ask for it, either. Her mother decided her fate before she'd taken her first breath, and she was content to go along with it, but that isn't the same thing. She never had a choice. A thought pierces her fevered mind, striking true—if she'd had a choice, she might have chosen differently, a life without poisons or subterfuge, without learning to pick locks or code letters, a life without lies.

Suddenly, it occurs to Daphne that she's tired of lies, of

pretending. She wants to touch him, so she does. She places a hand against his cheek, feeling the stubble rough beneath her palm.

"Daphne," he says, her name a whisper. At first she thinks he means it as an admonishment, but he doesn't pull away.

"I'm sure I would have liked Cillian," she tells him, though she doesn't mean to. The words fall from her lips before she can think to stop them. "But I don't think he would have looked at me the way you do."

"And how do I look at you?" he asks. He sounds like he doesn't know whether or not he truly wants the answer.

Daphne smiles, though even that hurts. "Like I'm a bolt of lightning," she says, tracing her fingers along his jawline. "And you can't decide whether I'll kill you or bring you back to life."

He doesn't say anything, but she feels the bob of his throat beneath her touch when he swallows.

"Daphne," he says again, and this time there is no mistaking it, the sigh in his voice, the meaning lurking just below the surface.

"I'm fairly sure that's how I look at you, too," she says quietly.

He closes his eyes, then opens them again. "You're sick. You need to sleep," he says. "You said you would."

Daphne nods, hugging herself tighter. "I'm just so cold, Bairre," she says. "Why is it so cold?"

"It's not," he says. "It's sweltering in here. It's the poison leaving you, making you feverish."

Distantly, she knows that makes sense, but it doesn't ease her shivering. She burrows deeper under the covers.

"Here," Bairre says with a sigh. "Roll over."

When she does, he brings his arms around her, settling her against his chest.

"Better?" he asks.

It's not, really, but she likes the feeling of his arms around her. It might not help the shivers wracking her, but it does make her feel safe. She feels his breath, steady and deep, feels the rhythm of his heart beating, and it grounds her.

"Much," she says, closing her eyes.

Silence falls over them and sleep begins to tug her under once more.

"Why are you here?" she hears herself ask again, though she doesn't remember deciding to ask. The words slip past her lips, half question, half yawn.

Bairre doesn't answer—asleep already, she thinks—but before she can join him there, she feels the low rumble of his chest as he speaks, his voice soft in her ear.

"I'm here because I want to be. Because you are lightning—terrifying and beautiful and dangerous and bright all at once. And I wouldn't wish you were anything else."

Sophronia

A ball is the last place Sophronia wants to be tonight. The crowd around her is giddy and boisterous, sipping drinks and making small talk, discussing the coming war with Cellaria as if it's the most recent tidbit of scintillating gossip rather than a devastating mistake for the country. If one more courtier congratulates Sophronia on it, she doesn't know if she'll be able to keep herself from striking them. But she understands that the optics matter—if they will be dragged into a war with Cellaria no matter what, it needs to appear to have been their choice. No one can know about Violie's forgery or that Leopold tried to go back on the falsified declaration. So she keeps her smile firmly fixed, even though she wants to scream.

Leopold passes her a crystal flute of champagne. "I've had no word from Pasquale," he tells her, keeping his voice low. "Have you heard from your sister?"

Sophronia shakes her head. After she sent coded letters to Beatriz and Daphne, she suggested Leopold write Pasquale as well. It's only been a few days since then, but Sophronia has been watching the post with a growing sense of desperation.

"We'll ship out our first troops tomorrow," he tells her. "Since it doesn't appear we can get out of this, I'd like the war over as soon as possible. If we ambush them on their land, we have a better chance of that."

Sophronia nods, though her mind is elsewhere. Her eyes track Eugenia as she crosses the ballroom floor in a resplendent gold gown. There is nothing forced about her smile—she is absolutely beaming, happier than Sophronia has ever seen her. And why shouldn't she be? In her mind, she is one step closer to getting exactly what she has been working toward—Temarin under Cellarian rule. Sophronia doesn't doubt her mother has a plan for that, too, though, and it gives her some petty joy to know that Eugenia's glee will be short-lived.

"Excuse me a moment," she says to Leopold before following Eugenia.

She catches up with the dowager queen on the other side of the ballroom, linking their arms and falling into step beside her.

"I know what you did," Sophronia tells Eugenia.

Eugenia rolls her eyes. "Please, my dear, this is a party. I'd like to enjoy it."

"Then why don't we get you a glass of sparkling wine? Tell me, was it bought from Cosella?" Sophronia asks.

Eugenia goes rigid for an instant before she laughs. "You truly are paranoid. No, as Leopold requested, any palace purchases that can be made in Temarin are. Including the sparkling wine. Might I suggest you partake in a glass?" she asks, plucking one from the tray of a passing server before handing it to Sophronia. "You really must relax."

Sophronia grips the glass so tightly she worries it might break. "I know that you've been conspiring with your brother," she tells Eugenia, barely bothering to keep her voice low. Eugenia narrows her eyes and tugs Sophronia away from the crowd, leading her out to the secluded balcony.

"I don't know what you're talking about," Eugenia says, but it is the most blatant lie Sophronia has ever heard.

"I know that you've been intentionally bankrupting Temarin, that you drained our war chest, so that when this war came, Cellaria would be able to conquer us with ease. I have a letter from your brother to you, and if you aren't gone from the palace tonight, I will show it to Leopold."

It's a bluff, but Eugenia doesn't know that. Without the letter, Sophronia can't prove Eugenia's treason—not conclusively enough that Leopold will believe her over his own mother, not without revealing her own duplicity. But Sophronia wants her gone.

Eugenia looks at Sophronia for a long moment, but Sophronia doesn't wither under her gaze. She holds it firmly.

"That's funny," Eugenia says finally, her smile a sprung trap. "Because your mother told me you sent the letter to her."

The ground shifts beneath Sophronia's feet. What did her mother say? *Leave her to me*. Before she can begin to wrap her mind around what those words actually meant, Eugenia continues.

"She explained that we had similar aims, she and I," she says. "But she wanted to know why I was doing so much work to serve another king when I could serve myself. So we . . . reconfigured our plans. I must say, I like hers better."

Through the open balcony door, Sophronia hears a wineglass shatter against the floor, but it feels like it's coming from a world away.

"What, to drive us into war? It's the same plan," Sophronia says, but something isn't right. She can feel it in the pit of her stomach.

"Oh, there won't be any war," Eugenia says, laughing. "You look absolutely parched, Sophie. Have a drink."

It's a bizarre non sequitur, but it isn't until Eugenia's hand closes around Sophronia's where it holds the wineglass, forcing it to her lips as another glass crashes to the floor inside, this time followed by a scream, that she understands. She struggles to get away from Eugenia and the glass, but Eugenia has her backed against the balcony railing.

"It's poisoned," Sophronia manages to get out.

Distantly, she hears Leopold call her name but realizes that Eugenia has positioned them out of sight of the ballroom. Still, she's relieved—if he's calling for her, he must be all right.

"Your mother said you were clever," Eugenia says through gritted teeth. "Ansel was so upset with Leopold, it was easy to convince him that the aristocracy was a threat that needed extinguishing. It was easy for him to convince plenty of other commoners."

Sophronia manages to shove Eugenia's arm with enough force that the glass goes flying, crashing against the stone floor, but she only takes two steps before Eugenia pulls a small pistol from the voluminous sleeve of her gown and levels it at Sophronia.

This time, though, Sophronia is ready. She lunges before

Eugenia can take proper aim and grabs hold of the arm holding the pistol, wrenching it backward at a sharp angle that leaves Eugenia no choice but to drop the pistol and let out a scream of pain. Sophronia grabs the weapon from the floor and has it pressed to Eugenia's temple in the space of a breath.

"I would kill you here and now, you know," she tells Eugenia, "if I didn't think I'd be doing my mother a favor."

Instead, she changes her grip and brings the butt of the pistol down hard against Eugenia's head, sending her crashing to the floor in an unconscious heap.

Leaving Eugenia behind, Sophronia starts toward the doors again, but as she draws closer, she sees that the ballroom has already been swarmed by a large group of what she assumes to be the peasant rebels Eugenia mentioned, some dressed in servants' livery. They check the pulses of the fallen nobles. When the Duke of Ellory moves to sit up, a man standing over him removes a pistol from his jacket and shoots him in the chest, the sound of the gun echoing loudly. She doesn't see Leopold, but there are so many bodies on the floor that it doesn't give her much comfort.

Sophronia stumbles back from the door, looking around the balcony for another way out. She is only on the third floor—climbing down the wall might be her best bet. She's about to hoist herself over the railing when she hears her name whispered from the darkened corner a few feet from the door.

"Sophie, through here," the voice whispers, a little louder.

Sophronia tiptoes closer, but before she can see who it is, a hand grabs her arm and pulls her into a dark passageway she didn't know existed. It's only when the door closes again and her eyes adjust to the dark that she sees Violie.

"Where are we?" Sophronia whispers.

"Servants' passage," Violie whispers back, beginning to lead her down the corridor. Sophronia has no reason to trust her, but since there are no other options at present, she follows.

A million questions run through Sophronia's head as they make their way in silence, but only one rises to her lips. "How did you get back in?" she asks. "I told you I'd have you arrested."

Violie glances back at her and shrugs. "If we manage to live through this, you're welcome to follow through on that threat," she says. "But to answer your question—Queen Eugenia had me brought to her before I left the palace. Apparently, your mother told her about me and passed along one last task—smuggling in the rioters and the wine."

Sophronia stops short. "*You* poisoned the wine?" she asks.

Violie glances back at her. "It was already poisoned, but I didn't know it. I didn't know what they had planned at first—your mother isn't fond of being questioned, you know."

Sophronia does know that, but still. "You didn't assume there was a reason the wine needed to be smuggled in? Surely you must have suspected it was tainted somehow."

Violie winces but doesn't deny it. "I intentionally didn't think about it," she says. "But once I realized it would be lethal, that the plan was to kill every aristocrat in the palace, I came to find you. To save you."

If she expects gratitude for that, Sophronia doesn't have

any for her. "Where's Leopold?" she asks instead. "And what about his brothers?"

"Eugenia had the princes removed from the palace this afternoon—I'm not sure where, but I believe she did it to ensure their safety."

When she doesn't continue, Sophronia presses. "And Leo?"

"His was the only glass not poisoned," Violie says after a moment. "When the bodies started to fall, Ansel had him brought back to your rooms and placed under heavy guard there."

Sophronia's immediate relief is quickly dwarfed by dread. "Why?" she asks, though she suspects she already knows the answer.

"His death needs to be public," Violie answers. "It's scheduled for the day after tomorrow at sundown. The rebels wanted to ensure there was time for word to spread. They want an audience."

Sophronia stares at her for a moment, shock coursing through her. "No," she says finally.

"Sophie—"

"No. That won't happen. I'm not going to let it—*we* aren't going to let it," Sophronia says, shaking her head.

"There's no stopping it," Violie says. "He's under heavy guard. I'm lucky I managed to find you. No, we need to get out of the palace, out of this city, out of this stars-forsaken country—"

"No," Sophronia says again, shaking her head. "No, there must be a way."

She does a quick inventory—she has Eugenia's pistol, Violie with her knowledge of the palace's servants' tunnels, and a wish around her wrist.

Her fingers go to the bracelet her mother gave her. *In case you have need of it.* She knows this is not what her mother meant, but here she is, having need of a miracle.

A plan forms itself around that wish—a mad plan, yes, and one she needs Violie for. She reaches out and grabs hold of the other girl's hand, squeezing it tight.

"I'm glad you saved me, Violie, but it doesn't make us even," Sophronia says. "It doesn't come close to making up for your betrayal."

Violie looks at Sophronia like she's physically struck her, but after a second, she nods. "I know that," she says. Sophronia prepares to hear more excuses, but none come.

"Help me save Leopold," Sophronia tells her. "If you help me save him, I will forgive everything."

Violie looks at Sophronia for a long moment and Sophronia worries that she is asking too much, but finally, Violie nods.

"What would you have me do?" she asks.

An hour later, Violie leads Sophronia down the deserted palace hallway with her hands bound behind her back by a strip of cloth from her dress and the pistol pressed to her temple. They stop in front of the hall that leads to the royal wing, where two men are standing guard—peasants, Sophronia guesses, based on their clothes and the mismatched weapons they carry. One holds a rusted ax, while the other carries a rifle.

"What's this, then?" the man with the rifle asks, looking from Violie to Sophronia.

"*This* is Queen Sophronia," Violie says. "I found her trying to sneak out of the palace. Apparently, she didn't drink any wine, but I thought Ansel might want her executed alongside the king."

The two men look at each other and shrug before letting Violie and Sophronia pass.

"This is a terrible idea," Violie whispers as they make their way toward the rooms Sophronia and Leopold share. Sophronia tries to ignore her, though she worries she's right. *I can't let Leopold die for my mistakes,* she thinks, pushing her doubt out of her mind.

More guards are stationed outside the rooms, but when Violie repeats what she told the first set, one of the men slips inside, and Violie can hear a brief, muffled conversation before the guard returns, Ansel with him. When he sees Sophronia, his eyes light up.

"Ah, Your Majesty, we were worried we misplaced you," he says, as if they are having a pleasant conversation over tea. Sophronia smiles tightly at him but doesn't bother with an answer. Ansel turns to Violie. "Well done, Violie. Better to execute two royals than one."

With that, he takes hold of Sophronia's shoulder and shoves her into the room.

Sophronia

Sophronia stumbles into the parlor where just this morning she and Leopold shared coffee. The cloud of the coming war had hung over them as they anxiously waited for their mail to be brought in, hoping for word from Beatriz and Pasquale or Daphne. Now, she would give anything to go back to this morning.

Leopold is there, on the settee with his hands bound behind his back, but a quick survey tells her he's unharmed—he's still dressed in the suit he wore to the ball, and there isn't so much as a tear or stain on it. Relief floods her, and she sees it reflected in his face when his eyes scan her, though his relief is quickly replaced by dread.

The door closes behind her and she hears the dull murmur of voices on the other side, Violie's and Ansel's.

"Sophie, thank the stars you're all right," Leopold says as she crosses the room to sit down beside him. It's awkward with her arms tied behind her back. Violie left the knots loose so she can free herself easily—but not yet. "I was worried you drank the champagne."

"No," Sophronia says. They don't have much time, and

there is so much she needs to tell him. "Though your mother tried to force it down my throat."

Leopold looks bewildered. "My mother did what?"

The urge to lie rises to her lips. It's such a natural habit, and she knows she could spin a story for him that will shift all the blame onto Eugenia while keeping her own hands clean, but he needs the truth now, and Sophronia is so tired of lies.

"Your mother has been conspiring with King Cesare to bankrupt Temarin and drain its war chest so that Cellaria can conquer it easily. She's been working against Temarin since you took the throne, maybe longer."

"No," Leopold says, frowning. "No, she wouldn't do that."

"She would and she did," Sophronia says before taking a steadying breath. "I know because I was supposed to do something similar."

Leopold's expression grows even more confused, though there's an added wariness to it now. "You . . . what?" he asks.

Sophronia bites her lip. "It's a long story, Leo, and you won't like me at the end of it, but I need you to listen."

Sophronia desperately wishes she had use of her hands, if only so that she could fidget. As it is, she looks around the room, scanning the centuries-old paintings on the walls, the breakfast table with its pressed white linen, the fire crackling in the hearth—she looks everywhere she can to avoid having to look at Leopold, but eventually, his gaze draws hers back to him and she lets out a deep breath.

"My mother was never meant to be empress," she begins. "Surely you've heard enough of her story to know that. She clawed her way to the throne and then she decided that it wasn't enough, that Bessemia wasn't enough. So when she gave birth to Beatriz, Daphne, and me, when my father died, she made a plan to rebuild the Bessemian Empire. That was where the betrothals came in. Ours, and my sisters' as well. She began plotting and planning to take over the entire continent, using us as her pawns, sent to Temarin, Cellaria, and Friv to destroy them."

Leopold sits up straighter. "She sent you here to . . . assassinate me?"

"No," Sophronia says quickly. "No, of course not. It would be too easy—her hand in it would have been clear and her reign would have been a tumultuous one." She pauses, taking a deep breath. "No, she sent me here to ruin your country, to urge you to a war with Cellaria that would weaken both countries so that she could conquer them herself."

Leopold shakes his head. "But I didn't need you for that," he points out. "I was destroying Temarin well enough on my own." He pauses. "Wait, you urged me *not* to go to war."

Sophronia laughs. "My mother likes to say that the stars played a cruel joke on her by giving her me," she tells him after a moment. "Daphne can be cold as ice when she wants to be, and Beatriz has her own sort of ruthlessness, but my mother has always said I'm too soft. I think now that she always knew I would fail her, that I would come here and fall in love with Temarin, in love with you. That's why she sent Violie."

"Your lady's maid," Leopold says, looking more confused than ever.

"My mother has an . . . effect on people. She senses weaknesses, knows exactly how to exploit them. She's done it to me often enough; apparently she did it to Violie as well." She pauses. "Violie was the one to send the declaration of war to Cellaria," she adds. "She forged your handwriting, sealed the letter with a stolen royal seal."

"How do you know?" he asks her.

Sophronia fixes him with a level look. "Because it was all planned, Leo. Daphne stole the royal seal from King Bartholomew and sent it to me—I'm the best at forging, so I was to write a letter in his hand, offering to support you in the crusade against Cellaria and forcing Friv into the war as well."

Leopold shakes his head. "Because Friv would never get involved in the disputes of other countries on its own," he says.

"Exactly," Sophronia said. "Meanwhile, Beatriz got close to the ambassador, close enough to frame him for sorcery so that I could push you into a war Temarin can't withstand. In a few months, all three countries would be ravaged enough that my mother could sweep in and pick up the pieces without much resistance at all."

"Then what?" Leopold asks.

Sophronia frowns. "Then my sisters and I go home to Bessemia," she says.

"And me?" he asks. "And Pasquale? And that bastard prince in Friv?"

Sophronia forces herself once again to look at him. "She wouldn't leave loose ends hanging about," she says quietly. "She would have exiled you to some faraway land, or so she said. I'm not sure I ever really believed that, though. My mother doesn't do things by halves."

"So she would have killed me," he says. "And you would have let her."

"I don't know," Sophronia admits. "If we had gotten to that point, I don't know if I could have stopped her—I don't know if I would have tried. As I said, my mother has an effect on people."

"But we didn't get to that point," Leopold says. "Because you changed your mind."

Sophronia nods. "But before I did, I wrote my mother about what I'd discovered about *your* mother, including a letter King Cesare had smuggled to her, thanking her for the work she'd done in draining Temarin's war chest and sowing discord." She doesn't tell him the harsher points of the letter, the personal cruelties they exchanged about Leopold himself. "I thought she would want to be aware of their plots, but instead she recruited your mother to her side as well as the rebels, organizing the riot, the poisoned champagne, and apparently our executions."

"You think our mothers want us killed?" he asks, shaking his head.

"I can't speak for Eugenia, but my mother isn't a forgiving sort," Sophronia says. "Though I have a plan to get us out of this. Despite everything I just told you, I need you to trust me."

For a long moment, he only stares at her like he's never seen her before. In many ways, she supposes, he hasn't.

"How much of it was real?" Leopold asks finally.

She leans her head against the back of the settee and

closes her eyes for a moment before letting herself look at him once more.

"I tried so hard to keep my heart closed to you. In the beginning, you even made it easy," she says. "There were so many lies, Leo. I know that, and I am so sorry for them. But when it came down to it, I chose Temarin. I chose you. I love you. That's the truth."

Silence stretches between them, and Sophronia all but holds her breath, waiting for him to speak or move or do *anything* but stare at her like she's some kind of stranger to him. After what feels like an eternity, he lets out a long exhale, his shoulders sagging.

"After we survive this," he tells her, "I'm going to be furious with you."

Sophronia forces a smile. "After we survive this," she echoes.

Daphne

When Daphne opens her eyes again, the throbbing in her head has faded to a dull ache and she can sit up in bed without pain spasming through her body. Bairre is sitting in the chair by her bed again, alone now, with a book open in his lap. When she stirs, his eyes jerk up to meet hers and he closes the book.

"All right?" he asks her.

Daphne does a quick inventory. Her throat is dry and rough, her muscles a bit sore. She desperately wants a bath and some food, though nothing seems appetizing at the moment.

"More or less," she tells Bairre. The words are hoarse but intelligible. "How long did I sleep this time?" she asks, afraid of the answer.

"You had a normal night's sleep," Bairre assures her with a small smile.

She leans her head back against the pillow and casts her gaze toward the ceiling. "Are there any updates?"

"Zenia's nanny along with her husband and brother," Bairre says. "All executed now."

She feels him watching her for a reaction and she wonders which one she should give him. Horror at the thought of their deaths? Sadness? Guilt? She's too exhausted to pretend any of those things.

"They tried to kill me," she tells him. "I'm not sorry they're dead."

He nods, glancing away. "They were interrogated thoroughly beforehand, but they didn't say who they were working with," he says.

He says *interrogated,* but Daphne hears *tortured.* She wonders if he knows it himself.

"But it wasn't the rebels," she says.

"No," Bairre says. "It wasn't the rebels."

Even though one of those rebels was holding a knife to her throat a week ago, she believes that. "I need to speak with Cliona," she says.

Bairre frowns slightly at the change of subject. "She's checked in on you a few times," he says. "But you should really rest some more."

"I'm fine," she tells him. "Actually, I'd like some fresh air. Can you ask Cliona to meet me for a walk through the garden?"

"You almost died, Daphne," he says, as if she is unaware of this.

"But I didn't," Daphne says, trying to sound surer than she feels. "We'll be careful, it's only the garden."

"*Careful* isn't enough. *Careful* won't stop an arrow or a bullet or a poisonous gas or—"

"Perhaps the assassins should consult you—it seems you've put a lot of thought into how best to murder me," she says.

Bairre fixes her with a dark look, one that reminds her of other things that were said while she was sick. *I'm here because I want to be,* he told her.

"This is serious, Daphne," he says.

It's different, she thinks, than the way he said her name before, when she had her hand against his cheek.

"So am I," she says, pushing the thought aside. "I know the risks; I'm the one they tried to kill. But I've been stuck in bed for a day and a half and I refuse to let fear keep me sequestered in this room any longer."

He holds her gaze for a long moment, his jaw tight. "Fine," he says eventually, getting to his feet. "But you'll take guards with you."

Daphne opens her mouth to argue, then closes it again. This is why she didn't tell anyone about the first attempt—she knew it would mean losing her freedom. But now that they've passed that point, there is no going back.

"Fine," she replies. "But I want Mattlock and Haskin," she says, remembering the guards who accompanied her and Cliona to the dressmaker, two of the ones Cliona said were with the rebels. Ones who will keep quiet about anything they might overhear.

He nods once. "Done," he says, starting toward the door. "I think I'll join you as well—a little fresh air sounds nice."

Daphne opens her mouth to protest, but he's already gone, the door closing firmly behind him. She flops back down against the pillows and lets out a groan. She can't very well speak freely with Cliona if Bairre is there as well.

If only she hadn't gotten poisoned, she would already have been able to talk with Cliona. The thought of it still rankles—of the three sisters, she's always been the most adept at creating and identifying poisons. The fact that one almost felled her is embarrassing.

Daphne frowns, a memory filtering back through her mind. Beatriz. The vial she sent. The poison she thought Daphne could identify. After failing so miserably with one poison, she's determined to redeem herself. She crosses toward the jewelry box on her vanity and sifts through it, finding the false bottom and pulling out the glass vial Beatriz sent, full of the dark red liquid.

Daphne unstoppers the vial and smells it. Wine. She puts the stopper back in the vial and holds it up to the sunlight streaming through her window, turning it this way and that. She squints, looking at the liquid, at the fine, siltlike flecks that sink to the bottom.

Someone is adding something to King Cesare's wine. Daphne frowns and digs through the hidden compartment of her jewelry box again. It's full of other vials of liquids and powders, funnels, and other necessities her mother's apothecary put together for her. Daphne finds a strip of white cloth and a magnifying glass and takes a seat at her vanity.

After shaking the vial, she spills a splash of the wine onto the cloth and watches as the liquid is absorbed, leaving a few grains of grit on the surface. She takes the magnifying glass and holds it up to the cloth, her heart beating so loudly in her chest that she wonders if the entire castle can hear it. The grains are rough and all different sizes, as if they've been ground up from something with a mortar and pestle, though she's quite certain by the uniform color that they come from the same source.

She pinches them off the cloth and brings them to her tongue—even if they *are* poisonous, such a small amount won't hurt her. That taste. She knows that taste.

Her hands begin to shake as she rifles through her miniature laboratory, searching for a vial. When she finds it, she opens it and spills some of the seeds inside onto her palm, comparing the color to the remaining grains. They are the same shade of brown—so dark it's nearly black. She pops one of the seeds into her mouth and bites down, crunching it between her back teeth. It tastes the same, too.

Daphne's mind is a blur as she closes everything up again. She rings for her maid and lets the girl change her into a fresh day dress and braid her hair, one thought echoing all the while in her mind.

She needs to talk to Beatriz. Now.

When Daphne finally makes it down to the garden, swaddled in so many layers of wool and fur she's actually sweating, she finds Cliona, Bairre, and Haimish already waiting, Mattlock and Haskin standing just a few feet away. Perhaps she should be surprised that Haimish is there, but she isn't. She can't think of much beyond Beatriz, though she knows that Haimish's presence is a lot less worrisome than Bairre's. She'll need to find a way to be rid of Bairre if she's going to get the stardust Cliona promised.

When Cliona sees her, she smiles, and even though Daphne knows better, she could almost swear the other girl looks genuinely relieved to see her.

"Look at you," Cliona drawls, taking her hands and

kissing her on each cheek. "No one would know you almost died just a day ago."

"Aren't you kind," Daphne replies, and Haimish has to hide his snort of laughter with a cough. Cliona glares at him anyway.

"If you aren't feeling up to this—" Bairre begins, his brow furrowed.

"I think a bit of fresh air is just what I need," Daphne interrupts, even though the cold is already getting to her. It doesn't matter, she reminds herself. Beatriz matters. If Daphne has to feel a little cold to help her, so be it. "Shall we walk?"

Bairre still doesn't look convinced, but he offers her his arm and she takes it, letting one of her gloves drop as she does. No one notices. Cliona takes Haimish's arm, and for a moment, they walk in silence. When they've gotten far enough away from the palace, Daphne releases Bairre's arm and makes a show of searching for her glove.

"Oh no!" she exclaims. "My glove! I must have dropped it."

Bairre looks at the ground around them. "Do you know where?"

Daphne bites her lip and shakes her head. "I *know* I had it when I came outside. Do you mind doubling back?" she asks him. "I'm sorry, I hate to ask, but it's so cold out and I don't want to catch a chill."

It's a cheap card, using her recent illness, and when his face goes a shade paler, a pang of guilt goes through her.

"Of course," he says. "You three stay here with the guards, I'll be right back."

As soon as he's out of earshot, Daphne turns to Haimish and Cliona. "Lord Cadringal's lands are troubled; he's overwhelmed by his new duties. If the rebellion approached him, he could be convinced to join, despite his friendship with Bairre," she tells them. "I did what you asked. Now I need that stardust."

They exchange a look she can't read. "We'll have to see if your reading of Rufus pans out—"

"I need it now," Daphne interrupts. She pauses, pressing her lips together into a thin line. She hates how desperate she is, how at their mercy, but she can't deny that she is. "Please," she says, softening her voice. "I need to use it to speak with my sister. It's urgent."

Haimish and Cliona exchange another look. "A wish like that will require a lot of power," Cliona points out. "Stardust might not be enough—"

"I know," Daphne says. "But I have to try."

Cliona looks like she wants to ask questions, but after a moment, she shakes her head.

"It'll be beneath your pillow after lunch," she says.

Daphne gives a nod. "Thank you."

"You can save your thanks—you owe us," Cliona says.

Daphne opens her mouth to argue, but she sees Bairre approaching at a jog, her glove clutched in his hand. She swallows down her protest and nods. "Fine," she answers through clenched teeth before greeting Bairre again with a smile.

Daphne makes excuses about not feeling well halfway through lunch. After the last few days, no one questions her. Two guards escort her back to her room and inspect every corner, the wardrobe, and under the bed before leaving her alone. She supposes their attention should make her feel safer, but instead it chafes. They're trying to keep her alive, she knows this, but she has too many secrets of her own to hide.

As soon as she's alone, she crosses to her bed and reaches under the pillows. It takes a moment, but she finds the vial of stardust from Cliona, along with a set of directions on how to use it to call on someone.

Daphne wastes no time unstoppering the vial. She reads the instructions and pours the shimmering black dust over the back of her hand.

"I wish to speak with Princess Beatriz," she says.

As soon as the words are out of her mouth, everything around her goes muffled: the wind whistling outside, the guards' voices on the other side of the door, even the sound of her own heartbeat.

"Triz?" she says.

She hears a sharp inhale, followed by a mad laugh that can only be Beatriz's. "Daphne?" her sister asks.

"It's me," Daphne says. "I don't have long—Frivians have a way of using stardust to communicate, but I don't know how long it will last."

"What—"

"No questions right now," Daphne says. "I looked at the wine you sent me. You were right, there was something off about it. Ground apple seeds." Daphne is speaking so quickly she wonders if she's making any sense at all. For a moment, Beatriz doesn't respond.

"Apple seeds?" she asks finally. "But . . ."

"They're a source of cyanide," Daphne says. "Surely you remember that from our lessons."

"I never paid nearly as much attention as you did," Beatriz says. "But I do remember that cyanide is lethal. King Cesare is very much alive, though I'm told his servants dilute his wine."

Daphne shakes her head, even though she knows Beatriz can't see her. "The wine you sent me wasn't diluted, but the dosage is small—it will be killing him slowly, though if they used any more than they have been, the addition would be noticeable. It may also be affecting his mind, depending on how much he ingests every day."

Beatriz goes quiet again. "He ingests quite a lot," she says. "And he's become more and more erratic. Pasquale says it's been going on for months."

"It will kill him," Daphne says. "Maybe not right away, but soon."

Beatriz lets out a long breath. "I wish you'd told me this days ago," she says, sounding annoyed.

Daphne rolls her eyes. "Apologies, I was only recovering from being poisoned myself. Perhaps if *you'd* paid better attention—"

"You were poisoned?" Beatriz asks.

"I'm fine," Daphne says emphatically, thoroughly tired of being fussed over. "How are you?"

That gives Beatriz pause. "Oh, under house arrest, currently. For treason."

"Are . . . you joking?" Daphne asks.

"Afraid not."

"But you have your wish to get you out of trouble," Daphne says.

"I *had* a wish," Beatriz says. "It's possible, though, that you just gave me what I need to get out of this mess."

Daphne bites her lip. "Beatriz," she says slowly. "How much trouble are you in?"

For a long moment, Beatriz doesn't answer. "It's only trouble of my own making, Daph. You know I've always been good at that, just as I've always been good at getting myself out of it."

She says the words lightly, and Daphne knows the truth of them, but it does little to unknot her stomach.

"Have you heard from Sophie?" Beatriz asks, changing the subject.

Sophie. Daphne's memories of the day she was poisoned are fuzzy, but at the mention of Sophronia, the letter comes filtering back. She closes her eyes. "She sent a letter," she admits. "Please tell me you managed to talk sense into her?"

For a moment, Beatriz doesn't speak, and Daphne worries that they've lost the connection.

"You and I both know I'm not the sensible sort, Daph," Beatriz says finally. "Besides, I happened to agree with her."

Frustration wells up inside Daphne, and she snatches a pillow from her bed and throws it across the room. It lands with a delicate thud, causing no harm and making Daphne feel no better. Appropriate, she supposes, given how helpless she feels at the moment.

"No wonder you got yourself into so much trouble,

Triz," she snaps. "If you both could just have done as you were told—"

"Do you think it's the right thing, Daphne?" Beatriz interrupts. "Tell me honestly now: Do you think Mama's taking control of Vesteria is in everyone's best interests? Or only hers?"

The next time Daphne sees Beatriz, she's going to strangle her.

"It isn't the right thing, or the wrong thing," Daphne tells her. "It's the *only thing*. You're under house arrest, Triz, so clearly your way of doing things isn't working out so well for you. Here's what you're going to do—write to Mama, apologize, beg for her help, and fix the damage you have done."

Beatriz is silent again, but this time Daphne knows she's still there. Hundreds of miles away and Daphne can still feel her sister's fury.

"I didn't get you into this mess," Daphne continues, because she knows that fury is directed at her. "And you know I'm right—Mama is your only hope now."

Another long pause.

"Of course," Beatriz says, again with that faux lightness that makes Daphne want to tear her hair out. "I'll get myself out of this. Try to avoid getting poisoned again, will you?"

She is gone before Daphne can respond.

Sophronia

Sophronia keeps an eye on the clock as night bleeds into morning, which gently fades into noon. Their execution isn't set until sundown the next day; while Sophronia isn't keen to cut too close to that deadline, she needs to give Violie enough time to reach the rendezvous point, as far from the palace as they dared. She tells Leopold the plan she and Violie came up with, simple as it is: when the clock strikes three, she will unbind her wrists and break her bracelet, wishing for her and Leopold to be transported to a cave on the far side of the Amivel Woods, where Violie will be waiting for them.

Like Violie, Leopold wasn't sure the wish would be strong enough to accomplish that, but she assured them both that it would.

The clock is only a few breaths from three o'clock when the door opens and Ansel enters. He appears to have changed into fresh clothes, but Sophronia doesn't think he's slept. There are dark circles under his eyes that weren't there last night. He glances between the two of them and runs a hand through his hair. He doesn't seem to know what to say, which is fine since Sophronia has a question for him and it will be the only chance for her to get an answer.

"When did my mother recruit you, Ansel?" she asks.

Ansel blinks in surprise. "Queen Eugenia reached out to me after Leopold declared war—"

Sophronia interrupts him with a laugh. "I'm sorry," she says. "I just expected my mother would hire a better liar. You were talking with Violie at the speech, and then you just happened to rescue the prince from the same crowd of rioters you're now leading? Contrary to what my mother might believe, I'm not an idiot."

Ansel looks at her for a long moment, then seems to make a decision. "Well, you'll be dead soon, so where's the harm?" he says, coming to sit in the armchair across from Sophronia and Leopold. "Yes, fine, I've been in contact with your mother for a year and a half. The fishing boat story was true enough, but I did go onshore once, when we were docked in Friv. Got into a bit of trouble at a tavern, cheated at cards, got into a fight. One of the men had a nasty right hook and when I came to, I was in one of the tavern rooms, and an empyrea was there offering to heal me with stardust."

"Nigellus," Sophronia says. Of course her mother's lapdog was involved.

Ansel shrugs. "Didn't ask who he was and didn't care. But he knew me—knew my name, my position on the boat, knew of my family in Kavelle."

"Don't tell me he offered to heal a sick family member for you, too," Sophronia says, remembering Violie's story.

Ansel laughs. "No, I'm a simple sort—he just offered me money. All he wanted me to do was return to Kavelle and begin stoking anger against the aristocrats. It wasn't even hard after King Carlisle died." He turns to Leopold. "You were very easy to hate, you know," he adds conversationally.

Leopold winces but doesn't reply, so Ansel continues.

"I didn't even realize your mother was involved until Violie sought me out. Then you arrived, Queen Sophie, and everything came together."

"Until it didn't," Sophronia says. "Until I went against my mother's plans."

For a moment, Ansel stares at her blankly; then he bursts into laughter. "Oh, maybe you aren't as smart as you think you are," he says. "You followed your mother's plan perfectly."

It's Sophronia's turn to be shocked to silence, the wheels of her mind spinning as she tries to make sense of that.

"No, I refused to push Leopold into war, I even tried to rebuild Temarin—"

"You behaved exactly as she thought you would," Ansel interrupts. "All of it. The only surprise, really, was Eugenia, and that was an unexpected boon. But this"—he pauses to gesture around the room—"this was always your mother's plan—a palace besieged by rebels, dead aristocrats, a beheaded king and queen, chaos around every corner. Her troops will arrive by the end of the week and their path will be clear. Thanks to you," he adds.

Her mother wants her dead—Sophronia knew this already, she told Leopold as much last night—but she thought it was because Sophronia had failed her. She thought her mother's anger toward her was her own fault, like always.

There is something strangely freeing in knowing it has nothing to do with her at all.

The clock behind Ansel chimes three, but he ignores it. Sophronia and Leopold exchange a glance, and she gives a quick nod. It's time. She twists her wrists at the right angle, with enough force, to break the bindings. Before Ansel has the chance to react, she grabs the bracelet around her wrist and throws it on the floor, positioning it under the heel of her boot.

"I'm sorry," she tells Leopold, who frowns in confusion.

It's strong enough to save a life, her mother told her and her sisters when she gave them the bracelets. *A* life. Not two, as Sophronia has led Leopold and Violie to believe.

She crushes the wish beneath her heel.

"I wish Leopold were with Violie, far away from here."

For an instant, time moves like honey. Ansel lunges toward Leopold, Leopold steps toward Sophronia. Then, as quick as a blink, Leopold is gone and Ansel is grabbing nothing but air. When he realizes, he whirls toward Sophronia with fury in his eyes.

"What did you do?" he yells.

Sophronia's smile is brittle. "Something my mother didn't plan for," she says.

Beatriz

Beatriz paces her locked bedchamber and tries to summon a plan. Daphne's words ring in her ears, but she focuses on the ones that are actually helpful—*ground apple seeds.* Anyone could have put them in the king's wine, she supposes, but there is one person she knows who had direct access to it, and who always smells of apples. And if Nicolo was the one putting them into the king's wine, she would bet anything that Gisella was the one grinding them up.

As the sky outside her sealed stained-glass window begins to lighten, Beatriz assembles the pieces of information she has into a weapon that will get her out of this mess—because contrary to what she told her sister, she would rather die than ask for her mother's help.

Soon, King Cesare will bring her before him, to pronounce her sentence if nothing else, and she can tell him about Nicolo's poison. She rehearses the story she will tell, how Nicolo and Gisella conspired together and threatened her if she didn't go along with their plans, how she is simply a victim in all of this, as much as the king himself is. The king's moods are unpredictable, but she's managed to wrap him around her finger before, she can do it again.

The door to the room opens abruptly, and Beatriz whirls around just in time to see Pasquale stumble inside, as though someone has shoved him. In seconds, she is across the room, her arms around his neck, holding him tight as her emotions go to war—relief that he is alive and rage that he is here, just as doomed as she is.

"Triz," he says, wrapping his arms around her waist and holding her so tight she isn't sure he'll ever let her go—isn't sure she wants him to.

"I'm so sorry," he says, his voice hoarse and heavy. "I don't know what happened—everything was fine, Lord Savelle got on the boat, he and Ambrose were just out of sight. Then the guards found me on the dock and arrested me."

There is some sense of relief in that—Lord Savelle and Ambrose made it out. Hopefully, they will manage to get to Temarin; the wish she used should place luck on their side.

"It wasn't your fault," Beatriz says, pulling back to look at him. "Nicolo and Gisella betrayed us." She catches him up on everything, even telling him what her sister found in the king's wine, though that requires even more explanations, and Pasquale listens in absolute silence as she tells him more, starting with her birth and her mother's grand plan. She expects him to be angry, to feel betrayed, to hate her for it, but instead he looks at her with tired eyes.

"We're all our parents' puppets, Beatriz," he says.

"You aren't angry?" she asks him, blinking.

He's quiet for a moment. "Not at you," he says finally. "I'd be a hypocrite, wouldn't I? To berate you for not going against your mother, when I've never once gone against my father." He pauses, considering. "Well, I suppose both of us rebelled, didn't we? And look where it's landed us."

Beatriz bites her lip. "If Nico and Gigi have been poisoning the king, we can use that," she says. "We can cast doubt on them, on their accusations. It won't be easy—they caught me standing in front of Lord Savelle's empty cell, with stardust—but perhaps we can think up a story . . ."

She trails off when Pasquale shakes his head and reaches for her hand, squeezing it between both of his.

"Beatriz, the guards arrested me last night. After that, they took me to my father, on his deathbed," he says.

Beatriz goes still. "He's dying?"

He shakes his head. "He died an hour ago," he says, and though he's discussing his father's death, his voice is calm and level. "Before he died, he wanted to be sure I knew what a disappointment I was, how I sullied our family line, how I was weak to be manipulated by my wife—that's what he thinks, by the way, what everyone will think, I suppose."

"Pas—"

"I've been disowned," Pasquale says. "My father decided, in his final moments, that the crown will pass to a cousin instead. And after months of loyal service as his cupbearer, plying him with wine and whispering in his ear, would you like to guess which of my many cousins he chose?"

Beatriz closes her eyes tight, the pieces falling into place. She knew they'd betrayed her, but she hadn't understood what their endgame was. "Nico is going to be king," she says quietly.

Pasquale nods. "Which means he will be the one deciding our fate."

Beatriz tries not to feel bad about drugging Pasquale that afternoon and mostly succeeds. He needs the sleep, there is no arguing that, and he is unlikely to find it on his own. Luckily, the guards who combed their rooms for anything suspicious left her cosmetics case alone—inside one of the jars, disguised as eye pigment, she found a sleeping powder and slipped some of it into his tea. He fell asleep still holding the mug in his hands.

Now, alone with only the sound of his deep and steady breaths to keep her company, Beatriz longs to take a dose of the sleeping powder herself. She craves the peace that would come with a blank mind, but she knows it would be a peace she doesn't deserve. And besides, someone has to stay on guard in case a scrap of news arrives.

Beatriz paces the dimly lit room, the only indication of passing time the slow dying of the fire in the hearth. She decides to take Daphne's advice and write to her mother after all. It won't be easy to get a letter to her under these circumstances, but surely her mother has allies in the palace, surely they will make themselves known to her soon, and she should be prepared when they do. But even the thought of begging her mother's help leaves a bad taste in her mouth.

It isn't for her own benefit, she reminds herself as she walks toward the desk, it's for Pasquale's. Beatriz might rather die than ask her mother for help, but she won't resign Pasquale to the same fate.

A quiet knock interrupts her thoughts, and she stops short in the middle of the room. The knock isn't coming from the door—the sound is too thin, the sound of knuckles against glass. She turns toward the stained glass and crosses toward it, making out the vague outline of a body on the other side. She hears the sound of a key turning in a lock, and with her heart pounding in her chest, she yanks the window open, causing Nicolo to lose his balance and nearly tumble into her room, catching himself on the frame at the last minute.

For a moment, Beatriz only stares at him, and, for his part, he refuses to meet her eyes, instead keeping his gaze on the stone floor.

"We need to talk," he says finally.

A few moments ago, Beatriz agreed with that sentiment. Over the last few hours, she's had countless conversations with him in her mind, she's railed at him and screamed and called him all manner of names. She's demanded answers and then slapped him before he ever got a chance to give them to her. She's thought of a dozen cutting remarks, each worse than the last but none of them quite awful enough.

Now, though, with him crouching before her in the window, his knuckles blanched where he grips the frame tight in his hands, the words leave her. Instead of telling him all the things she's rehearsed in her mind, she takes hold of the open window again and slams it closed, catching his fingers in the process and making him cry out in pain.

The sound makes her feel a bit better, but that lasts only an instant before the window pushes open again and Nicolo is still standing there, balanced precariously on the sill.

"We need to talk," he says again, and this time Beatriz hears the slur of his words.

"You're drunk," she says, biting out the words. "But I suppose you've been celebrating, *Your Majesty.*"

"Triz—"

She moves toward him quickly, grabbing him by the shoulders. "I could shove you out the window."

He doesn't look alarmed, doesn't even go tense, just appraises her with calm, cool eyes.

"Not unless you're keen on adding regicide to your charges," he points out.

Beatriz doesn't loosen her grip. "You reek of liquor," she tells him. "Any sane person would assume you fell to your death attempting something foolish."

"And you consider the members of the court sane?" he asks, his smile turning mocking.

"I think I'd like to test the theory."

She pushes him back, and his hands grip the window frame tighter. Fear flashes in his eyes, and Beatriz feels a jolt of triumph rocket through her. She could watch him die, she thinks. Not a full day ago she was kissing him, and now she's tempted to kill him with her own hands. How quickly everything can change.

"At least let me explain—"

"I assure you, I'm not so stupid I haven't figured out the gist of it myself."

"Gigi decided—"

Beatriz's eyebrows arch up. "Hiding behind your sister now? How brave."

He shakes his head, finally lifting his eyes to meet hers. "I didn't come here to make excuses, Triz—"

"Don't call me that," she snaps.

He lets out a long breath before trying again. "I came here to fix it."

Beatriz squares her shoulders and crosses her arms over her chest. "Oh?" she asks. "How exactly do you propose to do that? Let Pas and me go free? Relinquish the throne you stole to the person who belongs on it?"

It gives her some satisfaction to see him flush with shame. He forces himself to continue.

"Your marriage was never consummated," he continues. "If you annul it and marry me instead—"

"You must be joking." Beatriz laughs, then glances at where Pasquale is still sleeping and lowers her voice. "I wouldn't marry you if you were the last person in this wretched country."

He doesn't say anything for a long moment, but she can tell she's wounded him. *Good*.

"It's the only way you can make it through this. We can spin it, say your marriage to Pas was a sham and you were desperate. How none of this was your idea. How he used you."

Beatriz didn't think there was anything Nicolo could say that would anger her more, she thought her temper had reached its limit. She was wrong.

"Let me see if I understand this," she says slowly. "You would have me push all blame onto Pas in order to save myself?"

"There's no saving him," Nicolo says, shaking his head. "There are already powerful people at court who want him on the throne; pardoning him is too dangerous for me."

Beatriz's stomach tightens. "You'll execute him, then," she says.

He pauses, just long enough to let her know he's considered it. "No," he says. "It wouldn't do to make a martyr of him. He'll be exiled to the mountains. There's a Fraternia there that will take him. He'll be stripped of his title, his name even, and spend the rest of his days studying scripture and reflecting on his spiritual redemption within their walls."

Not death, Beatriz thinks, but Pasquale won't find it much better. She's heard stories about Cellarian Fraternias and Sororias—cold, minimalistic structures stripped of all comforts and luxuries, where the only entertainment to be found is in the pages of scriptures and the only conversation allowed is when a Brother or Sister says the nightly prayers to the stars. They have Fraternias and Sororias in Bessemia as well, where men and women devote themselves to the stars and the reading of them, deciding to live a life without personal or material attachments, but they aren't quite the same. *Deciding* being the main difference, she supposes. Perhaps some people choose the Sororia or Fraternia in Cellaria, but for most it's used as a punishment. Just like now.

"So are those my choices, then? Marry you or I'll . . . what? Be sent to the neighboring Sororia? I can see why

Cesare chose you to succeed him—banishing a girl to that place for rejecting him seems like something he would do."

Nicolo flinches. "I'm not trying to give you an ultimatum, but Pasquale is capable of protecting himself. He doesn't need you suffering alongside him."

Beatriz presses her lips into a thin line. "I want to make myself perfectly clear, Nico. I would rather be suffering alongside him than reigning beside you."

Nicolo deflates, sagging against the window frame like a sail losing its wind.

"I tried," he says after a moment. "Remember that."

"I don't think there's any chance I will ever forget this moment," Beatriz tells him. "I'll remember it until my last breath. They say boredom is a constant companion in a Sororia, but I don't know that I'll ever be bored, not when I recall the memory of you showing up in my bedroom—drunk, desperate, and disappointed. A pathetic excuse for a person, playing at being a king. I daresay the memory will bring me joy even in my darkest moments. Now get out, before I shout for the guards. What would they say, to find their new king sneaking into the room of accused traitors?"

For a moment, she thinks he will call her bluff, but eventually he turns away, climbing back onto the window ledge without another word. When he's gone, Beatriz slams the window shut, the sound echoing through the bedchamber.

"Triz," Pasquale says softly from the bed.

She winces. "How much of that did you hear?"

"Enough to know you just made a mistake. You should have taken his offer."

Beatriz shakes her head, sitting down on the bed beside

him. "No," she says. "We are in this together, Pas, and we will find our way out of it together."

Pasquale falls quiet for a moment. "You didn't tell him you knew about the poison," he says.

"No, that would have been foolish," she says. "Just now we're inconvenient, but if he knows we hold that secret, we go from inconvenient to dangerous."

Pasquale nods slowly, his brow furrowed. "Cosella," he says after a moment.

Beatriz frowns, and it takes her a minute to remember the winery she asked him about.

"What about it?"

"When Gigi and Nico were children, neither of them ever spent a moment without the other—Cosella was their collective nickname. Nicolo and Gisella combined. I'd forgotten all about that, but it's why it sounded familiar when you asked."

Beatriz closes her eyes, trying to make sense of this new information. It's remarkably easy—of course King Cesare was never conspiring with his sister; Beatriz had already suspected he didn't have the mental capacity for it. But Sophronia's information was valid after all. Nicolo must have used his position as cupbearer to intercept the letters. She's unsure whether Queen Eugenia knew who she was really corresponding with, but she supposes it doesn't matter now. It's more information that won't save her and Pasquale, and she doubts she'll be able to get a letter to Sophronia.

Pasquale looks at her again and attempts a smile. "Part of me is glad you didn't take Nico's offer, selfish as that might make me."

Beatriz bites her lip. "Well, part of me was glad you didn't sail off with Ambrose, so it seems we're both selfish."

When the sleeping powder drags Pas back to sleep, she tiptoes out of the bedroom and into the adjoining parlor, sitting down at her desk. She takes a sheet of parchment from the drawer and dips her quill into the inkpot before beginning to write.

Dear Mama,

I would rather die than ask for your assistance

She crumples up the letter and throws it into the fire.

Dear Mama,

I find myself in terrible trouble because of you

With a groan, Beatriz crumples and burns that letter as well. She takes a steadying breath and tries again.

Dear Mama,

I know that we have had our differences in the past and that I have not always been the most dutiful of daughters. I find myself now in a horrible mess of my own making, accused of treason along with Prince Pasquale. I fear for our lives and I beg your help.

Beatriz stares at the words, her stomach turning until she thinks she might be sick. It's too over-the-top, she thinks, her mother won't believe it. As she crumples that letter and adds it to the fire as well, she realizes what the problem is—her mother will not be moved by emotion or begging. She picks up her quill.

Dear Mama,

Our plans have gone awry and everything you've worked for is in danger. If you help us now, I will be forever in your debt.

Writing those words makes her sick too, but she knows that if anything will sway her mother, it will be that. She sets the letter aside and brings up a new sheet of paper, staring at it for a long moment and tapping the feather of the quill against her cheek.

She carefully transcribes the letter, using her mother's favorite code, the Delonghier Shuffle, to hide it within a simpering letter in which she begs her mother to maintain the treaty with Cellaria even in the face of her arrest.

When she's done, she seals the letter and burns the original before sitting back in her chair and letting out a long sigh.

The empress will come, she tells herself. She repeats the thought over and over again until she almost believes it.

Daphne

In the hours after her conversation with Beatriz, Daphne can't stop thinking about her sisters.

What they are doing is dangerous, Daphne has always known this—it's why they were taught to always carry a dagger holstered around their thighs, why she's smuggled a second one in her boot ever since her brush with the poison. But the danger to her seems inconsequential. It's her sisters she's worried about, and with every hour that passes with no news from abroad, that worry grows, along with the mounting frustration that they've gotten themselves into this position in the first place.

It helps that Cliona's decided to spend the next day with her. She arrives just after breakfast and helps Daphne go over the letters that have piled up while she's been recovering. At first, Daphne suspects Cliona has some ulterior motive, but as the day drags on, she can't figure out what that is. It's unnerving, which is why Daphne decides to confront her while they sip their morning coffee.

"We aren't friends," she tells Cliona. "You must know I

won't tell anyone about the rebels. I can't without incriminating myself."

Cliona glances up at her over the top of one of Daphne's letters—this one from an acquaintance in Bessemia, fishing for gossip. "Are you sure we aren't friends?" she asks, setting the letter aside.

"Yes," Daphne says, frowning. "Friends like each other. They don't threaten and blackmail and bribe."

"Hmm," Cliona says, pursing her lips like the thought had never occurred to her. "I guess I wouldn't know. I don't have many friends, and neither do you, come to think of it."

"I have friends," Daphne snaps, though as soon as the words are out of her mouth, she realizes they're a half-truth. She doesn't have friends; she has sisters. And that's the same in some ways, but not in others. A sharp thorn of regret pricks her when she thinks about her last conversation with Beatriz, but it goes away quickly. It's simply how they speak to each other; no doubt Beatriz has already forgotten it.

"You're interesting to spend time with," Cliona tells her, shrugging. "And whether or not I like you, I certainly respect you. Maybe that's enough for friendship."

Daphne looks down at the letter she's holding, frowning so deeply that she can hear her mother's voice in her mind, warning her about getting wrinkles.

"Besides," Cliona says, "if I didn't think we were friends, I wouldn't have given you that wish to speak with your sister."

At that, Daphne scoffs. "It wasn't a gift, remember? You said I'd have to pay you back. Ergo, not friendship."

"Yes," Cliona says slowly. "But I haven't asked for anything yet, have I?"

"There," Daphne says, pointing at her. "Maybe I don't know much about friendship, but I do know that friends don't go around threatening each other."

Cliona only laughs. "Please, you know you'd be hopelessly bored without me to keep you company, threats or no."

Daphne grits her teeth, but she realizes she can't deny it.

When they've gotten through Daphne's correspondence, Daphne and Cliona take a walk through the castle. With Daphne's wedding fast approaching, everything is in a state of chaos; twice as many servants as usual bustle about, and the visiting highland clans are everywhere Daphne looks. Cliona introduces her to everyone they pass, and though she recognizes the names from her studies, she pretends she doesn't. She also realizes that their accents have become a little clearer to her. When she says as much to Cliona, the other girl laughs.

"Just wait until they get some ale in them," Cliona tells her. "Even *I* can't understand them when they begin drinking."

Daphne smiles and they duck into the castle chapel, where she will marry Bairre in just three days. It's a strange thought, though she doesn't know why. She was ready to marry Cillian when she first arrived in Friv, and she feels she knows Bairre better than she ever knew his brother. And it's the last thing she needs to do to further her mother's plan. Still, she feels a sense of trepidation as they step into the space.

The glass roof lets in the light of the morning sun, making the space feel a little warmer than the rest of the castle. A dozen servants are hard at work, stringing up flowers, polishing candlesticks, laying a golden rug down the center aisle for her to walk on. She takes it all in, trying to imagine what it will look like when they're done, what it will look like the night of her wedding, with the stars shining down on her in her wedding gown, while Bairre waits at the front. She hopes no one forces him into a haircut before then—she's grown quite fond of his hair the way it is.

She's drawn out of her thoughts by the distinct feeling that she's being watched. It shouldn't unsettle her—of course she's being watched, she's the princess. Every servant's eyes were glued on her from the second she stepped into the chapel. But something about this gaze raises the hairs on the back of her neck.

"I think it will look splendid when it's done," Cliona says beside her, looking around the chapel.

"Yes, I suggested the white lily garlands—the florist said they were used for mourning in Friv, and it seemed like a fitting tribute to remember Cillian as well," Daphne says, though she barely hears her own words. She's following Cliona's gaze, taking in the details of the space, but also looking for anything more.

There he is, standing in the front pew with a broom in hand. Average height, with fair hair and broad shoulders. She doesn't let her gaze linger on him, but she doesn't need to. She recognizes him instantly.

"Cliona," Daphne says, letting her voice drop even as she maintains her bland smile and roaming gaze. "Do you see the man sweeping the front pew? Don't let him know you're looking."

Cliona shoots her an indignant glare at the last bit but then passes her gaze over the chapel. "Yes, I see him. Why?"

"Is there any chance he's one of your father's rebels?" Daphne asks.

"No," Cliona says without hesitation.

"You're sure? You can't know all of them."

"I promise you I can. I like knowing who I can and can't trust. Why? Who is he?" Cliona asks.

Daphne steers Cliona back toward the chapel entrance, dropping her voice even lower. "He's the man who was pretending to work in the stables, who set me up with a wild horse and a broken saddle. That," she adds, to be perfectly clear, "is the man who tried to kill me."

Cliona waits around the corner from the chapel, using a hand mirror to keep an eye on the door in case the would-be assassin leaves. Daphne hurries back to her rooms as quickly as she can, casting her eyes to the clock hanging on the wall. It's nearly noon, when the servant shifts change and the day workers take their lunch break. She doesn't have much time.

She rifles through her jewelry box, taking a large emerald ring with a hidden needle and a well of poison inside the gem and sliding it onto her right hand before delving into the hidden compartment and slipping a vial of truth serum into her pocket. She hates acting without a plan, but she also knows to take opportunities when they come, and she's not about to wait for another attempt on her life.

She pulls two fur cloaks from the wardrobe, one white and one gray, before leaving the room and running straight into Bairre, who steadies her with his hands on her shoulders.

"Daphne," he says. "I was just coming to tell you that the seamstress has arrived for your final wedding gown fitting. Should I send her up?"

She forces a smile. "Actually, can you make my excuses to her? I told Cliona I would help her with something."

Bairre frowns. "With what?" he asks, looking down at the cloaks draped over her arm. "Are you going somewhere?"

"Just for a walk," she says, her voice breezy.

"A walk is more important than your wedding dress fitting?" he asks, raising a skeptical eyebrow.

Daphne opens her mouth, ready to argue, but the sound of the clock chiming interrupts. Which means the morning shift is over, which means the man who tried to kill her will be leaving the castle for the next hour. Which means there's no time to argue.

"Yes," she says, pushing past him and hurrying down the hall, but Bairre matches her step for step and she realizes he isn't going to be swayed by anything but the truth. So she gives it to him as quickly as she can.

"We have to tell my father," he says when she's done.

Daphne snorts. "He didn't help much the last time, did he?"

"What do you think you can do instead?" Bairre counters.

"Follow him. See where he goes, who he talks to." She doesn't mention the daggers hidden on her person, the poison ring, the vial of truth serum.

"You're going to follow someone who wants to kill you, alone—"

"Not alone," she interrupts. "Cliona is coming as well."

He doesn't look terribly relieved by that.

"I don't suppose I can convince you not to join us," Daphne says.

"No, I don't suppose you can," he says with a heavy sigh.

They round the corner and find Cliona standing exactly where Daphne left her, the hand mirror still held up. When she hears them approach, she turns, taking in Bairre's presence with raised eyebrows.

"An unavoidable complication," Daphne grumbles, pressing the gray cloak into Cliona's hands and putting on the white cloak herself. She takes the mirror from Cliona and looks around the corner while Cliona dons the gray cloak.

"The way you say that almost makes it sound like a compliment," Bairre says, but Daphne waves for him to be quiet. There, in the mirror's reflection, she sees the fair-haired man leaving the chapel. The other workers cluster together, talking about lunch plans and laughing, but the man is on his own. He doesn't seem to know any of the others at all.

"Come on," she says, tucking the mirror into her pocket. "He's on the move."

It is alarmingly easy to slip past the castle guards amid the exodus of servants. Daphne supposes she understands why—no one expects the three of them to be leaving the grounds voluntarily. Under normal circumstances, the lax security might bother her, but just now she's grateful for it.

As she, Bairre, and Cliona follow the assassin at a safe

distance, she realizes how much easier it would be to avoid notice if she were alone, but still there is a part of her that is grateful she isn't.

"Cliona, you have a weapon," she says—a statement, not a question.

Cliona shoots her a grin and rolls up the long sleeve of her gown, displaying a slim dagger strapped to her inner left forearm.

It takes Daphne an extra few seconds to unsheathe hers from their hiding places in her boot and at her thigh, and she makes a mental note to ask Cliona where she bought that arm strap. When she passes one of the daggers to Bairre, he frowns.

"You just . . . carry daggers with you?" he asks.

He doesn't ask Cliona about hers, Daphne notes.

"Someone *is* trying to kill me," she tells him, though that's only half of the truth.

Most of the servants cling to the walkway that leads into the village, but the assassin meanders off alone toward the woods on the outskirts of the castle grounds. Daphne holds up a hand, indicating for Cliona and Bairre to wait.

"Let him get ahead enough that he won't see us," she says. The grounds are covered in a fresh sheet of snow, so they'll be able to follow his footsteps.

"I still don't like this," Bairre mutters.

"Then leave," Daphne says.

He grumbles something unintelligible under his breath, but he makes no move to walk away, and Daphne finds she's glad. She takes his hand, and though they are both wearing gloves, she suddenly feels a little warmer.

"Trust me," she says, and as soon as the words are out of her mouth, she hates herself for them. Because he shouldn't trust her, and neither should Cliona. Sooner or later, she will have to betray them, but today at least they are on the same side.

"I think he's gone far enough," Cliona says, and Daphne pulls her hand from Bairre's.

It's easy to find the assassin's boot tracks in the freshly fallen snow, and the three of them fall into their roles without discussion—Daphne following the tracks while Cliona listens for any sounds that don't belong; Bairre keeps his dagger drawn and his eyes roaming around them, looking for the slightest hint of a threat. Bairre is used to hunting, Daphne reminds herself; of course he knows how to track. And she's given up being surprised by Cliona's abilities. They continue like this for half an hour, until Daphne stops short.

"What's wrong?" Cliona asks.

Daphne doesn't answer at first. She drops to a crouch beside the boot prints and touches the edge of one with her gloved finger.

"These are different boots," she says, frowning. "They're a size bigger than the ones we've been following, and the heel shape is entirely different."

"Wait, here are some more," Cliona says, looking down. "But they're too small."

"There's more here, too," Bairre says.

Panic settles over Daphne an instant before the first arrow sails through the air, clipping Cliona's shoulder. To the other girl's credit, she is already turning toward the archer, dagger in hand, and barely flinches at the impact before throwing the dagger. A second later, a man screams.

"Careful, there are more," Daphne calls to her as Cliona slips into the woods to retrieve her dagger.

As though they were awaiting a sign, men begin to spill out of the shadows of the trees around them—Daphne counts six as she inches toward Bairre until they stand back to back, blades at the ready. The assassin she recognized from the castle is there, and when her eyes fall on him, he smiles.

"And here I thought it would be more difficult to lure you into a trap, Princess," he calls to her. "I do wish you hadn't brought friends, but alas—I was paid to kill only you. Though I suppose I can add a couple more bodies to the bill. My employer has deep pockets."

The man's eyes move to Bairre, then narrow. "Where did the other girl go?" he asks, looking around at his men—and they are his men, Daphne realizes. They look at him, waiting for instructions. One of them shrugs and glances away. "Murtag hit her, I thought."

The man frowns. "Find—" but he doesn't get the chance to finish his order. He crumples to the ground, revealing Cliona behind him, her dagger gripped tightly in her hand, now dripping blood. Her eyes meet Daphne's, and she nods once before all chaos breaks loose.

Daphne isn't sure what to expect of Bairre, has never seen him lift a weapon apart from the bow, but as soon as the first assassin comes toward him, Bairre reacts with a quick jab between the ribs before taking advantage of the man's surprise to grab his blade and turn it back on the man, slicing across his throat.

Daphne wishes she could watch him longer—there is something almost artistic about how simply he dispatched the man—but another assassin is walking toward her, raising a pistol in shaking hands—she knows right away he hasn't shot anyone before, so she uses the second of hesitation to knock the pistol from his grip with a jab of her elbow and bury her dagger in his stomach, to the hilt.

When she straightens up, she sees Bairre looking at her with the same shock and admiration she felt toward him just seconds ago. *If we make it through this,* she thinks, *we'll have a lot to talk about.*

Three men remain, and two of them converge on Cliona, while the third starts toward Bairre.

"Go," Bairre tells Daphne, raising his dagger again and nodding toward Cliona. Daphne doesn't hesitate, stopping only to grab the pistol from the snowy ground. It's already cocked, so she aims and fires, the bullet catching one of the assassins in the chest while Cliona slits the other one's throat. She turns just in time to see the last assassin fall to the ground, Bairre standing over him with the bloody dagger, breathing hard.

All three of them are standing, she notes, doing a quick inventory. Cliona's shoulder is bleeding from the arrow wound, Bairre has a gash on his leg that will likely need stitches, and she distantly notes that someone stabbed her in the stomach at one point, though she barely feels it and the wound doesn't seem terribly deep.

Daphne opens her mouth to speak, but out of the corner of her eye, she sees the fair-haired assassin pushing himself up on his elbow, raising his pistol with the other hand, the barrel leveled right at her. Before she can react, he fires and her world goes quiet and fuzzy. Distantly, she looks down and sees blood blooming across the bodice of her dress.

Too much blood, she thinks, before her thoughts go dark.

Beatriz

The morning drags by with Beatriz and Pasquale locked in their rooms. Meals are delivered every few hours; maids tidy up the rooms and empty the chamber pots; a servant boy comes to tend a fire in the fireplace. They are still treated with respect and dignity, still given every luxury available. There is no sign at all that they are under arrest except, of course, the fact that they aren't allowed to leave.

Just as they are preparing for lunch, there is a rap at the main door. They exchange looks across the room, him lounging on the freshly made bed with a book in hand, her at the desk, composing a letter to Sophronia she doubts will ever make its way out of the castle.

Before either of them can answer, the door swings open and Gisella slips in, crossing through the sitting room and through the open door to their bedroom, wearing a gown finer than any Beatriz has seen her in before—a day dress of pale blue silk, with a bodice embroidered with hundreds of seed pearls and dramatically voluminous sleeves that end above her elbows. Her pale blond hair is curled and coiled away from her face in an elaborate updo topped by a tiara of gold and sapphires that looks strangely familiar to Beatriz.

"Is that . . . are you wearing one of my tiaras, Gigi?" she asks, trying to keep her voice calm as she regards her former friend with a cold gaze.

Gisella ignores the acid in her voice, instead flashing Beatriz a blinding smile. "Technically, it was never *your* tiara. It belongs to Cellaria and the royal family, of which the two of you are no longer a part."

"Good riddance to that," Pasquale says under his breath.

"Careful, Pas," Gisella says. "Your father may be dead, but you won't be doing yourself any favors by speaking ill of him."

"I doubt you're here to dole out wisdom, Gisella," Beatriz says. "Did you come to beg forgiveness like your brother did? I can't imagine you intend to propose marriage to me as well?"

Gisella's eyebrows arch. "Did he really?" she asks, sounding more tired than surprised. "I'm not sure who was the bigger fool—him for offering or you for refusing."

"In my view, the biggest fool is you," Beatriz says, leaning back in her chair, her eyes darting up to the tiara again. "Do you think you're a princess now? That after all your scheming and betrayals, you are somehow safe? Above reproach? Untouchable? You aren't, you know. All you are is alone."

The words are daggers, and Beatriz can't help but feel like her mother's daughter for wielding them so expertly, for finding Gisella's insecurities and hitting them, for reveling in the look of naked fear that flickers over the girl's face.

"I'm not alone," Gisella says, lifting her chin. "I have Nico, and we have power. There is no one to control our destinies anymore, no one who will force me to marry an ancient stranger or push him to grovel before an ungrateful king."

Remembering how Nicolo looked last night, how quick he was to blame his sister, Beatriz wonders if Gisella really has him at all.

"At what cost?" Pasquale asks quietly.

Gisella shakes her head. "Do you think I celebrate bringing you low?" she asks. "I don't. But I won't apologize for seizing the only opportunity I was likely to get to climb."

Beatriz wants to launch out of her chair and slap Gisella across the face, she wants it more than she's ever wanted anything. But such an action would make her feel better only for a moment. In the long run, it would make their situation worse. So she grips the arms of her chair and fixes Gisella with a cool look.

"You were kind enough to offer us advice, so allow me to return the favor," she says, each word sharp enough to cut through stone. "You think you are safe because you have power? You'll never be safe, Gigi, no matter how many tiaras you wear, how close you are to the throne. Power is an illusion, and the more of it people think you have, the more determined they will be to tear you down. You should know that better than anyone, having been on the other side. How long do you think it will be before another *you* arrives with schemes and plots? You've climbed far, but that only means the fall will kill you."

"You're wrong," Gisella says. "Nico is king now. Who would go against him?"

Beatriz laughs, but the sound is cruel. "Who wouldn't?" she asks. "And you seem to forget that *you* are not king. You are not even a princess. You are the king's sister and *you* have no power at all. Nico already resents you for your scheming—"

"I made him king!"

"—how long will it be before he turns on you as well? Before you are entirely alone?"

Gisella fixes Beatriz with a glare strong enough to bend steel, but Beatriz holds her gaze, matching her hate for hate.

"I wish you all the happiness you deserve, Gigi," Beatriz says with a cold smile. "I think you can show yourself out."

Gisella holds her ground, eyes locked on Beatriz and jaw clenched. "I didn't come to fight with you. I came to let you know that the two of you will be leaving the palace in an hour, heading to the Fraternia and Sororia of the Alder Mountains."

"I'd rather die than become a Sister," Beatriz tells her.

Gisella lifts a shoulder in a shrug. "I'm sure that could be arranged," she says. "But I believe the words you're looking for are *thank you*."

Beatriz laughs. "Oh, I *know* I would rather die than say that."

"Thank you, Gisella," Pasquale says a beat later, his expression unreadable. "And pass our thanks along to the king, would you?"

Gisella looks at Pasquale, confusion etched into her expression, but nods. "Of course."

She turns to go, but Beatriz gets to her feet.

"Wait, there is one more thing—I have a letter I'd like sent to my mother."

Gisella turns and raises a single eyebrow. "You think I'll help you plunge us into another war?" she asks.

Beatriz fetches the coded letter she wrote her mother and presses it into Gigi's hand. "Go on, read it yourself."

Gisella frowns, scanning the short letter and letting out a laugh. "You expect me to believe this? That you are asking your mother *not* to help you?"

"I don't need my mother's help," Beatriz says, lifting her chin. "And I wouldn't accept it if she offered. I'm trying to do you a favor—you think Nico's reign can survive war? *Two* wars if he can't settle things with Temarin? His own people would eat him alive under the slightest threat of that."

Gigi's mouth purses. "And why should I believe you?" she asks.

"You shouldn't," Beatriz says. "But it's the truth. I don't want her help."

Gisella doesn't look like she believes Beatriz's bluff, but she pockets the letter anyway and sweeps out of the room without a backward glance.

When she's gone, Beatriz turns to Pasquale. "I can't believe you *thanked* her. What was that about?" she asks him, derision dripping from her voice.

Pasquale shrugs. "The same thing I'd wager was behind your letter," he says. "Let them believe we're defeated, Beatriz. Let them think we aren't a threat. They haven't seen the last of us, and soon enough, they'll wish they'd killed us when they had a chance."

The sun is high in the sky when Beatriz and Pasquale are finally escorted from their room, through surprisingly quiet palace hallways, and out into the open air. Nicolo was likely hoping to avoid a scene, but Beatriz can see the shadows of people watching from the palace windows, faces pressed up against the glass, hungry for the slightest glimpse of their discomfort or the smallest tidbit of salacious gossip.

She refuses to give it to them. She keeps her head lifted high and her arm linked tightly with Pasquale's.

"Chin up," she tells him under her breath. "We have an audience. Smile, like this is exactly what we want. Let them wonder what we know that they don't."

Pasquale follows her direction immediately, going a step further by laughing loudly, like she said something funny.

The guards beside them exchange puzzled looks, but Beatriz only smiles at them and winks at one in particular, whose face flushes crimson. Ahead is a carriage—not the ornate and gilded beast of a thing Beatriz arrived in, but a small one, all black and several years old, pulled by a pair of mismatched horses that look past their prime.

One of the guards opens the carriage door and the other offers a hand to Beatriz to help her inside, but she ignores it, lifting her skirt so that she can step up into the carriage on her own, followed seconds later by Pasquale.

The guard shuts the door with a slam that echoes in the small, dark space, before both guards climb onto the seat at the front of the carriage. Then, with no warning at all, there's a violent lurch and they are off.

Beatriz slumps back against the worn upholstered seat, closing her eyes for a moment. When she opens them, she sees Pasquale sitting across from her, leaning as close as he can to the window, watching the palace growing smaller and smaller.

"I'm sorry," she says after a moment.

He doesn't look at her, but his brow furrows. "What do you have to be sorry about?" he asks.

"It was my idea to free Lord Savelle, and I can't regret that, but I regret trusting Nico and Gigi."

"I trusted Ambrose," he points out.

"Yes, but he didn't betray us," she says.

"But he *could* have," he says, finally looking at her. "Trusting them was a chance, but it was one we took together. I can't regret that without regretting him."

His voice breaks on the last word, and she reaches toward him, taking one of his hands in both of hers. "He got out safely," she says, her voice low. "For all we know, he's in Temarin now. If he can get to Sophie, she'll protect him, at least until his parents can reach him."

Pasquale nods, but the worry doesn't leave his eyes. He looks out the window again.

"It's a strange idea, isn't it?" he muses. "To be in trouble and seek help from your parents? Neither of us did that."

"I sent a letter to my mother," she reminds him. "And you couldn't very well run to your father—he was on his deathbed."

He shakes his head. "I mean before that. From the very

beginning, from before the beginning. I could have told my father I didn't want to marry you and why. After you found out how I felt, you could have written to your mother about annulling the marriage."

Beatriz lets out a long breath. "I don't think either of us would have found much help," she says.

He laughs, but there is no mirth in it. "Exactly. But if Ambrose had been in that position, he'd have told them, and they would have done whatever they could to help him, to protect him, no matter the cost. I keep thinking about that, how ridiculous it sounds, but it's the truth. They would do anything to secure his happiness."

Beatriz doesn't say anything for a moment—*can't* say anything. Her throat feels so tight she can scarcely breathe.

"You had your mother, though," she points out finally. "At least for a while, you had your mother."

He shakes his head, his mouth twisting. "I love my mother, Triz, and I know she loved me, but of the two of us, I was her protector, not the other way around. And in the end, she didn't protect me—she couldn't. She wanted to, but that desire didn't outweigh her fear of my father. I know it isn't fair, but sometimes I'm angry at her."

Beatriz bites her lip. "Sometimes I'm angry at my father," she admits. "And all he did was die."

Pasquale nods slowly. "I guess what I'm saying is that I'm jealous of Ambrose, that he has someone in his life to love him so unconditionally, people who would lay down their lives for him. I never had that. I know you have your sisters—"

"It isn't the same," she says, shaking her head and

remembering her last conversation with Daphne. "I protected them, but they never did the same for me. They couldn't. Maybe I'm angry at them for that, too," she admits softly, hating herself for saying the words, hating that they taste like truth.

But as terrible as she feels saying them, there is no judgment in Pasquale's eyes.

"No matter what happens, Triz, I'll do whatever I can to protect you."

Beatriz holds his gaze and smiles, a small, tight-lipped smile. "And I'll protect you," she tells him. "No matter what."

Daphne

Daphne must be dead—she certainly *feels* dead. Though as soon as the thought enters her mind, she sees the flaw in the logic. If she feels anything, she can't be dead, can she? And certainly she wouldn't feel like someone has dug into her chest with a sharpened spoon.

She knows before she opens her eyes that she isn't in the castle. It is too warm here—almost sweltering—and she smells hay, hearth, and some spice she can't name. When she does crack open her eyes a slit, she sees a darkening dusk sky outside a small window.

"Daphne?" a voice says. Bairre.

She rolls toward him, wincing as she does, and opens her eyes a little more. They're in a small room, less than a quarter of the size of her room in the castle, and she's lying on a narrow bed mere feet from a roaring fireplace. The roof above them is thatched hay and the walls are a rough-hewn stone. Bairre is sitting beside the bed in a carved wooden chair with a wool blanket draped over him.

"We need to stop meeting like this," she tells him,

remembering how he stayed by her bed while she recovered from the poison. "Where are we?"

Bairre glances away. "With a friend," he says carefully before pausing. "After you were . . ."

"Shot?" she supplies.

He nods. "You were going to die," he says. "You *were* dying. I wasn't sure even Fergal would have been able to save you. But I knew someone who could, and she was nearer than the castle."

"Who?" Daphne asks, frowning.

At that moment, a woman pushes open the door and steps inside holding a tray. She looks about the empress's age, or at least the way Daphne thinks her mother would look first thing in the morning, before her hair was dressed and her face slathered with all the creams and pigments she uses. There is no varnish or polish on this woman—even her hair has gone gray, though in the bright sunlight it seems to glint silver.

She also looks familiar.

"Your mother," she says to Bairre, who nods.

"You can call me Aurelia," the woman says, setting the tray down on the foot of Daphne's bed and pouring steaming-hot tea into a chipped cup. She offers it to Daphne, who takes a small sip—bitter, but tolerably so—as she looks the woman over. Cliona said Aurelia was the greatest empyrea she'd ever heard of, but the woman reminds Daphne of her childhood nurse more than anything else. "I'm sure you feel like death itself," Aurelia continues.

"But I'm not," Daphne says. "Dead, that is. I'm assuming I have you to thank for that. Is Cliona all right? Her shoulder—"

"She's fine," Bairre says. "She went back to the castle to tell my father what happened, that we're safe."

Daphne nods slowly, taking another sip of tea. She thinks back to the events in the forest, how Bairre hadn't questioned Cliona's skill with a dagger, or her own. How he'd handled himself better than she expected him to. She thinks back further, to Cliona's implicit trust of him, despite the fact that her father was trying to overthrow his. To Bairre's resentment of his new position.

"How long have you been working with the rebels?" she asks him.

For his part, Bairre isn't surprised by the question. He holds her gaze, his silver eyes on hers. "It must be five years now?" he says, glancing at his mother for confirmation.

"Thereabouts," she confirms. "You were twelve."

Bairre nods, frowning. "I was in the woods one afternoon and a strange woman approached," he says. "She claimed to be my mother."

Aurelia shakes her head. "He didn't believe me at first, but as you noticed, the resemblance is uncanny," she says.

"But why?" Daphne asks Aurelia. "From what I heard, you put Bartholomew on that throne, you wanted to unite Friv. Why would you go through all that trouble and then assist the rebellion?"

Aurelia and Bairre exchange a look, but Bairre is the one to answer.

"She reads the stars," he tells her.

"And?" Daphne asks. "All empyreas read the stars."

"Not like me," Aurelia says. "I never had to learn it or train my gift. The stars have been speaking to me my whole life, telling me tales of the world to come. For so long it was war and bloodshed and death, so much death. I was young and tired of it all and foolish enough to believe I could stop it."

"But you did," Daphne points out. "There has been no war in Friv in nearly two decades."

"No," Aurelia agrees. "But I've learned that the absence of war does not equal peace. The stars still tell me a tale of war, Princess, but now I'm wise enough to know that war never dies, it only sleeps."

There is more Aurelia doesn't say, Daphne is sure of it, but Bairre seems to have accepted her reasoning easily enough, so Daphne holds her tongue. For now.

She thinks of her mother's plans for Friv, the way she's forcing them into a war with Cellaria that no one wants, the many people who will have to die for a country and a conflict that aren't theirs. She can't be angry with Bairre for keeping secrets, not when her own are far worse. If he learns the truth about her, he will never forgive her for it. Suddenly, she understands why her sisters went against their mother—she can't agree with their decision, but she does understand it.

"War is waking up now," Aurelia continues. "I've known it for some time. So when Lord Panlington came to me and asked for my assistance, I gave it to him, and we've been working together ever since."

"But why did you join?" Daphne asks Bairre. "To go against your father and Cillian?"

Bairre flinches and looks away. "I believed I could win Cillian over," he admits. "I still think I could have, if I'd had more time. As for my father . . . I love him. But you can love someone and still disagree with them."

Daphne considers this for a moment, leaning back against the pillows. "You must have been horrified," she says slowly. "When your father named you his heir."

Aurelia looks from Daphne to Bairre, her brow creasing. "I'm sure you're hungry," she tells Daphne. "I'll warm some soup for you."

When she slips back out of the room and closes the door behind her, Bairre lets out a deep breath.

"I wanted to wait," he says. "Once I inherited the throne, I could refuse it. It would have been an easy ending, but Lord Panlington, my mother—everyone, really—disagreed. So nothing changed when I was named heir—it was a crown I knew I would never wear, no matter what happened. The only thing that changed, really, was you." He pauses for a moment, and part of Daphne wants that pause to go on forever, because she knows where this is going, and even though it's exactly what her mother wants—what *she* wants—she also knows that if they continue down this road, it will hurt them both.

"After the poison, when you were delirious and feverish, you said some things," he says slowly.

Daphne nods, pressing her lips together into a thin line. "My memory is a bit fuzzy," she says. "But I remember you saying some things as well."

"Daphne," he says gently, but it is a warning all the same.

She ignores it and reaches for his hand, taking it and squeezing it tight, the way she did before they went into the woods, as if to say *I'm here, I'm not going anywhere.*

Another lie, she thinks, but one she wishes were the truth. He squeezes her hand in return, lifting it to his lips to brush a kiss over her knuckles.

Daphne understands, suddenly, exactly what she is—not a girl, not a princess, not a spy or a saboteur. She is a poison, brewed and distilled and fermented over sixteen years, crafted by her mother to bring ruination to whomever she touches. Poison is a woman's weapon, after all, and here she is, a weapon of a woman.

And Bairre sees it, maybe he has always seen it, from the second he handed her out of that carriage on the Frivian border. *Lightning,* he called her before, and that was before he saw her stab one man and shoot a second, but maybe there is a part of him that has always known what she is capable of.

She starts to pull her hand from his, but he surprises her, reaching up to cup her face. And then he is kissing her, and she is kissing him back.

It isn't her first kiss. When she and her sisters were fifteen, their mother dared them to see who could kiss the most boys at court over the course of a month. Beatriz won, of course, kissing five, and Sophronia was too nervous to kiss even one, but Daphne managed a perfectly respectable three. *Practice,* their mother had called it, to prepare them for this inevitable moment.

The thought seems ridiculous now, because nothing could have prepared her for this. It is nothing like those practice kisses, which were awkward and bumbling and pleasant enough, Daphne supposes. But kissing Bairre doesn't feel awkward or bumbling, and *pleasant enough* doesn't come close to describing it. It is a kiss that threatens to consume her, a kiss that feels as necessary to her as oxygen, but as hungry and desperate as it grows, the gentle touch of Bairre's hand on her cheek, his arm around her waist, make her feel safe and treasured and maybe even loved.

It is a new feeling, she realizes, but it is one she would drown in if she could.

They break apart when his mother returns, a bowl of soup in her hand, and her brow furrowed. When she passes the bowl to Daphne, she hesitates.

"I don't understand why you aren't dead," she says slowly.

Daphne frowns. "I thought we'd established that was thanks to you."

Aurelia shakes her head. "I told you the stars speak to me. Lately they've been all but screaming. *The blood of stars and majesty spilled.*"

"The stars said that?" Daphne asks.

Aurelia shrugs. "It's difficult to explain, but that is what I hear, at least. The words have been echoing in my mind for weeks now. Ever since you came to Friv. At first, I worried they meant Bairre; then when he showed up carrying you with what was very nearly a fatal wound . . ."

"*The blood of stars and majesty,*" Daphne repeats. "You used star magic to conceive Bairre."

"Just as your mother used star magic to conceive you," Aurelia says. "It's why you have the same eyes—star-touched. The blood of stars and majesty, meaning someone both star-touched and royal."

"My sisters," Daphne says, every muscle in her body going taut. "One of them is in Cellaria, with eyes like mine.

Last we spoke, she was in trouble—she seemed sure she could get herself out of it, but . . . I need to speak with them. I did it before, with Beatriz, using stardust. Do you have any?"

Daphne sits cross-legged on the bed with a vial of stardust in each hand and Bairre perched beside her. She uncorks the vials and smears the stardust on the backs of both of her hands.

"I wish I could speak to Princess Beatriz and Queen Sophronia," she says, closing her eyes.

For a moment, nothing happens; then the world around her softens and mutes and she hears the distant roar of a cheering crowd.

"Sophie?" Daphne asks tentatively. "Triz?"

"Daphne, is that you? Thank the stars," Beatriz says. "So much has happened—"

"What's happening?" Sophronia asks, her voice more tired than surprised. "Why can I hear you?"

"It's stardust—too much to explain, we only have a few moments," Daphne says. "Are you both all right?"

"Not at all," Beatriz says. "Is that a crowd cheering, Sophie?"

For a long moment, Sophronia doesn't speak. "It is," she says finally, her voice strained. "I believe they're cheering for my execution."

Sophronia

Sophronia squints when the guards lead her out into the sunlight, a burst of pain exploding in her head at the sudden brightness. Beyond that, she is numb. The furious shouts of the crowd of strangers watching her, the splintered wooden planks beneath her bare feet, the all-consuming fear she knows should be present in her chest—she doesn't feel any of it.

The execution had been postponed by a day while Kavelle and the surrounding areas were searched for Leopold, but when there was no sign of him, Ansel informed her it would be going forward this evening. Sophronia was almost relieved to hear it—the waiting had felt like its own kind of torture.

"Sophie, what are you talking about?" Daphne asks, her voice low in Sophronia's mind, but loud enough—mercifully—to drown out the screams of the crowd, screams crying out for her head.

"It's quite a long story," Sophronia says softly, her eyes focused ahead on the wooden platform at the center of the city square, at the glinting silver of the guillotine blade. "I only have a moment."

"Sophie, no," Beatriz says, her voice cracking. "That can't be right. Mama will save you."

At that, Sophronia laughs, the sound hysterical. "She will not," she says. "But I'm glad you're both here, even if I don't understand how. I love you both so much. And I'm so sorry I failed you."

"What are you talking about?" Daphne asks. "What's happening?"

But there is no time to explain it—not when Ansel is there, taking hold of her arm and guiding her toward the block of wood, still wet with dark red blood. How many have been executed today, she wonders. Have they saved her for last?

"There's no time," Sophronia says, focusing on her sisters' voices, on the presence she feels in her mind. She allows herself to be guided to her knees, allows her neck to be placed in the groove of the wood. She closes her eyes. "I have friends coming to find you—Leopold and Violie. Please help them. There is so much more at play than we realized. I still don't understand all of it, but please be careful. I love you both so much. I love you all the way to the stars. And I—"

Margaraux

Empress Margaraux understands the value of secrets better than most, and she knows that her own secrets are invaluable. She doesn't entrust them to her closest advisors, or her daughters, or even to Nigellus—stars know he doesn't tell her his secrets, either. No, there is only one person in the world Margaraux tells her secrets to.

And so she steps down from her gilded carriage, dressed in an elaborate black silk mourning gown, so heavy with onyx beads that it resembles armor. Her face is covered by a black net veil, though it is not opaque enough to hide her dry eyes or the hard set of her mouth.

It has been six days since the guillotine blade fell and Temarin dissolved into chaos, four days since her armies invaded in retribution for Sophronia's murder, two days since the rebels realized they'd been betrayed, that they were outmanned and outarmed, one day since she accepted their surrender and Temarin became hers. She conquered a country without ever setting foot in it.

The empress looks up at the towering stone fortress of Saint Elstrid's Sororia, a formidable and cold place so different from the palace, though it is only a twenty-minute ride from the palace gates. Cold and formidable as this Sororia might be, from what she's heard, the one Beatriz is in now makes it look like a palace.

She grits her teeth at the thought of her firstborn daughter, who should be dead right along with Sophronia. *Soon,* she tells herself.

The unvarnished wood door swings open and the mother superior steps out into the sun. Mother Ippoline has always struck the empress as the living embodiment of the Sororia, every bit as cold, hard, and unyielding. Though, for the first time in their almost two decades of acquaintance, there is a trace of pity in the woman's eyes. The empress doesn't care for it.

"Your Majesty," Mother Ippoline says, dropping into a brief curtsy. "What brings you to the Sororia today?"

"I find myself in need of solace, Mother Ippoline," Margaraux says. She has run the words through her mind so often on the way here that they come out unstrained. It isn't as though they are a lie, either. But she lets Mother Ippoline fill the gaps in herself, lets her make assumptions.

"Of course," Mother Ippoline says, bowing her head. "We were all devastated to hear of Queen Sophronia's death. Please, take whatever solace you can inside these walls."

"Very kind of you, Mother," Margaraux says. "I assume Sister Heloise is here?"

"Where else would she be?" the woman replies, eyebrows lifting. "She is in the usual place."

"Of course she is," Margaraux says, glancing back at her coachman, footman, and the rest of the entourage that accompanied her for this short excursion. "I'll be back in an hour's time," she says. Without waiting for an answer, she follows Mother Ippoline into the Sororia, through the dark, cold, windowless halls lit only by a few scattered sconces with dying candles.

"I don't think Sister Heloise enjoys your visits, Your Majesty," Mother Ippoline says.

It's a bold thing to say, but Margaraux appreciates the honesty.

"I don't enjoy my visits to her, either," she tells her. "But Sister Heloise and I understand each other. And I can't imagine she receives any other visitors."

Mother Ippoline doesn't deny it. She stops before a nondescript wooden door and pushes it open, letting Margaraux through. Margaraux doesn't have to ask for privacy, not anymore. Mother Ippoline closes the door behind her and Margaraux hears the steady fall of her footsteps retreating down the hallway.

It's only then that she takes in the room—the chapel, as dark and dank as the rest of the Sororia, but with the benefit of a single stained-glass window above the altar, a dark blue sky with pinpricks of gilded glass for stars. It doesn't let much light in, but Margaraux supposes that is the point—a room where it is always night, where the ersatz stars always shine.

A woman kneels before the altar, her plain homespun dress spread out around her and her hair bound underneath a wimple and hood. Her hair was pure gold once, the envy of every woman at court, though Margaraux supposes it must be going gray now, not unlike her own.

"Sister Heloise," she says.

The woman's spine stiffens at the sound of the name, but she doesn't turn around. Margaraux tries again, using a name the woman hasn't been called in nearly two decades, since she made her vows and joined the Sororia.

"Seline," Margaraux says, her voice sharper at the edges.

With a heavy sigh, the woman hauls herself to her feet and turns to face her. It takes longer than it should, Margaraux thinks, before realizing how much time has passed. The woman is no longer the regal and imposing figure who intimidated a young Margaraux to the point of tears on more than one occasion. Or, rather, she is still that woman, only now she has become old, her skin wrinkled and sallow from so much time spent in this room, her spine stooped from hours kneeling before the altar.

Margaraux realizes that she has aged as well. Time, it seems, stops for no one, not even empresses.

"You always were an impudent creature," the woman says, the words dripping venom.

"Yes," Margaraux says placidly, taking a seat in the front pew and pushing her veil back. "It is why I took your throne and you were sent here."

Age has not taken the woman's ability to lift a single dark eyebrow, to level a look so withering a lesser woman would be turned to ash at her feet. But Margaraux is not a lesser woman. Not anymore.

"And here I thought that was because you wrapped an empyrea around your finger and brought the heavens down to serve your purpose," she says.

Margaraux shrugs. "Yes, but I was *impudent* enough to do it, and you didn't have the strength to stop me."

"Strength I had, Margaraux," the woman says quietly. "But I didn't have the soul for it—or rather, perhaps I had too much of a soul."

"A lot of good your soul has done you," Margaraux tells her. "And it's *Empress* to you."

A ghost of a smile flickers across the woman's mouth. "Yes, I know," she says. "The title was mine before it was yours, after all. Before you pulled your strings and rewrote our fates, before I was sent to this place while you took my life, my husband, my country."

"None of it was truly yours if you couldn't hold on to it," Margaraux tells her.

"Perhaps you're right," the woman says, not sounding terribly bothered by it. "I understand Sophronia is dead."

She says it so flatly, so matter-of-factly. There is no apology in her voice, no simpering, no pity in her eyes. It takes Margaraux a second to remember she is grateful for it, that it's why she's here.

"And Temarin is mine," she adds softly. "Just as Cellaria and Friv will be soon."

"*Three daughters in the ground, three lands in your grasp,*" Seline says. "That is what you were promised so long ago, no?"

Margaraux doesn't deny it. It was the first confession she made to her onetime rival, a little more than sixteen years ago, when her belly was so swollen she couldn't stand for more than a minute at a time and had to be carried everywhere like a beached whale. She had truly hated being pregnant, but that had been the cost of power, so she'd paid it.

Three daughters in the ground, three lands in your grasp. That was what Nigellus promised her, and he has delivered on one count now. She does not doubt that the other two will be swift to follow—Beatriz has narrowly avoided a death sentence already, and then there is Daphne. After Prince Cillian's early death, Margaraux grew impatient and worried that his bastard brother might meet the same fate. She'd hoped she could manage to kill Daphne before she married Bairre. It would have been simpler, without tying her dynasty to Bartholomew's failing reign or Bairre's tainted bloodline, and Daphne's murder alone would have given her more than enough cause to send her troops into Friv—her troops and now Temarin's as well. They would have made quick work of Friv's ragtag rebellion.

Perhaps it was foolish to hire those assassins—perhaps she'd done too well in training her daughter to avoid them—but no one else in Friv seemed to aim for Daphne's death. Stars above, the rebels Margaraux had initially been counting on to kill her even came to *like* her. Margaraux feared if she waited too long, the rebels might rally around her.

"You raised those girls like lambs for the slaughter," Seline says, bringing her back to the present.

It is an accusation, fitted with knife points, but the blow doesn't land. It slides off Margaraux's back like water from a duck's wing.

"Yes," she says simply. "That is what lambs are for. I suppose you're going to tell me you will pray for their souls?"

If Seline hears the mockery in Margaraux's voice, she doesn't show it.

"I would if they were human," she replies evenly. "Star

magic can do many magical things, I will admit, but it cannot create a soul."

That surprises Margaraux, and she leans back, surveying the other woman thoughtfully. "You think they are not human?"

Seline falters for an instant before regaining her footing. "You forget that I was married to the emperor for more than two decades and I never fell pregnant."

"Perhaps you are barren, then," Margaraux replies.

"Perhaps," Seline allows. "And all the many mistresses who came before you? Were they barren as well? Because he never sired a single bastard. I always thought he was the barren one."

Margaraux purses her lips and doesn't answer. "You're speaking treason," she says after a moment.

"Our little talks have always been full of treason, haven't they? Treason and filicide and all of your dastardly schemes."

"Filicide implies that I killed them. I didn't kill Sophronia—Temarin did."

"You signed her death warrant before she'd even been born, before she'd even been conceived or created or however it is that she was made."

Margaraux doesn't speak for a moment. Instead, she settles her hands on her lap and fixes the former empress with a thoughtful look.

"Conceived," she says finally. "You aren't wrong—the emperor couldn't have children, not without help, without a good deal of star magic, more than even he had access to. That was where Nigellus came in. I assure you, Seline, they are human, mine and the emperor's, though, yes, perhaps there is a third part to them as well that is something else. I don't suppose it will matter in a few months' time."

A series of emotions flicker over Seline's face, and Margaraux reads them one by one. Surprise. Horror. Disgust.

"You are a monster," Seline says, sounding almost awed.

Margaraux doesn't flinch from the word. "All powerful people are monsters," she says quietly. "If that is the price I pay, so be it."

"You don't pay a price," Seline says with a harsh laugh. "*They* do. The daughters of your own flesh and blood, and they don't even know it. They must think you love them—"

"I do," Margaraux interrupts, her voice sharp.

Seline searches her face and barks out another laugh. "They are a means to your end and you are sacrificing them, their futures, their lives, to secure your own. That isn't love."

"I wouldn't expect you to know anything about children, Seline," Margaraux replies, her voice cold.

The former empress goes quiet, casting a gaze over her shoulder at the pane of stained-glass sky.

"Why are you here?" she asks. "Why do you insist on dragging me into this, telling me your horrible secrets when you know . . ." She trails off, shaking her head. "*Because* you know."

"That no one will believe you," Margaraux says. "The jealous spurned wife of the dead emperor, banished to a Sororia to make room for a younger, prettier, more fertile bride? Of course you're bitter and angry, of course you want nothing more than to see me laid low. No one will believe a word you say against me."

"I'm not," Seline says after a second. "Bitter. Or angry.

You were willing to sacrifice more for the throne, so you took it. I find I don't miss being empress. I don't wish to see you laid low, Margaraux. I merely pity you."

"Pity?" Margaraux asks, her lips twisting around the word with distaste. "*You* pity *me*?"

"I do. Because one day, when you have killed the only three people who have ever loved you, you will realize what you've done and you will regret it until the day you die, alone, unloved, and unwelcome among the stars. You took enough control to write the tale of your life. I commend you for that, I do, but the tale you've crafted for yourself is a tragedy."

Margaraux says nothing for a long moment.

"I tire of our conversations," she says finally, getting to her feet once more.

"And yet you will come back," Seline says. "You always do. The next time I see you, I'm sure there will be another daughter in the ground."

She means the words to wound, but Margaraux doesn't flinch. "Daphne and Beatriz will do their duty. Just as Sophronia did. I raised my daughters well, after all."

She turns and starts down the aisle, toward the door, but she doesn't get there before Seline speaks again, determined to have the last word.

"You didn't raise them, Margaraux. You built them. And now you will bury them."

Acknowledgments

They say writing books never gets any easier, and neither does writing acknowledgments. Trying to thank everyone who had a hand in making this book the best that it could be feels, as ever, an impossible task, but I'll try my hardest.

Thank you to my absolutely stellar editor, Krista Marino, for encouraging me to step out of my comfort zone with this book and for giving me a map when I lost my way. Difficult as this book was to shape, I know I came out of it a better writer, thanks to you.

Thank you to my marvelous agent, John Cusick, for all the support and encouragement and for always being calm and rational in the face of my many anxious emails.

Thank you to the whole team at Delacorte Press—Lydia Gregovic and Beverly Horowitz in particular—for believing in this book as much as I do.

Thank you to Random House Children's Books—the phenomenal Barbara Marcus; my incredible publicist, Jillian Vandall Miao (I'm sorry for naming the villain Margaraux—I swear it's a coincidence!); Lili Feinberg; Jenn Inzetta; Emma Benshoff; Kelly McGauley; and Caitlin Whalen.

Thank you to my dad and my stepmom for always being

a phone call away, and thank you to my brother, Jerry, and sister-in-law, Jill, for having my back. And thank you to my New York City family, Deborah Brown, Jefrey Pollock, and Jesse and Eden.

Thank you to the friends who talked me through the tough times of working on this book, and who celebrated every high and breakthrough: Sasha Alsberg, Lexi Wangler, Cara and Alex Schaeffer, Katherine Webber Tsang, Alwyn Hamilton, Samantha Shannon, Catherine Chan, Cristina Arreola, Arvin Ahmadi, Sara Holland, Elizabeth Eulberg, and Julie Scheurl.

And last but certainly not least, thank you to my readers. I literally could not do this without you.

About the Author

Laura Sebastian grew up in South Florida and attended Savannah College of Art and Design. She now lives and writes in London with her two dogs Neville and Circe. Laura is also the author of the *New York Times* bestselling Ash Princess series: *Ash Princess, Lady Smoke,* and *Ember Queen*, as well as *Half Sick of Shadows,* her first novel for adults.

laurasebastianwrites.com

Twitter: @sebastian_lk

Instagram: @lauraksebastian